MOTHER EARTH, BLOODY GROUND

A NOVEL OF THE CIVIL WAR AND WHAT MIGHT HAVE BEEN

R.E. THOMAS

BLACK GOLD MEDIA

BLACK GOLD MEDIA
Copyright © 2014 by R.E. Thomas
ISBN-13: 978-0988892224
ISBN-10: 0988892227
stonewallgoeswest.com
facebook.com/stonewallgoeswest

To My Old Kentucky Home,
which gave to me an appreciation for both sides
of my country's bloodiest calamity

ACKNOWLEDGEMENTS

Writing a book is mostly, but not entirely a solo act. This is my third book and my second novel, and the deeper I get into this craft, the more I come to appreciate both sides of that particular coin. While I could have produced a novel alone, it wouldn't have been *Mother Earth, Bloody Ground* without the help of others.

First I must start with my editorial and production team. On the editorial side, Scott Peters was back to help me shape and polish the text, this time joined by Alexandra Asher and Rebecca Kerins. On the artistic side, my old colleague Lianne Helper of Station 10 Creative graphic design returned to produce another wonderful cover.

Others contributed in very particular ways, assisting me in adding detail and color to the story. Steve Primm of Murfreesboro pointed me to take either a first or a repeat and much closer look at certain geographical features in Rutherford County during what was my third and final research visit in May 2013. John Brown of Stones River National Battlefield furnished me with some valuable assistance in fleshing out Fortress Rosecrans. Materials provided to me by the Lawrence County Archives, the Tennessee Historical Society, and the West Tennessee Historical Society continued to be useful for what is the most Tennessee-centered part of the trilogy. Finally, I owe a debt to all the caretakers of online archives and the authors of published works who unknowingly helped me along.

I must also thank some particular people for helping an unknown author draw some attention down on his first novel. Dr. Matthew Lively, author of *Calamity at Chancellorsville*, gave me my very first book quote, a favor I'll not forget. *The Daily Herald* of Columbia, Tennessee was the first newspaper to cover *Stonewall Goes West*, and Spotsylvania County was kind enough to invite me to launch my book at the 150th Anniversary of the Battle of Chancellorsville.

Lastly, there are the people in my encouragement category. That list is headed by those friends and family who offered moral support, chiefly my old friends Kurt Maitland and George Bouza; my father-in-law Raoul Santos; and the three most important women in my life, my wife, my mother, and my sister. In addition to George, many other old friends took the time and trouble to come and see me at Chancellorsville last year, and that meant a lot to me.

As important are the readers who warmly embraced *Stonewall Goes West*, proving that there was a real audience for serious "For Want Of A Nail" style historical fiction. Your reader reviews, e-mails and notes on my Facebook group have kept me enthusiastic for the project through the troubles I faced in getting things done. The past year was a hard one, but the thought of people who were anxiously waiting for me to finish this book kept things rolling.

PART I
SPRING WEATHER
AND
YANKEE COFFEE

MAY TO JUNE 1864

CHAPTER 1

May 17, 1864
Mid-Morning
Fort Darling, CSA
10 miles south of Richmond, Virginia

Standing on the parapet, Jefferson Davis peered with his one good eye through the burnished brass of a telescope tube. The day before, he had only field glasses with him and could see very little, but could hear much. The rattle of skirmishers firing, the ripping tear of massed musketry, the boom and crack of artillery. Today it was the opposite, as the only noise to be heard was the distant bleating of the bugles, but through the telescope, which was better suited to what sight remained him in any case, he could see billowing clouds of dust and sometimes even snatches of marching columns in blue and gray.

"Mr. President? If I may, sir?"

Davis recognized the voice and swallowed the bitter taste in his mouth before turning to face General Pierre Gustav Truffant Beauregard. He stepped down from the parapet with care, and joined Beauregard by the rounded butt of Fort Darling's mammoth, bottle-like 10-inch cannon.

Davis drew himself up, ramrod straight, making the most of his four inches of superior height over Beauregard, "The Little Creole," as he was sometimes called. "Yes, what is it General?"

"Mr. President, I am delighted to inform you that I can confirm our victory of yesterday. The Yankee Army of the James is withdrawing eastward. I must leave Fort Darling forthwith, to supervise the pursuit."

Suppressing a scowl, Davis forced graciousness out his mouth. "Yes, I surmised as much. You are to be congratulated, General Beauregard. Despite being outnumbered two to one, you have stopped that most awful of Northron villains, Benjamin Butler, in his backdoor attempt on Richmond. What shall you call this battle? Drewery's Bluff? Fort Darling?"

"I have not given any thought as to what to call it," Beauregard replied. "But yes. A great victory. Great. It could have been greater still, had I received those reinforcements I asked for. On more equal terms, I could have shattered Butler's army and driven it into the river."

Davis kept his outrage at Beauregard's slap in the face to himself, retaining his studied, formal manner. The Louisianan's ingratitude wasn't much of a surprise, after all, as the two men had been worsening enemies since almost the earliest days of the war.

As for the Little Creole's request for reinforcements, the plan as proposed was typical of Beauregard's preference for flashy, outlandish schemes. Davis could grudgingly admit that Beauregard wasn't a bad general, but only when forced to abandon his impossible flights of fancy, and even then the little frenchified peacock complained bitterly about what he could have done if only his counsel had been adopted, as he did just now.

Davis said coldly, "Reinforcements from Lee's army were impossible, General Beauregard, as I have already explained. At length." They were impossible because Robert E. Lee had been grappling with General Grant's bear, the main Yankee army, since the 5th of May.

The only reason you even have this command, Davis thought to himself consolingly, is because General Johnston refused it on the grounds that he would not serve under Lee, choosing instead to renew his dispute with the War Department over his rank.

"Very well, General Beauregard. See to your pursuit. You are dismissed."

Beauregard offered a limp salute, and left Davis to ponder who he despised more: the frenchified peacock before him, the vain and quarrelsome Joseph E. Johnston, or that nefarious Yankee, Benjamin Butler.

Beauregard and Johnston were the enemies within Davis's own camp, two troublesome generals with a grossly inflated sense of their importance and ability, and the darlings of every carping, complaining politician and newspaperman in the country who opposed his policies out of spite, poisonous ambition, or misguided and deluded principle.

Butler, on the other hand, was a turncoat former ally of both Davis and the South. A Massachusetts man and pro-Southern Democrat, Butler had actually put Davis's name forward for the presidential nomination at the 1860 Democratic National Convention. Instead of becoming a Peace Democrat, as he ought to have done, Butler donned the blue uniform and became a complete miscreant, confiscating slaves as war contraband, officially labeling the ladies of New Orleans harlots, and even filching silverware whenever and wherever he could. "Beast Butler" and "Spoons Butler" they called him, the very personification of Yankee perfidy.

Davis had responded by ordering that if Butler were captured, he would summarily be executed. No trial, for Butler deserved no judicial niceties, he thought. Just the hangman's rope or a firing squad. Pity that Butler escaped us this time, but no matter. We may catch him still.

Davis's bitter reverie was interrupted by the arrival of John Henninger Reagan, the Confederate Postmaster General. A burly and thick-bearded Texan, Reagan had accompanied Davis' for this visit to Beauregard's small army.

"Mr. President, shall we return to Richmond?"

Davis nodded. With Butler in retreat and Beauregard in pursuit, there was no reason to linger at Fort Darling. The few belongings they brought with them were gathered by negro servants, and the men were soon on the Richmond Turnpike and riding for the capital, less than 10 miles away.

His mind off Beauregard and Butler, Davis's thoughts instantly began sinking into grief. His son, little Joe, had fallen off a balcony and died not three weeks ago. He had allowed himself one day to grieve with Varina and the other children, and then promptly retreated into work. An idle ride back to Richmond was the last thing he needed or desired.

Davis looked over at his companion, the immensely able administrator who had turned the Confederate Post Office into the best functioning arm of the government. Reagan had also proven a decent strategist, the only member of his Cabinet who preferred reinforcing the West over agreeing to Robert E. Lee's plan to invade Pennsylvania during the previous summer. Davis too had felt it best to send troops directly to break the siege of Vicksburg, but eventually yielded to Lee and the majority of his Cabinet. But not Reagan, who objected to the end and was ultimately proven right.

Deciding the best distraction was seeking Reagan's counsel, Davis asked "If I may inquire, John, I would value your opinions on recent military events."

Reagan brightened, pleased to be asked for his counsel. "Things are better than I'd hoped for, Mr. President. It's true that General Lee is having a hard time with Grant, a very hard time indeed, but Beauregard has turned back Butler, and Breckenridge turned back Sigel at New Market. Richmond and the Shenandoah are safe for the time being, and you can now find reinforcements for Lee accordingly. And our Lee, he has defeated many such Northron invasions. I'm sure he will eventually send this one packing as well."

"No, I don't worry about Virginia. My cause for concern has always been the West, and it is Stonewall's victory at Lawrenceburg that gives the greatest cause for hope," Reagan continued. "I think it obvious that what Abe Lincoln intended was to push us everywhere at once, so Sherman's armies should have attacked us at the same time as Grant, Butler and Sigel. Instead, they're standing pat. Jackson spoiled them, and then sent General Forrest across the Cumberland to raid in Kentucky to spoil them some more."

"Things are going well for us in the West," Davis agreed. He left his feeling that things going well in the West was a welcome change unsaid. "We beat the Yankees in Louisiana too. The Red River. It has been a long time in coming, having good news from the West."

Reagan grinned. "You know that the Red River victory is near and dear to my heart."

Davis nodded. A Confederate defeat there would have meant the occupation of East Texas.

"Now," Reagan continued. "I reckon that if Jackson can stay in Tennessee, Lee can just hold back Grant, and Hardee's boys in northern Georgia can keep the Yankees out of Atlanta, and we can hold all that back until November, then Lincoln will lose the election. We'll get our independence. We might still have a lot of horsetrading to do with the Yankees, but independence will follow as sure as the sun follows the moon."

"Yes. That is very much how I thought of it." Davis continued gravely, "We might need to liberate more of Tennessee before then. Tennessee and Louisiana are back in the Union now, or so Washington says anyway. False state governments manned by traitors. Even the Peace Democrats won't be able to simply give them back to us. Your 'horsetrading' might get one state liberated, John, but not both. Not unless we stake a better claim."

"You mean liberating Chattanooga and Nashville?"

Davis said, "And hopefully Memphis too."

"That is a tall order for one summer's work, Mr. President."

"Perhaps. But Jackson is a hard worker. I will tell you this, John, I have no regrets about giving that command to Jackson and shelving Johnston. None. Whatever trouble he has brought me, his service to the country is more than fair compensation."

"You mean this business with General Loring?" asked Reagan.

Davis nodded. At the Battle of Lawrenceburg, Jackson had ordered the arrest of Major General W.W. Loring on charges of insubordination. He did not have Jackson's full report pertaining to Lawrenceburg yet, but the affair was all over the newspapers, and he already had a sheaf of letters from both Loring and his supporters, protesting his innocence.

Another letter came from his old friend, General Leonidas Polk, who had been Loring's immediate superior, and that missive made it sound as if Loring had merely made a hash of exercising his discretion as a division commander. Davis wondered about that. Loring had troubled every commander he had served under in this war.

Reagan went on. "What are you going to do about it?"

"Well, I do not have anything formal from Jackson as of yet, so I cannot assess the severity of the charges. At the same time, I do not want the commander of the Army of Tennessee distracted by some trivial feud. If it turns out that Jackson's charges have merit, I believe I will ask Loring to retire. With his pension, if not his reputation."

"And if he doesn't?"

"Then the court-martial can wait for winter, and let the damnation be on Loring's head."

The pair continued to talk as they rode on at a moderate pace, Davis first asking Reagan's opinion of the recently convened Confederate Congress, and then how to improve the Commissary Department. The latter was responsible for supplying the Confederate Army and a source of constant, bitter complaint, in the army, the Congress, and the press. On the Commissary matter, Reagan's opinion that the Confederacy's bad roads and lack of railways were at the root of the country's troubles rang well to Davis, but his suggestion that it was time to bring in new people and remove Colonel Northrop, the Commissary General and one of Davis's West Point cronies, was not so well received.

Davis began to half-ignore Reagan, allowing him to chatter on. By the time they reached the forts protecting Manchester, the town across the James River from Richmond, Reagan's polite, but ultimately insufferable critique of Northrop had left Davis wishing he had never sought Reagan's counsel in the first place.

Crossing the Manchester Bridge into Richmond, the pair arrived at the gray, neo-classical eminence of the Executive Mansion, where Reagan took his leave. Davis had just handed his horse over to a darkie groom when his secretary, Burton Harrison, jogged up to him bearing a clutch of papers.

"Mr. President! Mr. President! I have here the dispatches from General Jackson you've been waiting for!"

At last! Davis thought, visibly happier. Jackson had dutifully sent a string of short messages regarding his general situation starting on May 6th, and his communications were understandably hampered by the need to send his messages back to the telegraph station, at first in Tuscumbia, Alabama, and then extended to Columbia, Tennessee. The resources were not available yet to extend the wire all the way to the Army of Tennessee's headquarters in Franklin. The messages received merely teased Davis's thirst for more detail from Jackson on the Battle of Lawrenceburg, the condition of his army, and his future intentions.

Davis checked his watch. Quarter past eleven. "Burton, I want you to go around to Secretaries Seddon and Benjamin, and also General Bragg. Instruct them to come to the mansion for luncheon at 1 o'clock. We have a Cabinet meeting already scheduled for this afternoon, and I want to discuss General Jackson's dispatches with them before that meeting. Stop by the War Department before seeing Mr. Benjamin, so you can take a copy with you."

"Yes, Mr. President."

Davis waved his secretary off, his attention focused squarely on the report. He took them up to the privacy of his office, barely taking his eyes off them as he went. He read the papers, considered them, and re-read them until Harrison, who had returned from his errand in the meantime, came to the door to inform him that his guests had arrived.

Taking the report with him, he strode to the state dining room, where his high war officials and a lunch of butter and ham sandwiches with spring salad waited. Secretary of War James Seddon, ailing, but every inch the Virginia gentleman; General Braxton Bragg, his principal military adviser, a tall, cadaverously thin, scraggly man; and round and ruddy Secretary of State Judah Benjamin, easily the shrewdest man in the Cabinet.

As Davis approached the table, he motioned for them to sit. "Gentlemen, I do not mean to deprive you of your midday meal, but we have pressing news to discuss before the meeting of the full Cabinet this afternoon." Taking a seat himself, Davis continued, "Have any of you had the opportunity to read General Jackson's dispatches of this morning?"

Seddon swallowed a bite of greens and said, "I'm afraid just myself and, I presume, you, Mr. President. There wasn't time to make additional copies, just yours. I have the original."

Davis frowned, noticing that Benjamin ate only salad, and then remembered that as a Jew, he could not partake of the sandwiches. "Mr. Benjamin, my apologies. I'll send for some bread and cheese, or perhaps an egg or two if you prefer?"

Benjamin smiled warmly. "Boiled eggs would be lovely."

"Well, now to business. I'll summarize General Jackson's dispatches for you. First, the butcher's bill. The General reports that the Army of Tennessee suffered five thousand casualties at Lawrenceburg. Because he captured the Federal hospitals and had possession of the battlefield, he has a reliable estimate of enemy casualties, which he places at 700 dead, 3,700 wounded, and 4,100 captured. The wounded are, naturally, all prisoners as well, but counted separately."

"What does he intend to do with all those prisoners?" asked Bragg.

"Jackson writes that he sent to General Sherman in Nashville to negotiate parole and exchange, but in keeping with Lincoln's new policy, Sherman rebuffed the overture. So, he has sent those able to march back to Tuscumbia. The wounded remain in Lawrenceburg. He has detailed the regiments from Strahl's Brigade, which apparently was badly damaged at Lawrenceburg, to serve as guards in both places. The General also reports that he captured 18 guns and a large stockpile of supplies at Lawrenceburg, and while the foraging in that part of Tennessee he controls is sparse, he now has a supply line open to the new depot at Tuscumbia."

"I'm not familiar with the details there," Benjamin said. "Could you enlighten me?"

Davis motioned to Bragg and took a bite of his sandwich. Bragg said "Yes, Mr. President. After the Federals abandoned Corinth, Mississippi, Mr. Secretary, Jackson ordered General Polk to reoccupy the place and repair the railroads there. So, northwestern Alabama is again connected to Corinth, part of a railway running all the way back to Selma. The Army of Tennessee can subsist from the plenty of the Alabama black belt and the Mississippi prairie."

Of course, Davis knew it wasn't as simple as that, as did everyone else in the room. Confederate rolling stock was badly worn after four years of war. Southern industry simply could not keep up with the demands of maintenance or replacement. There were serious limits on how much food and materiel could be moved from the interior of the Deep South to Jackson's army in Middle Tennessee. Still, a trickle was better than nothing at all, and a trickle was all they could manage.

Davis continued. "As we know from earlier reports, the Army of Tennessee lost several generals at Lawrenceburg, not the least among them being John Bell Hood. His body is on its way back to Richmond for a state funeral. There are other command vacancies as well. General Jackson has several recommendations he wants to make for filling them. To replace Hood, he wants Patrick Cleburne promoted. To replace Cleburne at the head of his division, he wants Lucius Polk promoted. And to permanently fill the vacancy left by Loring's arrest, he wants George Maney of Cheatham's Division promoted."

Davis knew about Jackson's plans for Cleburne and Lucius Polk already, as the latter's uncle, Leonidas Polk, had already written ahead to encourage Davis to promote the two men, giving them both a fulsome endorsement. He had kept that to himself, however, preferring to wait and see what Jackson actually asked for, and in that he wasn't disappointed. Jackson, much like Robert E. Lee, didn't make demands. Instead, Jackson stated his preferences and asked for advice.

Seddon spoke up. "I don't see any problems with that. All three have an excellent combat record. Both Maney and Polk are among the most senior brigadiers in that army, if not the most senior. Promoting Cleburne means passing over Cheatham, however, as Cheatham is his senior. Very much his senior."

Bragg interjected, "Cleburne has an excellent record as a division commander, it is true, but that does not mean he is fit for higher command. Save a few years as a ranker in the Queen Victoria's army, he has no formal military training. I believe General Jackson is implying here that he doesn't want Frank Cheatham for a corps commander, and we should accept that, but that is no reason to give Cleburne the job, not when we have other officers who can fill the role."

"Who did you have in mind, General?" asked Davis.

"Major Generals French and Stevenson are already with the Army of Tennessee. Both went to West Point and both are senior to Cleburne. If that is not enough, Richard Taylor was confirmed as Lieutenant General just yesterday, and he has served under Jackson's command before. Now that the Yankee's offensive up the Red River is defeated, Taylor can be sent from Louisiana. I'm sure he would be grateful to serve with our famous Stonewall again."

Listening to Bragg, Benjamin looked up from his freshly delivered eggs and understood with alarm what the skeletal General was up to. Cleburne and Cheatham were Bragg's private enemies, both part of the faction that had practically chased him out of the Army of Tennessee.

Stonewall Jackson's wishes be damned insofar as Bragg is concerned, Benjamin thought, just so long as Cleburne and Cheatham do not advance. Bringing up Richard Taylor was clever too. Taylor is Davis's one-time brother-in-law. Best not to mention the hypocrisy that Taylor hadn't been to West Point either, Davis won't care for that, but I have to put a stop to this.

"Mr. President, I believe General Bragg's idea about General Taylor is a sound one, but it poses certain problems. Even if you were to immediately order Taylor to assume command of Hood's Corps, it would be weeks before he arrived. In the meantime, I agree that implicit in Jackson's request for Cleburne is that he prefers Cleburne over Cheatham, French, and Stevenson. Yet if he has to wait for Taylor, one of those men will inherit Hood's Corps by virtue of seniority. You see what I mean, sir? It causes our Stonewall a great deal of trouble in the short term, and I'm sure he wants his command sorted out before he has to fight another battle. You would also have to find someone to replace Taylor, and send them to the Trans-Mississippi Department."

Davis nodded, but said nothing. He liked the idea of giving the job to Taylor, and disliked giving it to Cleburne. The Irishman had talent, there was no doubt of that, but he wasn't a professional officer. As an immigrant, he wasn't even a real Southron. The last point was revealed in the most startling fashion last winter, when Cleburne proposed to free and arm the slaves. The only reason they could even discuss promoting Cleburne is because that proposal had remained confidential. If the Senate knew of it, they would never confirm him.

Benjamin went on. "I propose instead that we give Cleburne and Lucius Polk brevet promotions. That way Jackson can have the man he wants running Hood's old corps for the short term, and if you decide not to retain Cleburne or the Senate rejects his lieutenant generalcy, then Lucius Polk's promotion is just as temporary. Matters there would go back to the way they were."

Bragg soured. "We don't use brevet rank."

"True," Benjamin replied sweetly. "But it's still on the books. And therefore legal."

Well that, Davis thought, is better. If he brought Taylor in, it would mean no promotion for Lucius Polk, too. That would leave dear old Leonidas very disappointed.

Davis said sternly, "Very well. We brevet Cleburne and Polk as a temporary measure, while I propose to Jackson that we send him Richard Taylor to permanently replace Hood. And that we approve George Maney to replace Loring. Agreed?"

Bragg said nothing, but Benjamin and Seddon both concurred.

"General Jackson has one more request," Davis said. "He reports some success with recruitment and conscription. That is unsurprising, I think, since he controls an area our government has not exercised direct and uncontested control over since the fall of Nashville. As the Bureau of Conscription effectively doesn't exist north of the Tennessee River at present, he requests permission to incorporate anyone he gets his hands on above that line directly into the regiments, and once there to 'train the new men on the march' as he puts it, instead of sending them back to camps in the rear. I for one have no problem with that."

On this request, everyone agreed. Davis then passed his copy of the dispatches around for Benjamin and Bragg to read, and the four men finished their lunch.

June 8, 1864
After Midnight
The White House
Washington, DC

Abraham Lincoln stood up and laid his pen down on the desk. He blinked to clear his head, withdrew a hankerchief from his pocket, and wiped the ink smudges from his fingers and hands.

Turning around, he said to the men seated at various desks, chairs, and couches behind him, "Misters Seward and Blair, the missive to Dennison is finished, polished, and ready for the show. If you are done with me now, I would very much like to go to the telegraph office and await reports from Tennessee."

Seward, the Secretary of State, was reading near a window left slightly ajar and puffing on a cigar. His smoking was as much to discourage mosquitoes as it was to enjoy the tobacco. He looked up, smiled slightly, but said nothing, and went back to his newspapers.

Lincoln smiled in turn, half-amused. Anyone who asked why Seward always looked as if braced for news that his house had burnt to charcoal and ash had never seen the man smile. His drooping ears, narrow face, and prominent nose gave even a little smile a comical cast.

Montgomery Blair spoke instead. "Are you sure about that? The word from Baltimore will come directly and periodically. I know there is a battle going on in Tennessee, but it isn't of much import, not next to the convention."

Lincoln placed his hands on the small of his back, stretched out his long, lanky frame, and then replied, "Sir, we've got the convention in Baltimore as done as we can make it. There will be no surprises. I am to be nominated for President of these United States again, God help me. If anything causes our esteemed colleagues of the National Union Party to give pause and reconsider the wisdom of putting me before the country again, it could only be word of what transpires in a little place not so far from Clarksville, Tennessee. Now, I've tended to the needs of our good friend, the Honorable Governor Dennison of Ohio, and now I would like to go tend to the needs of the country at large."

"Yes, of course. If anything should come…"

"Yes, I know." With that, Lincoln put on his coat, picked up his hat and a hefty walking stick, and left the room.

In the hallway his chief private secretary, John Nicolay, sat behind a little desk that had been placed there. Nicolay continued to tend to his paperwork, but his main purpose was to send petitioners, office-seekers, and other such people packing. Those people usually did not come calling on the President at such unseemly hours, but Presidents were so rarely as certain of re-nomination as Lincoln was.

John Nicolay looked up from his stack of letters. "I'm surprised you didn't bolt the stable hours ago."

"Decorum dictates that a candidate cannot attend at his own nomination in person," Lincoln said, "but practicality demands some of his epistles must go in his stead."

Lincoln set the walking stick and hat down on Nicolay's desk. "Are any of these for me?"

Nicolay nodded and motioned to the small pile to Lincoln's right. Lincoln scooped them up, placed them in his hat, and then retrieved the heavy stick.

"This thing is a nuisance. But if I fail to carry it, somehow my wife always hears of it."

Nicolay didn't bother looking up from his correspondence. "If you would let us arrange a bodyguard for you, someone to be with you at all times instead of just sometimes, perhaps she would not insist you go around armed with that club."

"And what would they make of that? They would say I go around like a tyrannical Caesar of old, wearing a breastplate and proceeded by a phalanx of armed praetorians."

"The Copperheads already say that."

Lincoln chuckled. "Yes, but now it is all lie. Should I help them by making it a half-truth?"

Taking his stick and hat, Lincoln said goodbye to Nicolay and made his way downstairs and out the west side of the White House. Pausing to place his hat on his head, he frowned at how unpleasant the night air was. Stuffy, just a touch of rot hovering in the air. Washington's pestilential summer was just beginning to take hold, and he knew soon enough night would bring no relief from the steamy heat, nor the smells it brought with it.

Lincoln launched himself forward, using a brisk walking pace to shake out the discomfort from his joints. The stick he used not at all, but instead clutched it casually by his side. With his long stride, it took little time to reach the War Department, located as it was practically on the side doorstep of the White House. He tipped his hat to greetings of "Mr. President, sir" from the guards, all of whom were familiar with his habits and odd hours, and went straight to the telegraph office.

Walking through the door, Lincoln motioned to the cipher-clerks that they should remain seated. Gideon Welles, the Navy Secretary, was there. But Secretary of War Edwin Stanton was not, which meant he was next door in his office. Lincoln knew Stanton often slept in his office when a battle was in the offing or the running and made a habit of keeping late hours, battle or no. Awake or asleep, who knew?

As he went to the pile of recent messages, Lincoln asked the nearest clerk, "Has General Rosecrans' reply from St. Louis come in yet?"

The clerk, busily clacking away, replied, "Yes, Mr. President, it's in there. It came only a short while ago, so it should be near the top" without looking up from his telegraph key.

Lincoln plunged his hands into the drawer, lifting the pile of messages out and placing them on the desktop. He then removed his hat and set his other papers down alongside the War

Department messages. He started with the latter first, turning over the first few messages until he found the one he wanted.

William Starke Rosecrans, the former commander of the Army of the Cumberland, the loser of Chickamauga, was now out of the big show and serving as the commander of the Department of Missouri. Ostensibly, Lincoln and Rosecrans were cabling back and forth about some mundane matter of how to handle confidential communications, but Lincoln knew that Rosecrans' former chief of staff, James Garfield, headed the Ohio delegation to the Baltimore convention and that Garfield had wired Rosecrans earlier that day to inquire if Rosecrans, who remained popular with Ohio War Democrats, might be interested in the Vice Presidential nomination.

Lincoln also knew that Stanton, always a petty, vindictive man, had intercepted Rosecrans' reply, and as of yet, had neither released it or spoken of it.

If Rosecrans truly wanted to be Vice President, Lincoln thought, then he should also drop some hint of it here, cryptic as per his usual style. But there was no mention of it. Was there more? Would Stanton dare to doctor official War Department messages? Perhaps he would, but the document looked genuine, original.

The neighboring cipher clerk looked up from his desk, having finished keying his encoded message. "Mr. President, if you don't mind my saying so, I don't know how you can be here at a time like this. I know a battle was fought today and all, but those fellows up in Baltimore are talking about making you President again. Well, both are important, but I reckon…"

"Lieutenant, the convention of the National Union Party is as an African menagerie. Giraffes, a lion or two, a big white elephant, and far too many chimpanzees. Now I procured for myself, as the owner of any menagerie must, some able keepers from the circus, and I let them handle it. I prefer to wait here for those fellows to arrange the show, and not by the cages, which must by unfortunate necessity smell strongly of chimp and elephant dung."

The army clerk and Lincoln shared a chuckle. Of course, Lincoln thought, this young fellow knows little of what goes on in Republican party politics. I've brought the War Democrats and most of my fellow Republicans together into the National Union Party, and the nomination from them is tucked away like a week-old kitten in a neat silk stocking. Some of the Radicals left the herd and nominated John Fremont, mind you, but time remains to deal with them, persuade them to rejoin the fold.

Lincoln had been considering a story to tell the clerks when Stanton thundered in, coatless and open-collared, looking bleary-eyed and even more humorless than usual. He held a newspaper and shook it at Lincoln. "Have you seen this latest *New York Tribune?*"

Impassive, Lincoln replied, "Yes, I've seen it."

"Horace Greely's gone mad! Stark, raving, drooling mad! Calling for Fremont to replace Sherman and Hooker to replace McPherson! And while you are sitting there so calm and serene, Mr. President, you might give thought to what it means when a prominent editor such as Greely goes on the record for naming the figurehead of your party's malcontents as the man to solve the supposed leadership problems of our western armies!"

Lincoln grunted. "Oh, I know what it means. Senator Wade called on me this morning, threatening an investigation of the Committee on the Conduct of the War. Then Secretary Chase visited this afternoon, suggesting that if I were to swap Hooker and McPherson, it might be enough to sooth the feelings of the Radicals, cause them to heave Fremont over the side, and get back on our wagon."

"What will you do?" asked Stanton.

I've been giving some thought to that, Lincoln reflected. Although I'm rather fond of Mr. Joe Hooker, I have looked long and hard to find a man like my General Grant. Now I have got him, Sherman is his man in the West, and he and Sherman both want General McPherson to stay where he is.

"Let them talk," Lincoln shrugged. "If Wade, Chandler and the rest wish to investigate by means of a Congressional Committee, let them do that too. They can call their witnesses from the army, who I'm sure will say that James B. McPherson was indeed beaten by Stonewall Jackson, who was at the head of a larger army. They will also say this same Jackson danced circles around John Fremont, and whipped Joe Hooker, and in each instance Jackson did it with a smaller army. I know from personal experience that some in Congress suffer from deficient education, but I believe most can do that arithmetic."

Stanton was about to say more, but a clerk from the other side of the room shouted, "Mr. Secretary, I have received word from Nashville."

Lincoln sprang from his chair and in an instant stood behind the clerk, who was rapidly decoding and transcribing the message from the wire. Stanton waddled up behind them.

When the telegram was complete, Stanton snatched it up with a "Give me that!" Lincoln paid no mind to his War Secretary's rude bullying and presumption, choosing instead to wait affably for him to relate the contents.

Lincoln watched as Stanton's beady eyes darted back and forth across the page. When Stanton's mouth twisted up in anger, Lincoln knew. Forrest had beaten Sturgis.

"Sturgis is whipped!" Stanton spat, thwacking the message with the back of his hand, as if the paper were the very person of Brigadier General Samuel Sturgis. "Whipped at a place called Ringgold Mill. He writes that Forrest attacked him there, as he was trying to cut Forrest off from the bridges at Clarksville."

Lincoln slumped back into his chair. After a pause, he asked, "How stands Sturgis's command?"

"What? Oh. There is nothing here as to his losses, but he reports falling back on Hopkinsville, Kentucky. From what he says of his arrangements, it looks as though his expedition is intact. More or less. That Forrest must be the devil, the way he has our troops cowering! Our troops and our generals!"

"Forrest is no devil, but he is a hard man," Lincoln said softly. "He was a slaver, so I'm told, and those in such a profession must be hard men to achieve success in it. Very hard. He knows how to drive men, both his men as well as ours. I think we must endeavor to find a hard man of our own to match him, and spend less breath and ink on hellfire origins."

CHAPTER 2

June 8, 1864
Early Morning
Charlotte Road
South Bank of the Cumberland Rive near Clarksville, Tennessee

"Would the General care for some breakfast?"

Nathan Bedford Forrest looked over his shoulder to see a darkie cook standing behind him with a tin plate heaped with fried eggs and bacon, and a cup of steaming hot coffee. As soon as the aroma reached his nostrils, his stomach growled, and he suddenly remembered he hadn't had any food since breakfast of the day before, since before yesterday's battle.

He nodded, took the cup and plate, and sat down on a fallen tree trunk with a view of the Clarksville bridge, where the last of his supply train was crossing, a mix of the wagons that he had taken with him on his expedition to Kentucky and the wagons he had captured while he was there. Forrest dug into his breakfast, content that while some of those wagons were almost emptied of their contents of food and fodder, the others were crammed with valuable Yankee-made stores, medicines, ammunition, and other sundry items. He had just speared the last chunk of bacon with his fork when a small party of horsemen galloped in, coming up from the south. Five men, led by a captain.

Recognizing the officer, Forrest set his plate aside and called out, "Captain James Power Smith. What brings you out thisaway?"

Smith presented himself, saluting smartly. "General Forrest. It has been some time, sir. I come bearing orders from General Jackson."

Stonewall Jackson's chief aide-de-camp dismounted and proffered an envelope, which Forrest took. While tucking the message into his coat, Forrest asked, "What's all this about?"

"The only thing I know is that when headquarters received a copy of the *Louisville Daily Journal*, smuggled out of Nashville, that said you had left Munfordville and were heading south, I was given that envelope and ordered to ride out here to Clarksville. I was then to wait here until you arrived."

Forrest drained the last of his coffee. "And how are things on the Harpeth, Captain? I ain't heard nothing about a battle, so I reckon Sherman ain't come out of Nashville looking for a fight just yet."

"Quiet, General, all's quiet. Except for one thing. General William Hicks Jackson is under arrest."

Frowning, Forrest asked, "Red Jackson? What'd he do?"

"Well, sir, our cavalry patrols skirmish regularly with Yankee troopers right around Brentwood. I reckon you know he has a plantation there, Belle Meade. A couple of weeks ago he decided to go up there, have dinner with his wife, and bring back a few fresh horses from his stables. Of course, he did all of this without orders and only got back out again by the skin of his teeth. General Jackson was angry, mighty angry."

Forrest looked down and shook his head. He had never been able to make any sense of all that damned silly, dashing cavalier business, like war was some kind of game, a fox chase. That was the way old John Hunt Morgan went about his work, Forrest thought, and look where that got him. His command destroyed and an Ohio prison cell. Still, fox chasers like Red Jackson, with their dash and daring, they had their uses. A man just needed to keep a tight leash on them, that was all.

"Has the commanding general sent Red back to the rear?" If Red Jackson had been sent back to Alabama, Forrest guessed, it meant he was keeping time with W.W. Loring, and so both of them would be waiting for a court-martial.

Smith replied quietly, "No, he has not. If I may say so, I believe General Jackson is waiting on you, sir. I've seen this sort of thing many times before, back in Virginia. Sometime he arrests a man and leaves him there, as a punishment. Once the army gets moving again, he sets aside the whole business."

Rising to his feet, Forrest straightened his coat. "I need to go back into town. That's where my staff is. If you and your men will accompany me, Captain?"

Smith saluted. "Of course, sir." He turned around, his dissatisfaction firmly suppressed with military formality. He didn't care to be around Forrest, not after that ugly, mutinous display the cavalry general made in Jackson's own tent on the eve of the Battle of Lawrenceburg, more a month before. "Wizard of the Saddle" he might be, but Smith knew Forrest was also a base savage, without an ounce of real Christian civility in him. What he wanted most was for Forrest to read the orders, give him a reply, and then allow him to get away from here and back to army headquarters.

After mounting his horse, Smith's private disdain for Forrest boiled up when he noticed some of the men in the General's escort. Darkies. Two dozen riders were gathered around Forrest. Most were obviously hard-bitten fighting men, armed with a mix of six-shooters, sawn-down shotguns, and captured Federal repeaters. It looked less like a proper general's escort than like a gang of bandits. And among them were a pair of blacks, just as heavily armed as the rest, and wearing butternut field jackets.

"Is there something wrong, Captain Smith?"

Smith hadn't realized he had been staring. "Nosir. Nothing wrong."

"You may have heard, I reckon, that when the war started I was a slave dealer. I made a... a arrangement with some of them darkies. If they fought with me and stuck with me, win or lose, they would all be free. Well, they said yes, and they kept faith, I ain't never had any complaints."

"If you say so, sir."

And if them bloated sacks in Richmond knew half as much as they say about the black man, Forrest thought, they wouldn't hesitate to make that same bargain and arm every good darkie as could be found. Make some good darkies free and get them to fight to keep the rest down, that was smart business. If we lose, all the darkies go free anyhow. But most of the country is like Captain Smith here, ain't ready to hear that. Now most of them good darkie boys had gone running and joined the Yankees.

Forrest led Smith and their combined parties back over the bridge, now cleared of all wagons, to the north bank of the

Cumberland into Clarksville. In the town a column of almost a thousand captured blue soldiers had formed up, readying to be marched under guard across the river and, a long way away, onto prison.

"I took these here prisoners yesterday, at Ringgold Mill," Forrest said to Smith. "Can't just parole them, not now that we and the Yankees don't do that business no more. Couldn't keep them Yankees I captured up in Mundfordville. Too far behind enemy lines. Had to let them bluebellies go. But these fellows..."

Smith nodded, watching as the sullen, beaten-looking men in blue began marching by. Poor devils.

The riders went on, out of town and passing through throngs of Confederate troopers, busily tending to their horses and preparing for the day's ride. As soon as they saw Forrest on the road, they gathered around on both sides and cheered him wildly. Forrest paid no mind and soon was across the Red River and in an earthen fort, perched on a 200-foot bluff overlooking Clarksville and the confluence of the Red and the Cumberland.

As they passed through the entrance, Forrest told Smith, "We built this place. The Yankees call it Fort Bruce, but so long as we're here, it's Fort Defiance again. I detailed a regiment to garrison this fort while I was away, keep the damn Yankees from destroying that bridge while my back was turned."

Forrest dismounted and strode into one of the log buildings inside the fort, leaving Smith to wait outside. Motioning for his staff to go about their business, he pulled a stool up against a wall, sat down, withdrew and opened the envelope, and began reading. Slowly, carefully, painfully reading.

He thought he understood the message, but the last time he received a written order from Stonewall Jackson, he had misread it so badly he went and threatened mutiny at the man who was making him the Army of Tennessee's cavalry chieftain. So, Forrest handed the message to his chief of staff, seated at the table next to him.

"Major Anderson, what do you make of this?"

Anderson read the message. The meaning was easy and clear, but he wasn't surprised, knowing Forrest was half-literate at best. Sometimes Forrest gave incoming correspondence to him or one of the other staff for a second reading, but the General was sensitive enough about it to make the matter into a discussion rather than have the thing read aloud. Forrest's own written business, on the other hand, almost always went to either him or one of the other staffers for polishing.

"General Jackson desires that once you have your command safely on the south bank of the Cumberland, and en route for Franklin, that you should hand the reins over to General Buford and ride ahead to report to him and receive further orders."

Forrest nodded. He thought he understood it, but he wanted to make certain. That was why he made Smith wait all this time. No mention of Red Jackson, though, he thought. What to make of that?

"Draw up orders to Abe Buford for me to sign. You take them over to him yourself. He already knows who is doing what, but make sure he understands what roads to take and such."

After ordering Smith to wait on and travel with him, General Forrest lingered in Clarksville until late afternoon, when the last of his cavalry was over the river and on its way down the Charlotte Road. Overtaking the wagon train at the head of the column, they arrived in Dickson County's seat well after dark. With an escort and staff party numbering over a hundred, and not wanting to scatter them into beds all over town, Forrest put his troopers up on the benches and floors of the Dickson County Courthouse for the night. The next morning, they rode on to Franklin, arriving at Jackson's headquarters at Harrison House as the skies began to turn to the golden orange of an early summer sunset.

Forrest presented himself and was shown into the parlor, where General Jackson was in the midst of meeting with his senior staff, of whom Forrest recognized only Colonel Sandie Pendleton, the army's boyish 23-year-old master bureaucrat.

Returning Forrest's salute with his right hand, his only hand, Jackson said, "Gentleman, General Forrest has ridden a long way. Let us adjourn. Go get yourself some supper. We shall resume tomorrow morning, first thing."

As Sandie made his goodbyes to Forrest, Jackson studied his cavalry leader. He was a strongly built man, with a thick, vital shock of graying hair. When he last saw him, that strong build and Forrest's air of predatory menace reminded Jackson greatly of a prowling mountain lion. Now, that lion was dusty and sweat-stained, his eyes sunken and weary, his face more weather-beaten than before. The muscular frame and posture that once seemed so relaxed and full of power was now stiff, disjointed, and his hair looked grayer.

I've been that tired, Jackson thought. The strain and worry, the endless work of seeing to everything yourself. A man who wins victories and comes home like this, that is a man who has well and truly done his duty. Good, good.

After offering Forrest coffee and motioning for him to sit down, Jackson said, "General Forrest, we've had no word on your actions since you crossed the Cumberland, except what has come out in the Northern papers. That is proper, as you were ordered to exercise the strictest secrecy and take pains to befuddle the enemy, but now…"

"Yessir. I rode to Bowling Green with Buford's Division, aiming to wreck the railroad bridge there, but found the forts protecting the town and bridge situated on a ring of strong high ground, and the commander weren't inclined to give up. Your orders weren't to get into no siege, so I kept on north to the next target, the Green River bridge at Munfordville. I got there quick, surrounded the place before they knew what I was about, and bullied them into surrender."

Forrest grinned widely, the memory making him forget how worn he was. "The commander there was one Brigadier General Hugh Ewing, sir. Big plump fellow. Brother-in-law to none other than General Sherman. After disarming the bluebellies, I paroled them with instructions to go to Louisville, all except Ewing. I sent him and his staff down to Nashville, thinking Sherman might appreciate the company."

Jackson chuckled, deep and mirthful. "Please, do go on."

"Well, I captured enough wagons and teams to double the size of my train. After letting the boys eat their fill and piling the wagons high, we burned the rest of them supplies and the bridge and started south again. I set a slower pace, keeping the boys rested, pulling up plenty of track, and taking care of some recruiting. Brought back more than seven hundred Tennessee men, plus a hundred and fifty Kentucks."

"Good, good," Jackson said. "How many have horses of their own?"

"Half," Forrest replied.

Jackson took a drink from his coffee, and after setting his cup down, placed his scarred hand so the thumb stuck straight up. "Then you know the other half go to the infantry. That is the law. Only men who provide their own mounts stay in the cavalry service."

"Yes, General, but I don't reckon that will be any trouble. These boys are as eager to serve under you as they are under me."

Forrest continued. "About that time, two infantry divisions were coming down from Louisville under A.J. Smith. On account that I wrecked that bridge at Munfordville, they had to get out and walk, so I could stay ahead of them easy. But Sturgis was coming in from the west, with infantry and cavalry. They were coming on fast, looking to cut me off from my one good crossing at Clarksville. Not wanting to abandon those wagons, I went out to meet him.

"I made a dash to get in quick, before they were ready or rightly knew exactly where I was. We attacked Grierson's cavalry at Ringgold Mill, drove them back, and up came Sturgis's infantry. They were tired from marching at the double, what with all the heat, so I whipped them too. Took over nine hundred prisoners."

"Defeat in detail," Jackson said firmly.

"What's that sir?"

"You beat a divided enemy. First one part, then the other."

"Yessir. Now, if I may ask you, General, how goes with Red Jackson?"

Jackson sighed. "Brigadier William H. Jackson took advantage of a cavalry skirmish to push an entire brigade through the enemy's patrols and right up to Brentwood, exceeding his orders by a mile. While there, he dallied for a luncheon with his wife and family. The rumors that he collected some of his horses are false, as there are no horses left at Belle Meade. He denies none of it. General Jackson is very frank about what his intentions were: to show up the Yankees and visit his homeplace, all with the single stone."

"And what do you intend to do with Red?"

"Do you need him?"

"I reckon I do."

"Then he stays under house arrest until this army resumes active operations. If you go see him, you are free to reprimand him. In fact, I encourage you to do so, but say nothing about charges, court-martials, or any of that. Let him sweat over it."

Forrest smiled. "I ain't exactly pleased about that damned knightly foolishness neither. I figure I'll wait a day or two, make sure he knows I'm back, and then go have a few unfriendly words with old Red."

That was exactly was Jackson wanted to hear. Coming west, he already knew Forrest's reputation as a raider and a fighter, and now that he knew him first-hand, he also liked the man's hard-nosed, all-business approach to running his cavalry. As much as Jackson loved his friend Jeb Stuart, he thought the Virginia cavalier enjoyed daring too much for its own sake and unquestionably suffered the sin of vanity when it came to seeing his name in the papers. Whatever his other faults, that was not Nathan Bedford Forrest.

"Good, good." Jackson stood up. "General Forrest, you have industriously carried out your orders, and my report will indicate as much. See Colonel Pendleton about where to place Buford's Division, and get some rest."

Jackson extended his right hand. Forrest took it gladly, happy to at long last have a commander-in-chief who valued him.

CHAPTER 3

June 9, 1864
Mid-Morning
Rippavilla Plantation
Headquarters, Polk's Corps, CSA
Spring Hill, Tennessee

Featherston jumped up from his chair to salute as Polk strode into the parlor. Polk took his hand and gave it a strong shake, saying "Winn, will you walk with me?"

The pair left the house and walked away from that part of the estate where Polk's staff had set up their tents. After a few minutes and some bland chatter, Polk said "I'm afraid I have some unfortunate news from Richmond. I sent for you as soon as I saw the news over the wire."

Featherston stopped and swallowed. "I've been passed over."

Polk turned to face him and nodded gravely, while thinking to himself what a blessing it was to have his headquarters closest to the army's telegraph station in Columbia. It meant he received news hours before anyone else and therefore enjoyed some control over its dissemination.

"President Davis," Polk said, "has appointed George Maney of Cheatham's Division in your place. His promotion to major general has yet to be confirmed by the Senate, but I have no doubts it will be."

Putting his hands on his hips, Featherston grimaced and stood quiet for a time. Then he cried, "God dammit!" and kicked the chair. It was frustrated kick rather than a wrathful one, so the chair slid a few inches instead of falling over.

Polk's brows furrowed, and he said quietly "General Featherston, please…"

Ignoring him, Featherston ranted, "Oh, I saw this coming. I saw it when Jackson didn't give me or the division the credit we were due in his Lawrenceburg dispatches. You know this, General! I held the men back from that slaughter house at Coon Creek, and because of that we had the strength to renew the assault at the right time. I didn't need that thrice-damned Irishman to tell me to attack, but no! Cleburne got all the credit!"

Judging the moment was ripe, Polk added, "Cleburne has, in fact, been put up for a brevet to Lieutenant General."

"He what?!" Featherston cried. "Over Frank Cheatham! The Devil's blazes! That knocks it. Knocks it right out the window! Lee and Jackson. I'll not serve under these damned Virginians a moment longer. Those high and mighty, lordly bastards. They had to be dragged screaming and thrashing out of the Union, and then they turned right around and had the audacity to claim to lead us. Damn them, damn them all! And what was Jeff Davis thinking? He is a Mississippian for chrissakes!"

Polk reddened. "Winn, I beg you, Our Lord's name?"

Almost panting, Featherson snatched up his sword in its scabbard. "Do you know what I'm going to do, General Polk? I'm going to ride straight for Franklin. I'm going to throw this down in front of that man, the high and mighty Stonewall Jackson. I'm going to resign and go home."

"That is your right, of course," Polk said soothingly. "But I think you shouldn't. You'll win few converts to your side, resigning in protest in the wake of a victory."

"Then what do you think I should do?"

"Tell your side of the story, for one. You have friends in Mississippi and Richmond. Write to them. But if I may make a suggestion, avoid criticizing the man of the hour directly. Merely describe how your contribution has been slighted. May I trust in your discretion and be frank?"

Featherston nodded.

"I know you resent Cleburne, Winn, but the Irishman is a good soldier, and he had the sense to oppose that miscreant failure, Braxton Bragg. But I suspect many will be… uncomfortable with the idea of giving so high a posting to an immigrant, no matter how ardently that immigrant may espouse our cause. His rank is only temporary, and if he should stumble..."

"I thought you said he was a good soldier."

"Yes, to a point. But I recall General Hardee's sentiments that Cleburne was unsuited for higher command. And if anyone should know, it should be him. Wait, Winn. Be patient. Show some good grace. I know you aren't alone in your division."

Featherston said, "True enough. The other brigade commanders are also upset. Some say army headquarters persecutes us as part of some petty feud Jackson has with Loring."

Smiling placidly, Polk said, "Maney is new to your division, new to this level of responsibility, new to my Army of Mississippi. The other brigade leaders will look to you, who they know so well. Maney may come to lean on you too. He needn't be your enemy. Go back to your brigade, Winn. Go back and wait. As the saying goes, the Lord works in mysterious ways. Tomorrow might bring anything."

As the two men walked out to Featherston's horse, Polk basked in a satisfied glow. His other division commander, French, was nearly as upset over Jackson's battle dispatches as Featherston. Now he could count on Featherston and most of his colleagues as well. Polk knew George Maney and liked him, but the Tennessee brigadier was still an outsider. So, he needed to know that Maney's subordinates would be for Polk before Maney. And Stonewall Jackson.

Polk returned to his office and his work, biding his time for a far more personal and less satisfying appointment. He didn't look up to acknowledge the knock at the door. "It opens."

A clerk announced, "Lieutenant Bell to see you, sir."

Just this once, Polk thought, Bell was punctual. "Show him in."

Polk still didn't look up, but instead kept on writing. After spending a few minutes silently finishing the paragraph, he finally turned his eyes towards the young man standing at attention before him. Tall, blonde, immaculately uniformed, standing at perfect attention. Exactly the sort of appearance Polk liked in his entourage, except for the insufferably haughty gleam in Bell's eyes.

"I assume you know why you are here, Lieutenant?"

"Nosir, General, I do not."

That was a lie, Polk thought. Samson Bolivar Bell's father was one of the most prominent planters in West Tennessee, an old friend of the Polks. When young Bell appeared at Polk's Army of Mississippi headquarters just after New Year's with a letter of introduction from his wealthy, well-connected father, Polk happily gave him a commission as a two-bar, first lieutenant and a place as aide-de-camp.

It had proved an unhappy choice. Bell had soon shown himself to be a fractious, dissentious presence in Polk's military family. When he wasn't whoring, drinking, gambling, or some combination of the three, the boy was challenging one of the other lieutenants to fight or crudely politicking for a step up into a captain's slot somewhere. Polk wanted nothing more than to court-martial him and send him home to his papa in disgrace, but Bell's father was not a man Polk wanted to alienate. Even Isham Harris, the exiled Governor of Tennessee, had stopped by two weeks before to lobby Polk on Bell's behalf.

"Give him a company," Harris had said. "It would make the Bells happy."

So, Polk suffered the whelp and waited for an opening to transfer him away out of his command. Now he had it, and Bell knew it, knew it without being told.

The little fool, Polk thought, smiling pleasantly. Too pleased with himself to see what lies in store for him.

"Then allow me to surprise you and congratulate you." Polk reached to a stack of several folded papers, and lifted the first bundle off the top. "This is your transfer and your promotion to captain."

Bell gleamed. "Transfer, sir? I am to leave your service?"

Behind his serenity, Polk's loathing for the boy sharpened. Bell couldn't be bothered to make even a failing effort at appearing disappointed to leave the staff. "Yes, Lieutenant. Not Captain yet, Bell. Your rank becomes official upon your transfer. You are going to the infantry. A company is waiting for you in the 41st Tennessee Infantry, Maney's Brigade, Cheatham's Division."

Bell stepped forward and took the envelope. "It has been my absolute pleasure to serve under your command these past six months, General Polk. Your leadership is an inspiration to everyone under your command."

The way Bell emphasized the word "pleasure" almost snapped Polk's patience. "I wish you well in your new posting, Bell." Returning to his paperwork, Polk dismissed him with a "that will be all."

Polk tried to continue his office work after Bell sauntered away, but he couldn't. Instead, he got to his feet and stuck his head outside his door.

"Do we have any of that ham and biscuits left over from breakfast? Good. Give Mrs. Cheairs my compliments, fetch that up with a pot of tea, and put it in the parlor for me."

Polk stewed in his dissatisfaction with the shackles that prevented his humiliation of Bell until his tea was ready, so by the time he settled into the Cheairs family parlor, he was in full sulk over his general unhappiness with his place in Stonewall Jackson's Army of Tennessee.

Polk grudgingly admitted to himself he had some cause for contentment. He was finally part of a successful army, an army that had won a clear victory at last month's Battle of Lawrenceburg. They had liberated a large swathe of Middle Tennessee from Yankee occupation. The Northrons quaked with fear behind their entrenchments in Nashville and northern Georgia, too frightened to come out and fight. And his corps, his Army of Mississippi, was encamped in the northern half of Maury County, the family seat.

More than tipping the scales against that was Polk's firm belief he had not received anything like the credit he deserved for the victory at Lawrenceburg. Indeed, in Polk's opinion the victory would have and should have been all his in the first instance, because it had been his plan to invade Middle Tennessee, a plan Jackson stole from him with the connivance of Jefferson Davis.

My plan, he thought. My men that crushed Veatch's Division against the bluffs of Shoal Creek, and yes, Cleburne's Division were my men, because they were operating under my command at the time, were they not?

Polk felt even more slighted because while he was in Maury County, he did not even have the satisfaction of setting up headquarters in Columbia or the Rattle and Snap, his family estate. No, he thought, he had to stay here, in Spring Hill, so he was closer to Franklin.

Such an inconvenience. What difference would an extra 10 miles make if the Yankees came, he wondered. Surely there would be plenty of warning.

Polk polished off the last of the biscuits and drained his cup of tea. There was one benefit to staying in Spring Hill, he thought. Poor old Major Cheairs is off in a Yankee prison, while his family had been evicted and living in a cabin behind Rippavilla House. They were grateful just to have the family home back, volunteered to Polk the rooms for his personal quarters and office, and gladly catered to the needs of himself and his staff.

Polk stood and patted his round belly. "That Mrs. Cheairs keeps a pretty kitchen." He would have to invite and escort Mrs. Cheirs to the banquet he was planning with his brothers, as an act both charitable and gracious.

June 9, 1864
Late Afternoon
Camp of the 41st Tennessee Infantry, CSA
Hillsboro, Tennessee

After his servant darkie, Abel, packed his things, Bell and Abel set out from Spring Hill for Hillsboro.

Away from old Bishop Polk and excited at getting a leg up on the rest of Polk's stuffy, pious junior aides, Bell mused over his prospects on the ride. He could make a name for himself leading a company of fighting men, and after covering himself with glory, a promotion to major would drop into his hand like a ripe plum.

"Major Bell," he said to no one, as no one was there but his darkie, Abel. He liked the sound of that. It would be a title he could wear with pride until the next war with the Yankees came around, because another war surely would. Then he would be heir to the plantation, and that would make him Colonel Bell, ready to whip the Yankees again.

Hillsboro was half a day's ride, and Bell was too eager to assume his new rank and take a look at his company to do what he would ordinarily do if he was off on his own, namely stop in a tavern for whiskey, and hopefully a fetching, lonely, and cash-strapped local girl to go with it.

Instead, Bell and Abel rode straight for Cheatham's Tennessee Division. After navigating his way through the different camps, he soon found Maney's Brigade and presented himself to the colonel of the 41st Tennessee.

"You've arrived just in time, Captain Bell," Colonel Tillman said. "We're seeing off our brigade commander today."

Bell replied, "Yes, Colonel. How's that?"

"George Maney has been promoted to major general. We found out about it this morning. He is taking over Scared Turkey's, er, Loring's Division. A coincidence, eh? You've come to us from Polk's staff on the day Maney is going over to Polk's Corps."

"Polk prefers to call it the Army of Mississippi."

Tillman chuckled at that, since Bell's arrival put him in a good mood. With Maney moving up, Francis Walker of the 19th Tennessee was replacing him as permanent commander of the brigade, with a brigadier general's wreathed stars to go with the new posting. Tillman was now the senior colonel in the brigade, and with a Bell of Haywood County leading one of his companies…

Tillman said, "The brigade is turning out to see Maney off, but your company is excused. You should come, though. Six o'clock."

"Why is my company excused?"

"You'll see for yourself soon enough. They're over there. First Sergeant Halpern is running things, so ask for him."

Leaving Abel behind to put his things away, Bell walked to where Tillman indicated, out of the tent village of the regiment's camp, and as he came over the crest of the small hill, he found himself confronted by a small crowd of very nearly naked men lolling about under the shade of a grove of trees. Nearby on a patch of flat ground was a smaller group of half a dozen men who were in uniform, tending a pair of small, steaming iron cauldrons and racks fashioned from lashed tree branches, festooned with drying clothes.

After a few seconds, Bell realized he was gawking. He stepped into the tree grove and bellowed, "What in God's name is going on here?"

A man crowding 40, graying hair at his temples and a small, but solid-looking pot belly gracing his middle, grunted and got to his feet. Bell felt relief that this man, at least, had a wide sheet of torn canvas wrapped around his waist. He ambled up and offered a salute.

"I'm First Sergeant Halpern, sir. May I help you, Lieutenant?"

Bell sniffed, "It's Captain now, Sergeant. Captain Samson Bolivar Bell. This is my company, as of this instant. Now, answer my question. What's goes on here?"

"Lice, Captain."

"Lice?"

"Yes, lice. When the brigade came here a few weeks ago, it was our first real stop since we left Georgia, so everyone's uniforms were crawling with vermin. So, we did what we always do. We stripped off and boiled the little bastards and their damned infernal tiny eggs out of the seams of our clothes."

Halpern gave a nod to behind his shoulder. "The thing is I detailed them new boys to the job, and they made a mess of it. New recruits. Always the same. The lice came right back again, so here we are, boiling our clothes a second time. This time I've got Grimes keeping an eye on them."

Bell grimaced. "And what punishment did you give to those men? The conscripts?"

"Well, by now our lice had spread to their clothes too, Captain. I figure making them wear those itchy clothes for an extra day while they take care of the rest of us first will do."

"The Colonel tells me you are excused from the farewell ceremony planned for General Maney."

"Yes, that's right," Halpern drawled. "They haven't boiled it all properly yet, so not all the boys will have dry clothes by then."

Bell wanted at least some of his company with him to see General Maney off and considered ordering the conscripts to accompany him, but then thought better of it. By all reports, they were lice-ridden, and the thought of standing next to them filled him with disgust.

"Alright. Introduce me to the other non-commissioned officers."

"Yessir. Marks and Grimes, front and center!"

Two sandy blonde, wiry men, one of them well over six feet tall and wearing a plump and pink, L-shaped scar on his cheek, got to their feet. Before they could stand at attention, a nauseated-looking Bell waved them off.

"Don't do that," Bell snapped. "You're both in scraps of canvas. Jesus Christ, you look ridiculous. Like some gang of catamites."

The two men stood at ease, both replying, "Yessir!"

Halpern said, "This here is Sergeant Edward Marks, raised from corporal just two weeks ago. The tall fellow is Corporal Willard Grimes, also promoted just a couple weeks ago."

Bell stared at Grimes. "Aren't you a bit young to be a corporal?"

"Captain, sir, I been with the colors since '61. Only private in the company with as much time served as me is my older brother, Nathan, and he don't want no stripes, sir."

If Willie was annoyed at having a boy captain who looked to be about the same age as himself complaining about his youth, he didn't show it. Bell showed every sign of being a rich man's son, and that was how things were.

"Very well. Sergeant Halpern, have the company ready for separate inspection, before breakfast. I wouldn't be surprised if General Walker doesn't parade us tomorrow, and I want you all looking like the best company in this regiment." Bell smiled. "We should have an advantage, with your freshly washed clothes, what?"

"Yessir." Halpern stifled the temptation to shake his head or roll his eyes. Instead, once Bell had taken a few steps, he turned to Willie. "Grimes, you'd better look in on your detail. Some of those nincompoops would chew nettles thinking it was mint."

Willie grabbed one of the sheets of canvas they had handy for anyone who needed to leave the grove, and went over to where the lice-boiling station had been set up. At once he saw that the fires hadn't been kept up, so the clothes were at a low simmer.

Willie demanded, "Why haven't y'all thrown any wood on these fires?" Looking over to the wettest clothes on the rack, he suspected he couldn't trust the job that had been done on any clothes since he left the detail to get out of the sun for a while. Pointing to those suspect clothes, he said, "All this here will need boiling again!"

"Go fuck yourself, Corporal!"

Willie turned to see Raglan Lloyd standing a few feet off, wearing a contemptuous smirk.

"What did you say to me, Lloyd?"

"You heard me."

Willie quickly realized what had happened here. The other conscripts were boys of 17, 18, or 19. All his age, come to think of it, but all as green as he had been in '61. When the army came here, it was the first time the Confederacy had enjoyed sway over this part of Middle Tennessee since Earl Van Dorn got himself shot by a cuckolded doctor. Plenty of young men had come of age since then, young men who didn't have the gumption to leave home and volunteer, but who weren't going to run off when the conscription officer came calling either.

Lloyd was different. He was 27 and a hardened draft dodger who was caught napping when that conscription officer came around. Word had it that he had turned to robbing. Most men in his position did, but there had been no proof and no trial. So he was a robber and a draft dodger, and now he had set himself up as boss of these conscripts and was trying to bully his way up the chain.

Willie raised his voice. "You've kept out of it for long enough, but you're in the army now, Private. You're talking to a corporal. You'll do what you're told, and you'll like it."

Lloyd took two steps forward. He was very close now. They were the same height, and glared easily into each other's eyes. Lloyd's face was splotchy, framed by scraggly, long blonde hair, and his breath stank.

Lloyd sneered "What are you going to do about it, Corporal."

Willie struck fast. He moved to step forward, but instead of punching, he jabbed his heel into Lloyd's foot. As Lloyd began a howl and moved to throw a roundhouse punch, Willie's other leg came up, smashing a knee into his groin. Lloyd doubled over, instinctively shielding his privates with his forearms. Willie brought a short right cross down on the corner of his mouth. Lloyd collapsed, dazed.

"Now, you sonofabitch, you listen good. This here is a Tennessee regiment, and that's how we do things in the Tennessee volunteer infantry! Get your ass up and get to work. And the next time you give me any lip, I'll give you to Halpern, and he ain't so gentle!"

As Willie put the other new boys to work, and Lloyd moaned on the ground, Nathan Grimes sat watching from the edge of the shady grove, where he was playing dice with some of the other soldiers. Good for you, little brother, he thought. Good for you.

Nathan knew Lloyd was going to be trouble as soon as he laid eyes on him. He reckoned Halpern knew it too, which was why he put Willie on him. Willie's first test. If he couldn't put Lloyd in his place on his own, he ought not to be wearing those stripes.

Even so, Lloyd would bear watching. If I've got his measure, Nathan thought, he's a mean and yellow sonofabitch. Ain't worth beaver shit on a penny, but he still ain't going to lay down. He'll either try and get his own back, or he'll run off and desert. Good money says he won't run off before he tries and get even first. Willie's back needs watching.

"Your turn, Nathan."

Nathan took the tin cup of dice from Jim Marsh, a veteran of a year's service. After giving the dice four shakes, he threw them down onto his unrolled gum blanket, on which six numbered squares had been drawn with charcoal.

"Dammit!" All of Nathan's Chuck-A-Luck bets had gone sour on that roll.

"That's it, boys," he cried. "I'm broke!"

June 9, 1864
Evening
Headquarters, Cheatham's Division, CSA
Hillsboro, Tennessee

Cheatham had just finished his first tumbler of bourbon for the night when there was a knock at his door.

"What is it?"

The aide called through the door, "General Cleburne is here to see you, sir."

Damn, Cheatham thought. I was hoping to put this off until my mood was better. I'd scheduled a full day in the saddle tomorrow, inspecting the division to avoid this very thing! Leave it to Old Pat, honest, Irish, no drinking Cleburne to stumble in and shoot that idea full of holes.

Cheatham grumbled, "Show him in."

He rose and shook hands with Cleburne and then motioned for him to take a seat.

Cleburne said, "I prefer to stand, Frank."

"Suit yourself."

"This is a nice place you found here, Frank. Fine, fieldstone farmhouse."

"Yeap, that it is. I'd prefer to go home, of course. It's right over there." Cheatham motioned to the north. "Just some miles or so. You still in tents? You know, even Old Jack has set up his offices indoors at Harrison House. He just sleeps in a tent."

"Yes, I know." Cleburne shuffled his feet, but kept his dark eyes fixed on Cheatham. "You've heard, Frank?"

That's Pat, Cheatham thought. Sincere to a fault, never much good at small talk, finesse, or beating around the bush. Still, I might as well help him out.

"I have. I suppose congratulations are in order."

"Dammit, Frank, I feel terribly over this. I never sought promotion. You're the senior man here, senior by a league. You have a fine record. It ought to be you replacing Hood, not me."

Cheatham grunted. "Pat, I ain't going to lie to you. I've been passed over, and that hurts. It makes me a little sick in my stomach, and I don't mind telling you that. But God dammit, my ambitions and pride don't make me blind or stupid. You are the best damn division commander this army has. And by army, I mean the Confederate States Army. I'm disappointed and bitter, but I ain't mad at no one for it. Besides, you're my friend. You deserve this. I wish it ain't coming at my expense, but that don't change the fact that you deserve it."

Cleburne's eyes became watery. "Frank…"

"Oh, none of that sentimental crap. I ain't in the mood for it. Can we just celebrate your good fortune and put the rest to bed, Lieutenant General Cleburne?"

"Brevet Lieutenant General."

Cheatham burst out laughing. "Are you screwing me up, Pat? You!?"

Cleburne smiled, chuckled even, although his dark eyes still reflected sadness. "It's true. I could be back at my division tomorrow."

"Aw hell, that brevet is all just Richmond politics. I'll tell you plain, I don't think Jefferson Davis was too pleased with the idea of putting a man who ain't been to West Point at the head of a corps."

"Or a foreigner."

"That too. But come to think of it, I ain't been to West Point myself. So where does that leave me? Anyway, will you just leave it all alone. I'm happy for you, Pat. Leave it at that. Will you celebrate with me?"

Cleburne nodded. "Pour yourself one and give me the flask."

Cheatham shot Cleburne an incredulous look. Cleburne was a devoted temperance man. "If that's what you want, but that ain't what I meant by celebrating."

"I know. But just this once. And just a sip."

Cheatham poured another two fingers of bourbon into his tumbler, and handed the now almost empty flask to Cleburne. Cheatham had a drink, and Cleburne had his promised sip.

"Now," Cleburne said. "Let's take up our pipes, share a smoke, and talk about running this Corps."

CHAPTER 4

June 9, 1864
Early Morning
Carter Stagecoach Office
Nashville, Tennessee

Sherman watched as the big sixteen-passenger coach made its way down the Gallatin Road. Once it had traveled a few hundred yards, he mounted his horse, struck a match, and lit a cigar.

After a few hard drags, still watching the departed coach and drumming his fingers on the pommel of his saddle, he grumbled, "Alright gentlemen, back to the office."

As Sherman and his pair of escorting aides crossed the fortified bridge leading to the southern bank of the Cumberland and into Nashville proper, he wasn't sure which left him in a fouler mood: sending his brother-in-law away, or the docket of unpleasant business piled up and waiting for him clear through late afternoon.

Poor Hugh, Sherman thought. A good man, solid division commander, or at least he had been when he was serving under me. So how did he come to surrender his post without firing a shot? And this is after I wired him orders, in plain language directing him to give Forrest a fight? What did that devil have in him that scared a man like Hugh Ewing into staining his pants?

Perhaps it was his health? Sherman knew poor health had a way of wearing a man down, breaking his will. Hugh had been down with a frightful case of dysentery a couple of years before and was suffering badly from rheumatism now. The latter was the reason Ewing was commanding garrisons in Kentucky, and not leading men in the field.

Chewing on his cigar, Sherman muttered bitterly, almost inaudibly, "I'll crucify Forrest if it costs ten thousand lives and empties the Federal treasury." Paroling Ewing and sending him to Nashville instead of Louisville had been a deliberate insult, of course, and it had worked. Sherman boiled over the gesture, which was why Ewing was riding the stage out of Nashville at this very moment. Despite being family and a childhood friend, Sherman couldn't bear having him around any longer.

Forrest was also the reason Ewing had to take the stage and not the train. The last of the track Forrest's raid had torn up would be repaired in a day or two, if it wasn't repaired already. Sherman's efficient railroad repair gangs would see to that. The Munfordville bridge was another matter entirely and would require another week before it was rebuilt.

At least they wouldn't starve while they waited for the supply line to Louisville to be restored, Sherman thought. Nashville held a mountain of supplies, and the garrisons in places like Murfreesboro, Pulaski, and Decatur were well-stocked, as was George Thomas and his Army of the Cumberland down in Chattanooga.

Sherman's reverie came to an end with his realization that he had arrived at his headquarters, and that brought him to the day's second unpleasantness: Brigadier General Samuel D. Sturgis.

He found Sturgis, a thick-set man with a mop of curly black hair, waiting in the foyer. Motioning for Sturgis to follow him, he said, "Come on, General."

Sherman took a seat behind his desk, and regarded the man standing at attention before him. Early 40s, stout, very anxious. He reviewed the details of Sturgis's career in his thoughts, clear as if it were from paper. West Point, Class of 1846; Mexican War service, 1st Dragoons; Indian fighter; fought at Wilson's Creek, South Mountain, Antietam, Fredericksburg, Dandridge, and Fair Garden; current Chief of Cavalry for the Department of the Ohio.

"Well, General, I won't draw this out. Let's have your report."

As Sturgis began describing his actions for June 7th's Battle of Ringgold Mill, Sherman saw immediately how it all went wrong. His own stratagem had worked well enough, of that Sherman was certain. The fact that Sturgis drew Forrest into battle was proof of it.

With Nashville and the Army of the Tennessee encamped to the east, A.J. Smith with 10,000 men marching down from the north, and Sturgis with 8,500 coming in from the west, Forrest was effectively hemmed in. All Sturgis had to do, as the most mobile element of the plan, was either interpose himself between Forrest and his crossing at Clarksville or, failing that, to attack. Listening to Sturgis tell his tale, it was clear to Sherman that he had woefully mismanaged the battle. In his haste to get in front of Forrest, Sturgis had allowed his cavalry to get too far ahead. Forrest was able to lick first one part of Sturgis's force, and then the other.

Sherman ruminated that if there was a flaw in his plan, it was that only one pincer could move quickly. He had wanted to send a third expedition after Forrest, Minty's cavalry plus infantry, but Minty was needed patrolling the outskirts of Nashville. The Rebels were playing merry hell there, and the papers were full of William Hicks Jackson's "visit" to his home of Belle Meade. There just weren't enough men in the saddle to both chase Forrest and keep the Rebels out of the Nashville's hinterland.

But at least he had fought, that was something, Sherman thought to himself, reflecting on his brother in law. Fought badly, but fought.

"General Sturgis, you know why I brought you here, from Memphis to Nashville?"

Sturgis was still at attention, staring straight ahead. "Yes, sir. I attempted to carry out my mission to cut off or engage the Rebel Forrest to the best of my…"

Sherman interrupted. "No, that became your mission only after you left Memphis. Granted, it was only a few days after you left Memphis. What was your original purpose?"

Sturgis gulped. "To bring reinforcements, particularly Grierson's Division.

"Yes, and when you got here, you were to assume command of Grierson and Minty and run the cavalry for the Army of the Tennessee. That isn't possible now. I have half a mind to send you back to Memphis and your old post as cavalry chief there."

"There isn't that much cavalry left in Memphis, sir."

"Exactly," Sherman said curtly. "You are to make your way to Louisville, how I leave to your discretion, and once there await further orders regarding resuming your duties or a new assignment. Dismissed."

Sturgis saluted and left. Watching him go, Sherman felt grateful that at least Sturgis had accomplished his original mission and brought reinforcements. Grierson's Division was intact and would effectively double his cavalry.

Sherman promptly attacked his paperwork, happily losing himself in facts and figures until there was a knock on his door, announcing the arrival of his third unpleasant appointment for the day.

"General Hooker is here to see you, sir."

With some reluctance, Sherman said, "Show him in."

Hooker entered the room and strode confidently up to Sherman's desk. A tall, strongly built man blessed with handsome features and wavy blonde hair, Hooker offered a jaunty, lazy salute and then motioned to one of the chairs.

Sherman nodded, "Please, Joe, sit down. What can I do for you?"

Hooker plopped into the chair. "Nothing, Bill, nothing at all. It's what I can do for you." He pulled out a folded up newspaper from the inside of his coat and gently tossed it onto Sherman's desk. "Have you seen this? It's the *New York Tribune* from Monday."

Sherman nodded again. He knew the paper and its contents. That particular rag was what Horace Greely had intended for every Republican delegate to the convention in Baltimore to take with him onto the floor. The lead editorial was harshly critical of Lincoln and the direction of the war in the West, and called for John C. Fremont, the famous Pathfinder and darling of the Republican Radicals, to replace Sherman, and for "Fighting" Joe Hooker to replace James B. McPherson at the head of the Army of the Tennessee.

"Well, I wanted you to know I had nothing to do with it. I haven't been in communication with Greely or Wade or Chandler or anyone in Congress or the press, and if I had been, I would have told them I want no part in being a pawn in their schemes against old Abe Lincoln."

Sherman noted that Hooker didn't put Treasury Secretary Salmon Chase on that list. According to his younger brother, Senator John Sherman, Chase was Hooker's most vocal advocate in Washington.

"May I offer you a cigar?" Sherman asked.

"Yes, Bill. I'd love a smoke."

Sherman drew two cigars from the box on his desk, and handed one over, along with some matches. After taking his first few puffs, Hooker said, "Anyway, I wanted you to know. I have nothing against General McPherson, who enjoys my full support, and I'm delighted to have this opportunity to even the score with Stonewall Jackson. In fact, I have a proposal for a small operation that might clear up our difficulties out by Brentwood."

Same old blabbermouth, Sherman thought. Offers McPherson his unqualified support one moment, and then makes a blatant end run around the chain of command the next. Classic Joe Hooker. Sherman took a couple of drags on his cigar to keep the contempt off his face.

"What did you have in mind?"

Hooker got up and moved towards a local map that was tacked on the wall. "My XX Corps has been in the Nashville lines since we arrived. Minty's boys have been skirmishing with the Reb cavalry almost every day in Brentwood, past the Forrest Hills on the Granny White or Hillsboro Pike, or out here on Mill Creek. That Minty is a good man, by the way. Bully call on giving him that star."

"Mac will be pleased to hear you say that. Minty was his choice."

Hooker continued, as if Sherman hadn't said anything about McPherson. "Now, the enemy has been using this gap in the hills below Brentwood, Holly Tree Gap, to move back and forth unobserved. My boys aren't doing anything right now but drilling and tossing pebbles at each other. What I propose is to advance and seize those hills. They abut the Harpeth on the west, so we'd secure that flank, and the heights dominate the Franklin and Wilson Pikes. With infantry in those hills and cavalry on those roads, we'd have Jackson's mounted arm stymied."

Sherman nodded, but immediately saw the flaw in Hooker's plan. Jackson would know Hooker was mustering for an advance before the first soldier had filed out of the entrenchments, and from there that soldier had to advance 15 miles. Jackson had Clayton's Division in Franklin, less than five miles from the ground Hooker wanted to seize. An advance by a small force would certainly be checked, while an advance by Hooker's entire corps might bring on a large-scale engagement. But that might very well be what Hooker wanted.

"I'll take it under advisement," Sherman said. "You should submit a written proposal to Mac, of course."

Hooker replied flatly, "Naturally."

"Well, I appreciate your stopping by, Joe, and your frankness about this Greely business. Journalism! I do believe the Lord made journalists so harlots would have someone to look down upon."

Chuckling, Hooker gave his salute and left.

Sherman stood staring at the closed door for a time, puffing energetically on his cigar. He had known Joe Hooker in California and had never liked him. Although a man without a vice or two wasn't much of a man, Sherman thought, Hooker was a man stooped under the weight of his vices. A gambler, drinker, whore-chaser, debtor, and endowed with a tongue that wouldn't stop wagging even after getting caught in a sausage grinder.

"Fighting" Joe Hooker couldn't be trusted. He was senior to McPherson by five months, and Sherman was certain that if Hooker wanted to go his own way on some matter, it would be that seniority that Hooker would rely upon. At Sherman's request, Halleck had confirmed the War Department order dictating that a Presidential appointment to the post of department or army commander trumped any issue of seniority in rank, for all the good it did. Many officers in the army thought the order and the policy behind it dubious. Given the need and the opportunity, Hooker would exploit the ambiguity.

So, I just need to guarantee Hooker never gets that opportunity, Sherman thought to himself.

With the day's unpleasantness behind him, Sherman went back to work and kept at it until late afternoon and his supper with McPherson and John Logan came around. After washing the ink from his fingers, Sherman called for a small escort and rode back over to the north bank of the Cumberland, where the XV Corps was encamped, and sat down for a meal in the townhouse where Logan kept his quarters. None of the trio of generals wore fancy dress to supper, each preferring to come as he was, as all had spent the day either bent over a desk with paperwork, out in the saddle, or both.

After helping himself to some cornbread, Logan asked, "Mac, pass me that crock of butter?"

McPherson handed the crock over, saying to Sherman "I heard you had to send Hugh home, Bill. It's a damn shame. He was a good man. Damn shame."

Sherman toyed with some salad greens. "I've been thinking about that. Hugh is a good soldier, but he hasn't been well. Hasn't been well for going on two years now. I think that took something out of him, I could see it this morning. He had a good spell for a while, but that wasn't the same Hugh Ewing that went with us to Vicksburg. To stare down the devil, I think a man needs to have all his faculties."

McPherson nodded, grunting, "Forrest."

"What will he do now?" asked Logan, just before popping a chunk of butter-smeared cornbread into his mouth.

"Well, I doubt I can get him a field command. Or a garrison command. Not for a while, if ever. But I can get him a nice desk job. I'm going to put him in quartermaster or commissary in Louisville. I need a man I can trust and with some weight back there, back there permanently, caring for my supply affairs. I grew up with him, he is an Ohio Ewing, and he has a star on his shoulder strap. I believe that makes him perfect for the job. After some months at that, if his health improves, maybe I can bring him back to something better."

Logan said quietly, "Everyone deserves a second chance."

"It's more than that," Sherman replied. "And it's more than just family. I owe him. When they all said I was crazy, it was Hugh who fought for me in Washington."

"Well, you won't hear of any Illinois Union Democrats jumping on the bandwagon to tar and feather him. That I can promise you," declared Logan.

McPherson shifted in his seat. Having felt the lash of Radical Republican criticism himself lately, he sympathized, but had no taste for conversation of Washington or politics. "What of Sturgis?"

Sherman swallowed his food, and said, "I haven't made up my mind about that. And I may need to put someone on the shelf for all the damage Forrest did. So we'll see."

Suddenly perturbed, Sherman set down his cutlery. "Damn me, but I don't understand it. Hugh, Sturgis, these are West Point men. Professionally trained soldiers! Neither man is a coward, neither is stupid. How does one surrender a perfectly defensible fort without trying to fight for it, and the other stumble into battle half-cocked and with his trousers around his ankles?"

"If you ask me," Logan replied playfully, "You fellows who have been to West Point put far too much weight on having been there! You tend to overlook the merits of men who aren't from your academy, and at the same time ignore the deficits of men who have been." Logan chuckled, "If you like them, that is. If you don't, all bets are off."

McPherson grinned and pointed a fork in mock accusation. "Why Jack, are you thinking of yourself?"

"No," Logan said slyly. "Honestly, I was thinking of Bobby Minty. Who led the horse before? Judson Kilpatrick, that's who, a hothead, whoremonger, scoundrel and fool of the first order, out of West Point and not even 30 yet. Ed McCook, well, he's there because of politics. Kenner Garrard, another West Point man. McCook and Garrard aren't bad men, but they aren't what you want for things like, well, fighting Nathan Bedford Forrest. All the while you have fine, able fellows like Minty, Ben Grierson, and John Wilder, and they couldn't get up the ladder because they haven't got the political backing and they haven't been to West Point."

"Well then, you should be happy now," Sherman beamed. "Your army's cavalry is led by Minty and Grierson, and neither one has been to West Point."

McPherson stood up. "May I offer a toast, gentlemen? To true fighting men who have not been to West Point!"

As they laughed and clinked glasses, the supper plates were brought out. Logan had found some servants who had run away from Travellers Rest, the Nashville estate, and promptly hired them to provide for his headquarters, at least so long as they were camped north of the city.

The three generals sat down to plates of steak with fried tomatoes and potatoes, served with a light gravy. The men were quiet for a few minutes, as they eagerly dug into their suppers.

McPherson broke the silence. "It's been a while since we were together like this. How are the families?"

"Mary is well," Logan said. "Busy with her pen, as always. And she writes that little Mary is healthy."

"Your girl is six now?" asked McPherson.

"Yep."

As Logan spoke, Sherman kept his attention focused on his steak. He didn't want to talk about home just now. He was still grieving for his son, Willie, carried away by typhoid fever almost a year ago, and the letter he had received from his wife just that very day had rubbed salt into that most tender of nerves. Ellen meant well enough, but now was not the time for her to renew her pleas for him to embrace Roman Catholicism.

Between Willie, my poor, dear boy, and the burden of my duties, particularly trying at this time, he thought, what with all the reporters in Nashville anxiously waiting with their breaths held for him to make a single misstep and the Radicals eager to put Hooker in his place just to embarrass Lincoln... Christ on the cross! Couldn't she see now wasn't the time to worry about my immortal soul? Worry about my living skin instead!

Sherman spoke up. "What about that lass of yours, Mac? Miss Emily? I did warn you that if you didn't go make your wedding, you wouldn't get another chance." Sherman added teasingly, "Has your ardor for the young lady cooled? I'm suspicious of long engagements, you know."

Flustered, Mac earnestly protested, "Not at all! How could I go back east and think about things like weddings and honeymoons when the army needed me here. My feelings haven't changed a whit, why..."

Logan's thigh-slapping laughter brought Mac instantly to a halt. Even redder than before, he adjusted his napkin and quietly said, "Pardon my outburst, gentlemen."

Sherman grinned. That was their Mac. Brilliant fellow, usually so relaxed, but on some things, just a little too uptight for his own good.

The men finished their dinners over small talk, and retired to the veranda for cigars and bourbon. Once the servants left and the sentries were out of earshot, McPherson said "Bill, there is something I've been meaning to raise. I know Nashville doesn't have room for XV Corps, let alone XVII Corps once Smith gets here with his boys, but I just don't like having the Cumberland split our army like this. I know your reasoning, but I think we should all be on one side of the river. It's safer."

Logan added, "And I wonder if Kentucky really is under threat. Part of the reason for our being here was so some of the army would be in a better position to pursue quickly if the Army of Tennessee crossed the Cumberland. If Jackson hasn't done that yet, I don't think he will. The maximum aggressive would have been to cross the river as soon as his supply wagons came up, and they passed out rations. He's been standing pat for a month. He has something else in mind, I'd stake my bones on it."

Sherman shrugged. "You might be right, but you know how things are. If I brought you across the river, I would need to advance the entire army beyond the Nashville fortifications. Smith gets here tomorrow, and that brings our strength up to 60,000 men. The city proper hasn't got the room. The sewage alone... the boys will be down with fevers in a week's time! And if we move beyond the works, then..."

McPherson finished the sentence, "... then we might bring on a battle before we're ready."

With his cigar clenched between his fingers, Sherman pointed emphatically at McPherson. "Yes. Once I start that ball rolling, I don't want to stop for lack of supplies, and for that we need more transportation. Well, those wagons and mule teams will get to us one way or another, whatever damage Forrest did."

Sherman studied his most trusted subordinates. Did they know? he wondered. His secret plan was for the Army of the Tennessee in Nashville and the Army of the Cumberland in northern Georgia to launch joint offensives starting on June 15th, only six days away. As the field commander, McPherson had drawn up two plans: one for a pursuit into Kentucky and one for an advance on and around Franklin. Only George H. Thomas, the Army of the Cumberland's commander, knew about June 15th. It was Sherman's intention to give McPherson 48 hours' notice on putting the second plan into effect.

Besides, Sherman thought, I'm not as sanguine as Logan about Stonewall Jackson's intentions. He is a tricky one, and if anything would put a bee in Washington's bonnet, it would be Jackson marching on Kentucky. I have to wonder that if I brought the entire army south of the Cumberland, and then didn't advance on Franklin, would Jackson instantly start a foot race for the Bluegrass behind some diversion?

CHAPTER 5

June 9, 1864
Early Afternoon
7th Pennsylvania Cavalry, USA
South bank of Mill Creek, west of Concord Church
14 miles south of Nashville, Tennessee

Spear spied movement. "Lieutenant," he called out in a clear, level tone, not taking his eyes from the place where he saw the flutter. "There's some fellows behind the crest of that hill yonder."

"Rebs?" Webster said back.

"Can't say. Could just be local farm boys. Not runaways, though. They're white. All I know is I saw some movement, and I saw a face and a hat."

"Well, let's have a look." First Lieutenant Webster called the dozen and a half troopers of his advanced guard to a halt, took out his binoculars, and quietly watched the ridge across from Mill Creek for a few minutes.

"Yep, I see them. They're hiding in the grass, but they're there. Two men, both armed. Let's flush whoever's up there out. Sergeant Spear, take two men with you, catch up with the point, and loop around behind them. Your job is to bag whoever gets away."

Spear motioned to his chosen pair, Rose and Crowder, both Pittsburgh glass blowers just like himself, men who had left the glassworks and signed up with him back in '61. As he put the spurs to his horse, Webster was sending a rider back to bring the company up. By the time Spear's trio had caught up to the pair of troopers at the very head of their patrol, the first shot cracked, followed by several more.

Spear gripped his reins and shouted, "Dig those spurs in. We've got ground to cover, cover quick!" The five men galloped headlong for half a mile, before slowing their horses and turning in around behind where the shooting had been heard. Now Spear led his four troopers at the trot, creeping in behind a line of trees, until they came upon half a dozen Rebel troopers racing across the open field before them.

"Horses," he commanded. Spear and his men yanked their Spencer carbines up, and each man fired four, five, or even six shots in the space of half a minute. One butternut horseman fell from his saddle. Another was tossed from the saddle when his horse tumbled over.

Spear cried, "Hee-yaw!" and led his troopers out of the trees. The Rebels who were still mounted rode on, the riderless horse following right behind them, leaving the downed pair to the Pennsylvanians.

Riding up, Spear found one Reb had crawled over to help the other, whose trouser leg was already thickly stained with blood. His men already had the pair covered with their Spencers, so Spear laid his carbine across his saddle and asked placidly, "Throw down your arms and surrender."

The healthy Johnnie yanked a six-shooter out of his belt, clutching it by the cylinder, and threw it away. He did the same with his comrade's revolver. "Do you have a tourniquet for my friend here, Billy Yank, before he bleeds to death?"

Spear fished his tourniquet out of his saddle bag, and casually tossed it over. Looking over to Crowder, he said, "Jim, they need a horse, and you're the smallest of us. Dismount, and ride with Riverboat Charlie. Help that wounded man into the saddle, bind the hands of that other one, and no complaining about it either."

Once his prisoners were mounted, Spear declared, "Now, don't you two fellows get ideas about running off. My friend Jim here is mighty attached to that nag you're on, and we all like Jim. If I even think you're trying to escape, you'll be dead before you hit the ground."

Spear took his prisoners back, where he found that the rest of the company gathered. Lieutenant Webster had grabbed a few prisoners of his own, plus some horses. Two corpses, both shot in the chest, lay on the ground.

Captain Vale said, "Lieutenant Webster. Sergeant Spear. Good work. I reckon I'll have a look around, see if the rest of their regiment is not hereabouts."

Spear nodded. The plan wasn't as foolhardy as it might have sounded. The 7th Pennsylvania as a whole was well above normal strength, so their company had almost a hundred men, each one armed with a seven-shot Spencer repeater. Rebel horse outfits often had 200 or less, and the Rebs were carrying with muzzle-loaders.

"Lieutenant, since your guard took these prisoners, you take the sergeant here and six men, and get them back to camp. The main camp, not the battalion bivvie."

Webster and Spear saluted, gathered their detail, mounted their prisoners, and started the six-mile trip back to Owens Store, where the bulk of the Saber Brigade was camped. After turning over their prisoners to regimental headquarters and Lieutenant Colonel Seibert's staff, they unsaddled their horses, and began the tasks of watering, grooming, and feeding their mounts.

Spear was in the midst of tending to his horse when Webster came over. "Put on your clean shirt and your best jacket, George. You're going into Nashville."

He kept on with brushing his Morgan horse. "What's that?"

"Colonel Siebert is handing out a 24-hour pass to each company. As it turns out, we're the only boys from our company here, and that makes assigning that pass my job. I figure if it's you, I won't need to bail anyone out of jail in the morning."

Spear chuckled. "I reckon you're right. I do like my stripes." He gave Webster a knowing look. Before becoming a lieutenant, Webster had been a sergeant major. So had Second Lieutenant Brandt for that matter. The officers in their company were very wise to how things were in the ranks, as well as having firsthand knowledge of what went on in the fleshpots of Nashville.

Webster said "Now, don't forget to thank Stonewall Jackson. He chased all the working ladies out of his territory, so I reckon they must have all landed in Nashville. What with all that choice, you ought to get a good deal on a poke."

I won't be needing choice, Spear thought. *I know who I'm looking for and where to find her.*

After tending to his horse, Spear put on his clean shirt and retrieved his best uniform jacket out of the battalion baggage. He stacked his carbine, gave his boots, pistol, holster, sword and scabbard a quick spit polish, saddled his horse, and set out for Nashville. As the only man in the regiment with a pass who had not spent the day in camp, he left hours after the others and made the short, eight-mile journey alone.

After presenting his pass to the provosts on the Nolensville Pike, Spear rode first through the outlying pickets in their rifle pits, and then the massive earthworks of Nashville's fortifications, a forbidding wall of dirt, stone, and wood studded with iron cannon and girded by row upon row of sharpened stakes, *cheval de fries*, and deep ditches. It was well after dark by the time he entered the city proper, but he knew the way, straight down Broadway to Smoky Row. He turned onto 2nd Avenue, left his horse with a stable there, and went straight to his favorite brothel, the Red Filly.

Stepping through the door, he peered through the haze of tobacco smoke to see the 7th Pennsylvania's regimental commissary and quartermaster sergeants at a table, sharing a bottle of whiskey. The other tables were also occupied by blue uniforms, singly or in small groups, and a quick glance around yielded mostly corporals and sergeants, a few lieutenants, and a captain.

Spear smiled. He liked the Red Filly because the house's girls didn't cheat and bribe for their clean bills of health from the doctors, nor their licenses from the Army. Just because every prostitute had to have a doctor declare her disease-free and a license from the Army to work didn't mean all those papers were gotten squarely. Also, the prices at the Filly kept the common privates out. This was a middling place for men with stripes on their sleeves, and the thriftier fellows with bars on their shoulders.

He called to the bartender for a beer, and then sat down with his fellows from the regiment. "Evening. Do you know who all these other fellows are?"

"Bunch of fair-weather soldiers," spat the commissary sergeant. "From the 180-day regiments they raised to thicken up the Nashville garrison, in case Stonewall comes knocking."

"This lot are Buckeyes," muttered the quartermaster sergeant. "I've heard one big fat regiment of them 180-day boys came in from Iowa, Illinois, Indiana, and Ohio each. Story is when the recruiting officers said they were forming a new regiment for a six-month term, men signed up like nobody's seen since '62, all of them figuring six months in Nashville beat sitting around waiting their turn in the conscription lottery."

"Where's my manners?" said the commissary. "Spear, isn't it? Will you have some whiskey with us? It's rye, not corn."

The barkeep arrived with a mug of beer and a shot glass, placing both before Spear. "I'll have one drink of whiskey with you, sure," Spear replied. "But I'll stick to beer after that."

The quartermaster stood up. "To the 7th Cavalry, 80th of the Line. The boys who put the sharp tip on Minty's Sabers!"

The trio of sergeants clinked shot glasses, swallowed, and sat back down. "Oh, I almost forgot," the quartermaster said. "Be sly about it, but there is a general in the room. Over there, in the back."

Spear slouched in his chair, and looked back over his shoulder to see a thoroughly miserable-looking man, thickset with a thick head of curly black hair, sitting in a dark corner and drowning his sorrows alone in a bottle of whiskey. Now that he was looking right at him, Spear could see the star on his shoulder straps.

"Who in God's name is that?" Spear whispered.

The quartermaster replied quietly "Barkeep said that is Sam Sturgis, the fellow got himself whipped by old Nate Forrest the other day."

Spear was about to say something when he felt breath on his ear and heard a whispered feminine drawl. "So lovely seeing you again George."

He grinned, his whole body tingling, but didn't look back. Instead, Spear sat up straight and opened his lap a bit. "Ms. Higgins, lovely seeing you as well."

A raven-haired girl of ample, fetching curves and not much more than 20 years plopped down side-saddle on Spear's lap. Placing her arms around him, she said, "Are you with us long, George?"

"Just 'til morning, I'm afraid. Would you join us for a drink, Molly?"

"What a sweet suggestion. Don't mind if I do." Molly took Spear's empty shot glass, poured herself a whiskey, and held it towards the pair of supply sergeants and nodded before knocking it back.

"To answer your question, Molly, not long. I need to go back in the morning. My intention was to have a few more beers here, and then see about a bed to sleep in tonight. Mind if I share yours?"

"That," Molly purred, "would be delicious."

June 10th, 1864
Early Evening
Camp of the 41st Tennessee Infantry, CSA
Hillsboro, Tennessee

Willie asked the darkie cooks, "So what have y'all done with the game we done brought you today?"

One of the cooks handed over some hoecakes and ladled out some stew onto Willie's tin plate. "See for yourself, sir."

Nathan and Willie Grimes had had a very good run of trapping, bringing in two groundhogs, a rabbit, and a couple dozen squirrels. Usually the enlisted men in the regiment cooked their meals in small messes, but on occasions when special food was available, the negroes who tended to the officer's mess cooked for everyone. With fresh meat on the table, today was such a day, and the cooks had combined it with captured Yankee salt pork, navy beans, and fresh wild onions into a stew.

Taking his supper, Willie walked off to the First Sergeant's tent, just a half-shelter fashioned out of one of the many dog tents captured at Lawrenceburg. It wasn't much, but even so, First Sergeant Halpern was the only enlisted man in the company with a shelter all his own. Willie still ate breakfast and dinner with his brother Nathan and his old mess, but since making corporal, he joined Halpern and Sergeant Marks for supper.

Halpern was sitting in a camp chair under his lantern post, and Marks had the tree stump, leaving Willie to sit on the ground. Halpern asked, "Where's Nathan? I reckon he should have been back by now."

Nathan had been dismissed with a pass after the new afternoon skirmish drill instituted by Old Pat Cleburne, allowing him to take some of his squirrels off to trade as a reward for bringing them in. Most likely he had it in mind to trade for cheap, pop skull whiskey, seeing as how he had gambled his pay away and Jackson had ordered all the captured Yankee whiskey destroyed, excepting some kept for medicinal purposes.

Willie said, "I ain't worried. He's got papers this time, and it ain't like he's going to run off. Besides, he ain't the only one. Where's the Captain? He weren't in the officers' mess."

Halpern chuckled, "His boy told me that Captain Bell would be joining some of the other captains and going over to the widow Ross's house for cards tonight."

Willie said sullenly, "I knew that lady weren't right. Captain Fletcher wouldn't go do something like that. Gambling. Drinking. Loose women."

Marks sopped up some stew juices with a hoecake. "I suspect the only reason old Captain Fletcher wouldn't do such a thing is likely because Tillman wouldn't grant him the pass."

Halpern grunted and Willie reddened a little. They all knew some of the regiment's other officers, including Colonel Tillman, didn't much care for their old company commander, on account of his stridently Whig sentiments. They also knew Tillman was very favorable towards their new company commander, the young Samson Bell, scion of one of the biggest land owners in Haywood County.

After a few bites of stew, Willie asked, "How is Fletcher, anyhow? Any word from back in Lawrenceburg?"

Halpern shrugged. "Regimental quartermaster told me just before afternoon drill that Fletcher was out of the hospital. Going home to his pa, to his homeplace out on Big Rock Creek."

Marks said quietly, "Shame he lost his foot."

"If he'd stayed or come back, reckon he would have made major?" asked Willie.

Halpern said flatly, "Yeap. I reckon with Miller killed, it would either be Fletcher or nobody."

Suddenly uncomfortable with the subject, although he wasn't sure as to why, Willie said, "Now I like this here stew, but that Sunday dinner we just had was better. Rhubarb crumble! I ain't had it so good since…" Willie's voice trailed off. He honestly couldn't recall when he had last had any crumble, or cobbler, or pie. Confederate rations weren't often so tasty, and it wasn't like his bitter old pa set a good table either.

Halpern said, "Fresh asparagus too."

"Ain't like there aren't farmers in these parts," said Marks. "They just ain't growing as much, because they ain't got the hands. And they ain't got full barns and smokehouses neither, because they've been picked clean. We been fighting here all through '62 and '63. Armies are hungry things. Only difference I can tell is we got a piece of paper saying we requisition things on behalf of Jeff Davis, while the Yankees got them a piece of paper saying they requisition things on behalf of Abe Lincoln."

"When the piece of paper is bothered with," Halpern added.

"You fellows reckon we're here to stay?" asked Willie.

"Well, Corporal," replied Halpern, "I can't rightly say. I do know one thing. Stonewall Jackson ain't no Bragg or Pemberton. If he decides to leave, it'll be because he wants to go, or because the Yankees well and truly licked us. We finally got ourselves a general with some iron in his back and fire in his belly, not like back in Mississippi or Chattanooga."

Willie polished off his meal and stood up. "Well, if you don't mind, I have affairs see about in the latrine." He walked out of camp and to where the regiment had erected an outhouse, where the smell wouldn't offend and the leavings wouldn't contaminate the water.

Concealed in a fold of ground nearby, Nathan watched as his brother closed the outhouse door behind him. A few seconds after doing so, three figures emerged from the trees marking the edge of the field, and quietly covered the short distance to the regiment's latrine. In the moonlight, he could see each bore a club.

He had guessed that since everyone knew he was out of camp that day, a yellowbelly, draft-dodging bucket of scum like Raglan Lloyd would take his chance to even things and bushwhack Willie. The only thing that surprised Nathan was that a couple of the other draftees could be bullied into joining him. Apparently they were all too stupid to realize that while little problems in the regiment were dealt with by some informal discipline, like the whupping Willie gave Lloyd the day before, laying into a corporal with clubs was the sort of thing they shot a man for.

Nathan got up, pulled what had once been Captain Fletcher's Navy revolver from his belt, and crept up behind them in the darkness. When he was a few yards away, he pulled back the hammer on the revolver and said, "If y'all don't drop them clubs, I'm going to have to shoot you in the leg."

Alarmed, the men spun around. When the two boys saw Nathan standing there with a pistol, they dropped their clubs. One of them said, "This ain't what it seems. We is just…"

"Oh, stuff it," spat Nathan. "Lloyd, drop that stick."

"You'll get yours, Grimes. You'll get yours."

Nathan smiled at Lloyd's attempt to brazen it out. "Drop that stick, or I'll put a ball in your thigh."

Lloyd dropped the stick. Willie threw open the door of the outhouse and stepped out wearing a confused look, buckling his belt up as he went.

"What is…"

"Willie, these fellows were laying in wait right over yonder," said Nate, taking a nod at the trees, "with them sticks on the ground there. Aiming to whup you. Or worse. Reckon with this piss-yellow bastard Raglan here, worse."

Willie collected up the clubs. "Let's get Halpern and take them to the Sergeant Major."

The next morning Captain Bell returned, bleary-eyed but with a pleasant, dreamy look on his face, having been successful in winning the attentions of the widow Ross last night away from his fellow captains. No charm had been involved, just some hard coinage. She was a somewhat plain woman, but had satisfied under the circumstances.

I know he is a religious man, Bell thought, but why did General Jackson have to send all the whores packing anyway? It left scanty picking.

Arriving at where the little road met the camp of the 41st, Bell found a man trussed up outside the camp, and recognized him as one of his soldiers. Damn, he thought, what's this man's name? Oh, what difference does that make. What the hell is he doing out here and hogtied?

Raglan Lloyd had been bucked and gagged. He was crouched in a sitting position, with a pole run under his knees and over the crooks of his arms, with his wrists and ankles lashed together. A piece of wood had been placed in his teeth, bound in place by twine wrapped behind his neck.

Bell rode into camp, found Halpern, and demanded, "First Sergeant, one of my men put in the stocks outside of camp?! This is disgraceful, a damned disgrace. What in God's name happened?"

Halpern said pleasantly, "Good morning, Captain. Private Lloyd and a couple of the other new fellows took it into their heads to show Corporal Grimes they don't care much for army discipline. With clubs, you understand. I talked it over with the Sergeant Major and then we talked it over with Colonel Tillman. He was mite displeased, and ordered us to buck and gag Private Lloyd from sun-up to sundown, placing him right where we did so everyone could see him."

Bell was speechless, so Halpern continued. "Didn't you see the paper hanging around his neck? It said 'attempted assault of a non-commissioned officer.' Tillman said he would leave it at that, but if Lloyd ever got up to any kind of insubordination again, he would have that man court-martialed and shot. Said a few choice words about the quality of men conscription was bringing into the ranks too."

"What about those others?" stammered Bell. "You said there were more."

"You didn't see them sir? Sergeant Major took them with him into Hillsboro with the supply wagon, wearing packs loaded down with rocks. Orders were if they stopped for any reason, other than the wagon itself stopping, they were to be bucked and gagged on the spot."

Bell said reluctantly, "Well, if that is what Colonel Tillman ordered..."

Halpern nodded "You had better go see him yourself, Captain."

Flustered, Bell rode off. Nearby, Nathan stood looking out towards the edge of camp, where Lloyd lay.

He won't let it go, Nathan thought. Not that one. He's yellow, but yellow like the dog who bites only when your back is turned. He'll wait until we're in a fight, and if he doesn't skedaddle straight to the next county, it'll be to wait and kill either Willie or me or both, and then skedaddle.

CHAPTER 6

June 11, 1864
Early Evening
Rattle and Snap Plantation
Maury County, Tennessee

"Leo, I cannot begin to tell you how relieved myself and every man of dignity and substance is in this corner of Mother Earth that your army has arrived to relieve us from Northern tyranny. The loss of property has been terrible. Not just black property either, but valuables? Why, George and I had to pool what silver we could hide away from vile, grasping Yankee hands just to make a suitable presentation this evening!"

Bishop Polk smiled pleasantly at his older brother, Lucius J. Polk, owner of Hamilton Place. He had already heard a similar tale from his eldest brother George, master of the family seat of Rattle and Snap.

"This," his older brother continued, raising his frosty, silver julep cup "was part of a set of 18 I kept for entertaining. I lost the six I kept on display two years ago, to some filthy, jumped-up Pennsylvanian cavalrymen."

"I do appreciate your efforts, Lucius. And your difficulties. Sincerely, I do. By the grace of God, our army is in Tennessee to stay, and with His blessings, I hope the family fortunes will be repaired after this terrible war is justly won."

Polk surveyed the scene. The double parlor had seen better days, what with some of its better pieces of decoration and furniture gone missing, but the veranda and garden were as lovely as ever.

Enjoying either mint juleps or a non-alcoholic punch in the splendor of Rattle and Snap's hospitality were all the division commanders of the Army of Tennessee: nephew Lucius Polk, Frank Cheatham, William French, Carter Stevenson, Henry Clayton, and George Maney. Also present were some two dozen members, gentlemen and their wives, of the region's prominent families, such as the Carters and the Websters.

"You know, Leo," the older brother Lucius said chuckling, "I think we should perhaps refer to nephew Lucius as Lucius the Younger, and to myself as Lucius the Elder. So as to not confuse our guests."

Polk smiled, half-sad, recollecting nephew Lucius's father William, gone to God four years before. "Or General Lucius? Our nephew has become quite a soldier. Billy would be proud."

Older brother Lucius nodded, sadly and slowly. "That he would."

Keeping an eye on the space behind his brother, Polk saw the moment he had been waiting for had arrived. Carter Stevenson stepped away from small talk and went out the back for some air. Polk excused himself from his brother and followed him.

"A lovely evening, is it not, General Stevenson?"

"Yes, indeed it is," Stevenson agreed. "I was just thinking to myself how much I am obliged to thank each and every one of your family for this hospitality. A reminder of what we're fighting for, truly. So thank you, sir. Thank you."

"We all make our contributions, as we must. My brothers told me if they could help lift spirits, then they would bring the silver out of its hiding place, clear out the secret smokehouse, and retrieve the last of the fine wine from under the cellar stones."

"But insofar as spirits are concerned," Polk continued, "and morale, I must confess disappointment that General Jackson's dispatches did not make greater mention of the contribution made by you and your division to our victory at Lawrenceburg. Most of the credit went to poor John Bell Hood, which is only appropriate of course, that report being his eulogy and all. But then the remainder went first to Cleburne, and then to Forrest and Cheatham. Only a few words were said about anyone else."

Polk studied Stevenson's long, drawn face carefully. He knew French, Featherston, and most of the brigadiers in his corps were aggrieved that Jackson had not praised their role in the Battle of Lawrenceburg to their satisfaction. Although Cheatham had been uncharacteristically silent to date about Stonewall Jackson, he was a proud man who had just been passed over for corps command, so Polk was sure Old Frank would soon grow more hostile towards the commanding general. Nephew Lucius was blood and could therefore be counted upon.

Against that, all the other senior officers in the army — Clayton, Cleburne, Forrest, Stewart, even George Maney in his own Army of Mississippi — owed their elevation to Jackson. They would be unlikely to side against Jackson in the event of a dispute. Stevenson was the only one Polk was unsure of, and because Stevenson was from A.P. Stewart's Corps, Polk had not been able to sound him out as of yet.

"I thank you for your sentiments, General Polk. I appreciate them, but I must confess I thought Jackson's report a fair one. Stewart's Corps was assigned to pin down the Federal XV Corps, and that is what we did. It was not the most glamorous task that day, but we did our duty, and the record reflects that."

"But Jackson, perhaps unfairly, said nothing of your valiant effort at trying to head off the Yankee retreat to Nashville. You very nearly made it."

"True," Stevenson said, "and we strove mightily, but did not succeed. And we were not criticized for that failure, so I feel we were treated very fairly by army headquarters. Very fairly."

Polk surmised Stevenson was not being cautious or polite, but meant what he said. There would be no nursing this one's grievances with Jackson, Polk thought, because he has no such grievances to nurse.

Noticing that a very well-attired darkie servant was speaking to the string and brass band that was serenading them with a dignified rendition of "Dixie," Polk shifted his attention towards the front of the double parlor while continuing polite small talk with Stevenson. George and Sally had taken up a position there, waiting to greet their most honored guest. Stonewall Jackson was here.

The same well-attired servant returned, and then disappeared into the entry hall for some moments. Even the least observant of the guests took note of that and surmised what it meant. The room quieted before the servant returned to announce "Ladies and gentlemen, the commander-in-chief of the Army of Tennessee, General Thomas J. Jackson."

The band began playing "Stonewall Jackson's Way" as Jackson stepped into the room. He wore his best uniform, a parting gift from Robert E. Lee and Jeb Stuart, a thing of restrained splendor, adorned with just the right amount of gold trim and braid. The room broke into loud, enthusiastic applause.

Jackson smiled weakly, his cheeks colored bright red. I should never have allowed Sandie, he thought to himself, to talk me down from ordering that song banned. "Good for morale"... in a pig's eye! It's an embarrassment, the way they play that tune everywhere I go.

After shaking hands with George Polk and kissing Sally's proffered hand, Jackson found himself mobbed by a small crowd of mostly civilian well-wishers. Politely mobbed to be sure, but mobbed all the same. No one noticed J.P. Smith or the saddle bags he wore over his shoulder, especially as Smith didn't enter the double parlor, but slipped away to the adjoining day parlor.

By the time Jackson had finished becoming properly acquainted with every civilian present, the time for the banquet had arrived. The party, some 32 in attendance, was led out of the house and to a flat patch of ground between the carriage house and the pond. Lanterns had been hung and a canvas windbreak erected.

George Polk joked "I beg your forgiveness for the outdoor seating, but when I designed the house, I'm afraid in my abhorrence of company, I never anticipated the need to sit more than two dozen at my table."

While the others laughed, Jackson stared at George Polk for a moment before the jest occurred to him. "Oh yes. Yes," he muttered. "Good. Hah."

The table was lavishly adorned with richly colored tablecloths, and brilliantly polished silverware and candelabras, and was heavily laden with sumptuous food. At the head of the table was a roast turkey and a roast chicken, both golden brown, while a roast suckling pig and a fine, glazed ham sat at the foot. Occupying the table's center was a succulent round of beef and a whole roast lamb. Filling the spaces between were dishes of rolls, cornbread, field greens stewed in bacon, roasted potatoes and carrots, and corn on the cob, along with bottles of wine, tall-cut celery stuffed into stands and sauce boats with cranberry sauce and gravy.

Jackson took up the place of honor, to the right of George Polk, who as host sat at the head of the table. Sally Polk sat to Jackson's right, and across from them were "Lucius the Elder" and Leonidas. From there, the arrangement continued down in a fashion that mixed protocol with the intention of spreading the assembled major generals around.

The house slaves began the banquet by pouring wine and serving not from the offerings on the table, but by ladling out a creamy oyster soup to the guests. Jackson placed his hand over the wine glass, and as a lifelong dyspeptic, looked down at the rich soup with little enthusiasm. While Leonidas Polk tucked into his soup bowl with relish, Jackson took a few spoonfuls over long intervals, consuming just enough of the broth to meet the standards of politeness.

George Polk asked discretely, "Would you care for some pepper for that soup, General?"

Jackson shook his head. "No, no. I do not care for pepper, as it weakens my leg. But I am much obliged."

"George, if you don't mind my asking, where on earth did you find oysters for this soup?"

Jackson looked down and across the table to see the woman who inquired of the host was seated next to Lieutenant Colonel Abram Looney. He remembered her name, Sally Todd Looney. The Looneys owned an estate in Spring Hill, and Cheatham had asked that Abram Looney be excused from his duties with the 1st Tennessee Infantry and permitted to attend, as he hadn't seen his wife in years. Jackson had gladly assented, as it didn't interfere with his intentions for the night.

George replied, "You can thank my dear brother the Bishop for that. Excuse me, Leo, the General. Well, the General here was able to find us some canned oysters, brought up from Mobile. Like so many other things here — the servants, the silver — assembling things into a civilized affair, the way we had them before the Yankee invasion, is not impossible, but still requires ingenuity and a combination of our efforts."

With Jackson looking straight at them, Sally asked, "General Jackson, I hear tell you are from Lexington, Virginia? Neither my husband or myself have been there. Could you tell us about your homeplace?"

Jackson placed his spoon down, grateful for a means to avoid eating any more of the overly rich broth and its shellfish meat. "Lexington is the seat of a county of prosperous small farmers, framed by green mountains to the west and east. A river runs through it, a river sharing the name of this very place, Maury. I hold if we are much different from the rest of the Upper Shenandoah, it must be because of our institutions of higher learning. We have two such places, Washington College and the Virginia Military Institute, where I was honored to serve as Professor of Natural and Experimental Philosophy, as well as artillery instructor."

The conversation at the table became more subdued, as everyone wanted to listen to what Jackson had to say, even about such mundane things. Sally Looney continued, "Will you go back there? After the war?"

Jackson nodded. "Yes, yes."

"And not pursue a career in the army?" asked the elder Lucius Polk. "You are still a relatively young man, General Jackson. If I recollect, 10 or 15 years younger than the other men of your rank. I imagine Lee, Johnston and the others will retire before too long. You are, if I may say so, in line to become the top general of our army just a few years down the road."

"General Bragg is only seven years my senior, and General Beauregard only nine. But I have no such ambitions beyond returning to my wife and daughter and raising a family among my friends and neighbors."

Bishop Polk said, "I once suggested that after the war, our General Jackson here and General Stewart too should come to Sewanee and help build up the University of the South into a national university our Confederacy could be truly proud of, something to rival the hallowed halls of Oxford. I'm afraid he declined, but I was not entirely persuaded by his protests."

Jackson looked across the table to Polk and smiled amiably. "I fear I would have a terrible time persuading my dear wife to come to Tennessee."

Polk smiled back, the picture of serenity. He had discussed the matter at length with Jackson during the past month and knew a powerful ambition lurked beneath his modest, sometimes awkward manner. He doubted very much that Jackson would refuse an offer to, say, found the Confederacy's military academy, and he was certain that Jackson's ambitions were channeled along two narrow channels: the army and the academy. He was no threat to Polk's own ambitions of succeeding Jefferson Davis and becoming the Confederacy's second president.

Sally Polk said, "And how is your family, sir?"

Jackson countenance darkened instantly. "Fled to Roanoke. A Federal army under David Hunter is approaching Lexington and may be there even now."

Many paled at the news, and Sally Polk said, "Surely not. I saw in the papers that the Yankees were moving south through the Shenandoah Valley again, but I thought we would turn them back, as the gallant Breckenridge did in May."

Shaking his head, Jackson said "No, no. I have no knowledge of what General Lee plans to do about Hunter's army, but I am certain he plans something. With the blessings of Providence, the invaders will be repelled."

George Polk stood and thrust his glass forward. "To the liberation of Virginia and Tennessee, and our victory in this war!"

The toast met with many "hear, hear's," the glasses were clinked all around, and when the party resumed their seats the main course was served. None noticed how Jackson had turned his eyes down, nor how they were wet and glistening. His family were refugees and Hunter would be in Lexington soon, where he would no doubt put his beloved VMI to the torch, perhaps even his house. Jackson put nothing beyond the perfidy of some Yankees.

He burned to hit them back, to smash Hunter as he had Nathaniel Banks at Winchester. But he was here now, in Tennessee. Providence must find another to punish Hunter, he thought, for my duty is to deal with Sherman. That must be my consolation. That and, as the scriptures say, knowledge that "judgment is without mercy to one who has shown no mercy." Hunter will pay for his sins, of that I have no doubt.

When Jackson had made his plate, all he had on it was a piece of cornbread, a helping of roasted vegetables, a pair of celery sticks, and a chicken leg, which was easier for him than meat that required a knife and fork. George Polk leaned over and whispered "My dear General, is everything alright?"

"You have set a pretty table, Mr. Polk," Jackson said in a subdued tone, "but one that is, for the most part, too rich for my constitution."

"Leo warned me of that. You needn't worry. Dessert will be more to your liking. "

That dessert lived up to George Polk's promise: a simple bowl of fresh cherries and peach slices. Jackson was delighted, and ate with great pleasure. After dessert, the ladies returned to the double parlor, while the men went to the back porch and garden. Most partook of brandy and whiskey, accompanied by pipes or cigars. Jackson was furnished with a tall glass of fresh milk, and Bishop Polk took coffee.

Jackson was approached by James Webster, an older gentleman in his early 60s. After introducing himself, Webster asked, "General Jackson, if it is not imprudent, some of the papers wonder quite vociferously why you didn't keep on going north. I was wondering..."

Frank Cheatham came up and slapped a friendly hand on Webster's shoulder, "I'm afraid, Jimmy, that you won't get much from General Jackson. He likes keeping his secrets. Why, once back in Georgia, when I asked him about nothing so innocent as what training he had planned for my division, you know what he said? That if his coat knew his plans, he would take it off and pitch it on the fire."

"I've known Jimmy and his family since I was a small boy. General Jackson here knows so little of these parts. Why don't you tell him about your daddy? Just so he doesn't come away with the impression that Maury County isn't a fiefdom of the Polk clan."

Jackson listened attentively as Webster described how his father, a Revolutionary War veteran, came over from Georgia in 1807 and staked his landholding, which he and his brothers later built upon. As Jackson listened, he thanked Cheatham with a nod of his head. It was a stridently democratic country, sometimes too democratic, and many prominent civilians used to getting their way thought they had a right to know of military matters that were none of their business. Just last week Tennessee's governor, Isham Harris, and Senator Landon Hayes came calling with inquiries as to his future plans and were fended off with lamentably less tact.

When Webster finished, Jackson said, "Pardon me" and checked his watch. "Gentlemen," he called out, "if Mr. Polk will be good enough to lend me the use of his day parlor, all general officers will join me there."

Jackson's stentorian tone left no doubt among the generals that the party was at an end, politely made their goodbyes, and followed their leader into the hallway. In the day parlor, they found Jackson's familiar aide-de-camp, Captain J.P. Smith, waiting for them with several fat envelopes.

Jackson turned to face Polk. "Lieutenant General Polk, I apologize for using the hospitality of your family as part of my deception, but military necessity must take precedence."

Lucius Polk came up beside his uncle. "I think I see, sir. You see, Uncle Leo, it's Saturday, and General Jackson's observation of the Sabbath is well-known to the enemy. We're more than 40 miles from army headquarters, and they must know we're here."

Polk nodded slowly. "Yes, I see." They might catch the Yankees napping and would at least muddy the waters. Whatever Jackson had planned, he had just gained a day's head start.

"Captain Smith has copies of your marching orders. You are not to share them with anyone outside your immediate chain of command. Generals Cheatham, Clayton, Stevenson, and Polk, your senior brigadiers will see to starting the march, under the supervision of Generals Cleburne and Stewart. You are to continue with whatever plans you had for the night, and join your divisions on their routes of march in the morning."

Stevenson said, "Sir, I would like to ride to my command at once. Would it not be better for us to be there as soon as possible?"

"No, no. I saw this as an opportunity to give your deputies some experience in handling larger responsibilities. And their deputies as well." And, Jackson thought to himself, Cleburne and Stewart are there to supervise.

Looking to Polk, Jackson continued, "Your corps is closer at hand, and keeping that in mind I excused yourself and your officers to attend. Again, I thank you for your generosity, but you, General Maney, and General French must depart at once and implement your orders."

The Bishop saluted. "Of course, sir. I would prefer to study our orders here, so if there are any questions…"

Jackson nodded, "Yes, of course." He dismissed Captain Smith to his bed, left the assembled generals to study their orders, and went out into the hallway.

"Mr. Polk," he said audibly, standing in the doorway so the generals in the day parlor could see him. "You have such a lovely home. May I have a tour?"

George Polk replied, "I would be delighted, General. Delighted."

Having designed and built the house himself, George Polk knew every detail and wanted to start with the front. Jackson grinned as they stepped outside. His officers and the civilians would think it strange, but sometimes people found a show of nonchalance very encouraging.

June 12, 1864
3:15 a.m.
Camp of the 41st Tennessee Infantry, CSA
Hillsboro, Tennessee

Sergeant Marks shook Nathan gently on the shoulder. "Get up, Nathan."

Nathan's head hurt, thick with hangover. He grumbled, "What? Hell's bells, Ed. It's Sunday, and I didn't hear no horns."

Lying next to him under the half-shelter, Willie woke and muttered something inaudible. The other men nearby were waking as well.

Marks said in a level voice, "All of you up. Get up! It's assembly, so fall in. But don't make a fuss. No bugles, no bells, and no shouting. That's an order."

Once he was sure at least Willie was awake, Marks went off to rouse the others. In a matter of minutes, the company was dressed and moving to assembly, where Captain Bell stood watching and waiting in the dim lantern light. He gave a long yawn as he turned around and the company lined up beside him, along with the other companies in the regiment.

With the regiment assembled, the Sergeant Major gave a hoarse, hushed call of "T'shun!" Then Colonel Tillman stepped out.

"Boys, we're moving out. Marching orders came down just a little while ago. See to your breakfast. We're to issue what remains of the Yankee coffee, so boil it up and drink it while you can. Then strike the tents, roll up your gum blankets, fill your canteens, draw five days rations of that Yankee hardtack and salt pork, and 40 rounds for your cartridge boxes. We are the tail of the division this time around, so see if you can't scare up a bandana or bandage to keep the dust out of your mouths. We're on the road at six o'clock. Dismissed."

The assembly broke up, with the officers meandering off either to their quarters or their mess, and the men sifting themselves out into their own mess groups, whereupon they set about the business of starting cooking fires. With three hours to do what for most was one hour's worth of work, they enjoyed a leisurely breakfast of hoecakes and bacon.

Savoring what he believed would be the last cup of coffee, the real rio, he would see for weeks or months, Nathan looked across the fire to Marks. "Care to place a wager on where we might be going, Ed?"

Willie shot Nathan a look, to which Nathan smiled back pleasantly. With the coffee and some bacon grease in him, he felt much better, and pulling Willie's leg was so easy. Damn, Nathan thought, I need to pinch Willie's Bible thataway more often.

"I reckon that Lucifer's beard will sport icicles before Old Jack tells us where we is going," Marks replied. After stuffing a small plug of tobacco into his cheek, he continued "Democratic, that man. We ain't got no idea, colonel ain't got no idea, them other generals ain't got no idea. I guaran-damn-te you of that."

"Ain't that more like a kingly way?" asked Willie. "Sitting at the top, not saying nothing to nobody."

Nathan said, "Naw, just the army way. Only more army." Grinning, he raised his feet and wiggled his toes. "I declare, I'm looking forward to this one, wherever we be going. These here brogans from them Yankee prisoners from back in Lawrenceburg they gave me, these are the best shoes I've ever had. And I've had a few weeks to break them in, too."

The Johnnies kept chatting over their precious coffee until the appointed time came, and the regiment assumed its marching formation. There were no bands and no bugle calls, just the

Sergeant Major calling out, "Forward... March!" They soon fell in behind the rest of Walker's Brigade, which in turn came up behind the rest of Cheatham's Division.

They were marching south, towards Hillsboro and the crossroads. That scrap of knowledge told them they weren't going straight down the Hillsboro Pike to Nashville. An hour later, they were in the village of Hillsboro, marching towards the crossroads.

Waiting for them there was not Cheatham, who the Tennesseans expected, but Brigadier General Vaughn. No one knew that Old Frank was riding from Maury County to meet them, so rumors began flying up and down the column that he had finally done something to prompt Jackson to order his arrest for drunkenness.

It was full morning daylight by then, and as they approached the village, the men could see the billowing clouds of dust stomped up by the thousands of pairs of feet, clearly marking where the rest of the division was. And they were going west.

Nathan looked over at Sergeant Marks. "Kentucky?"

Marks nodded. "I reckon so. Ain't much point in going to Memphis."

PART II
WAGON HUNTING

JUNE 1864

CHAPTER 7

June 13, 1864
9:30 a.m.
Thompson's Mill
Headquarters, Minty's Division, USA

The courier found Minty in his tent and working at his camp desk, looking over the commissary paperwork for his horse fodder. Minty looked at the man as he saluted from the tent flap: dirt spattered, sweaty, agitated, but restrained. Whatever he wants, Minty thought, it must be urgent. Minty motioned for him to come into the tent.

"Message from Colonel Klein, sir!"

Minty didn't take his attention from his papers for more than a few moments. He went back to work, and without looking at the courier, said, "On the desk, please. Then wait outside."

After the courier left, Minty picked up and read the scrap of paper:

Monday, June 13
Quarter to 9 o'clock
Headquarters, 1st Brigade of Cavalry
Brentwood, Tennessee

To: Robert Horatio George Minty
Brigadier General of Volunteers, USA

Sir,

I report to you the following facts: 1. My forward patrols relieved my night pickets early this morning, as per standing orders; 2. These patrols bore reports of no Rebel presence to their front; 3. I ordered all patrols forward all the way to the Harpeth, reconnoitering the crossings at Franklin and the Hillsboro Road before I encountered any resistance. Franklin bridges destroyed, Hughes Ford occupied in force. Requesting further orders.

Lt. Col. Robert Klein
Cmd'ing 1ˢᵗ Brigade

Folding his arms over his chest, Minty considered Klein's message. He was certain it was the first sign that Stonewall Jackson was finally on the move, and he had been anticipating it for some time now. He understood Sherman's reasons for waiting in Nashville well enough, but he had expected it would be Jackson who went first all the same.

Minty stepped out of his tent and set his cocked, feather-plumed hat on his head. To his chief of staff, he said, "Major, we'll be postponing that inspection of the 4ᵗʰ Michigan's horses for another time." Turning to the courier, he said, "My compliments to Colonel Klein. Go back to him and tell him to send a patrol out to the crossing at Harding Pike and report back. In the meantime, he is to issue rations and ammunition to his men. We might be in the field for a few days."

His next orders were to Smith's Brigade, now patrolling the Mill Creek line, and to his old Sabers, who were resting in reserve nearby, along with his horse guns. They too were to issue rations and ammunition, and be prepared to ride at moment's notice. Only after that was in motion did he send a message by telegraph back to army headquarters, relaying the news to McPherson and requesting permission to cross the Harpeth for a reconnaissance in force. That done, Minty kept himself occupied by seeing his saddle and tack polished, his saber sharpened, and his accoutrements generally made dandy.

He didn't need to wait long. In less than 20 minutes a signals clerk was at his headquarters stables.

"Your reply from General McPherson, sir."

Minty asked placidly, "And what does it say?"

"And I quote: 'You are hereby ordered to cross the Harpeth River at whatever point is most convenient, and ascertain the movements and position of the enemy, proceeding as far south as the Duck River if that be necessary. Good hunting.'"

Minty smiled knowingly. The orders could have been much more restrictive, but even so he wasn't to ride south of the Duck. Minty knew McPherson trusted him—it was McPherson who had gotten him his star—but not two months ago that damnable fool Judson Kilpatrick had abused just such a mission and was badly beaten at Holly Grove Crossroads for it. James Birdseye McPherson was a cautious man and wouldn't be burned twice.

"Thank you." Minty jumped up, strode from the stables, and found his chief of staff. "Dispatch a two-gun section to Klein and tell him that if the Harding Pike Ford is unoccupied, he is to send a regiment across, and that they are to reconnoiter towards Franklin from the west. His remaining regiment and the artillery are to demonstrate before those Rebels now in possession of Hughes Ford. The rest of the division and myself are crossing by way of Trinity Ford, and will approach from the east and southeast."

3:30 p.m.
7th Pennsylvania Cavalry, USA
Winstead Hill, near the Columbia Pike
Franklin, Tennessee

Thus far the "reconnaissance in force" hadn't required much in the way of force, Spear thought. He had heard some of Klein's Kentucky boys had a bit of a scrap at Hughes Ford, but once the artillery showed, the Rebs skeddadled. The Sabers came right over from Trinity Ford and on into Franklin without seeing so much as a scrap of butternut, easy as you please.

Now the Pennsylvanians were posted on the hills due south of Franklin, so as to block any Rebel approach coming up from

Columbia or thereabouts. They knew the country well from much prior service there, including covering the retreat from Lawrenceburg the month before. Taking advantage of the break, Spear and the other troopers who weren't on picket duty had broken into their messes, boiled up some coffee, and set about making a late dinner of skillygale, or crumbled hardtack fried with salt pork.

Spear muttered, "We really ought to mount those negro women we hired to cook for us. They can always make something tasty, even out of iron rations."

Walther Rose puffed on his clay pipe from across the cooking fire. In a light German accent, he said, "I say this many times. You put a little water in the pan before you fry the sliced pig flesh. Then you take the pig flesh out, and cook the biscuits in the fat. Then you put the pig back in. But you never listen."

Jim Crowder commented, "Besides, if we put them cooks on horses, we'd like as not have to put them in uniforms. Or at least them negro menfolk, anyhow. Then half-blind, hairless old sourpuss like Thaddeus Stevens would be all up in our faces about it, saying those negroes should have a Spencer, a six-shooter, and a saber too. They best stay with the wagons. Colored regiments is one thing…"

Finishing Crowder's sentence, Spear said, "… but we don't want them in here with us. Yes, I know."

Spear messed with his glassblowing chums, friends who all worked in the same Pittsburgh works where he had been a junior foreman and who had followed him to the recruiting officer and into the cavalry. Because he had brought half a dozen troopers to the flag with him, and knew a little something about managing men, Spear had started the war as a corporal.

When they all signed up, Spear thought, hardly anyone cared a whit about slavery. Well, Walt was something of an abolitionist, but not hardly anyone else, and Walt's father had some pretty strange notions about work and freedom that he had brought with him from the old country. But even Walt had joined mostly to preserve the Union, and Jim had signed up because he thought riding a horse and swinging a sword would be more exciting than blowing glass. So had I, come to think of it.

Then they all went to Tennessee, patrolling the state far and wide for pretty much the whole year of 1862. Seeing the "peculiar institution" up close had done more to harden their attitudes towards slavery than a hundred anti-slavery speeches. By the time Stones River was fought, they were all abolitionists, to the very last man. Being abolitionists didn't mean they wanted negroes lining up with them at assembly, though.

Thinking about Walt's father prompted Spear to say, "I'll tell you again, Walt, your pap should have done like my grandpap and made his name all American. Less trouble that way, what with the Know-Nothings and all. Clinging to the old country and all is well and good, but not if it gets your teeth broke."

Walt shrugged. "And what do you suggest? 'Rose' is spelt the same in English as German. I think this makes little difference. And when your grandpap came to the three rivers, the place was still full of wild Indians, and people thought all Germans were Hessians, come to kill them for the English King."

Spear dug his spoon into the semi-burnt, imperfect skillygale. Bad as it was, at least he had strong, sweetened coffee to wash it down with. He had just taken his first bite when Crowder asked a question.

"Do you think we'll bivouac here tonight, Sarge?"

Spear swallowed a spoonful and took a sip of coffee. "I believe we will, Jim."

"How so? I imagine they'll be hot to know where the Rebs went to, back in Nashville. There is plenty of daylight left."

"Well, the way I see it is this. Us and Smith's boys have already been in the saddle for 30 miles today. Now you are right, and there is plenty of light left, but to go on far enough to do any good pushes our horses hard. And we've got some good ground here, plus those fortifications back in Franklin if things go wrong. This is a right good and safe place to make camp for the night."

After another bite of food, Spear said, "Our Bobby Minty, now that man is a trooper. He's got cavalry in his blood. We might mount up before dawn and ride like the devil tomorrow, but I can't see him wanting us to wear out our horses only to bed down in some God forsaken place where Forrest could turn around and hit us."

Rose said placidly, "The rumors say Stonewall Jackson went west."

"You never can tell with that one. We thought we were dealing with Polk and two corps at Lawrenceburg, and Jackson was over in Georgia."

After a pause, Spear spat, "That man is full of surprises."

Crowder asked, "Where do you reckon he's going?"

Rose shrugged. "He may go to Kentucky. I believe that is very likely. We all thought he wanted to go to Kentucky before. But..." Rose paused to puff on his pipe for a time. "Perhaps he goes to Memphis and Vicksburg. To undo what Grant did last summer?"

"Well Walt, I promise you this much," Spear said. "Wherever Jackson is going, our Bobby Minty will be out looking for his rear guard tomorrow."

Both Spear's deductions proved sound. Minty elected to remain around Franklin for the remainder of the day. By nightfall, the wire was extended from Nashville, and a telegraphy station was in operation in Franklin, not that Minty chose to remain there for very long. Hopeful of catching the butternut pickets napping, the Irish cavalry general made sure his men were up, breakfasted, mounted, and riding west well before dawn. Smith's Brigade took the route south on Carter's Creek Pike before moving west towards Charlotte, while Klein's Brigade took the direct route by way of Hillsboro. The Sabers came up behind them.

Minty's troopers found less sport than at Lawrenceburg. Buford's horseman had been soldiering under Nathan Bedford Forrest for months by then and knew better than to fall asleep while on duty. Klein's and Smith's advanced guards exchanged shots with small groups of watchful, dismounted gray troopers in the early morning mist. The Federal cavalry pushed on, but soon found themselves stalled along the line of South Harpeth Creek.

The South Harpeth wasn't much of an obstacle, and in mid-June men and horses could cross it at just about any point. Even so, Minty still needed bridges and fords to cross his artillery and the small wagon train carrying his ammunition and fodder. He dispatched the 7th Pennsylvania to feel its way cross-country to the gap between Klein's and Smith's fronts, whereupon they plunged across the creek, scattering the gray skirmishers they found screening the bank. Minty's Division was across the South Harpeth before noon.

The blue troopers pressed on, slowed by fallen trees and the need to keep strong skirmish parties on their front and flanks to guard against ambushes. Then they reached Turnbull Creek and again found the crossings defended. Minty responded as he did at the South Harpeth, this time sending the 4th Michigan, his old regiment, across the creek. It was late afternoon by the time the division was across the creek and had Klein, Smith, and part of the Sabers gathered for a hard lunge into Dickson County. That was when Nathan Bedford Forrest came calling.

The Battle of Turnbull Creek was a small and inconclusive affair. Forrest hit hard with his initial foray, but was firmly repulsed. Minty dismounted, shook out a line, and stood his ground, while Forrest spent the few remaining hours of daylight shelling the Union front and feeling around for their flanks. After nightfall, Minty withdrew to the east bank of the Turnbull.

June 14, 1864
After Midnight
Headquarters, Military Division of the Mississippi, USA
Nashville, Tennessee

Major Audenried burst into Sherman's office, where he found Sherman and McPherson standing before the map table.

Holding out a folded piece of paper, he said, "Sir, a wire from General Minty!"

Sherman took a staccato series of short, hard drags on his cigar as he snatched the message away from Audenried. His eyes danced quickly across the lines of text:

June 14
8:30
Headquarters in the Field, 1st Division of Cavalry,
Army of the Tennessee
Brig. Gen. Robert H.G. Minty Cmdg

To: Maj. Gen. James B. McPherson
Cmdr, Army of the Tennessee

Sir,

My division's progress was halted at Turnbull Creek, where we fought an action this afternoon against a mixed force of horse and foot. Unconfirmed reports sighted Gen. Forrest on the field. Enemy regiments involved known to have been from Buford's Division, which has been contesting my progress all day, and from Featherston's Mississippi Brigade, plus 10 guns. I have withdrawn to behind the Turnbull for the night.

Today's action suggests a strong Confederate presence in Dickson County. I propose to move around south of Turnbull Creek in the morning, swing around their right flank, and directly ascertain the strength, position, and direction of movement for the enemy's main body.

Confirmation requested.

R.H.G. Minty

Sherman handed the message to McPherson, took a few more draws on his cigar, and then stubbed the butt out in a clay ashtray. "Since Grierson reports the crossings of the lower Harpeth strongly covered by elements of Red Jackson's Division, that paints a clear picture. Stonewall Jackson is about Dickson, and because he is about Dickson, he must be making for Clarksville, or somewhere near it. I imagine that new garrison there will see scouting parties sometime tomorrow."

McPherson looked up from the message. "Who is out there now?"

"Rousseau sent a colored regiment and a veteran Ohio regiment, plus a new set of cannon. They should be settled in by now. Round about a thousand men. Not that it matters. Forrest captured the place with a gaggle of cavalry and a few boats last time. Jackson has upwards of 40,000 infantry, several thousand cavalry, roundabout

150 guns, and a bridging train. I've already ordered that bridge there demolished."

"I agree if he's going for Kentucky, he will cross near Clarksville. Probably throw a pontoon bridge across downriver. The Cumberland is narrow there, so it's an awful place for our gunboats to contest a crossing. They'd be fish in a barrel." McPherson added in a heavier tone, "I just wish I were certain he was indeed going to Kentucky."

Sherman drummed the table with his fingers. "He isn't going to the Mississippi. If he were doing that, he should have gone west from Selma a month ago, not north. And Forrest left that bridge in Clarksville standing for a reason, for all the good it will do him. No, Kentucky is the only place Jackson can go that draws us out of Middle Tennessee and the only place he can easily live off the land and provide for his army. The way I see it, he has always had two options: march on Kentucky or march on Chattanooga. Dickson isn't on the road to East Tennessee."

McPherson couldn't argue with Sherman's logic. What bothered him was how according to script it all was. If his battle with Stonewall Jackson had taught him anything about the man, it was the primacy Jackson put on playing close to the chest and keeping his trump cards safely tucked away in his sleeve. Invading Kentucky was certainly audacious and was the move they had been dreading from this very headquarters all the way to the War Department in Washington. Yet because it was so feared, an invasion of Kentucky was also what they expected, and doing the expected didn't sound like the man he fought at Lawrenceburg.

"Well," McPherson said with resignation, "we can't simply sit here in Nashville, whatever he does. I'll put the army in motion. The boys will be on the road for Springfield before dawn."

"Cheer up, Mac." Sherman smacked him on the shoulder. "Tomorrow is June 15th. We were moving out in the morning even before word of this reached us. Now we're going north instead of south. We'll catch Jackson, fight it out with him, chase him back down to the Cumberland, use the gunboats to cut him off, and destroy him. And best of all, Old Slow Trot is moving out in the morning too."

McPherson nodded. Whatever might be happening in Middle Tennessee, George Thomas's Army of the Cumberland was poised to give Bill Hardee a good, hard kicking in the mountains of northern Georgia. And by the grace of God, McPherson thought, that is exactly what Thomas would do.

June 15, 1864
10 p.m.
Headquarters, Army of Tennessee, CSA
Charlotte, Tennessee

Sandie walked up to the front door of the Dickson County Courthouse, a simple brick building adorned only with a central cupola at the top. J.P. Smith had told him it was where he had spent the night with Forrest's party on the ride back from Clarksville little more than a week ago. Now it was army headquarters for the night, although in keeping with Jackson's dictum, they only worked indoors and slept in tents on the courthouse lawn.

Going straight to Jackson's office, he passed the guards and aides and knocked at the door. Upon hearing a muffled "yes, yes" inside, Sandie entered.

"Sir, General Cheatham is here to see you on an urgent matter." Sandie then deepened the tone of his voice and said, "In the company of a Dr. Coleman."

Jackson spun out of his chair. Sandie saw a spark of light in his eyes. Oh yes, Sandie thought. He hasn't said a word, but he has been anxious about this one.

Composing himself, Jackson said steadily, "Bring them to me. Good, good."

Sandie called for Cheatham, who soon ambled into the office in the company of a wiry figure wearing an ill-fitting, borrowed uniform coat with a trio of captain's bars about the collar. The rest of the thin man's clothes contrasted sharply with the coat, as they were impregnated with dust and dried sweat, and he was visibly both animated and weary.

The dingy thin man saluted and spoke with a mild Scottish accent. "General Jackson, sir. May I tell you, sir, this is quite an honor. Captain Alexander Gregg, reporting as ordered."

Jackson took a step forward and extended his hand. "Nonsense, Captain. The honor is mine."

The day after arriving in Franklin, Jackson had summoned Cheatham to headquarters and inquired about what had been Bragg's intelligence service in Tennessee, since he knew Old Frank had had a hand in organizing it. In this way, Jackson took up the reins of the Coleman Scouts. He had never met their current leader, Captain Gregg, before tonight, but to Gregg's personal supervision went the most important assignment of all: monitoring the movements of the Federal army in Nashville.

"I take it," Jackson continued, "that McPherson and Sherman are on the move?"

Gregg ran his hand over his head, slicking back his sweaty, dirty hair. "Yessir, General. The XV Corps and XVI Corps were both on separate roads before dawn, bound for Springfield. By sunrise, XX Corps was crowding the bridges and coming north. All of this I saw with my own eyes. As soon as I saw Hooker's boys crossing the river, I knew the whole army was really on the move. All in all, about 60,000 infantry I reckon. I departed to find General Cheatham at once, as ordered."

Jackson nodded. His total strength was more than before Lawrenceburg, what with volunteers, conscripts, the lightly wounded returning to duty, and other returnees. Yet with Strahl's Brigade detached to train its large helping of green troops and garrison his rear, he had about the same number of men as before the march into Tennessee.

Sherman has taken the bait, Jackson thought. If Providence stays with us…

"Sandie, summon all the senior officers. And retrieve those written orders you were instructed to prepare. You know the ones I mean. And see to it Captain Gregg here gets a tent, a wash basin, and a proper meal. And have some coffee sent in for General Cheatham."

"There is no coffee left, sir. We still have some of that ground sweet potato stuff, though."

Cheatham nodded, saying "Much obliged." Sandie saluted and left, his satisfaction bringing a rosy character to his cherubic features. The Tennessean pulled up a chair close by the window, watching Sandie leave as he did so, and realizing that whatever Old

Jack was planning for them, that the boyish, 23-year-old colonel who had just walked out the door had known about it for days. Perhaps even weeks or even for the last month.

We all think it's Alex Stewart that Jackson confides his secrets in, Cheatham thought, but it's not. Hot damn, it's not! Not all the time. It's that boy right there who truly counts as Old Jack's inner circle.

Cheatham opened a window, sat down, and began rummaging through his pockets for his pipe and tobacco pouch. Jackson returned to his chair by his camp desk, while Captain Quintard, one of his newer western aides, came in to set up a map table.

The two generals sat quietly for a time, Cheatham puffing on his pipe and Jackson ramrod erect in his chair, arm resting on the desktop with his thumb stuck straight into the air.

After a few minutes, Cheatham spoke. "Perhaps you will find this amusing, sir. Have you heard that when I rejoined my division, after leaving the Rattle and Snap banquet, the boys were gossiping that you had finally had enough of my drinking and put me in arrest!"

Surprised, but not amused, Jackson asked, "Why would they think that?"

"I imagine a mixture of finding Alfred Vaughn in command and our mutual reputations."

Jackson's expression soured. "Let me assure you that any complaint I have with your drinking, General Cheatham, is at this time strictly personal and private, or else you would have heard about it."

Cheatham chuckled. He had seen that Jackson was one of those who took themselves too seriously long before. It wasn't that the man had no sense of humor, but that it was walled off in places.

"You've never had much taste for liquor yourself, sir? If I recollect, the Presbyterians don't take to drink all that often, but nor do they abstain."

"That is true," Jackson replied. "I must confess I like the taste of whiskey, and some other spirituous liquors as well. That is why I avoid them."

Jackson considered Cheatham for a moment. He didn't care for the Tennessean's drinking, it was true, but Frank Cheatham was hardly the first hard-drinking officer Jackson had served with. More importantly, Cheatham's fondness for whiskey never seemed to interfere in his duties, despite the stories. He was an able division commander, but not, Jackson felt, one endowed with the aptitude for higher responsibilities.

The two men did not delve further into small talk while they waited. Instead, Cheatham returned to his pipe and Jackson to his thoughts. It was only when the other generals began to appear that the idle conversation began in earnest. First came A.P. Stewart, Henry Clayton, and Carter Stevenson. As was his custom, Jackson kept Stewart's Corps nearest to army headquarters. Then Patrick Cleburne and Lucius Polk arrived, followed by Nathan Bedford Forrest. Bishop Polk, Samuel French, and George Maney arrived last, and by that time the hour was approaching midnight.

After greeting Polk's party, Jackson dispensed with any further pleasantries. "Gentlemen, the hour is late and you all have duties to attend to. I shall be brief. This army is turning east."

Jackson gauged the expressions of his assembled generals. Whether by temperament or by cue, most followed the example of their corps commander. Like Stewart, Clayton and Stevenson looked impassive. Cleburne, Lucius Polk, and Cheatham were all astonished and made no effort to disguise it. Only Polk's people showed signs of incongruity. Polk himself appeared content, while Maney looked confused and uncertain, and French was visibly upset.

French said to Jackson, "We're not marching for Kentucky, sir?"

"No, no."

"May I ask why, General?"

"No, no."

"Can you at least tell us if we are turning back?"

"No, no." Jackson paused, and when no one asked further questions, he continued by explaining how the army would now march east, more or less following the same routes used thus far, only in reverse and with much longer days on the road. In two days time, Stewart's Corps was to be on the Peytonsville Road and in the vicinity of White House Post Office, while Cleburne and Polk were to be in Spring Hill.

"Gentlemen, Colonel Pendleton has your new written orders. You will receive further directions upon reaching your assigned destinations. Return to your commands and have them ready to march as directed. You all have long days ahead of you. General

Forrest, will you remain here for the specific instructions for your cavalry?"

Sandie handed each corps commander a bundle of envelopes as he left the room and then followed them out, leaving Jackson and Forrest to discuss the cavalry arrangements alone. He watched as they broke into groups and went to their horses and escorts, his eyes lingering on Polk, French, and Maney.

I must watch Polk more carefully, Sandie thought. Much more carefully. Old Jack is very taken with our Bishop. But he's not a very good general, more's the pity. He plays the part. Many of these western old timers seem to love the man. But he's not up to the job of leading a corps. And if what I have heard has even a half-measure of truth, Polk spends no little time in the shadows, encouraging discontentedness.

But Old Jack likes him. Well, the General has more than his fair share of our Southern fondness for men of the Good Book. I was taken with him too, for a time. Reminds me a bit of my father. It's like old, bumbling Pastor Dabney. It took us an Old Testament age to make Jackson see that Dabney wasn't much of a chief of staff, however well-meaning he was, and Dabney had to go. Pastor Dabney even wanted to go. Polk won't, and he's much worse. So, I must watch him carefully, spell out every order, even beyond Jackson's usual exacting standard, and take all the care in the world with handling that one.

As Sandie looked on, Polk and his generals made their way off the courthouse lawn, through the tents, and to their party of aides, escorts and horses.

French muttered to Polk, "I can't believe it. Has that crackbrain lost his nerve!? We haven't gotten to Kentucky, haven't even so much as crossed the Cumberland yet, and we're already in retreat! It's a damned disgrace!"

Maney said consolingly, "It's not like that Sam, not that way at all. There is an old Greek saying. I can't recall who said it, but it goes, "If the lion skin won't cover it, we must patch it out with the fox's." You know Old Jack. He likes heaping confusion on the enemy. This whole march to the Cumberland was a diversion. If we're turning back, it's because the Yankees swallowed the line."

"A diversion?" French shot back. "Involving the entire army? Not likely. And he won't tell us the new objective, if we have such an objective. It's not proper army, I tell you. Not proper army at all."

Polk listened, enjoying French's displeasure with the commanding general, but slightly unnerved by the reactions of Maney and the other generals. Under Bragg, he could count on at least half the high command being in opposition, whatever Bragg might order. With Stonewall Jackson, only French and a few brigadiers found their commander so distressing.

After mounting his horse, Polk looked down to his generals. "Gentlemen, shall we carry on?"

June 16, 1864
4 p.m.
41st Tennessee Infantry, CSA
Beech Grove
Maury County, Tennessee

Willie said, "Nathan, how far do you reckon we've gone today?"

Nathan shrugged. "About 20 miles. Same as yesterday."

Once Nathan moved his shoulders, he compulsively kept rolling, shaking his back and neck out. But he never stopped loping forward. He ached, and not just in his feet and back.

"Reckon whatever Old Jack had in mind with them short marching days is done," Nathan said. "We all back to foot cavalry now."

Forty foot miles in two days had a way of making a man tired and raw all over and just about equally, he thought. That and the parched, dusty coating in the mouth. The heat. Ugly. Just ugly.

Looking at Captain Bell, struggling alongside the company, he saw the clear signs of a man who was struggling with blisters and an unbalanced load. The way Bell moved his feet, avoiding the tender spots. The jerks in his movement. Nathan grinned at the sight.

But what bothered Nathan more than the customary aches of marching was the drudgery. They had used up the exciting talk yesterday, the rumors of Old Frank under arrest for drinking and what mischief Old Jack might be making by marching them all back and forth. The band and pretty music from their dinner stop was a couple hours behind them, and their campground for the night, wherever that was, lay a couple hours ahead of them.

There was one thing for it. Nathan took a swallow from his canteen, and started singing.

John Brown's body lies a-moldering in the grave
John Brown's body lies a-moldering in the grave
Damn him straight to Hell!

Glory, glory hallelujah
Glory, glory hallelujah,
And damn him straight to Hell!

Brown gone to Harper's Ferry,
To set the darkies free.
He were a scoundrel and a villain,
Set on killing you and me.
Damn him straight to Hell!

Glory, glory hallelujah
Glory, glory hallelujah,
And damn him straight to Hell!

Brown hid out in an old factory,
He called out "do your worst!"
So they called for Bobby Lee.
Lee got him out and Virginie hung him from a tree.
And damn him straight to Hell!

They loved that traitor Brown all around the North,
But the traitor's noose and traitor's grave
These were all that he was worth.
And now he rots deep in the earth.
Damn him straight to Hell!

First the regiment picked up with singing the song, then the whole brigade. They sang on, one rollicking tune after another, passing the time until the bugle sounded "Halt!" and the sergeant major barked, "Dis-Missed!" The ranks broke up and fanned out into campsites in the adjacent fields, whereupon they regrouped into their messes.

Most of the men plopped out onto the ground and pulled off their shoes. Some set about collecting firewood, as it was their turn, and a dozen soldiers gathered around a lieutenant to form a canteen detail. These unfortunates began collecting canteens from everyone in the regiment, and were soon trekking to some local creek for water.

Using his blanket roll as a pillow, Nathan lay on the ground with his slouch hat over his face, while the other fellows in the mess lit a cooking fire. Old Jack is right about one thing, he thought. Lying down really is the best rest.

With Willie off to supper with Halpern and Marks, Nathan was the most senior man in the mess, as well as the chief forager and scrounger for the company, if not the regiment. So, only Nathan didn't have a mess chore, not beyond setting out his tin cup with some crumbled hard tack and water to soak for the skillygale.

A hesitant voice said, "Private Grimes, um, sir?"

Nathan grimaced and reluctantly raised the brim of his hat. It was one of the conscripts. Or was he a volunteer, Nathan thought.

Not that it made a whit of difference to him. After he had caught Lloyd lying in wait to bushwhack Willie, Halpern broke up the "new fellows mess" and distributed them out to all the other messes. His mess got two of the greenhorns, neither of whom were with Lloyd that night. Nathan didn't know their names, and didn't care to.

Nathan spat, "Don't call me 'private.' We're the same rank, dummy," and placed his hat back across his eyes.

The boy replied, "Yessir. Mr. Grimes then."

Well, Nathan thought, that didn't sound half as stupid, at least. "Boy, what do you want?"

"They say all around that you is a mighty bold fellow. I thought you would be the one to ask, excepting them officers and all... is there a battle up ahead?"

"Yep," Nathan said. "Scared?"

"Well Mr. Grimes, I don't mind saying I am."

"Yep. Me too. Any man who tells you different is just plain ignorant or a damn fool liar."

The boy was quiet for a time, so Nathan continued. "If there is one thing I learned in this army, it's that we're all scared together, and we all help each other out."

The boy still didn't say anything, so Nathan raised his hat. The other green boy was there with him now, so he met both their eyes. "There's a fight coming, that's for sure. But it ain't got to be a bad one. Lawrenceburg was bad, and Chickamauga worse. But we hardly got shot at all at Raymond. Jackson, that was somewhere in between. Sometimes you get lucky and wind up in a place where ain't hardly no Yankees shooting at you. So when the time comes, you stay close to Willie and me or Sergeant Marks or First Sergeant Halpern. Find a nice, thick tree or a big, fat rock to stand behind, and do what we do. You'll be alright."

Tired of talking, Nathan rolled over onto his belly. A few dozen yards away was Captain Bell, sitting on a camp stool while his grizzled old darkie, Abel, pulled his boots off. Bell had been able to ride as an aide to Bishop Polk, but now he was an infantry captain. In the infantry, only regimental headquarters and on up got to ride. In the infantry, a man walked. Abel walked too, leading Bell's unused horse along with the baggage. As to why Bell still had a horse, Nathan could only guess it was because his status as the son of one of the richest landowners in West Tennessee spared him from the full extent of Army regulations.

Nathan watched as Bell's servant tenderly ministered to his master's feet, placing salve over the blisters, and then went on to prepare his shelter and his meal.

Rich man's war and a poor man's fight, Nathan thought. That's what the Yankees teased us with in prison, that and 'why do you fight so some planter can keep his slaves?' Well, that is how things were everywhere, and he didn't figure North or South made a damn bit of difference about it. It's always a rich man's war, poor man's fight.

Nathan knew why he joined the army, and what he was fighting for. Initially, he ran off and enlisted with his little brother, both underaged, to get away from Nate Grimes, Sr. Kindly Captain Fletcher understood that, and overlooked their age. He'd grown into a man in the army, and his brother too.

Nate, Sr. had always been a hard man, but not always a violent drunk. That came after Nathan's mother died of giving birth to

Willie, and it got worse when Nate, Sr. lost his land to debt and the neighboring planter. Nathan grew to scorn the idea of working like his father had, only to lose it all and make a rich man richer. If he wouldn't do that, he sure as hell wasn't fighting to help a rich man could keep his darkies.

No, the one thing Nathan knew he had, even as a poor dirt farmer's son, was that he wasn't as low as a darkie. He was white, and that was the ultimate guarantee. He would always be better than any free darkie. Nathan knew slaves and he knew free darkies, and he didn't believe that they would run loose killing, raping, and thieving if they were freed, the way the preachers and the slick politicians said. He didn't believe that any more than he believed the Yankees came South out of the goodness of their hearts or to save the Union.

But that didn't mean he wanted the darkies freed, freed so they could take what little Nathan could get out of life away. He knew that if darkies came up from slavery, they would become the same as the least of the white men, and that meant they would all become something only a little better than slaves together. It wouldn't bring the darkies up, but instead would drag the lowest whites down, and he didn't like his chances when should that happen.

June 17, 1864
7 p.m.
Port Royal, Tennessee
45 miles northwest of Nashville, near the Kentucky border

Sherman paced in the confines of the front room of the Port Royal post office in his shirt sleeves, taking short, sharp drag after short, sharp drag on his cigar as he went. Even with the windows open, the front room of the modest, two-room clapboard building were thick with tobacco smoke.

He came to a stop, having smoked the cigar down to the nub. He tossed the butt aside and went to his coat, hanging from the back of a chair. He retrieved another cigar and lit it, tapping his foot violently against the floor all the while, and then resumed smoking and pacing.

"Jesus Christ, how long do they need to find out why the telegraph in Franklin is down?"

Sherman had learned of the telegraph failure that morning. That small piece of news didn't worry him at the time, because telegraph service frequently failed and for any number of reasons, such as Rebel partisans cutting the wire, or a poorly set telegraph post falling down.

Then McPherson sent up the reports from Grierson and Minty that afternoon. Rebel cavalry was still on the south banks of the Cumberland opposite Clarksville, but they were nowhere else. The day before, the southern banks had been alive with Confederate patrols, just as they should be for an army setting up security and preparing to bridge a major river. Today, those patrols had vanished. He immediately ordered his own patrol sent out to ascertain why the Franklin wire had failed and then settled in to wait. And how he hated waiting.

Then he thought he heard a faint clacking. Sherman spun on his heels and threw the door open into the next room, where the field telegraph had been set up.

"God dammit, is that from Nashville? About Franklin?"

The signals officer said, "Yessir and nosir. It is from Nashville, but not about Franklin."

"Then what the hell is it?"

Used to Sherman's nervous excitability, the signals man was unruffled. "I'll have that for you in a minute, General."

When the cipher clerk was finished, the officer took the paper and promptly handed it to Sherman, whose eyes darted rapidly through every line. The message was about Franklin, just not about the Franklin telegraph. Instead, it reported that two reliable Union sympathizers, both men with an established track record for providing sound intelligence, had come separately into Nashville with the story that Jackson's army had moved back into the area between Franklin and Columbia. Sherman's Nashville intelligence office discounted the stories, but forwarded them anyway.

"Fools," Sherman scoffed. "I left nothing but blind men and fools in the Nashville headquarters." He sprinted out of the telegraph office and out the front door.

"Get McPherson," he shouted. "And get him now!"

As Sherman had made a point of keeping his headquarters near Hooker, and McPherson had been keeping his closer to the center of the army, summoning McPherson took nearly an hour. Sherman was outside the post office and in the street, pacing back and forth and slurping down black coffee from a tin mug when McPherson galloped into Port Royal and saluted.

Sherman beckoned him into the post office and said, "Close the windows, Mac" before seeing to the doors himself. Alone and with a margin of privacy, Sherman began "You were right, Mac. You were right. Jackson's been about his trickery again. He is marching east. East!"

McPherson shook his head. "I can't believe that, Bill. I always thought there was something more to this, but I never thought that. His whole army has been moving west. Such a movement cannot be merely a diversion."

"It can and it is." Sherman handed him the message from Nashville. "Think about how long it will take us to turn about, cross the Cumberland, and catch up to him. He has hoodwinked us again."

McPherson read the message and said, "I know the movements of the Rebel cavalry are strange, but you want to me turn on the word of a pair of civilians?"

"I do. I've known Jackson was throwing sand in our eyes and marching east for hours now. This is my confirmation. He waited for us to set off after him, and once he knew we had, he turned himself around and marched east as fast as he could. It's almost 50 miles back to Nashville, and then we must cross the entire army. It will be four or five days before we are south of the Cumberland and ready to give chase."

"Perhaps," McPherson said slowly, "we should send Grierson across the river in the morning. Have a look around, just to be certain."

"I," Sherman said firmly, "am certain. What is more, that mission would take all day, and then only to confirm the Rebel army isn't in the vicinity of Clarksville. Actually finding it would be days more. I'm not waiting for that."

McPherson sighed. "Since you put it that way... I'll turn the army around. I'll force the march and get back to Nashville, quick as I can."

Sherman clapped a hand down on McPherson's shoulder. "Good, Mac. Good. The boys can rest a little when we get to the river. Crossing the bridge will take time, and we need to put the entire army across before we can move on."

June 17, 1864
Shortly Before Midnight
Headquarters, Army of Tennessee, CSA
Spring Hill, Tennessee

Captain Quintard spoke quietly from outside the closed tent flap. "Sir, General Forrest is here as requested."

"Good, good. Let him pass."

Jackson got up as Forrest entered the tent and motioned for him to come over to the map, laid out on a card table and anchored with flat stones. Only then did he look at Forrest, who appeared rested and restored.

Good, good, Jackson thought. He will need his strength in the coming weeks. We all will.

"General Forrest, could you indicate to me the current positions of your cavalry?"

"Yessir." Forrest pointed to different points on the map as he spoke. "I do not know the exact whereabouts of Rucker's Brigade. You know we left him south of Clarksville to deceive the Yankees, sir, and his orders were not to leave that place until after sundown today. Buford is screening us from Nashville, in about Franklin and Petersburg, and Red Jackson's boys are facing east, at Jordan's Store and Riggs Crossroads."

"Good, good. General Forrest, tomorrow I want your cavalry to go to Murfreesboro. I am informed you fought a small battle there in July 1862, so I gather you know the roads and the country."

Forrest was astonished. He had been expecting a move to cut the railroads, but not this. "Murfreesboro, sir? Yes, I know the roads and the country. Very well, I reckon. I also know that down Murfreesboro way is Fortress Rosecrans, and after Nashville, that be the greatest fortress I know of."

Jackson nodded. "You are not wrong. It is a formidable place. Truly. I reckon the defensive power of Nashville and Washington about equal, and if my reports are accurate, Fortress Rosecrans is not far behind them. But you need not concern yourself with that. Your orders are to advance Buford down the Franklin and Bole Jack Roads, and Red Jackson down the Salem Pike, with strengthened leads, flankers, and advanced guards. When your divisions encounter Federal roadblocks or patrols, or when they close to within ten miles of Murfreesboro, whichever should come to pass first, they are to dash forward and descend upon the town."

"I want any enemy resistance encountered on the roads broken up. You are to select two parties of a few dozen picked men, one for each division, and when you make your lunge into Murfreesboro, these are to ride out and cut the wires going north and south. When you arrive in Murfreesboro, you will surround the fortress and isolate it. You are not to attempt an assault on the fortress."

Upon hearing he wasn't to attack Fortress Rosecrans, Forrest felt some relief. Even so, he asked, "Not even if I see an opportunity?"

"No. Not under any condition. You may parlay with the enemy, and attempt to procure their surrender, but only if they agree to the general terms described in your written orders. Your main task is to silence all communications coming from the fortress and the town. I do not want even a single runner or Unionist traitor sneaking out of either place and bringing word to Nashville."

"Yessir. I'll wrap them up in a gum rubber bag for you."

Jackson handed Forrest his written orders. "Good, good. Then be about your business. Dismissed."

As he watched Forrest leave, Jackson couldn't help but muse about what his strict secrecy had wrought. He had his staff prepare sets of orders covering several eventualities, as was his habit, both because he liked to be prepared and because it kept even those closest to him guessing about his intentions. He assigned the Coleman Scouts and other not just Murfreesboro, but many other things to spy upon. Only Sandie and President Davis knew what he had intended for weeks now, and Davis had only been informed by means of a message hand-delivered by a trusted courier on the day before the march began. Thus, the President had been given due notice and sufficient time to object and cancel the new campaign before it began, and he had not.

Even now, Jackson thought, part of me wants to cross the Cumberland. It is the audacious thing to do. But it was too dangerous. Far too dangerous.

Three times before, Southern armies had abandoned their base to invade the North. In Maryland and again in Pennsylvania, Lee had used the country he passed through to feed his troops, relying upon Virginia only to supply ammunition and medicines when needed, and then only periodically. Bragg had done much the same in Kentucky, as had Winfield Scott in the Mexican War. Jackson had first-hand experience of Mexico and Maryland, had studied Pennsylvania and Kentucky, and came to his own conclusions about the advantages and disadvantages of the practice.

He knew that when an army brought its "tail" with it, it had no rear to defend. That army could therefore move more rapidly and was spared the need to leave garrisons behind it. A large army operating so had to disperse, so it could cover more ground and gather more food and fodder. But when an enemy approached, that army would have to concentrate, and in doing so its supply base would become only what it had with it in the wagons at the time. The army's flexibility in terms of where, when, and for how long to fight would instantly shrink to the size of its wagon train.

That knowledge had weighed heavily upon Jackson's mind when he considered whether or not to go through with going over the Cumberland and into the fatter country of northern Tennessee and southern Kentucky, but more important was how he might get back if he should suffer a reverse. When Bragg invaded Kentucky, he did so knowing he had a line of retreat through Cumberland Gap and back unto Chattanooga. That route was now closed to Jackson, so he would have to fall back the way he came, over the Cumberland River.

Federal gunboats could blast a pontoon bridge to matchwood, and there were only a few places where such a bridge could be protected from them. That made any crossing of the river a hazardous undertaking, let alone a crossing made on the retreat with a hostile army at his back, and Jackson doubted that Sherman or McPherson would allow such an opportunity to slip through his fingers. They would strain every muscle to trap him and annihilate him.

All these considerations together persuaded Jackson that he needed to do two things before he could cross the river and carry out his original plan of cutting the railroad to the North and compelling the Federals to abandon the invasion of Georgia. First, he needed to increase the size of his wagon train, to enlarge the "tail" he would bring with him. He had once told the War Department he couldn't invade barren East Tennessee without an additional 900 wagons, and he needed a similar number to mount an invasion of Kentucky. Second, he needed to wear down the reinvigorated Army of the Tennessee in battle.

Hence Murfreesboro. In Jackson's mind, the taking Fortress Rosecrans would solve many problems. He would capture supplies, but most importantly wagons, horses, and mules. Also, the fortress had several heavy guns, guns that he would need if he needed to lay siege to Nashville or fortify his river crossing against Yankee gunboats. And finally, it was both a move that the enemy expected least and a move guaranteed to draw the enemy out of Nashville on his chosen terms.

Having finished his reflections, Jackson muttered, "The time has come. After a month, it has arrived." He raised his hand into the air and quietly prayed.

CHAPTER 8

June 18, 1864
Noon
Fortress Rosecrans, USA
Murfreesboro, Tennessee

The first hint Major General Robert Milroy received of his predicament was when the telegraphy to Nashville and Chattanooga went out, but he paid that no mind, as that was a common enough occurence. So, Milroy was taken aback when his cavalry patrols came rushing back inside the earthen walls of Fortress Rosecrans, with tales of huge masses of gray troopers on the roads to the west, not more than a two hours' hard ride from Murfreesboro.

Milroy pondered his situation as he waited for his senior officers to arrive in his office, an affair improvised with camp furniture in a stout log building. Charged with defending the Nashville and Chattanooga Railroad, he transferred his headquarters to Fortress Rosecrans upon hearing that Stonewall Jackson's entire army was moving into his territory, bringing some reinforcements into the fort with him. Fortress Rosecrans was by far the strongest post in his area of responsibility and therefore the least likely place to be attacked. The Rebels might send their infernal horsemen to try to cow them into surrender, but nothing more. Milroy had decided that Stonewall Jackson himself would never want to become bogged down in a siege trying to take the place.

He looked to Brigadier General Horatio Van Cleve, as if to confirm his assessment. A thin, balding man with a flowing beard and spectacles, he resembled a kindly old professor. Milroy knew Van Cleve had been banished to Murfreesboro after a poor showing at Chickamauga.

Van Cleve was a good enough man, Milroy thought, but lacking in the fire needed to purge this wicked land of its sins. Standing up, Milroy decided that if the design of Providence put him in this place, it must be to stiffen the spines of these men.

Milroy cut a fit, fiery figure as he stepped forward to confront Van Cleve and the gathered colonels. "Gentlemen, I'm sure you have all heard that our cavalry has been driven in. A large force of Confederate cavalry is on the roads to the south and east of Murfreesboro, perhaps two brigades strong. It seems the Rebels are about to raid this place in force, and we're going to meet them. We will hold this fortress, and if they are imprudent enough to relax their vigilance, we will strike at them."

Van Cleve sat, phlegmatic, his arms folded across his chest. "You have my support, sir, and I'm sure the support of all present. But if I may say one thing?"

Milroy nodded, so Van Cleve went on. "This fort is more than 200 acres square. We have less than 3,000 men to hold more than two and a half miles of walls, a place that was built to accommodate an army of 50,000. If a sizable force of cavalry makes a determined attempt at storming this place, I fear we will be too thinly spread to repel them. In my opinion, we should contract our lines. We can throw up a line of new earthworks behind Stones River and between Redoubts Thomas and Wood, pull back behind it, and abandon the western third of the fort. That will shorten the perimeter up nicely."

Milroy recalled his last attempt to hold a fortress in the face of a Rebel army, when Dick Ewell rooted him out of Winchester the previous June. The only thing his resolute actions had earned him there was the indignity of a court of inquiry, and he knew General Sherman was adamant that no post was to be given up without a fight.

"No, I will not yield one inch of this fortress to the enemy. The walls are high, the stakes in the ditches sharp, and we have ample artillery. If they come here, we will kill every last Rebel. You all have your assignments. Take care to make sure your men remain rested and alert, especially for night duty. Dismissed."

But as the day wore on, and butternut troopers blocked the roads leading out of Murfreesboro one by one, Milroy's determination to hold the fortress faltered. It also seemed to him that after Winchester, he was censured for holding his ground when he should have retreated, so he became worried by doubts that perhaps withdrawing from Murfreesboro was the proper course of action. He also fretted over the fate of his regiment of colored soldiers, should they fall into the hands of the Rebels.

A devout Presbyterian and abolitionist, Milroy had embraced the war with religious fervor, seeing in it the hand of Providence, the Lord's will that the slave-powers be thrown down, broken, and trodden from memory. That black men now bore arms, wore blue, and served as the instruments of their own liberation was only further proof that the destruction of the South was God's own intention. Yet the damned Rebels massacred colored troops whenever they could, more proof in Milroy's mind that Southerners were a wicked and vile people. He knew that if he surrendered the fort, or worse, if the fort were taken from him, most of his coloreds would be slaughtered, and the survivors put back into bondage.

Finally, he contemplated his own fate in the event of defeat and capture, growing sicker with worry as he turned the matter over in his mind. Everywhere he went in this war, Milroy took it as his righteous duty to punish slave owners and traitors. In retaliation, the Rebels had labeled him a criminal and put a price on his head.

Milroy doubted he would be afforded the treatment due his rank if he were captured. Instead, he was liable to find himself on trial for capital crimes. By nightfall, he had changed his mind about holding Fortress Rosecrans, and had instead decided to break out under cover of darkness.

"Begging your pardon, General Milroy," Van Cleve protested, "but that course of action is most unwise. Needlessly desperate. We were taught at the Academy that night actions are prone to great confusion and can only be made by well-disciplined troops with the proper training, which I imagine is why they are so rarely undertaken in this war. Half our troops, including the coloreds, are green. I'd count on them to stand behind the walls, but in the open field and at night..."

Milroy said impatiently, "Your concerns are noted" as he watched his cavalry, his regiment of U.S. Colored Troops, and two cannons mustered at the sally port between Lunettes Granger and Rousseau.

Van Cleve grew more alarmed as Milroy refused to be budged. "Yes, sir. Even if you should break out... most of the convalescents are fit enough to man the walls, but not to make a rapid march. We would be abandoning those men to certain capture, and we don't need to! We can still pull back behind Stones River in the dark, concentrate the garrison and make a stand."

Milroy turned and snapped, "Enough, General Van Cleve! I will lead the sally. You will command the fort in my absence, and when we have forced through the Rebel cordon, you will follow. Those are your orders, understood?!"

Van Cleve stood to attention and saluted. "Yessir. I'll see to my men, sir." He turned on his heels and stalked away.

At half past midnight, Milroy struck out to the north for Castlewood Farm and the Lebanon Pike, his cavalry providing strong detachments of advance guards and flankers. They marched quietly in the dark, moonless night, creeping forward so stealthily that the first Confederates knew of the breakout attempt was when Milroy's advanced riders stumbled right over the rifle pits of the dismounted Southern pickets.

Hearing the shots and seeing the orange flashes in the black up ahead, Milroy ordered his cavalry forward and his infantry to shake out a line. To the colonel leading the colored troops, he said, "Once the cavalry locates the Rebel main line, you pin it. I'll bring up the guns, and we'll tear a hole through the Rebel scum."

Milroy placed himself between the foot soldiers and his cannons, and watched with satisfaction as they moved up to support his troopers. From the scattered stabs of fire up ahead, he could see the Rebel cavalry had little more than a skirmish line up ahead. He grinned when his colored soldiers tore loose with a massed volley, instantly smothering the flashes of Rebel musketry with smoke.

Riding behind the men, who were busy reloading, Milroy cried, "That's it, boys! Keep at it! Keep at it! Drown them with balls, and then sweep them aside. Lieutenant, bring up the guns!"

Then Milroy heard a chorus of hundreds of yips and yells. Turning to the source of the noise, he saw dozens of muzzle flashes on his left flank, and then watched with horror as Rebel cavalry charged into the flank of his infantry. The scene dissolved into a confused murk of darkness, powder smoke, and thrashing horses, punctuated by the nearer bursts of flame.

Above the screams of men and horses, Milroy thought he heard cries of "Darkies! Kill all the damn darkies!" Then he heard his own horse scream, felt it buck, and was sent flying back through the air. Milroy felt the dim awareness that he was on the ground, and then nothing.

June 19
Early Morning
Headquarters, Forrest's Cavalry, CSA
Hickey Farm
Murfreesboro, Tennessee

Jackson came thundering down the Franklin Road at the head of several dozen riders. He would have preferred a smaller and less obtrusive entourage, but Sandie insisted that, if he was riding ahead of the vanguard of Stewart's Corps, he go with an entire company of escorting cavalry. Since Sandie was coming as well, there was no way to refuse him.

He looked over at his chief of staff, galloping beside him. Still just a boy, he thought, even with the years of war and all the responsibility he bore. Sometimes I look upon him as family, as if he were my nephew, but sometimes the boy is just a plain nuisance, a clucking, bothersome mother hen.

They came to a halt upon encountering a camp, where the smell of horses vied for notice with the aroma from the many mess fires cooking up almost a thousand breakfasts. There they were directed down a country lane to the Hickey farmhouse and Forrest's headquarters and found Forrest himself in his shirtsleeves, sitting just outside the house in a rocking chair.

Forrest rose to meet Jackson as he rode up at a walk. Grinning, he offered a salute and called out "Good morning, General. I trust you enjoyed a pleasant ride?"

Jackson came to a stop before him, and returned the salute. "Very pleasant. Invigorating even. Your report, General Forrest?"

"I blockaded the fort, concentrating on the roads and Murfreesboro. General, we've only 6,000 men here, give or take, and I have to hold a perimeter of, oh, I reckon about eight miles. We're stretched mighty thin. The enemy made a stab at busting out, and I must tell you, we repulsed them only because they was stupid enough to try it at night. If they try again this morning, I ain't sure I can stop them."

"You needn't worry," Jackson replied. "We just left Clayton's Division. They are on the Salem Pike, and only four miles away. Now tell me about this fight."

"I weren't there myself. Yankees came out with a strong force of cavalry and infantry, I'm told, over by the Lebanon Road, just a ways north of Murfreesboro. I went around and told every regiment to prepare for them to come out that night myself, so they was ready. Them Yankees came onto one of my patrols, and the shooting brought Lyon's Kentuckians coming up from town, who fell on their flank."

Forrest's expression hardened. "General Jackson, I regret to tell you that one of the Federal outfits were all colored. Darkies in the blue suit, sir. Well, once they got started, the boys didn't stop. With the killing. I heard this morning they killed hundreds of them, hundreds. Only took two dozen prisoners, and half of them were white officers."

Jackson's expression soured, his feelings mixed. He felt a Christian duty to tend to the welfare of the negroes, but at the same time knew divine Providence sanctioned the institution of slavery, at least in this time and place. The North's practice of turning negroes into soldiers was merely a gilded form of slave insurrection. Even so, he wanted no part of any massacre. Such false retribution was not only lawless, but sinful, the sin of wrath.

As Jackson said nothing in response to this Forrest looked at him and said "We also captured Major General Robert H. Milroy, sir."

"Milroy?" Jackson recalled from the name from the Battle of McDowell. "Is he not a wanted man?"

Forrest smirked. "A regular black abolitionist villain, sir. He's a bit beat up, his horse shot out from under him and all, but he ain't too badly hurt."

"Milroy can wait. Have we heard from the fort yet?"

"No."

"Then I suggest we open the parlay." Jackson twisted in his saddle to look back at Sandie. "Colonel Pendleton, go with a few members of the escort and inform the enemy commander of my arrival. Tell him that if he does not surrender his post before noon today, I will attack him. To avoid the unnecessary effusion of blood, I call upon him to surrender, etcetera, etcetera. Then invite him out for a word."

Almost two hours later, Pendleton returned with Van Cleve, whose blindfold was undone only once he was within the Hickey farmhouse.

Sandie made the introductions. "General Van Cleve, it is my honor to present General Thomas J. Jackson and Major General Nathan B. Forrest, Confederate States Army. Gentlemen, this is Horatio Van Cleve, Brigadier General of Volunteers, commander of Fortress Rosecrans, United States Army."

Van Cleve shook hands with first Jackson, and then Forrest. "General Jackson, it is an honor. Truly, sir."

Jackson said "General, I will be brief, as you have only two hours, twelve minutes before my deadline of noon arrives, and I assault your lines."

"Before you begin threatening me, General Jackson," smirked Van Cleve, "may I inquire as to the fate of General Milroy and his expedition?"

Jackson stammered, "We have prisoners, including General Milroy. But there was much loss of life."

"I see. Please, commence with the threatening."

Forrest chuckled, amused with Van Cleve's sarcastic style of bravado. Jackson shot Forrest a look to shut him up before speaking.

"General Van Cleve, Stewart's Corps is here, so I have four full divisions at my disposal. My intelligence informs me that you do not have the strength adequate to hold such a large fortress against a serious assault. Even if I should fail in my first attempt at noon today, my entire army will be here by this afternoon. My second attempt will succeed. I will have Fortress Rosecrans before nightfall. And we all know full well what happens inside a stormed, taken fortress. After what occurred last night, I warn you, I will not be responsible for the untold bloodshed that will result if you should force me to breach your works."

Van Cleve felt queasy and struggled to keep his composure. He was putting on a brave show, but he left Fortress Rosecrans knowing he had no choice but to surrender it. Milroy's folly had cost him a quarter of his strength. Oh, if only Milroy had sent me the reinforcements and stayed in Tullahoma, Van Cleve thought. I would be sitting behind fat earthen walls, flanked by big, black cannon, and thumbing my nose at Stonewall Jackson, Forrest, and the whole damned lot of them!

"What terms do you propose?"

"If you turn over the entire contents of the fort to me, undamaged, I offer to parole every white prisoner taken in lawful arms. After they are properly booked, naturally. Officers may keep their side arms, but all mounts and flags are to be surrendered."

"I see. And what of the officers from the colored regiment, and the colored soldiers themselves? And General Milroy?"

Jackson placed his one arm behind his back. "General Milroy is already in my custody, and I have no intention of negotiating with you regarding his status. As for the colored soldiers and their officers..." Jackson paused for a time, to give the appearance of thinking things over, but his mind had been made up on the issue before Van Cleve's arrival. "I will parole them as well."

Van Cleve nodded slowly. "Very well. I accept. If you will write up and deliver those terms, I will surrender the fort to you at... noon?"

"Good, good. Sandie, see General Van Cleve back to the fort."

As Jackson watched Van Cleve being blindfolded and led away, he felt satisfied with the day's events. With Fortress Rosecrans surrendered, he could turn all his force against the Army of the Tennessee. As for the parolees, his plan had always been to disencumber himself of any prisoners, and that was exactly what he would do, with the exception of Robert H. Milroy. Milroy would go back to Richmond.

"Providence has blessed us with an easy victory on this, his day," Jackson whispered. Then more audibly, he said, "General Forrest, you are familiar with the area, are you not?"

"Yep, I am."

"I would be pleased if you would show me the ground west of Murfressboro."

June 19, 1864
Northern Georgia

While Jackson and Sherman built up their strength in Middle Tennessee through May and into mid-June, George Thomas and his Army of the Cumberland had not lain idle in Chattanooga. Thomas's infantry labored for weeks repairing railway tracks and beds, improving old roads, and cutting new roads through the forest, while his cavalry reconnoitered east of the Confederate defensive position on Rocky Face Ridge and their base at Dalton.

Thomas also kept his three infantry corps busy by shifting their positions, always on the move, which posed a problem for William Hardee, commander of the Confederate Army of Georgia. Between the rough, mountainous terrain and the lack of direct contact with his enemy, Hardee had to rely on the reports of scouts, spies, and the occasional foray by Wheeler's cavalry to provide him with information on Federal movements. Hardee's knowledge of the whereabouts of Thomas's infantry was soon rendered unreliable.

As per Sherman's orders, Thomas set his plans into motion on Wednesday the 15th. While feinting to the east of Dalton, the Army of the Cumberland probed Buzzard's Roost Gap and Mill Gap on the Confederates' main defensive position of Rocky Face Ridge. Behind this activity and the thickly forested hills of northern Georgia, Thomas sent John Palmer's XIV Corps south to Snake Creek Gap, an opening in the mountains situated some dozen miles south of Dalton. Palmer's column was spearheaded by John Wilder's Lightning Brigade, a crack mounted infantry force armed with Spencer carbines.

Hardee had ordered Wheeler, his 28-year-old cavalry chief and an old crony of Braxton Bragg's, to defend Snake Creek Gap and vigorously patrol its approaches. Wheeler posted Humes' Division to defend an area that stretched almost 30 miles, from Resaca to Rome, and then ignored Hardee's order to "vigorously patrol its approaches," preferring to spare his horses the wear of frequent rides over the rugged landscape. Neither Hardee or Wheeler bothered to inspect Humes' arrangements in person, both of them focused on the Army of the Cumberland's actions to the north and east of Dalton.

Although suffering from dysentery and lingering typhoid, Colonel Wilder had lost none of the fire in his belly, and his men were full of fight. When the Lightning Brigade arrived at the western side of Snake Creek Gap, they found a single regiment of Arkansans dug in there, and promptly chased them out of their rifle pits and lunettes. After plunging through the four-mile defile of the Gap, Wilder's men emerged on the other side, ran headlong into Harrison's Brigade of Confederate cavalry, and easily swatted the butternut troopers aside. Palmer marched his infantry through the gap and onto Resaca without firing a shot, and was astride the Confederate railroad line by mid-afternoon.

Here Thomas's plan went astray. Palmer, whose XIV Corps had almost as much infantry as Hardee's entire army, was ordered to advance on the Rebel's left flank "if practicable." Palmer decided it wasn't practicable, despite having more than five hours of daylight left in the day. He assumed a defensive position and thus one of Thomas's pincers became an anvil instead.

Hardee withdrew overnight, using the inferior roads to the southeast. Peremptorily ordered by Thomas to march north at dawn, Palmer completely missed the bulk of the Army of Georgia, then on roads several miles east of Resaca. Thomas's pincer movement caught only the Rebel rear guard, Kelly's Division of cavalry. Kelly took a hard drubbing, but Hardee's infantry and wagon train escaped unmolested. Both armies were slowed by the muddy, rain-sodden roads. Hardee didn't stop retreating until he was across the Etowah River, some 55 miles south of Dalton, on the morning of June 20th.

June 20, 1864
Midday
41st Tennessee Infantry, CSA
Stewartsboro Road
11 miles west of Murfreesboro

Nathan removed his slouch hat and wiped his brow clear of sweat and road grime, put the damp hat back on, and took a drink from his canteen. Water was the only amenity he had a full supply of. The three-day supply of corn meal, bacon, and salt they were issued four days ago was gone, and the regiment had marched more than a hundred miles over those four days. He was sore, tired, hungry, and caked with sweat and road dust, just like every other foot slogger in the regiment.

The bugle trumpeted "Halt!" while the Sergeant Major called out, "10 minutes! 10 minutes boys!"

They were near a crossroads, although what the other road was Nathan had no idea, nor did he care. He trudged off the road with his brother Willie for the regulation 10 minute rest given them every hour. Avoiding the smooth, flat patches of limestone that pock marked the ground, Nathan laid down on the rich, early summer grass with the rest of the company. Some smoked, some chatted, but most doffed their gum blanket rolls and lay spread eagle on the ground.

A few minutes later a column of cavalry came up that other road at the walk, heading west, and stomping up a dust cloud that spawned groans from the resting foot sloggers.

Nathan sat up and shouted, "Hey, who ever seen a dead cavalryman?"

The horsemen laughed. One stopped and shouted back, "Had enough of that walking? Ready to join the cavalry and have yourself a good time?"

Nathan grinned. "What do you hear, buttermilk boy?"

The trooper drawled, "Well, Mr. Web Foot, we captured Fortress Rosecrans yesterday. Reckon we'll all be on Yankee rations again before long. And we got that rat bastard Milroy too."

Nathan's stomach growled at the mere mention of food. "I'd rather have me hoecakes and sow belly any day. Good Southern food. But I reckon I am ready for some more of that Yankee coffee!"

"Me too. You take care there, blister boy."

"You too, saddle sore."

The mood of the whole regiment brightened, the air full of animated chatter and no one caring about the thick cloud of dust tramped up by hundreds of horses riding by. Fortress Rosecrans captured! Between Jackson and Forrest, that was four victories in a row: Holly Grove Crossroads, Lawrenceburg, Ringgold Mill, and now Fortress Rosecrans.

The men were soon up and marching again, skipping the customary halt for dinner. With no rations to cook, there was little point. After another four hours of marching north, stopping for the regulation 10 minutes every hour, the regiment and the rest of Walker's Brigade arrived at the crossroads, turned east, and went over a wooden bridge crossing Stewart's Creek.

As he marched over the bridge, Nathan observed with relief that a cluster of wagons was parked on the other side, just a couple hundred yards distant. The wagons meant no going hungry that night. He knew they sometimes out-marched their supplies in this army, like they did Lawrenceburg, but they went hungry not nearly as often under Jackson as they had under Bragg.

With a veteran infantryman's eye, Nathan examined the ground around him. Behind him lay an expanse of flat pastures and cedar thickets. Before him was Stewart's Creek. It was a shady stream, both banks lined with trees. The creek itself wasn't much to speak of, only about a foot deep in most places. But its banks were steep and four or five feet high, like walls made of gnarled tree roots, small boulders and hard, compacted dirt. It was a natural obstacle, and better still, the bank on their side was higher than the western bank, so they could easily shoot down on anyone trying to get across.

Nathan turned to Willie, who was studying the ground in much the same way. "If we build a breastwork here, it's as good as standing behind the walls of a fort."

"We don't need muskets to keep this place," Willie said. "We could do the job with broomsticks."

The Sergeant Major began calling, "Gather around! Gather around!" Nathan saw that the officers were already clustered around Colonel Tillman and realized what was coming. Tillman was telling the officers what he wanted done. The Sergeant Major was going to tell them, the ones who would actually do all the work, how to do it.

"Men, you might have seen all them rock outcrops hereabouts. The ground here is just too stony to dig in properly, so we are going throw up a barricade. Fetch the axes and the shovels from the wagons. Chop down them trees on the other bank, to clear out a field of fire. Haul the trunks over to this side, and stack them up against the trees on this side. Fill in the little gaps with rocks from the creek, and pack the whole thing in mud. You understand me?"

The Sergeant Major was met by nods and murmurs of "Yep, sarge" from the more than 200 soldiers gathered around him.

"We have a lot of ground to cover. 250 yards of it. The regiment is stretched out in a single line, boys. So get busy."

The regiment broke up, with some men going to fetch tools and some going to fetch food. Before long, the designated cook in each mess had a fire going and was busy preparing a meal while the men set about fortifying the ground. All except Nathan and Willie, who shot the breeze with their mess cook while waiting to be detailed to foraging, as they usually were.

Captain Bell left the officer's meeting pleased with himself. Finally I'll take this company under tight reins, Bell thought, and make it shine. I'll see our part of the fieldworks erected first and best.

Returning to the company, Bell immediately went to First Sergeant Halpern, pointed at the mess cooks, and demanded, "Sergeant! Why aren't those men at work?"

"Because," Halpern replied in a businesslike fashion, "the boys are hungry and need to eat. The other companies are doing the same thing, sir."

Bell looked around quickly and saw what Halpern said was true. "What about those two?" he blustered. "That corporal and the man with him over there. Corporal..."

"Corporal Grimes and Private Grimes, sir. I was just about to ask you about that. Those two are the best foragers and trappers in the regiment. Old Captain Fletcher used to excuse them from duties like this, so they could rustle up some more vittles for us."

"Absolutely not," Bell replied indignantly. "The fortifications come first. If they want to go off in search of food, they can do that later."

"Captain," Halpern said patiently, "sometimes the Grimes boys bring back enough to fatten the cook pots for the entire regiment. Even Colonel Tillman appreciates it."

"That may well be so, but this is my company. They work on the fortifications first, and then go foraging if they have time." Bell then spun about on his heels and walked away, leaving Halpern to mumble, "Yessir, Captain, sir."

Halpern went over to the Grimes brothers. "Boys, Captain won't let you go until we finish fortifying this place. Ed is already seeing about the axework. Nathan, you go join him. Willie, you go take charge of getting rocks out of the creek."

The brothers glumly trudged off to the creek. Nathan briefly considered going off foraging anyway, but then he saw Raglan Lloyd sneering at him. Thoughts of escaping hard labor and going foraging were replaced by a sweet desire to beat Lloyd's face against a rock. Before now, Nathan could sneak away and no one would have said a word about it, not even Halpern. He could at least lay traps before Bell noticed he was gone. Not anymore. Now Lloyd would run to the Captain crying "Deserter! Deserter!" as soon as he was out of sight.

Nathan sighed, took up a hatchet, and began hacking branches off a felled cedar trunk. He looked over to Willie, who stood bent over at the top of the bank, hoisting up the stones that were handed to him by the men in the creek bed and piling them up.

He smiled and went back to work. My little brother, he thought, the foreman.

CHAPTER 9

June 21, 1864
3:00 a.m.
Rowlett's Farmhouse
Headquarters, Army of Tennessee, CSA

Smith gently shook Jackson by the shoulder. "Time to rise, sir. Do you hear me? Do you hear me, sir?"

"Yes, yes," Jackson replied, sluggishly rising from his cot and blinking his way to wakefulness.

"Breakfast is waiting outside. I've gotten a few couriers up to join us on the ride. If you don't need me, I'll see to your horse now."

Jackson nodded, so Smith turned and ducked under the tent flap. Having slept in his trousers and shirtsleeves, Jackson spent only a few moments splashing water on his face at the basin and dressing. He emerged from his tent wearing a rumpled, sweat-stained uniform, and after a quick visit to the outhouse, sat down at the rough-hewn wooden table standing under the canvas shelter extending out from the front of his tent.

Before him was a tin plate bearing cornbread and sliced peaches, plus a cup of hot tea, the latter a recent capture from the Federal's stores. The cornbread was made with milk, courtesy of his hosts, the Rowletts, but with the bare minimum of salt. Jackson had long ago fixed upon simple, plain food with a minimum of seasonings as the curative for his dyspepsia. Even so, he adored fresh fruit, and peaches most of all, so his plate was piled high with them. He also made a point out of a good breakfast, as the pressures of the day often caused him to forget to eat.

After devouring his meal with relish, Jackson joined Smith and a pair of couriers at the horses. They mounted and made their way down the country track to the nearby road in the starless, overcast early morning darkness. Upon reaching the road, the party turned right, picked up their pace, and rode to Fortress Rosecrans.

Even if they hadn't already known the way, there was no risk of becoming lost in the gloom. The noise of freight being shifted and of men shouting reached their ears long before the torches and lanterns around the fort came into sight. Just outside the walls was a gathering convoy of hundreds of wagons and dozens of hulking black cannon.

Jackson soon found the men he was looking for among the bustling crowd of mules, teamsters, and wagons. There amid the seeming chaos were his chief quartermaster and chief ordnance officer, Lieutenant Colonels John Harman and William Allan; his cavalry chief, Nathan Bedford Forrest; and Colonel Edmund Rucker, commander of the cavalry brigade assigned to escort the convoy.

Returning the many salutes with one wave of his hand, Jackson asked, "Harman. Allan. Report, please?"

Allan started. "More of the guns in the fort turned out to be six-pounders than we were expecting, sir, exactly the sort of cannons we don't need more of. I've spoken to Robertson, and he agrees, although he was happy to lay claim to the Napoleons. But there are still plenty of the heavier pieces you wanted."

Jackson said eagerly, "What about the heavier pieces?"

Allan replied as if he were reciting a grocery list. "Eleven 8-inch siege howitzers, eleven 24-pounder rifles, four 24-pounder smoothbores, and four 30-pounder Parrot rifles."

Unconsciously, Jackson licked his lips. The gunner in him felt warm satisfaction at the idea of having possession of such a train of guns for sieges and garrisons, like a man who unwraps a gift and finds it to be exactly what he desired.

Allan looked to Harman, who took the cue. "Due to the necessity of providing captured animals to pull those guns, sir, I've only found myself able to add 64 wagons to the army's transportation. 64 exactly. But that plus the empties will allow us to haul away a small mountain of valuable supplies. As you can see, the convoy is coming together. We'll be ready to head out by dawn, as promised."

"Good, good. You do fine work, Colonel Harman. Fine work." Jackson looked at his longtime quartermaster, who now wore a broad, toothy smile. Harman was the most efficient mule-driver he had ever know, as well as perhaps the most profane man in the entire Confederate Army. Harman would have preferred to spike the guns and expand the wagon train, but Jackson knew he would need them should Providence see his plans to fruition.

After a pause, Jackson continued. "We will have more work tomorrow. Hot work. But for now, we must tend to our gains. General Forrest?"

Forrest tilted his head towards his subordinate. "Colonel Rucker here will provide the escort."

Rucker's hand shot out. "General Jackson, if I may, I have not yet had the pleasure, sir?"

Jackson shook hands with Rucker. "The pleasure, and the honor, are mine, sir. I know General Forrest regards you highly."

Rucker beamed as Forrest spoke. "Rucker's boys have ridden farther and harder than any of my other cavalry of late. He is a good man for an assignment like this, but a spell of escort duty will give his horses a rest too."

"Good, good. Now Colonel, you understand your task." Jackson began gesticulating at the columns of heavy cannon. "To see this convoy to Columbia unmolested, where you will hand it over to General Strahl? Mind the enemy strongholds at Pulaski and Shelbyville?"

"Yessir," Rucker said with enthusiasm. "I understand my assignment perfectly."

"Good, good. General Forrest, I wish to speak with you. Privately."

The two men withdrew a short distance from the fort and the road, across the clearing and into a stand of cedars.

"I received your report last night," Jackson said quietly. "About Federal cavalry occupying Stewartsboro and Smyrna."

"Yep. Bluecoat pickets will be giving big old Abe Buford and his boys dirty looks across the Murfreesboro Pike Bridge just after sun-up, I reckon. You still sure you don't want me to go on ahead and have that bridge burned?"

"No," Jackson said firmly. Appearances were important. A closely watched bridge was no danger to him, but leaving it standing implied he might want to come across Stewart's Creek for a lunge at Sherman's railroad supply line. "General Forrest, in the fight that is coming, I want you to stay with Red Jackson's troopers. I anticipate that the enemy will attack us tomorrow morning and attack us on our left. If you must withdraw Red Jackson from his present position on Scales Mountain, your highest priority is covering the Salem Pike, not screening the army's immediate left. Do you understand?"

Forrest's brows furrowed. Covering the Salem Road, miles to the south of the army's position, would mean exposing the army's left flank, sure enough. "You are sure that is what you want, General?"

"Yes, yes. You shall receive those orders in writing later today. Safeguarding the Salem Pike is your paramount concern. I also want that you should speak to no one of this until the battle opens."

Forrest frowned, dissatisfied. The instructions to abandon the left flank in favor of screening a road were bizarre. But he knew Old Jack wouldn't explain why it was to be that way, even if he demanded to be told.

When Stonewall Jackson goes to meet his maker, Forrest thought to himself, he'll admit to all his sins easy enough, but refuse to say a thing about why he did any of them, even if Saint Peter threatens him with the fires of Hell. It all comes down to if I trust the man. Do I? I reckon I do.

Forrest drawled "Well, I reckon you are right about needing me there on the left, to make sure Red falls back like you want. He won't want to leave Clayton's flank in the air like that, any more than he'll care for me looking over his shoulder. But, if that is what you want, that is what I'll give you."

"One last thing. What of the prisoners?"

"I ordered the boys to drag all the, oh what do you call those things... cheevahl dee freeze?"

"Cheval de frise."

"Yep, them things. I had the boys drag them out to the backs of two lunettes, one next to the other, along with some of the six-pounders that your chiefs there didn't want. Loaded the guns with double canister. What with men on the walls and behind that line of... cheval de fries... I reckon that will do for prisons. The Yankees have been nice and quiet."

"Good. Good." Jackson dismissed Forrest, collected Smith and the rest of his party, and rode away from the convoy and the fortress. Jackson felt both satisfied and yet also slightly annoyed by his meeting with Forrest as he led his followers to the hamlet of Blackman, where the headquarters of Polk's Corps had been set up in a schoolhouse. He was pleased by Forrest's performance, but annoyed by the need to take Forrest ever so slightly into his confidence.

In Jackson's mind, orders were to be obeyed without question, and certainly not with explanations of intent. That was his duty as a soldier and a God-fearing man, and so should it be for every man in the army. Beyond that, secrecy was a prime military virtue. But his present army was twice the size of any command he had held in Virginia, and that simple fact demanded a grudging concession in the way he went about things. It was necessary, but he still didn't care for it. Not one little bit.

Arriving before the schoolhouse porch, Jackson found Bishop Polk seated there, idly eating a breakfast of biscuits and gravy while thumbing through his pocket New Testament. Seeing Jackson approach, Polk got up from his table and greeted him.

"Good morning, sir," he said pleasantly. "I was just preparing for the service I intend to give later today, for those men of my Corps who wish to attend. After your mandated period of drill, of course."

Jackson dismounted from his horse, saying "Commendable, General Polk. Commendable. What shall you use for your sermon?"

"I was considering Romans 13:4."

Jackson paused for a moment, and then recited, "For he is God's servant for your good. But if you do wrong, be afraid, for he does not bear the sword in vain. For he is the servant of God, an avenger who carries out God's wrath on the wrongdoer."

Polk beamed. "Very good, sir. Excellent, in fact. The Lord has blessed you with a clear and sound memory."

Jackson smiled, slightly embarrassed. "No, No. I fear I know that for the same reason I know anything, by the labors of rote." Jackson paused, and then said, "If I may say so, I have always been fonder of a different passage from Romans, Chapter 13."

"Allow me to guess? Um.... Let every person be subject to the governing authorities. For there is no authority except from God, and those that exist have been instituted by God. Therefore whoever resists the authorities resists what God has appointed, and those who resist will incur judgment. For rulers are not a terror to good conduct, but to bad. Would you have no fear of the one who is in authority? Then do what is good, and you will receive his approval, for he is God's servant for your good."

"Yes, that is exactly the one."

"Perhaps I shall use it instead, and preach on the Yankees, and their betrayal of our liberties, hard-won by our forefathers in the Revolution."

"General Polk, I wish to inspect Cockrell's Brigade this morning and inquire about how they are faring with those captured Henry rifles. Will you accompany me, and while we ride you can inform me as to the standing of your Corps?"

Polk smiled affably, but beneath his kindly demeanor he was half-irritated at having to refer to his command as a "corps" in the Army of Tennessee. He was still the department commander for Alabama and Mississippi, and his "corps" was part of the Army of Mississippi. Among his own people, he always referred to it that way.

But only half-irritated, because the mention of the Henry rifles recalled his little headquarters victory. Several hundred of the dreaded sixteen-shot repeaters had been captured along with the 64th Illinois by his troops. The Irishman, Patrick Cleburne, also had a claim to the weapons, but Polk had prevailed in the dispute, so they went to arm Cockrell's small brigade of Missourians. So small, in fact, that most of Cockrell's soldiers were able to exchange their muskets for Henrys.

Leaving his breakfast behind, as he could always have another one made for him later, Polk roused his staff and assembled the style of entourage he deemed proper to a Confederate lieutenant general: one of his senior staff officers, two aides, two enlisted couriers, his guidon-bearer, and two armed escorts. All were nattily turned out and created a vivid contrast with the ragged, weather-beaten appearance of the commanding general, if not with Jackson's own much smaller party. The contrast was only magnified when Polk himself emerged from the schoolhouse, wearing a finely tailored, exhaustively brushed coat, brightly decorated with gold embroidery and braid. Polk was as dandy as Jackson was seedy.

Still mounted and sitting behind Jackson, Smith shook his head despite himself. He had never quite understood the sheer extent of Jackson's tolerance for the pious, and he knew that Old Jack would never have waited patiently for almost half an hour for such a gaggle of military pomp to be assembled for anyone who wasn't a Bishop Polk or a Reverend Dabney. Not that Dabney would ever have made him wait.

The now large party rode down a country track and through the camps of Maney's Division, formerly Loring's and then Featherston's. The Bishop was cheered by the men at their breakfasts, and so was Jackson, but with noticeably less enthusiasm.

Jackson noticed the tepid reception and privately dismissed it as the lingering demoralization left by Loring's flawed leadership, and perhaps the resentment the men felt at having George Maney, an outsider, placed over them. It bothered him only very slightly, for he cared little for cheering except as a display of the men's morale, feeling as he did that feeling any further interest in adulation would cause him to succumb to vanity.

Polk knew better. Maney's soldiers resented their new general alright, believing Jackson had slighted them for Loring's sins, and so they felt the bitter animus of both the unjustly wronged and that of the spurned and unloved. He knew too that Featherston simmered in his own disappointment at having his hopes of retaining command of the division dashed, that some of the other brigadiers supported Featherston as one of their own, and they encouraged the bad feelings in the ranks.

But Polk said nothing of this, for if the men resented Jackson, they remained his by default. The sentiment they were seeing in the camps just now proved it.

Jackson and Polk entered the area occupied by French's Division, and soon came into the camps of Cockrell's Brigade. There both generals were popular, and the cheering rose in volume accordingly. As they approached the tents of the Cockrell's headquarters, a fife and drum band struck up "Bonnie Blue Flag."

Jackson climbed down from his horse and found Cockrell, a man who would have looked unremarkable except that he was a brigadier at 30, waiting for him with a salute and an excited greeting.

"General Jackson, this is a magnificent surprise! It is an honor to have you in our camp, sir, a great honor!"

Jackson acknowledged the flattery with some slight nodding. "General Cockrell, I've never seen one of these pieces of Yankee ingenuity that they raise so much fuss about. I want to see one of your Henrys, please."

Cockrell motioned to the nearest private. "Hanks! Yes, you there, Private Hanks! Cheer up, it's not every day Stonewall Jackson wants to inspect your rifle."

The private gulped as he jumped forward into attention and presented his rifle. At Cockrell's request, he showed Jackson and Polk how the weapon was loaded and fired and how the sights were operated.

"And how does it operate in practice?" Jackson asked. "Is it sturdy? Does it misfire often, or the mechanism bite your fingers? I know of a breechloader or two that worked fine in the shop, but were not fit for field use."

Calmer now, the solder replied, "It needs more love and care in the camp than an Enfield, sir. But the rifle is no dog, sir. I reckon that for sure."

"May I?" Jackson took the rifle, examined it, and murmured, "Hmmmm. No place for a bayonet."

Polk said sourly, "Infernal Yankee artifice."

"I wish we had more of these 'infernal Yankee artifices' General," Cockrell said, "and more ammunition to accompany them. I'll say this, those guns are hungry. I had to set the standard ammunition issue at double, up to 80 rounds per man. We captured enough cartridges for two, maybe three big fights at Lawrenceburg, but I'm told our country lacks the industry to make these newfangled metal cartridges, nor did we capture any more of them here at Murfreesboro. We make do for now by collecting the brass casings after practice, but we won't be able to do that in a battle, sir."

Jackson became downcast. "Before the war, the fire-eaters and charlatans were too prideful, scorning the Northrons as a race of pasty mechanics. Unworthy, they said. I fear that we have come to regret the hubris of such men in so many ways, and this," he said, holding up the Henry, "is just one of them."

Polk nodded earnestly, saying quietly, "Amen."

A grave silence fell over the group. Finally, Jackson said, "General Cockrell, assemble your men." The bugles sounded, and as Jackson pulled himself back onto his horse, the Missourians ceased their drill and formed up.

Bringing around and himself before the assembly, Jackson addressed them. "Missourians! The trials of divine Providence have brought you far from your homes and families. I do not come from a speechmaking profession, so I have no sweet words of comfort for you, nothing to assuage the homesick. So I also will not tell you that with a tomorrow and a hurrah that your country shall be redeemed for you. Nor should you need such reassurances. We are all veteran soldiers here. So I promise you this. If we defeat our enemies tomorrow, we shall remain here, in Tennessee's good Mother Earth. Do that, and Nashville shall fall. Take Nashville, and West Tennessee shall fall. And from that place, your country lies just across the Mississippi."

Jackson's brief speech was met with buoyant applause and cheers, as hats flew into the air and Missouri Johnnies broke ranks and mobbed Jackson. By the time the troops were persuaded to fall back into line, Jackson's one hand was painfully sore from too many firm, manly handshakes.

When Cockrell's men returned to their morning drilling, Polk walked up to Jackson. "Sir, unless I am mistaken, you are about to move along? May I have a word before you depart? In private?"

Jackson agreed and dismounted. As he did so, Polk said, "General Cockrell has offered us the use of his tent." They went inside, and Jackson found the battered furnishing familiar, with the only novelty being the faded state banner of Missouri, sewn into one of the tent panels.

Drawing the tent flap behind him, Polk said, "General Jackson, I know the vicinity very well, having fought here at Second Murfreesboro, a year and a half past. In hindsight, I believe General Bragg made a serious error in fighting on the ground that he did. It offered no particular advantage to either attacker or defender. Now, I know you have put yourself on very different ground, with Stewart's Creek as our front, a strong position and immeasurably superior to Bragg's choice. But I must tell you, I have always thought Overall Creek, just behind where my corps is camped now, is the best ground to be had in these parts. It offers all the strengths of Stewart's Creek, but only more so. Sir, I must urge you to retire behind Overall Creek. We still have time. The Federals should not arrive at this place until this afternoon, perhaps not until after dark."

Yes, Jackson thought to himself, Overall Creek is the best defensive line hereabouts, and that is why I cannot occupy it. The enemy would never attack it. I don't know Sherman, and while some say he is crazy, the record speaks to competence. I know McPherson better, and he is both cautious and able. Instead of attacking a position like that, such men would choose a turning movement instead. And that is not what I want.

But Jackson offered none of his design, instead replying, "We make our stand on Stewart's Creek. Your corps stands in reserve, ready to support Stewart's Corps, should that be required."

"May I at least know more of your intentions for battle, sir?"

Instead of becoming irritated, as he often did when pressed for more information, Jackson said patiently "General Polk, do you know of Benjamin Franklin's advice on secrecy?"

"No. What did esteemed 'Poor Richard' have to say?"

"That a secret between three is kept only if two are dead."

Displeased, Polk blinked twice, but otherwise retained his composure. "I see. Yes, I see. Well, you must want to call on the remainder of the army, and I must attend to my own affairs. Including my service. Thank you for hearing me out, sir."

"Of course, General Polk. Of course."

Jackson joined Smith and the couriers, and they rode back to and down the Bole Jack Road, past the bulky, towering, forested mass of Burnt Knob, a dominating U-shaped chain of hills. He could see where some trees had been cleared and his signals men had erected wig-wag stations. The flags were already in motion, sending trial messages back and forth. A little over three miles from Polk's camps was a large knoll, where A.P. Stewart had tucked his headquarters in a fallow field just behind the rise, and Jackson noted with approval that caissons for several guns dotted the east slope. Coming among the tents, Jackson found Stewart just as he was preparing to mount his horse.

"General Jackson," Stewart cried, genuinely pleased. "I was just about to inspect my lines. Will you join me?"

"That," Jackson said, eyes dancing and smiling warmly, "was exactly what I had in mind."

Jackson found the renewal of his acquaintance with A.P. Stewart one of the few real pleasures of his western command. He had first met the gaunt, bookish Tennessean when Jackson was a cadet at West Point, where Stewart had been a junior artillery instructor. Both men had left the army to become professors. But most important of all to Jackson, Stewart was a good Presbyterian, and the kind of quietly competent officer who did what he was told, with no complaints and offering his opinion only when asked for it.

Stewart began his tour with Clayton's Division, lying between the Franklin and Bole Jack Roads, and dug in behind a line of breastworks that wound through pastures and fields, incorporating the cedar thickets, stands of scrub trees, and rock outcroppings wherever possible. Everywhere along Clayton's front, the field of fire was clear for at least two hundred yards. His line was tied into Red Jackson's cavalry pickets on Scales Mountain on its left, and Stevenson's Division and the headwaters of Stewart's Creek on its right.

Stevenson's Division extended the line north, behind the eastern bank of Stewart's Creek. Here the infantry were protected not by earthworks, but by tree trunk barricades. The creek itself was a natural ditch, improved by the plethora of sharpened stakes that were driven into the soft, muddy bottom. Along this stretch of creek the field of fire was clear for up to a quarter mile in places, but Stevenson's men were spread more thinly than Clayton's. Behind them was an expanse of pasturage, and then the rugged heights of Burnt Knob.

After Stewart indicated where he had formed his reserve, a brigade each from Stevenson and Clayton, Jackson ordered Smith and the other attendants to remain behind. He took Stewart with him out into one of the overgrown fields between the creek and the hills.

Noting the tall weeds and bald patches of flat limestone, Stewart observed, "Horses and cattle should be grazing here, don't you think, Tom? And there are none." With more sadness in his voice, he continued "See how poor two years of war makes a country. How shall we cope with all this? Our devastated land?"

"We shoot the Yankees. Then we rebuild." To himself, Jackson acknowledged that Middle Tennessee looked more ravaged than anywhere he had ever seen in Virginia. "What do you think of this ground, Pete?"

Stewart grimaced slightly and met Jackson's eyes. "It's a good hard shell, but that big hill worries me." Stewart nodded toward Burnt Knob, then continued. "If I get pushed back, I'll have a stark choice of splitting my corps or falling back to the north, away from Polk. Stevenson has to fall back on Cleburne whatever happens, because the mountains back there are in the way. They will break up any formation trying to cross it."

"You are perfectly correct, Pete." Jackson paused, looking up towards the gray sky and shifting uncomfortably in his saddle. "Sherman may still try to turn us out of here, but I don't think he will. As far as he is aware, Milroy and Van Cleve are still in Fortress Rosecrans. So he will think us in a desperate place."

"Yes, I thought that might have something to do with it. Didn't Napoleon once say the worst place for an army was between a powerful fortress and an enemy army?"

"He may have. I want Sherman to think you, Cleburne and Forrest are facing him, while Polk is back screening the fort. Because your left extends beyond the creek, and because you have Burnt Knob in your rear, I expect he will fall upon your front and flank and try to drive us onto Stones River for destruction."

Jackson began pointing south, jabbing with his finger. "If Clayton is hard-pressed, withdraw him back to here. Pull his line back like a door on its hinges. Polk will then counter-attack directly west."

Stewart digested that. It was a simple enough ambush in its conception. The only complicated parts were pulling Clayton back and preventing the enemy from rolling Stevenson's flank up as he did so.

"Yessir. I understand."

Jackson smiled warmly. No protests, no doubts, no questions. Not from Stewart.

A light drizzle started coming down. Stewart said, "Will you come in out of the rain with me? Take some dinner with me, perhaps?"

The mention of food made Jackson remember he needed to eat, which in turn made him feel a little peckish, so he decided a light meal was in order. "Yes, yes. That sounds lovely."

Returning to Stewart's headquarters, the two men doffed their damp coats and hats and chatted about the captured heavy cannons with the spirit that only a pair who were both academics and gunners could muster. After a while, a meal of split pea and bacon soup with hardtack was brought to them, all of it made from captured Northern rations.

As he spooned up the last of the hearty soup, Stewart asked, "Have you been to see General Milroy yet?"

Jackson didn't look up from his bowl. "No. Nor do I care to. The man is a criminal, not a soldier."

"Did you know he was a Presbyterian?"

"Yes, yes. I fought him at McDowell more than two years ago. I learned a bit about him then. I have never understood how our co-religionists in the North could be so deluded about the intentions of Providence in this war, but I dismissed those who were both Presbyterians and abolitionists as misled or deluded years ago."

Stewart set his bowl aside and reached for his cup of coffee. He had never wanted secession or this war, but felt much the same way as Jackson that Southern society was the way it was because God wished it so. If they had grown so far apart from the North for it to come to war, that was divine design as well. Such was the course of human events, all of it predetermined. He was just less certain than his friend and commander of God's ultimate intentions.

After draining his cup, Stewart asked, "What do you intend to do with him?"

Jackson replied flatly "Our government wants General Milroy on charges. I captured him, and my duty ends with handing him to the proper and relevant authority. So, I will send him to the rear, and from there Richmond can do what they want with him. Incarcerate him as a prisoner of war, exchange him, parole him, try him, deport him to Cuba, I don't care, so long as my duty is done and the outcome is proper and legal."

Stewart said softly, "Yes, I'm sure you're right." Except that Stewart was not sure. Richmond had inflated Milroy into one of the greatest Yankee miscreants, and he worried about what the government might do. Having possession of Milroy was trouble, political trouble, Stewart was certain of that. He was equally certain his country had more trouble than it could handle as it was.

He changed the subject to something happier, namely resuming their teaching careers after the war. He renewed the conversation over his idea that if the War Department did not offer one or both of them the role of founding the Confederate Military Academy, perhaps Jackson should come to Tennessee and join Stewart in establishing a private military college along the lines of the Virginia Military Institute.

When the rain ended, Jackson said his goodbyes and rode on with his small party to Cleburne's Corps. He found Lucius Polk's front was much the same as Stevenson's. The men were stretched out in a single rank behind the steep banks of Stewart's Creek and a wall of interlaced standing trees and felled tree trunks. Small details were improving the fortifications and tending to other camp duties, but for the most part the men were idle now, and thus Jackson was met by smiling faces and much waving of hats wherever he went. There was no cheering, for he had ordered all cheering and noisy displays stopped while enjoying his dinner with Stewart.

Jackson was just coming upon the joint between Lucius Polk's and Cheatham's Divisions when he encountered Cleburne himself, riding the other way. Upon seeing Jackson, Cleburne put the spurs to his horse, but then had a frantic job of stopping again. Old Pat rode right by Jackson and his party at a gallop, coming to a stop only after riding a few dozen more yards. A shame-faced Cleburne then brought his horse around back at the walk.

"My apologies, sir." Cleburne muttered. "I fear I have never been much of an equestrian."

"No, no. You have nothing to apologize to me for. My own horsemanship is lacking, and I barely manage to get along with this old mare here. Truthfully, I haven't had a horse I was comfortable with since I lost my Little Sorrell at Chancellorsville."

Cleburne gave a single, heavy nod. "Yessir."

Jackson smiled slightly at that. He felt he was coming to like Cleburne's character and manner, earnest and severely grim as they were. "General Cleburne, would you share your thoughts on the advantages and disadvantages of your position with me?"

"Yes, General. The line itself is a strong one, well-protected. To storm the breastworks, the enemy will need ladders. Furthermore, those hills to the west are a mile or more away along most of the front, so our line would be on the outside of the effective reach of any long-range bombardment."

Cleburne audibly drew a breath before continuing. "Against that, the lines of trees and fences that border the fields, as well as the wood lots and cedar thickets, obscure the enemy's advance across that mile of low and rolling country between the creek and the western hills. And the line of the creek itself is held by less than two men per yard. Less than two men per yard for more than five miles of front. And as for my own corps, Cheatham's Division is less by Strahl's Brigade, as you know, sir. I have only one brigade in reserve. To my right, Buford's cavalry is spread out even more thinly. Finally, if I am forced back I cannot retreat towards the southeast, towards the rest of the army, due to the presence of Burnt Knob."

Jackson's eyes sparkled. "You will not need to fall back. You will hold this ground, General Cleburne. You will hold it. I expect you to hold it."

Already sitting straight up in the saddle, Cleburne stiffened even more. "Yessir!"

Jackson was about to take his leave when a young lieutenant galloped up to the generals, sending clods of soft, damp sod flying. He snapped off a salute to Cleburne and said, "Sir, Federal troops have been spotted occupying the heights west of the creek!"

Oblivious to the dirt and grass clinging to his coat, Jackson looked at his watch. Quarter past two, he thought. A little earlier than I had anticipated.

Cleburne said, "General, I had an observation post cleared atop Grindstone Knob, alongside the signal station, and my largest telescope placed there. Would you care to see for yourself?"

Jackson agreed and followed Old Pat away from Stewart's Creek, across the weedy fields to a dirt track that led up Grindstone Knob, the western spur of Burnt Knob. The path was too steep and rugged for the horses, even if it hadn't been slippery from the recent drizzles, so they had to walk.

To Jackson, Cleburne said, "Take care, sir, I pray you. One of my people has already had a bad fall on this trail. Slipped and snapped his ankle." The two generals, 41 and 36 respectively, scrambled up the knob, leaving their younger attendant behind. They quickly reached the top, panting and sweaty in the warm, humid air.

Jackson whipped his hat off, exultant. "I tell you, General Cleburne, I have long thought of the simple act of walking the best form of exercise. I have not had the time for a strenuous walk up a hill like this one since the earliest days of the war. I once made a habit of such walks. I do miss it. I have had to make do with the saddle."

Cleburne nodded, still too short of breath to reply. After a short rest, during which time their followers caught up, the pair went to the telescope tube. Jackson noted with satisfaction that Cleburne had the brass tube wrapped in old rags, a measure to prevent its polished surface from attracting attention. The lieutenant who had been manning the telescope directed Jackson where to look on the opposite ridge, two miles away.

There he could see the work parties of shirtless men with axes, picks, and shovels felling trees. Carefully observing the fields between the enemy-held heights and Stewart's Creek, he could see the small parties of bluecoats gingerly exploring the countryside and setting up a picket line.

Jackson observed the enemy for several more minutes before giving the telescope over to Cleburne and bidding him farewell.

First he penned an address to the troops, warning them that battle was expected tomorrow and admonishing them to do their duty in the sight of their country and almighty God. That was followed by orders for his generals, directing them to ensure the men filled their canteens and cooked four days' rations over supper that night; to make sure every infantryman carried at least 60 rounds and that ammunition wagons were kept in a shelter, but convenient location; and that the pickets were to be replaced at 3 a.m., to ensure fresh men were there to provide sufficient warning of the enemy's advance.

After handing the papers over to Sandie for copying and distribution, Jackson returned to his tent. There he read from his Bible and prayed for a time, before joining his available senior staff – Sandie, Wells Hawks, William Allan, and Dr. Hunter McGuire, all followers from Virginia – around a camp fire for supper. Taking a lantern back to his tent, he added several more pages to a letter for his wife, Anna, knowing it would be the last letter he would be able to write for days, perhaps even weeks to come.

He folded the pages up, wrapped the thick letter in paper, tied the bundle up, and addressed it to his home in Lexington, Virginia, content in the knowledge that Jubal Early, his wicked former subordinate, had driven Hunter's army out of the Upper Shenandoah and into Virginia's western mountains. The Virginia Military Institute had been burned, but not his house, so Anna and his daughter had a home to return to.

June 21, 1864
9 p.m.
Headquarters, Army of the Tennessee, USA
Western outskirts of Rutherford County
22 miles southeast of Nashville

Bringing his horse from a canter to a halt, Sherman dismounted without waiting for any of his attendants to catch up to him, ignored the salutes from the men working around headquarters, and walked straight over to a lantern post. Once there, he checked his watch. Hearing his party catching up to him, Sherman spun on his heel and stepped forward to meet one rider in particular.

"Very good!" Sherman called out. "We have arrived right about when you said we would. I commend you, Corporal!"

Sherman's guide, a corporal assigned to Nashville's signals staff, tipped his hat. "Thank you kindly, General Billy. I reckon I ought to know this country well enough, seeing as how I spent the last year mending telegraph wire all up and down it."

Looking to Audenried, Sherman said, "Major, you and the others see if you can't find yourself some supper. It's been a long day. I'll send for you if I need you."

Sherman, Audenried, and the others had left the army before dawn, returning to Nashville to attend to Sherman's business as commander in chief for the western theater. After a change of horses, they then rejoined McPherson that afternoon. The pair had studied the ground together and discussed battle plans, whereupon Sherman left McPherson to deploy his army and rode off again, this time to Smyrna to look into the establishment of the temporary supply depot. By the time Sherman's party found McPherson's new headquarters, they had put in more than 40 miles in the saddle that day.

Yet Sherman's sole concession to all those horseback miles was to put his hands in the small of his back for a stretch. He then lit up a cigar and strode forward to the little roadside cabin serving as McPherson's office. Sherman entered to find McPherson seated across the corner of a map table from the grizzled, gray figure of A.J. Smith, the two men playing a game of checkers. In the back, the bullish John Logan wolfed down a plate of chicken and dumplings.

Motioning for everyone to remain seated, Sherman said, "Good evening, gentlemen. Aren't we missing someone?"

McPherson said, "Hooker should be along shortly" before double-jumping Smith's pieces, prompting the latter to muter a curse.

Catching the scent of Logan's supper, Sherman's mouth began watering. He hadn't realized how hungry he was until now. "Is there any more of that?"

McPherson called for his cook, who like so many of the servants attached to Union generals those days, was a former house slave from a great estate who now worked for pay. The cook returned with a tin plate of hot, savory supper for Sherman, who pulled up a chair in the back corner of the one-room cabin and ate quietly. He was just sopping up the last of the gravy with a cracker when simultaneously Smith let out a triumphal hoot, double jumping McPherson in turn, and Hooker burst through the door.

As Hooker stood in the doorway and offered his jaunty salutes, Sherman observed the rosy cheeks. A bit of bottled courage, Sherman wondered?

He then dismissed the notion. Sherman knew Hooker to be many things, most of them immoral, and being overly fond of the bottle was part of that. But the man was no drunk. Sherman accepted a cup of hot coffee from the negro cook, thanked him, and then settled in to watch the meeting. The army was McPherson's, so this was Mac's show to run, and Sherman was there merely to observe.

After having the checkerboard cleared away, McPherson was about to speak, but was stopped before he could start by Hooker.

"General, if I may? I have something I want to say before you begin?"

McPherson nodded his assent. Sitting in his corner, Sherman plucked at and thumbed one of the buttons on his coat. Typical Hooker, he thought. The man hasn't changed a whit since San Francisco.

Hooker said, "I know we must assume Fortress Rosecrans is still resisting the Confederates, and therefore must be relieved as soon as practicable. However, I believe attacking Jackson is unnecessary. We can still swing around through the south, around these easily defensible creek lines, and force the Confederates to abandon Murfreesboro. Coming up from there, we could then drive the enemy onto Stones River, and break them up."

"I appreciate your thoughts on the matter," McPherson said graciously. "But such a turning movement would detach us from the railroad and lay our supply line open to attack. You know as well as I do we have only half the transportation an army of this size requires for such an operation, and we cannot live off the land in a country already picked clean by two years of war."

Sherman kept fidgeting with his jacket, consciously choosing a quieter alternative to drumming his fingers or tapping his foot. He thought he recognized Hooker's game, believing that Hooker had to know his suggestion was impractical. It didn't matter so much what Hooker said as much as that he said it, because in the event of a setback he was now on record as having proposed an alternative. Doing so cost Hooker nothing, but might help his case in winning the army command away from McPherson.

Yet Sherman was pleased when McPherson continued, confidently laying out his plan as if Hooker had said nothing at all. "XX Corps will open the attack at six o'clock, striking Scales Mountain with the aim of pinning and flanking the Confederate left. XVI Corps will support XX Corps. Now A.J., I want you to attack the headwaters of Stewart's Creek with one division, while holding your other two divisions in reserve. You understand?"

"Yessir," said Smith.

"Good. XV Corps will demonstrate against the Confederate right. Jack, in addition to the usual display against their front, I also want you to mount a diversionary attack to force the Murfreesboro Pike Bridge over Stewart's Creek."

After taking a moment to consider, Logan said, "I have a lot of ground to cover, but I can manage a diversion. I'll keep the Rebels preoccupied with my end, at any rate."

"Good. When Hooker is engaged with the enemy left, I'll send word for you to begin your diversion against their right flank. That ought to divert at least some of any reserves they have available. Then we will roll up their left, and push the whole lot of them back onto Stones River. The enemy main body destroyed, we will then relieve Fortress Rosecrans. Any questions?"

When there were none, McPherson gave his corps commanders a final word. "Make sure your men have full canteens, at least 60 rounds per man, and to get them up early so they can have a hearty breakfast. The weather might stay cloudy tomorrow, but hot sun or no, I expect a long, hot day's work tomorrow."

CHAPTER 10

June 22, 1864
3:00 a.m.
41st Tennessee Infantry, CSA
Stewart's Creek

Nathan awoke in the darkness to the whispers of Sergeant Ed Marks. "Up. Up. Picket detail. Get up."

He sat up, rubbed his face, and looked over to Willie, who looked haggard. He usually slept alright the night before a fight, when we knows the fight is coming, Nathan thought. Having them stripes must be keeping him up.

The company mustered behind the regiment's stretch of log barricades, and First Sergeant Halpern made a silent head count, not including himself and Captain Bell. Nathan watched as Halpern told Bell what must have been "all present and accounted for," and then went over to pull two of the greenhorns out of line, the same pair from the day before who he had been doing his best to ignore since.

Halpern brought the pair before Willie, and said quietly, "Corporal Grimes, you've got these two."

Willie whispered back, "Yes, Sarge."

Halpern then glared at the visibly displeased Nathan, hissing, "Do you have a problem with that, Private?"

Nathan muttered, "No, Sergeant," but of course he didn't like being saddled with a pair of raw recruits, not for any reason, but especially not on picket duty. Skirmishing and picketing could be loose, unpredictable business, and Nathan didn't want to be looking out for anyone other than Willie. He skirmished with his brother, and just his brother. That was their custom.

"Good," Halpern said quietly. "I would hate to think I had inconvenienced you."

Once Halpern was out of ear shot, Nathan looked at Willie and muttered, "Your being a corporal is making me prone to all manner of complaints."

The company filed out through a crude sally port, a place where the barricade could be pulled down and there were no stakes in the creek bottom, permitting an easier passage. Even so, climbing out of that creek was a dirty chore without a ladder or a helping hand. That very point was made by Lloyd, who had to scramble up the steep bank on his own now that the rankers were making a point of shunning him.

Watching Lloyd slide down the bank in the gloom, Nathan reckoned it was only a matter of time before the failed draft dodger deserted. He hoped Lloyd would leave them sooner rather than later and find himself at the end of a rope before long.

Colonel Tillman's adjutant, a lieutenant, led Bell and the company forward half a mile, through fields and lines of trees. It was easy going despite the dark, as the country was almost flat. Finally the lieutenant stopped them at the edge of a fallow field, behind a line of trees, where another company was spread out over more than 200 yards of ground. On the other side of the trees was a field of young corn. Halpern motioned to Willie to go left, so he took Nathan and the greenhorns down to the far left end of the picket line and relieved the men who were waiting there.

Nathan hunkered down and whispered to a corporal from the other company, "Where are the Yankees?"

"Nathan!" Willie hissed. "That's my job!" More softly, Willie said, "Frank, where are the Yankees?"

The corporal chuckled quietly. "Nathan. Willam. Good morning to you too. Them Yankees is on the other side of the cornfield. They ain't been talkative or nothing, just over there minding their own business."

Nathan muttered, "That sure ain't going to last."

"Nope," the corporal said back. "I reckon not. See you boys back at the creek."

Willie motioned for the greenhorns to crawl forward. "Listen. We're here to give the main line a good warning when the Yankees come up, and ain't supposed to make a real fight here. When they come over, we shoot and skedaddle, you understand? Follow Nathan here and me back to the next line of trees. We work in pairs, just like in the skirmish drill. Alright?"

The boys, both only a year younger than Willie himself, nodded hesitantly.

"Alright then. Jimmy, you're with Nathan. Pete, you're with me. Just stick close, do what we do, don't make any noise before them Yankees come cross the cornfield, and you'll be fine."

Nathan snatched Willie by the arm, but before he could say anything, Willie spoke first. "I know, I know. But I got to look after these boys. I ain't going far. And anyhow, I reckon I got to look after you too, seeing as how I'm a higher rank and all."

He couldn't help but smirk at that, but with more seriousness Nathan said, "Don't you go off seeing about them fellows down our right. This ain't their first dance in the nettles or nothing, and you ain't been given that job. Let Halpern worry about them."

He could see Willie happily smiling back at him in the gloom. "Alright. You want the end there?"

Nathan nodded, patted the boy he now knew was named Jimmy on the shoulder, the same one who had pestered him with questions the other day. They went down the line of trees for several more yards, Nathan counting the paces as he went. He was still annoyed at being separated from Willie, now "Corporal Grimes," and at having to look out for a greenhorn.

Even so, Nathan thought, I reckon little brother is finding his feet. The notion gave him a warm, proud feeling, but he was still annoyed.

Hours passed and the sky slowly grew brighter, into a soup of smoky gray. Nathan absently chewed on a hardtack cracker. When it grew light enough, he looked down the line, making sure not only of where Willie was, just 30 feet away, but also where Halpern and Bell were, down off the center.

When the Billies came, they came on without preamble. There were no bugles, no shouts, no artillery, just a line of four dozen men in blue, stepping out from behind the trees and brush and into the half-grown stalks of corn.

Nathan leveled his musket, cocked the hammer back, and squeezed the trigger, adding to the musketry crackling to his right. Standing behind his tree, he set about reloading while keeping an eye on the flashes of blue amid the corn stalks. He didn't spare even a glance for Jimmy, but instead kept his ear cocked as he reloaded. Soon enough he heard the crack of Jimmy's musket, and Nathan gave a slight nod of satisfaction and he tamped a ball down his musket barrel.

A bullet zipped through the branches just above Nathan's head, sending sticks and twigs bouncing off the brim of his slouch hat. Bringing his musket up cocked, Nathan waited for the spot of blue he had been tracking to reappear, which it did a couple of seconds later. He pulled the trigger and set about reloading, this time sparing a worried glance down the right. He looked first to Willie, then tried to find Halpern.

"What are we still doing here?" he muttered. The Yankees were coming on, careful but still moving forward, and pickets weren't supposed to stand their ground like this. Nathan knew perfectly well they should have fallen back right after the first shots, especially as the field behind them was just knee-high grass and weeds, with no cover all the way back to the next line of trees. If they were going to stand and shoot a spell, it should be back there, and not here.

Nathan had been efficiently shooting, loading, picking a target, and shooting again for little more than a minute, but it felt much longer. The Yankees were halfway across the field now, with the flashes of blue and puffs of smoke growing steadily larger. His gut was already clenched solid when two balls struck the front of his tree, one "thwack" right after the other.

He was about to call out to Willie when Halpern came running down the line, hunched over and hissing, "Back! Back!"

As Willie barked, "Go! Go! Go!" Nathan shouted, "Run!" at Jimmy. Once he saw Willie was off, Nathan fired one last shot, right into the belly of a charging, hollering Yankee. Then he spun around and ran, flat out ran, sprinting right past Jimmy as the boy stumbled forward, red splashing out of his middle back. Nathan only stopped when he crashed through the underbrush of the next tree line and then dropped to the ground and slid to a halt. From there, he rolled over, and saw Willie and the other greenhorn had made it.

What was his name? Nathan thought. Pete. That's it.

Crawling back up to a thick tree, Nathan saw the spurts of flame and smoke coming from their abandoned position. The Billies themselves were only dark shadows in the tree shade and dim light of the early, overcast morning. Jimmy was in the field, some 50 yards away and crying for help.

Nathan shot Willie a hard look that said "No," and was relieved when Willie gave him a reluctant nod in agreement. No one could get that boy out of there without getting shot, and they both knew it. Nathan started reloading his musket and tried not to look at the back-shot boy sobbing his and Willie's names.

As soon as Halpern made his rounds, the company fell back again, this time in a more timely and orderly fashion. They turned again, fired a couple more shots each at the advancing bluecoats, and then made their dash for the creek. Soon the company was across and with the regiment again.

Backs up against the barricade, Nathan, Willie, and Pete sat catching their breaths. After a few minutes, they were joined by Sergeant Marks.

Nathan spat, "Ed, what in the name of sweet Jesus happened back there?"

Willie wheezed "Blasphemy" in a scolding tone. Nathan ignored him, set on Marks.

Marks avoided Nathan's eyes. "Bell wouldn't leave. He wanted to stay and fight. It didn't take but a couple minutes to change his mind, but..."

"Did we lose anyone else?" Willie asked.

"Just that greenhorn of yours."

"Jimmy," Willie said angrily. "You know his name, Ed. His name was Jimmy Sturgill."

Marks shrugged. A cannonball tumbled through the branches above them to strike the ground dozens of yards off, plowing up dirt and chips of stone. Hard on its heels was the distant, muffled thunder of artillery. Another solid flew through the trees, followed by another that struck ground well before the creek, only to bounce over the barricade and on into the field behind. A shell burst overhead with a loud crack, but did no harm.

Artillery had played only a small part in the battles Nathan had fought up until now, so although the bombardment had done no damage insofar as he could tell, he still found it disconcerting. Peering through a loophole in the barricade, he could see no bluebellies, but he knew they were out there. They were behind the line of trees bordering the open field, about 150 yards away. Leaning against the log wall of the barricade, Nathan settled in to wait for either something he could see and hit, or else orders to begin shooting up those trees.

7:30 a.m.
Red Jackson's Division, CSA
Scales Mountain

From his perch near the crest of Scales Mountain, Forrest studied the country below through his field glasses. He could see the entire southern end of the battlefield. For two miles, from the foot of the mountain to Stevenson's front, the fields boiled with bluecoats. He could even see the party of officers and the flapping guidon in a clearing just under the mountain, where a line of guns had set up and were even now flinging ball and shell into the wooded slopes of the mountain. The flag was emblazoned with a simple emblem, a single star, signifying the XX Corps.

"That there, Bill, is Fighting Joe Hooker and his eastern bluebellies," sneered Forrest.

William Hicks Jackson, known to most as "Red," replied, "Yep. I reckon his entire corps is bearing down on us now. There is at least a whole division of Yankee foot sloggers to my front, and as plain as day there is another working around the western end of this hill. I'll be flanked directly. Very directly."

Unbothered, Forrest said, "Get ready to withdraw. As soon as your pickets come a-running, pull your entire division back behind this here hill, and take up that new line I showed you on Indian Mountain."

"Sir, I can hold on here a while longer just by pulling back and refusing my left flank. I don't have to leave just yet."

That's right, Forrest thought, he don't have to leave just yet. But Red would get busted trying to hang on to this here hill, maybe busted up bad, and he would have to leave it all the same, Old

Jack's orders or no. That was five to one odds down there, and that is too much, even by my standards.

"I know, but if we're going to make a fight of it, I prefer Indian Mountain. It'll take the Yankees all morning to come up over and around this here mountain and get to us there, and they can't bring their artillery with them. Putting down cannon on the other side of a big wooded hill like this would take all damn day. I like them odds better."

Red shot back, "But we can't pull back. If I leave, I expose Clayton's flank."

Forrest was suddenly very glad he was here. Red didn't want to leave, so he would have argued against an order sent by courier or wig-wag. In the meantime, he would have gotten himself chewed up in a real fight with Hooker. What was more, Forrest knew the enemy would need to drive them off Indian Mountain too if they were going to come down on Clayton's flank.

Forrest gave Red a hard look. "We've all got our orders, Bill. I'm going on back to Indian Mountain. Pull back your boys like I told you, and let me worry about Clayton."

Red hesitated, and resignedly said, "Yessir."

9:00 a.m.
Headquarters, Army of the Tennessee, USA
Western outskirts of Rutherford County

McPherson stood bent over a table writing a message in the signals station, the open-sided tent situated next to a prominent semaphore tower built from green logs, and easily the busiest place in the headquarters. But this message wasn't for transmission by wig-wagging flags. Instead, McPherson handed it to a courier and said "Take that to General Minty."

He then proceeded to write a second message, this one for encoding by a signals clerk and bound for the semaphore tower and transmission to Logan. It was a last-minute adjustment, acceding to Logan's request to call upon Smith's Brigade of cavalry, then screening the hamlet of Stewartsboro, to exploit any success his diversionary attack should gain. McPherson liked the idea, since it would mean more chaos on the enemy right, and therefore a greater distraction.

But he liked it most of all because it meant Logan was feeling optimistic. McPherson shook his head. Old Blackjack was as solid a fighter a man could want, but he could also be so pessimistic at times.

Aggression and gloom was a most strange combination in a man, he thought. But hell, if Logan can capture that bridge, I would give him Minty's whole division to send around the Confederate right, were it not that Bill is so nervous about guarding the railroad.

Thinking of Sherman, McPherson looked down to where his superior was energetically pacing back and forth in front of the little log cabin he was using as his quarters and office. Sherman had the military affairs of the entire region between the Appalachians and the Mississippi to attend to, and most of the time that so occupied even Sherman's capable braincase that McPherson was left alone to manage the day-to-day affairs of the Army of the Tennessee.

Today was different, and McPherson understood that. There was a battle underway, and Sherman was here in person. Today, his army was the sole focus of Sherman's thoughts. So Sherman was over there, painfully restive and burning his way through his third cigar of the morning, but doing his best to stay out of the particulars of running the army.

He's letting me do my job, McPherson thought with a warm, appreciative smile. He doesn't care for it, but he is getting on with it. Bless him.

A clerk handed McPherson a new message from the semaphore station. He read it, folded it up, and walked down to Sherman.

"Message from Hooker," he said, handing the message over. "He says the Confederate cavalry screen has withdrawn from Scales Mountain, but assumed a new position immediately to the southeast on Indian Mountain. He wants to take the new position before beginning the main attack."

Sherman glanced the message over, then raised his eyes to meet McPherson's. "Well, it is Hooker. I'm going down there to see what he's about."

"Yes, that's best. After all, it's a big part of why you wanted to be here." Sherman had always said part of his reason for traveling with the Army of the Tennessee was to make sure Hooker didn't start some argument over rank, because while McPherson was the army commander, and served at the pleasure of the President of the United States, Hooker technically outranked him. It was a murky gray area, but Sherman clearly outranked Hooker on all counts, thus solving the problem.

Sherman mounted up and rode away fast, leaving a string of escorts and aides behind him. McPherson was glad to see him go, because it meant Sherman would have something to occupy him.

After a quick ride of a little over two miles, Sherman arrived at Hooker's headquarters, whom he found standing with some of his staff under an open-sided tent, all studying a map.

Hooker came out from under the canvas and greeted Sherman with a salute. "Good morning, sir. I was expecting General McPherson."

Sherman returned the salute. "Well, you've got me. I'd like to see this other mountain of yours, if you can spare me the time."

"Of course." Hooker motioned for his horse to be brought over, mounted up, and led Sherman and their combined attendants up the slopes of Scales Mountain by way of an old dirt track.

Sherman immediately admired the view. The entire southern end of the battlefield could be seen from there. The scene would have even been something like idyllic, were it not for the bursting of Rebel shells onto the wooded slopes below.

"You should put in an observation post here."

Hooker nodded. "Already on it. That and a new signals station. It will save time, what with couriers having to ride over or around this damn hill all the time." He pointed at the ridge just across a rugged, narrow valley from them. "The new Rebel position is right over there. It's just dismounted cavalry, but as you can see, the terrain is very difficult, and clearly the positions were planned and prepared. Geary is in the valley now, on the Rebel front. Butterfield is moving around the flank and rear of that mountain, through the woods. It takes more time, but impairs observation. Give me a little more time, and I'll crush those bastards, rout them off those heights or bag the whole ugly bushel of them, and clear the entire left. Then I'll swing Butterfield and Geary around, and do the same to the Stewart's Creek line."

Sherman's mind clicked swiftly through Hooker's plan, weighing its merits and analyzing its variables. "I agree that you must clear those heights. If we make progress against the enemy's main line and get beyond Scales Mountain, those guns will pound our right flank as soon as it comes into sight. But you've still driven a wedge between the enemy flank and its cavalry screen. Call up reinforcements from XVI Corps if you need to, but I want you to get on with the main assault. Don't wait to clear these hills. Do both at the same time."

Hooker said, "Yessir. I'll get to it." Taking out his pocket watch, Hooker added, "My guess is that making the necessary adjustments will require an hour, give or take. Start at 10:30?"

Sherman nodded in agreement. As Hooker saluted and rode back down the mountain, Sherman sat calmly on his horse, neither fidgeting or feeling the need to light another cigar, and watched the skirmishing and light artillery fire taking place in the plains to his left and in the valley to his right. He plucked the spent cigar butt from his mouth and threw it away. He decided to stay where he was for the time being, leaving it to Hooker to notify McPherson of the change.

"The main action today will be here, he said to Audenried. "Here, on our right. And this is as good an observation post as any. I'll commandeer Hooker's wig-wags, once those are in operation."

Audenried replied, "Yessir. Shall I go hurry Hooker's signals people along?"

"Capital idea. Yes, go to it."

10:00 a.m.
Headquarters, XVI Corps, USA
Christopher Farmhouse
15 miles west of Murfreesboro

Upon receiving Hooker's detailed written message brought by courier about the delay, McPherson made two decisions. The first was to order Logan to go ahead with his diversionary attack as soon as he was ready. The second was to ride down to the army's right himself and smooth out the arrangements in person, starting with XVI Corps, which was headquartered only a mile or so down the country road from his own headquarters.

He arrived outside the house Smith was using as a headquarters to hear a full-bore shouting match from within, which McPherson soon recognized as between Smith and Hooker. Waving off the aides who tried to slow or stop him, he went inside.

Smith, with his bald head, white whiskers, and merely average frame, always seemed much older than he actually was. When McPherson entered the room, he saw Hooker looming over him oppressively, trying to bully Smith with his sheer size.

Hooker picked the wrong man for that, McPherson thought. Andrew Jackson Smith might look feeble, but the man's as steady as Gibraltar.

"God dammit, Smith, Sherman's orders are for you to reinforce me, and this is the quickest damn way to do it. Send Sweeny around the right, and flank their God damned entrenchments!"

Looking straight up and into Hooker's eyes without flinching, Smith retorted, "I know Bill Sherman, and I know he didn't mean a God damned thing about breaking up my corps and feeding it in piecemeal. Either sidle over like I told you, or send up for clarification, because that is the only way Sweeny is moving one inch."

So intent were the two men on each other, they hadn't even noticed McPherson enter in room and were surprised to hear him speak. "Gentlemen, maybe this is how they conduct business in the Army of the Potomac, or down in Louisiana under Banks, but not in the Army of Tennessee," he said sternly. "Your staffs can hear you outside."

After saluting, Smith said, "Yes, sir. Of course." Growing slightly ashamed, he added, "I should have known better." Hooker merely saluted and glowered.

Now to attend to the dispute itself, McPherson thought. I'm certainly not handing Hooker control of another division. He already has my largest corps. If I start giving over Smith's divisions to him, he'll have supervision of half the army.

"Mower's Division is already in position, yes?"

"That's right. He's in front of the southern end of Stewart's Creek."

"Alright. Hooker, have Williams sidle over so Sweeny can come up. So now you," McPherson said, motioning to Smith, "have full charge of attacking the Confederate left-front. General Hooker, you are now responsible for attacking their left flank with Williams, and driving into their left-rear with the rest of your corps. Thomas Kilby Smith's Division is my reserve. Understood?"

Smith and Hooker concurred. "Good. Now see to it. Dismissed." Watching them leave the room, McPherson felt satisfied. Sherman had made the call over his head, of course, but Sherman was his superior. More to the point, Sherman had left the details to McPherson, as was their understanding. Hooker had tried to elbow out some more authority for himself, of course, but hadn't directly challenged McPherson's authority, at least not yet.

10 a.m.
7ᵗʰ Pennsylvania Cavalry, USA
Smyrna, Tennessee
East Bank of Stewart's Creek
12 miles northwest of Murfreesboro

Spear listened to the muffled, dim booming of cannon, miles off in the distance. Nearby, Crowder napped with his hat over his face, while Rose doodled, drawing crude figures in the dirt with his pocket knife. Sitting with his back up against a tree, Spear plucked a pebble from the dirt. With a disgusted grimace on his face, he flung it.

"Sometimes, I think stars make a man stupid. What in God's name are we doing here?!"

The company was on picket duty near the banks of Stewart's Creek, not far from the confluence of that creek, Overall Creek, and Stones River, on the extreme northern end of the Union line. Their task was a simple one: screen the northeastern approaches to Smyrna, where the railroad station and the growing supply depot were located.

Rose said, "You know what we are doing. The Saber Brigade guards Smyrna. Smyrna is where our supplies are kept. Any general worth his salt, he always casts an eye over his shoulder, thinking to himself 'the next wagon load of crackers and cartridges, where comes it from?' For us, that is a particular problem, yes? What with Forrest stomping around?"

"I know. But I think we could do the same job just as well by crossing that there creek and raising some hell in the Rebel rear. We might even raise that siege around Fortress Rosecrans and do some real damage. Dammit, Walt, you know what I mean. We're the Sabers! We fight as good or better than any Johnnie bastard Forrest ever had."

Rose shrugged. "Still. I believe Uncle Billy wants to be sure. Nothing is more certain than having us here."

"I'll tell you this much. Buell didn't know nothing about how to use cavalry. Old Rosey had something of an idea, I reckon, but whether Uncle Billy does, well, we're just going to have to see about that."

"See about it or not," Rose said, "today we guard the railroad."

"I don't know what you're fussing about," murmured Crowder. "What, do you want to get shot at? Now will you keep quiet and let a man sleep?"

CHAPTER 11

Noon
Headquarters, Stewart's Corps, CSA
The Confederate Left
Near the Bole Jack Road

Jackson and Stewart stood side by side atop the hillock located just west of where Stewart kept his headquarters, observing the fighting taking place just a mile or so away. Stewart's entire corps was under heavy attack, with the enemy taking advantage of every row of trees, every wood lot, and every overgrown cluster of boulders for cover. They hadn't tried to storm the breastworks yet, but were instead laying down a terrific fire of musketry, shot, and shell.

With the care of the one-handed, Jackson put his field glasses back in their case. His eyes sparkled brightly, and he aggressively scratched his thigh as if chasing a painful itch. He turned about as if to leave, but then stopped and returned.

"I wish I had some lemons, Pete. A lemon would be very pleasant, very settling."

Stewart still had his binoculars raised. "Message from Forrest. I can see the flags on Indian Mountain."

In just a few minutes, the message was transcribed and decoded by Stewart's staff. The clerk was about to hand it to Stewart, but he shook his head slightly and tilted it towards Jackson, who received it instead.

Jackson read and became even more animated, snapping his words out in small barks. "It's Forrest. Reports strong Federal column working around Clayton's flank. From Scales Mountain. But we can see that. Also, Red Jackson under heavy attack. About to be out-flanked too. Will withdraw soon."

"Then it's time," Stewart said. "With your permission, I will tell Clayton to pull back, as per his instructions. And I want to put that counter-attack in myself."

Jackson nodded vigorously. Stewart had already explained to him his specific plan: to speed up the withdrawal, Clayton's brigades would let go of Stevenson's left flank and keep only loosely aligned with each other. To prevent the enemy from pouring through the gap that would open up between Stevenson and Clayton, Stewart would punch right into that gap with his reserves.

"Good, good."

More hesitantly, Stewart said, "Tom, may I suggest you leave this place. I know I have some artillery up here, and Polk's whole corps is supposed to come through here, but if something goes astray… this little hill will become an island in a sea of Federal troops. You should go on back and join the Bishop."

Jackson looked annoyed, and said testily, "Yes, yes. You are right, of course. I'll not tarry here."

Stewart mounted up and rode away, taking his immediate attendants with him. Jackson watched as the party cantered across the fields, the road, and into the woods at the base of the Burnt Knob escarpment. Right about the time Jackson saw Clayton begin his withdrawal, he also saw Holtzclaw's and Pettus's Brigade's, practically an improvised demi-division of Alabamians, move forward.

Jackson looked back over his shoulder, although all he could really see was the black and brass cannon lined up behind him. Polk is three miles away, Jackson thought, but the enemy would see him coming up from about two miles away. He decided to wait a little while longer before calling on Polk. So he sat down on the grass, watching and waiting.

After about twenty minutes of this, a courier galloped up. He swung over and off his horse and almost leapt the final steps up to Jackson. "Message from General Cleburne, sir!"

Jackson didn't get up, took the message, and started reading it without saying a word.

Wednesday, June 22
Noon
Headquarters, Cleburne's Corps of the Army of Tennessee
Patrick R. Cleburne Commanding, Brevet Lieutenant General of
Foot, CSA

To General Thomas J. Jackson
Commanding General, Army of Tennessee and Western
Department

Sir,

General Buford reports his position severely tested by Federal infantry, and that the enemy has captured and been driven from the Murfreesboro Pike Bridge once already. I went north to personally inspect Buford's circumstances myself, and believe the Federals will make another attempt to force a crossing of Stewart's Creek north of the position of my corps, in Buford's territory. For this reason, I have instructed General Buford to fire the Mufreesboro Pike Bridge, and dispatched my reserve of Granbury's Brigade to bolster his line.

I may require reinforcements should the enemy press my front and the far right under Buford in greater strength. Please advise.

Your obedient servant,
Patrick Cleburne

Jackson folded the message up, put it in his pocket, and said, "Inform General Cleburne that the main Federal effort will be here, on the left, and not on the center or right. I condone his actions, but have no reinforcements to send him. He must hold with what he and General Buford have."

The courier saluted, and as he turned and sprinted back to his horse, Jackson checked his watch and noted that it was quarter to one o'clock. He then returned to his vigil, and broke into a broad smile as he saw Clayton's planned withdrawal had begun.

Clayton's Division had once been Stewart's and labored and fought in accordance with Old Straight's methodical style. Each of the three brigades on the firing line left behind a single regiment, spread out loosely, to keep up a masking fire from behind the earthworks. Then went those batteries assigned to directly support Clayton's line. Torn up by Federal counter-fires, the gunners left behind them scenes of dead horses, dead crewmen, and shattered limbers.

Only when the cannon left did the Billies of Sweeny's and Williams's Divisions begin to realize that the butternuts might be pulling back, and even then some blue field officers believed the guns were withdrawn only so as to replace them with fresh artillery. It was several minutes after even the skirmishers were gone that they went forward, leaving their trees and rocks, crossing soft, damp fields pock-marked by bombardment, working their way around felled trees that had been carved into abatis, and finally into the abandoned earthen embankments themselves.

Upon reaching this point, the profane and fiery Irish general, Thomas Sweeny, sent back word to his superior, the XVI Corps' commander A.J. Smith, that Mower should throw his men forward in an attempt to storm that end of Stewart's Creek, because he would soon be assailing its flank and rear. Sweeny pivoted then his line to face north and northeast, while the hard-eyed, bristle-whiskered Alpheus Williams drove his division forward due east in pursuit of Clayton's graybacks.

Sweeny sent Rice's Brigade straight up the east side of Stewart's Creek, where they almost immediately ran into Cumming's Georgia Brigade, their line refused through a dense copse of trees and into headstones of the McClaren family cemetery. There they stood for twenty minutes, until Bane's Brigade came around and poured a volley into their side and rear.

Riding along with Bane, Sweeny was exultant. To an aide, he said, "Go back and tell General Smith that I've seized Johnny Reb by the neck, he's gone and pissed himself, and I'm cutting his balls off! If Mower comes down now, we'll kill every last God damned traitorous, sister-loving bastard on this field!"

The aide was looking to the rear, studying the busy flapping of the XVI Corps semaphore station. "Yes, sir, I'll leave right now, sir. But General, you should look to the wig-wags…"

"Damn the wig-wags, Captain! I'll attend to those fucking wig-wags when I've got this line rolled up like a plug of tobacco. Now move!"

In the same instant Sweeny's aide put his spurs to his horses, blue flank guards came in hasty flight from out of rows and copses of cedars and scrub oak to the east, followed by the densely packed ranks of Stewart's reserves, the "demi-division" of Alabamians. With a resounding crash, a massed volley slammed directly into the backs of Bane's Brigade, causing an instant rout. They fled directly into the right flank of Rice's Brigade, throwing it into confusion. In a matter of minutes, thousands of Illinoisans and Iowans were recoiling in confusion.

The blue torrent carried a violently distraught Sweeny along with it. Slapping fleeing bluecoats with the flat of his saber, the one-armed Sweeny screamed, "Rascals! Blackguards! Scoundrels! Yellow bastards! Get back in there. Don't you see we have them whipped!"

Sweeny's protests were to no avail. Some of his men fled as fast as their feet could carry them, while others withdrew with more dignity and order, but all ignored the demands of their officers, right up to the swearing, spitting, flailing Irishman with the single star on his shoulder straps. Disgusted, Sweeny put the spurs to his horse and rode off to find Burke's Brigade, then coming up in support.

While Sweeny struggled restore order to his muddled ranks, Stewart rode out between the two Alabama brigades, where he could be seen by all. Pointing his sword west, he shouted, "Forward my Southrons! Chase them! Drive them! Give them hot fires and the cold steel!"

Almost four thousand Alabama men cheered back at him, "Old Straight! Old Straight!" and surged forward in pursuit. Stewart steadied his horse, and once the thick rows of butternuts passed him by, made to ride back to the rear, but he encountered Carter Stevenson first.

"Well handled, General Stewart, well handled! General Cummings is already reforming those men who ran," Stevenson said.

"Thank you, Carter. Now, what I need you to keep on with the good work. You can have Pettus back, but tell Holtzclaw to march back into the rear, back into reserve. Use Pettus to lengthen and partly refuse your line. I'll bring Clayton back on your left. Understand?"

Stevenson nodded. Stewart said, "Good. Now go," and rode off in search of Clayton.

After the generals concluded their brief conference, the Alabamans stepped out of the trees that fringed almost every field in the county and into the open, only to discover Burke's Brigade lying in wait on the other side of the embankments of Clayton's abandoned field fortifications. In the center of Burke's line was the 66th Illinois, the Western Sharpshooters, a regiment several hundred strong and armed with Henry repeating rifles. The torrent of fire felled dozens in a matter of seconds. Shocked, the Alabamans halted on the spot and scurried back to the cover of the nearest row of trees and brush, despite their greater numbers. Stevenson arrived shortly thereafter and set about stiffening his line.

1:15 p.m.
The Hillock by Stewart's Headquarters, CSA
The Confederate Left

From his vantage point on the low hill, Jackson beamed as he watched Stewart's counter-attack ambush and smash Sweeny's advance. Without taking his binoculars from his eyes, he called out, "That is the hand of Providence, Sandie! Providence!"

Sandie, who stood just behind and to the right of Jackson, was also watching the fighting through field glasses. "Yessir. The Lord surely smiles on us." More nervously, he said, "But shouldn't we be bringing General Polk up now?"

Jackson lowered his binoculars and gave Sandie a reproachful look, but then softened. That was the second time Sandie had asked that question, on top of Stewart saying as much before his leaving. But his chief of staff was right. The enemy blue closely pursued Clayton's brigades even now, and heavy columns of blue were just then emerging from the forested hills to the southwest. It was time.

"Very well. Have those written orders sent to General Polk. Bring him up."

Sandie said, "Yessir, at once. In fact, General Jackson, by your leave, I will deliver the message personally."

Jackson stared quizzically at Sandie for a time, but finally nodded and said, "If you think it so important, then alright."

Sandie got into the saddle and rode back towards Overall Creek, relief and determination replacing anxiety. He had absolute faith in Old Jack's plans, but little or none in Bishop Polk's ability or willingness to carry those plans out. Sandie had heard the camp gossip, studied and followed up on the field reports from Lawrenceburg, and decided Polk was a bungler and just possibly a troublemaking font of insubordination as well.

Jackson wouldn't hear of it, Sandie thought as he went on. Of course he wouldn't. Piety mattered most to him. It would never occur to Old Jack to make sure his orders were obeyed, because he would never believe a Christian soldier like Leonidas Polk wouldn't obey to the best of his ability, divine blessings showering down upon his works and all. Well, this time I'm going back and making sure things get done.

Back on the western slopes of the hillock, Jackson watched the enemy pursuit of Clayton's brigades with rising alarm. The bluecoats followed aggressively, coming on at the double quick. Half a mile from the hillock, the pursuer's finally came to grips with the rearguard of one of the retreating Confederate brigades, forcing it to turn and offer support. But Jackson could see what his infantry could not, namely a loose, fast-moving mass of enemy troops coming up behind a thick belt of cedars to their south.

Jackson spun around and snapped at the gunners behind him, stabbing violently at the flanking Yankee mass almost 900 yards distant. "Open fire! I want fire placed on that enemy brigade, that one right there!"

The artillery crews set about loading and aiming their pieces, and even before Jackson had reached his horse, all eight of the Napoleon smoothbores and three-inch rifles on the hillock had fired their first shots. As he mounted his horse, Smith came up and seized his mount by the halter.

"Sir! I know your intent. You must not endanger yourself in such a manner!"

Jackson bent over the neck of his horse, eyes burning, and snapped, "Jimmy, those boys are going to break. If they do not break, I'll be in no danger at all. If they break and fail to rally, then our whole line is in danger. Let go of this horse." When Smith did not obey, he shouted "That is an order, Captain!"

Smith reluctantly let go of the halter. "I'm coming with you."

"Very well." Jackson put the spurs to his horse and galloped off as quickly as the sturdy old mare would carry him, with only his guidon bearer following immediately behind him.

A quarter-mile out, Jackson met a mob of fleeing Johnnies in an open field. He turned his horse, pacing back in forth before the oncoming rout.

Over the din of shells bursting just a few hundred yards away, Jackson roared, "Men! Stand your ground! If you will rally and stand your ground with me, I will stand this ground with you!"

They stopped, but rather than rally, they approached and surrounded him, pleading, "Leave! To the rear! Leave!" One man, a hatless, sweaty sergeant, gently placed his hand the shoulder of Jackson's horse and looked up. "We'll stand, sir. Wherever you tell us, we'll hold that ground. But we cannot afford to lose you, General. This is no place for you, so get back at once."

A general rode up at the head of a formed body of men, whom Jackson recognized as Alpheus Baker, promoted to brigadier only three months before.

Jackson commanded, "General Baker, reform your men at the foot of that hillock yonder, under the guns. Reform them now." Looking down to the sergeant, Jackson said more quietly "I shall do as you ask, Sergeant."

Leaving the men behind, Jackson trotted back towards the hill, and was met by Smith and another aide about halfway there. He was about to call out to Smith when several cannonballs shrieked overhead, smashing into and exploding about the artillery positions on the hill beyond. An instant later, Jackson was deafened and flung from his horse.

Dazed, he pressed himself from the ground with his one arm. An explosion, Jackson thought. A bursting shell. But when his vision came into focus, it was no longer day, but dark, which left him more confused. Have I been unconscious, he wondered.

Then he noticed he was no longer in an open field, but in a thick, overgrown wood. Before him, propped up against a tree was Keith Boswell, sitting there with two dark, red stains plainly visible through his butternut coat. Jackson stared at his pale, smooth face, youthful and lifeless. Jackson shook his head as he rose clumsily to his feet. When he looked again, it was not Boswell, but Smith who was lying there.

Jackson rushed to him, dropping to his knees. Smith's neck lay open, his head resting in a puddle of blood, but he gurgled and blinked. He was still alive, but Jackson knew he would not be for much longer.

Not again, Jackson thought. More fine young men killed on account of me. As the tears came to his eyes, he scorned his guilty regret. I mustn't do this now, he thought, not when Jimmy needs me.

Jackson took Smith by the hand, and said softly, "It's alright, Jimmy. Go across the river and lie down in the pasture. Our Heavenly Maker awaits you there."

Smith blinked at him, and then he was gone. Jackson gently passed his hand over Smith's face, closing his eyes. At the same moment, he heard Captain Quintard shouting behind him, "General! General! Are you alright, sir!?"

Rising painfully to his feet, Jackson turned and mumbled, "No, no. I believe I am unhurt." He dimly realized that Baker and his aides were galloping to him as well, with hundreds of men sprinting up behind them.

I must act. I must act now, he thought, urgency further clearing his head.

Gently pushing Quintard aside with one hand, Jackson stepped into view. "I am unharmed! Unharmed!"

That brought the mob of alarmed soldiers to a relieved halt, and their officers set about putting them back into order. Baker rode on though, and as he came up, he called out to Jackson.

"General Jackson, with all due respect, I must insist that you retire to a place of greater safety at once! What a calamity nearly befell our country this hour! I say it again, this is no place for you!"

Jackson frowned. Still wracked with guilt, his lips quivered. "Yes, you are more in the right than I think you know, General Baker. A calamity has befallen us just now."

Baker looked confused, but Jackson did not explain himself. "General Baker, if you would assign some stretcher bearers to assist Captain Quintard here, I would be grateful."

Looking to Quintard, he said, "You see Captain Smith's body back to General Stewart's tents, behind that hillock yonder. And Quintard, I fear I must ask for your horse. I cannot accompany you. When you have seen Captain Smith to shelter, make your way as best you can either to rejoin me with General Stewart, over by the creek, or to army headquarters."

Quintard nodded, slightly, gravely. "Yessir. If I may say, sir, I always liked him. He was a good man."

Jackson nodded, biting his lip, saying nothing.

CHAPTER 12

1:30 p.m.
XX Corps, USA
The Federal Right

Hooker sat on his horse in the open field, watching Williams' troops march away and a battery of guns unlimber, when Dan Butterfield rode up. He grinned like a schoolboy at the sight. Besides being one of the few general officers in the Army of the Tennessee that Hooker genuinely liked, Butterfield was a brave, intelligent man, as handy at the head of troops as he was wielding a pen. Hooker thought him the perfect man for the task ahead.

"Dan!" Hooker cried. "You've come at a good time!"

Bringing his horse to a halt, Butterfield saluted and said, "How goes, Joe?" He was a broad-shouldered man, but that part of his appearance was overshadowed by his bulging, egg-like forehead and bushy moustache.

"Marvelous, Dan. It is marvelous. Old man Williams has bent the Confederate line back into a big wedge. That wedge is anchored there," he said, thrusting his gauntleted finger northeastward with so much force his horse had cause to steady its footing.

Butterfield followed the finger to a hillock, the top of which was visible above the trees lining the field. He could see several Confederate guns below the crown and that those guns were already taking fire.

"They are hoping to keep me down, Dan, Sherman, Halleck, and all the rest of them. They are hoping I'll blunder into something insubordinate, something they can charge me with, so they can hook my backside and hoist it up a flagpole. But I won't give them the satisfaction, no, I will not. I'll beat them on the merits. I'll get what's coming to me because I'm the better soldier."

As Butterfield, his old crony, nodded in agreement, Hooker thought how it was all so ridiculous. He knew the reason Sherman insisted on accompanying the army was because Sherman hated him, had hated him since California, and was determined to ruin him. Just as the U.S. Army's chief of staff, Henry Halleck, was determined to ruin him. He wouldn't give them the chance.

"Take that knoll, Dan. Take that knoll, and we can enfilade the whole damn Rebel line. We'll push them back on that big damned mountain there, or onto the creek, and break up the whole lot. Take that knoll, and we destroy Stonewall Jackson's army."

Grinning, Butterfield said, "And you want me to have that honor?"

"You have it, my good man. You have it. Mass your men here. I'm going to see about bringing Geary up to cover your right flank now, but I'll be back shortly. I want to say a word to your boys, but don't wait too long. If I'm not back soon, you go on in."

Butterfield spent the next twenty minutes making his dispositions, putting the brigades of Ward and Wood side by side in double line of battle, a phalanx of roughly 4,000 men from northern states stretching from Wisconsin to Massachusetts. By the time Butterfield was done, Hooker had returned.

He rode out in front of what was the bulk of Butterfield's Division. "Boys, you're hard-fighters and life-takers. Many of you fought at Gettysburg and Chancellorsville, but you don't get any credit for it, do you?"

"No, no!" the men loudly groaned back.

"And they scorn us out here, don't they? They call us all tin soldiers, jealous because we can march straighter and wear real uniforms, don't they?"

"Yes, yes!" the men shouted.

"Now is your chance to shut them up. Shut them all up, once and for all. Take that hill up there, and no one will say anything about the 70th Indiana, or the 55th Ohio, or any of us ever again. They won't talk about Gettysburg or Chancellorsville, but only about the day Butterfield's boys took that hill and whipped Stonewall Jackson!"

"Huzzah! Huzzah!" the men roared. Some shouted in broken English, "We fights mit Hooker!"

Hooker moved his horse out of the way, Butterfield taking his place to lead them into the attack. Bugles sounded the advance, and the men stopped their cheering and began steeling themselves for the carnage they knew lay ahead. As Hooker watched Butterfield go forward, McPherson rode up.

Hooker quickly explained his situation to his superior. McPherson approved of Hooker's intentions, his only comment an admonition to bring Geary up as quickly as possible.

As McPherson rode away and the cannon in the field boomed, Hooker leaned over and said loudly to an aide, "He's too cautious for my taste, Candler. A good man, McPherson, but too cautious for an army commander. Not that it matters. I'll win the day for us here, and that done, we'll see if they still want James B. McPherson in command of this army after Joseph Hooker covers himself in a fresh coat of glory."

1:45 p.m.
Headquarters, Polk's Corps, CSA
Blackman Schoolhouse
Three miles behind the Confederate left

After a hard dash, Sandie and his mount arrived at Blackman, both gasping for air. Sandie jumped down, spent only a moment composing himself, and then strode right up and into the schoolhouse, pushing past the aide who tried to stop him for a proper announcement. Bursting through both the door and Polk's staff, Sandie went directly to the Bishop, who turned away from his camp desk and serenely met his urgent stare as the young colonel came rushing forward.

"General Polk, your corps is ordered forward, sir. I have your written orders, but briefly, Clayton's Division has pulled back towards the north. You are to advance your corps directly west and counter-attack the Yankee right."

Polk seemed unmoved by Sandie's urgency. "Thank you, Colonel Pendleton. You have obviously applied great energy to delivering this message to me in a timely fashion. Rest assured that I will apply myself with matching vigor, my corps shall advance, and we shall smite the enemy with all our might."

Sandie stood waiting, while Polk looked back placidly. Finally, Polk said, "You may go now, Colonel. My staff and I have much to do. In private."

Sandie placed an envelope on Polk's desk, drew himself up, and saluted. "Yessir."

Once the army's boyish chief of staff was gone and the door closed, Polk turned his chair back to face his desk. His own chief of staff asked, "General, shall I pass the word to Generals French and Maney, putting them on notice..."

"Silence!" Polk snapped, as he pondered what to do next.

The Bishop had been in a sulk ever since Jackson had rejected his proposal for a stand on Overall Creek and refused to share his plans for battle. He had fretted that Stewart's Creek was too easy to turn, had been half-certain that a stand there would lead to disaster, and now it looked as if that might be happening. Polk imagined that if he stayed where he was, perhaps the army could still fall back on Overall Creek, or rally behind him there if it came to the worst.

Yet at the same time, Polk knew he was too close at hand to simply ignore his orders. The army's chief of staff had delivered them in person. Even more important, what would the people say if he stood by and did nothing after receiving such orders, even if his actions saved the army and the country? He knew such choices had a way of turning rotten, regardless of intention or outcome. The slanders needn't be true to mire his post-war political ambitions.

Polk opened the envelope Sandie left on his desk, and slowly leafed through the pages. He read each line carefully, not to look for extra guidance, but to buy extra time before the eyes of his waiting staff while he fretted over what to do.

Outside the schoolhouse, Sandie pulled himself into the saddle, where he waited, watched, and worried anxiously for several minutes. When no aides or couriers emerged to relay the orders and begin the advance, he turned his horse and rode straight to Maney's Division.

2:15 p.m.
XX Corps, USA
Hell's Hillock
The Federal Right

Baker's Alabamans had sufficient time to form and steady themselves on the lower slope of the hillock, soon to be spoken of as Hell's Hillock, but not enough to dig in. They laid down in the tallish grass, still wet on the humid, overcast day, so as to avoid the worst of the careening solids and ripping bits of iron from exploding shells. Behind them, their own artillery fired back, flinging metal at the guns massed on the eastern spur of Scales Mountain, about a mile to the southwest. There they waited, but not for long.

The Yankees came forward, out of the cedar thickets that covered a low ridge 300 yards away. First to emerge from the dark green of the cedars were the skirmishers, coming on in a loosely ordered mass stacked three deep. These men advanced in small groups, hid in the tall weeds and grass of the abandoned field, taking turns snapping off musket balls at the gray line on the hillock, reloading, and sprinting forward. Ignoring the skirmishers, the Alabamans waited out the preliminaries, waited for the true elephant to come out of the woods before them.

After the skirmishers had closed half the distance, the main Federal lines stepped out of the trees, a picture of trim, well-ordered ranks crowned with serried rows of bayonets. The butternut gunners stopped firing at the distant Northern cannons, reloaded their pieces with canister, and turned to chopping at the advancing blue coats, each boom of a gun spewing dozens of inch-wide iron balls. Baker, riding behind his brigade, ordered his men to stand up. Almost as one creature, they rose, brought up their rifles, squeezed their triggers, and unleashed a wave of flame, smoke, and lead.

That was where the Billies stopped, instinctively responding to the aggression heaped upon their persons by returning it. From a distance of 75 yards, the front ranks of Northern infantry stood in the open and exchanged blows with the graybacks on the hillock. The space between the fields and the hillock filled with a dense smoke, and men steadily fell from their respective firing lines, groaning, screaming, or deathly quiet. Southern cannoniers on the hill suffered badly from overshooting musket balls, which fell among them like a light rain.

On both sides, brave men stood in their places, ignoring the familiar dangers and intent on the mechanical process of seating powder and ball down barrels, capping gun nipples, and pulling triggers. As the minutes ticked by, bravery gave way in some, and those who felt they had endured enough began helping wounded comrades off the field. The truly craven did not bother with pretense and scurried away, sometimes under the curses of their sergeants, barely audible under the din. The ranks of both attacker and defender were remorselessly torn down, shred by shred.

Colonel Wood and General Ward spent the time hard at work, shifting some of the men from their second, supporting lines out onto the flanks. Butterfield brought his third brigade, Coburn's, up onto his far right, leading them into position in person. Federal artillery continued to hammer their rivals at the top of the hillock, and one by one the Rebel guns went silent, either smashed by a conical rifle shot or because there were too few surviving crew to man them.

Half an hour into the fight, Coburn's Brigade charged Baker's left, crashing into it at a dead run, bayonets leveled. Baker, his horse shot out from under him, ran to his left and tried to steady his men, but to no avail. The Alabama brigade's already tattered left collapsed and fled. The rest of Butterfield's division surged forward, yelling and screaming with triumph. Outnumbered by more than six to one, the Johnnies were chased off the hillock and into the woods beyond.

Sherman, McPherson, and Hooker had watched the fierce but lop-sided contest from the shelter of the wooded ridge. Now they rode out into the fields, among the wounded, the dead, and the detritus of battle.

"See what my boys did!" Hooker crowed. "Are they not fine? Are they not magnificent?"

McPherson replied flatly, "A solid victory, General Hooker. But I do worry that Geary's Division hasn't come up yet."

Hooker couldn't restrain himself from snorting. And that is why I need to take charge of this army, he thought to himself. Too much caution. Some fighting spirit, that is what is needed here.

While Hooker issued a fresh set of orders for Butterfield to a courier, McPherson chose to overlook Hooker's bad manners and focused instead on studying the bluecoats advancing up the hillock. All the while Sherman sat in his saddle, no longer fidgeting, chain-smoking, or chattering like a runaway telegraphy machine. He sat stock still, all his senses tuned what was going on around him, even as he swallowed his personal distaste for Hooker.

Finally, Sherman said to Hooker, "Congratulations seem to be in order, but General, I think there is a party of men over there bearing up a prisoner."

The trio went over and found three soldiers and a lieutenant escorting a Confederate general, who shuffled along unenthusiastically and needed a periodic shove from one of the rankers. He had high cheekbones, a largish nose and a bushy goatee, and the fact that he was hatless revealed a prominent forehead and a prematurely thinning crown of hair.

The three Union generals all looked to each other, none of them recognizing the man. Finally, McPherson politely introduced himself and his colleagues, and asked, "Who are you, sir?"

"Brigadier General Alpheus Baker, sir. Volunteer, Confederate States Army."

"Baker. Baker," murmured Sherman. "Ah, yes. Are you the same Alpheus Baker who was listed as colonel of the 54th Alabama? I believe the record indicated you were wounded at Champion Hill."

Baker stood up straight and tried to muster an air of defiance. "That's right."

McPherson looked to his friend, astonished by the feat of memory. Noticing this, Sherman gestured as if it were of no importance, saying, "Just something I read in a captured newspaper."

Hooker jumped in. "Well, General Baker, your brigade put up a good fight. Don't worry yourself about your capture. By nightfall, you shall have plenty of company."

Baker shot back, "By nightfall, General Hooker, I hope to see that Old Jack has whipped you. Whipped you, I say, just as he did at Sharpsburg and Chancellorsville."

Hooker snapped, "He did no such thing in that fucking cornfield, damn your eyes, you ignorant rascal!"

Sherman burst out laughing, and even McPherson smirked, bringing a halt to the conversation. Hooker told the lieutenant to go on taking Baker to the rear. Sherman and McPherson accompanied them, along with their people, while Hooker left to find Geary's Division.

Over on Hell's Hillock, Butterfield had finished his horseback inspection of the captured Rebel cannon, as well as supervising the collection of fallen Alabama standards, and turned his attention to getting his men regrouped. He rode up and over the top of the rise and found some of his troops organized and chasing off routed butternuts to the north and south, but to the east Wood's Brigade was milling about a cluster of tents.

He was about to go down into the captured camp and order Colonel Wood to restore order to his men and consolidate the position when a shocking blast of musketry flared from the thick woods just 50 yards to the east of the camp. Wood's men recoiled out of the camp and onto the foot of the hill in shock, and for a few seconds there was silence, as a dense belt of powder smoke drifted in the space between the camp and the woods. Then came the Rebels, advancing from the trees with a piercing shriek.

3:45 p.m.
Maney's Division, CSA
Hell's Hillock
The Confederate Left

"I owe you some thanks, Colonel Pendleton," Maney said, beaming. "Another 15 or 20 minutes, and the Yankees might have pulled themselves back together and gotten artillery up here. Should that have happened, it would have been much harder for me to retake this ground. And more costly."

Sandie reddened. "I merely did my duty, sir. I reckoned that since I had to ride by your direction on the way back to army headquarters, I would deliver General Jackson's orders to you personally."

"So you say." Maney smirked. "But I do declare, things have had a way of going astray in this army. At least they did until recently. So once again, thank you."

Sandie nodded thoughtfully. He had met George Maney years before, during the ill-fated Romney Campaign. Sandie was a junior lieutenant on Jackson's staff, while Maney was the colonel of the 1st Tennessee and was one of the few who did not conspire with the now disgraced W.W. Loring to undermine Jackson's command. Sandie had known if anyone in Polk's Corps could be relied upon to act, it was Maney.

A slight drizzle started to come down, prompting Maney to pull the brim of his hat down. "Now, if you'll be good enough to excuse me, Colonel, I need to see about placing my division. The Yankees will be back soon enough."

"You'll not continue the attack?" Sandie asked.

"I will not," Maney said emphatically. "I surprised the bluebellies and caught them separated just now, and they withdrew. Might have been a disorderly withdrawal, but I didn't break them. They are over there in those woods reforming right now, and I ain't in contact with Clayton yet, nor has French come up. So, I'm bringing up some fresh batteries and staying right here."

Maney grinned. "I like it here. Reckon I'll dare the Yankees to throw me off this hill. Now, you get back onto Old Blue Light and relate that to him."

"Yessir." Sandie saluted, leaving Maney to his business.

3:45 p.m.
Headquarters in the Field, Army of the Tennessee, USA
The Federal Right

McPherson trotted his horse up to join Sherman and A.J. Smith in the open field, near where Thomas Kilby Smith's Division lay in reserve. Smith saluted and Sherman nodded by way of greeting.

McPherson said, "I think we've got a good hold on the Confederate right and center. All along Stewart's Creek, we've moved up, dug in, and have the Confederates in a long range firefight. Jack has probed the far right in force and gotten troops over the creek twice and through the screen, only to be thrown back. Now, he says if we could reinforce him…"

"And he can't do that from his own corps?" Sherman asked.

Shaking his head, McPherson replied, "No, not if he is to keep his grip on Cleburne's Corps. He might be right, you know. The Confederates are very strong here on the right, and they are relying on that God damned creek like a moat to strengthen their center. They must be weak on the left. It's simple logic. Now if we were to give over to Jack either Minty or Kilby Smith, or simply tell him to go over with his whole corps…"

Sherman considered that. If Logan said the Rebels were weak on the left, they likely were. What was more, it tallied. Their defensive line was very long. They couldn't possibly extend it all the way down Stewart's Creek to Stones River in strength.

But, Sherman thought, we've already been through this. If we break through on the left, all we accomplish is pushing the Rebels out of Murfreesboro, a fruitless victory. They will have an open door to escape to the south, where they can find better ground for defense and destroy more track. If we succeed here, on the right, we can push the enemy back on those mountains or the river, pinning them and breaking them up. In any case, we're already committed, and I refuse to risk Smyrna. I'll be damned if that devil Forrest gets even the slightest chance of sneaking into the henhouse, wrecking my rolling stock and depot.

He noticed both Smith and McPherson were waiting for him. "No, Mac. We aren't changing horses in the middle of the race. Tell Logan to keep on as he is. Hooker will go in shortly with both Butterfield and Geary. Williams, Sweeny, and Mower will support. Kilby Smith will stand in reserve to exploit our success or work around the flank, as needs be. Understood?"

4:00 p.m.
Polk's Corps, CSA
Hell's Hillock
The Confederate Left

After he had wrestled with his uncertainty for a time, Polk had finally summoned General French for his counsel. Not as a means of making a decision, but to further postpone one. Hidden away in his schoolhouse, he had not learned that Maney's Division had marched to the front until French came in and told him. That finally forced Polk's hand.

Arriving behind Hell's Hillock, Polk found Maney in the remains of what had been Stewart's headquarters, busily issuing orders. Seeing the thick-bearded Tennessean, Polk's lips curled and trembled with rage. Then he recalled his reaction when French told him of what Maney had done and dismay capped his anger, for he had exploded into a rare public temper tantrum. Polk turned slightly queasy at the memory of how he hurled his silver inkwell through the window, how he turned over his desk, how he drop-kicked his chair across the room, with General French and the senior members of his staff all looking on.

Polk shook with ill displeasure. How unseemly, he thought. George Maney would pay for that, oh how he would pay. But not today. *Later, when my unpleasantness is no longer such a fresh and lively memory.*

With all the congeniality he could muster, Polk said, "General Maney, please report."

Maney saluted. "General Polk, you are just in time. I'm tied into the left of Stewart's Corps, so we have a continuous line now. But my own left is in the air, just a few hundred yards yonder." Maney gestured to the south, then continued. "The Federals are reinforced. I'll be under attack shortly."

"Cantey's Brigade is coming up right behind me, and General French is bringing up the rest of his division. I will ride back and tell Cantey to form on your left, lengthening your line."

"Thank you, sir."

Cantey's soldiers filed through the woods and into place on the left of Scott's Brigade, General Scott having recovered from the foot wound received at Lawrenceburg. They arrived just as the bombardment of Hell's Hillock began. Dozens of cannon, placed on rises to the east, southeast, and south, fired as fast as they could be loaded and aimed for 30 straight minutes, a crossfire that burned through over two thousand solids, exploding shells, and rounds of case shot. The downpour of iron nearly tore the top off the hill and decimated Maney's artillery. Then the guns quieted, and the Billies went forward.

Williams's Division attacked in support, moving on Clayton's position. Butterfield sent his men back across the open field between the wooded ridge and Hell's Hillock, the weeds and tall grass now thoroughly trampled, the ground still littered with the dead from the first attack. They stood in with Lowry's and Quarles' butternuts, two lines of musket-armed men proficiently loading, firing, and killing at a range of less than 100 yards.

Geary attacked the left flank, sending Candy's Ohioans and Pennsylvanians against Scott's Alabamans, and Buschbeck's New Jersey, New York, and Pennsylvania men against Cantey's Alabama and Mississippi boys. The Johnnies enjoyed the advantage of being able to fight on the edge of the woods that flowed down from the mountains of Burnt Knob to behind Hell's Hillock and out onto the plain, while Geary's Yankees had to stand and shoot in the open. While Candy and Buschbeck pinned the graybacks from the front and suffered a withering fire, Ireland's Brigade crept through the dense woods from the south, feeling their way forward for the Confederate flank.

Ireland's flank attack landed on Cantey like a splitting maul, driving in the flank guards before landing on the main line only minutes later. With no chance to refuse, Cantey's line melted under the pressure of Ireland's steady, organized fire-and-advance attack. Cantey himself was wounded in the hand while attempting to rally his men and refuse his line, losing his sword but escaping capture.

Sitting well behind his firing line, Geary saw Cantey's Brigade come unraveled. A giant, bearish man with a bristly carpet of a beard, Geary put his spurs to his horse and galloped up behind his troops. "Charge!" he cried. "They won't stand! Charge! Charge!" Candy's and Buschbeck's bluecoats swelled forward, crashing into Scott's line and sweeping away whatever semblance of resistance was left in Cantey's.

Despite being outflanked, Scott's graybacks stood their ground and began a brutal and barbarous contest, one of officers slashing with swords and firing or hammering with pistols, while the rankers stabbed with their bayonets, clubbed with their musket butts, and in some instances resorted to their fists, rocks, and even teeth. The bulk of Geary's Division broke around Scott's flank and rear, leaving him behind and surging up the south flank of Hell's Hillock. There they were met by Featherston's Brigade, coming over the crest and into the wreckage of broken gun limbers and caissons.

Dismounted, Featherston walked slowly behind his ordered ranks of Mississippi Stumpjumpers, as shells screamed overhead and cannonballs plowed through their ranks. He called out in clear, stentorian tones "Ready! Aim! Fire!"

The deluge of musket balls brought the disorganized blue surge stumbling to a halt on the foot of the hill. As the Confederates at the top of the hillock fired at will, the Northern field officers struggled to restore their lines to order. Their efforts were only partially successful, and the blue rankers shrank back into the cover of the woods.

Ignoring the artillery pelting the hilltop, Maney galloped over the crest and up to Featherston. "Good work, General! Good work. Now fix bayonets and drive those Northon scoundrels back."

Exultant, Featherston momentarily forgot his ire at being superseded by Maney. He was also anxious to get his brigade out of its exposed position. "Yessir! My boys will drive those Yankee Dutchmen clear back to Nashville."

Maney nodded. "Good. Restore the line. That done, do not pursue. I'm heading into those woods, to help Cantey rally his men."

Cries of "Fix bayonets!" rose up and down the line, Featherston motioned to his bugler, and the call to "Charge!" was sounded. His graybacks rushed down the slope with piercing whoops and howls, intent on blue bloody murder, but they struck empty air. Faced with the serried mass of sharp, pointy and onrushing steel, the Yankees instinctively pulled back into the woods. There Geary's men took up positions amid the trees and brush, and stood their ground. They met Featherston's advance with a stand-up musket fight at an appallingly close range.

With Ireland having halted Featherston's counter-attack, Geary shifted his efforts to dislodging Scott, ripping into the Alabamans on front and flank. Scott's Brigade wilted under the pressure, men streaming back through the woods and onto Hell's Hillock, where the buzzing swarm of bullets flying over the heads of Maney's main, westward-facing line drove them back down off the hill and into the relative shelter woods. There they churned as a mass of nervous and frightened men, unable to find anywhere truly safe to skedaddle to.

Colonel Ireland kept a watchful eye on his right flank, which stood in the air. When his flankers came running in reporting a new Confederate brigade moving up, he was prepared and smoothly shook out the pair of fresh regiments he had held back, placing them perpendicular to his main firing line. Behind the foot of his L-shaped position, Ireland watched as several hundred Rebels, about the same number of men now covering his refused flank, became visible through the trees and underbrush at about 40 yards distance.

The new arrivals came under fire within seconds of coming into view, but none of that bothered their leader, Francis Cockrell. As balls whizzed overhead and landed with wet thunks among his men, he called out the simple firing orders as he withdrew his pocket watch.

Time to see if this works, he thought to himself before shouting, "Ready! Aim! Fire at will!"

The several hundred men of Cockrell's Brigade, standing shoulder to shoulder in two ranks with leveled Henry Rifles, began firing. Each man aimed, pulled the trigger, worked the lever, and aimed again, over and over as Cockrell monitored his watch, watching the seconds tick by as a cascade of lead fell onto Ireland's flank. When 60 seconds had passed, and the volume of fire had noticeably slackened, Cockrell yelled, "Charge!"

The Missourians ran forward at the bugle's sounding, screaming themselves hoarse and they rushed through the pea soup of powder smoke created by the firing of 11,000 cartridges in just one minute. Hearing the Rebel yells, Featherston's Mississippians joined in, and Ireland's lacerated brigade panicked and bolted from the woods. Within a matter of minutes, Geary's entire division had been forced back in disarray.

With Geary no longer pressing hard on their right, Butterfield's attack petered out. The infantry of the XX Corps retired back out of musket range, to the cover afforded by woods and low ridges. There they tended to their wounded, caught their breaths and sipped from their canteens, and waited for whatever was to come next.

5:45 p.m.
Headquarters in the Field, Army of Tennessee, CSA
Hell's Hillock
The Confederate Left

Riding through the woods and skirting the foot of Burnt Knob, Jackson and Stewart reached the soiled tents that had once served as Stewart's own headquarters, a single-file line of staffers following behind them. Even before arriving there, they were greeted by the scent of churned mud, copper, and, just faintly, the stink of feces. The place had become a kind of forward aid station.

The two generals cantered in behind the medical camp, where they were ignored by the stretcher bearers and orderlies, all busy loading those too badly injured to walk onto ambulances. It took care, as the grass was slick from the light rain shower. Those who could walk were another story, and a small group of such men called out, "Stonewall! Old Straight!"

Jackson, still feeling disoriented and not quite himself, forced a smile. He asked the closest of the group, a man who had his arm in a blood-stained sling, "Where were you hit, son?"

"On the other side of that there knoll, sir. I'm from Quarles's Brigade. Damn Yankees brought down artillery on us like I never did see. All hell and iron and fire. One of them God damned shells burst right over our heads. Got me an arm full of splinters to show for it." The Southron brightened. "I reckon I'm lucky, though. All them splinters, surgeon says I ain't got even a one that broke a bone or cut a bleeder."

Jackson nodded weakly. "Good, good. Indeed, Providence has been kind to you. But may I make a suggestion, soldier?"

"Yessir?"

"Mind your profanity. Most especially taking the Lord's name in vain. Providence may not be as kind again."

The soldier sheepishly replied, "Yes, sir."

Jackson and Stewart motioned for their staff to remain where they were and rode slowly through the camp. Wounded were still trickling in, carried or helped back from the front. Some sobbed and some screamed, while others were doing their best to wait their turn in silence. Still others were had the quiet of the dying, and sometimes there a dead man lay among living, only recently departed and noticed only by his neighbors. Amid this grisly setting, they found General Scott, under a tarp and lying on a cot, and sitting next to him on a cracker box was General Cantey, his shoulder and hand wrapped in reddened bandages.

Scott saw them first. Propping himself up, he said, "General Jackson, General Stewart. Sirs. I fear I have been wounded. And in the foot again! Can you believe that? At least I was struck my left one this time, and it is not the same foot!"

Stewart asked, "Are you badly injured?"

Scott shrugged, feigning nonchalance despite being clearly pained. "I'm afraid I'll lose the foot this time. The surgeon says the ball smashed two bones in the middle. There is nothing to be done."

Stewart nodded slowly, and whispered, "I'm sorry to hear that."

Jackson asked Cantey, "And you, sir? I recall your gallantry at Winchester and Cross Keys, and I hope you are not lost to the service for long."

Cantey beamed, pleased that Jackson recollected him from the Valley Campaign. "No, no, I do not think I shall be. I was hit by shrapnel in the shoulder, but my arm still works. My hand too. I can wait to have the iron pulled out, so I told the surgeons to attend to other men first."

Jackson and Stewart then inquired for details of the recent fighting, and after listening to the two brigadiers for a few minutes, wished them well and left for the hillock. Dismounting just behind the rise, they walked over the crest and into a scene that, if only moderately less gory than the campsite behind them, was much more macabre. Once over the top, they were surrounded by the bodies of smashed and shredded horses and men, broken limbers and caissons, and dismounted cannon. The ground was largely torn up clay, bare with but a few splotches of green coming from bits of sod that lay blown off and loose.

They had only been studying the Federal positions across the way for a minute when a horse and rider came thundering up. "What do you two think you are doing?!?" Sandie shouted at the generals. "Pardon my saying so, sirs, but you must be mad or fools or maddened fools! Look around you. I demand you both withdraw from this awful place at once!"

As the last word left Sandie's tongue, a cannonball whipped through the air not ten feet to their right. Stewart had been about to laugh, but instantly became more serious. "Pendleton is right, Tom. They've seen us. We'd best get back down."

Jackson nodded wordlessly and followed the other two off the crest. Once there, they saw the guidons gathered a short distance from the tents, indicating Polk, French, and Maney had come. Rather than get back up onto horseback, Jackson and Stewart walked over to them.

If they had been expecting a council of war, Jackson disabused them at once. Looking up to Polk, he said, "General Polk, prepare to renew the attack. Your corps will advance upon the enemy and drive them back, with Clayton's Division attacking on your right in support. We have not more than three hours of light left, so we must move quickly. Start with the far left, and proceed *en echelon*."

"General Jackson," Polk protested, almost sputtering. "I fear Maney's command has suffered very badly in the recent fight and shot off nearly all their ammunition besides. They are in no condition to attack."

Jackson looked to Maney, who frowned. "I'm afraid General Polk is correct, sir. I don't think my boys have much more than about five rounds a man right about now, and I won't be surprised if the reports later tonight come back saying I've lost a quarter of my men."

"And," Polk added, "observers atop Burnt Knob say the Federals have several thousand men massed in reserve. One or two divisions, fresh divisions."

Jackson felt himself getting stronger, his blood rising. "Nevertheless, you shall attack."

Polk was about to protest further when Captain Quintard thundered up. "General Jackson, General Jackson! The Yankees are withdrawing on the left, sir."

Jackson spun about. "What did you say?"

"They are pulling back! That is what came over the wig-wags. I went up for a look myself, and it's true. They are retiring due west."

Now Stewart and Jackson mounted, and they rode with the others to the top of the little hill. As they made their way up the slope, the drizzle swiftly grew into a deluge. When they all arrived at the bald, shell-ravaged top of Hell's Hillock, what had been damp earth had become a bog.

The dense sheets of rain obscured much, but blue columns could still be seen marching away.

"Good heavens" Polk murmured. "The boys can't fight in this. Their cartridge boxes will be soaked as soon as they pull back the lids."

"They will likely stop at the mountains over there," Stewart said, pointing to Scales and Indian Mountains. "I would. Tie my flank into there."

Inwardly, Stewart felt relieved. Before, when he was alone with Jackson, he had opposed renewing the offensive, and for much the same reason Polk did. He could see that such an attack might drive the Yankee line back, but only until those fresh reserves were put in. When that happened, Stewart was certain the attack would be stopped cold and perhaps even reversed.

Inside, Jackson felt a squirm, as if it shouldn't matter that the troops had been in a fight or that the powder would be wet, since that would apply to the enemy as well. But it was only a squirm, for mostly he felt tired, unsteady, and heart-worn.

Jackson sighed. "Very well. We will advance, but only to straighten our front and put it on more defensible ground. No attack." Jackson, Stewart, and Polk spent several minutes working out where to establish that new line, and that done, the generals returned to their commands.

8:00 p.m.
41st Tennessee Infantry, CSA
Stewart's Creek

The rain stopped and the cloud cover finally broke up just before sunset, allowing the fading rays of the sun to filter through the clouds and dark, thickly wooded hills. Nathan, Willie, Greenhorn Pete, and some of the other fellows from the company all knelt, sat, and laid together close to the barricade.

Willie looked to Nathan with relief. "Sun will be down soon. I reckon we can refill the canteens."

Nathan nodded and passed his half-full water bottle over. Willie took a swig and passed it down. They all had gotten the musketman's gunpowder tongue, and Nathan was the only one with water left in his canteen. No one dared venture over the wall and down into the creek for more, for fear of being shot.

"Only one man wounded today, and him only just a little," Nathan murmured, thinking of the fellow that got a few wood splinters when a roundshot struck the barricade. "Didn't even need to go to the rear."

"The good Lord was with us," Willie said.

Pete whispered glumly, "Jimmy."

Nathan asked, "What?"

"Jimmy too. Jimmy was killed."

Nathan said nothing. Willie asked, "Were you from the same place?"

Pete shook his head. "No, Corporal. We wasn't. Didn't meet him until I got to the army."

Still keyed up, Nathan was growing irritable. The mention of Jimmy had made him think of Captain Bell and stew in how rotten it all was. Captain Fletcher had been a good man, but the Colonel didn't like him or his politics. Now they had this rich boy who didn't know straw from hay for a captain. All the lieutenants in the regiment, even the whole brigade, had been passed over, all to make Bell a captain. Worse, the Colonel was happy to have Bell, that much was clear.

A bit down the line, Lloyd said loudly, "Well, that weren't nothing. I don't know what all this fuss is about. That weren't nothing! " He then chuckled nervously.

"Bastard!" Nathan cried.

He stalked down to where Lloyd was sitting, also leaning against the barricade, and hissed, "So you a big fighting man now? Is that that? Give me your cartridge box."

Lloyd sneered back, but shrank from a reply. Sergeant Marks, sitting nearby, did nothing.

"Give it to me!" he yelled.

Lloyd hesitantly handed over the cartridge box. Nathan stood over him, heedless of the musket ball that zipped past his shoulder in response to his yelling.

Examining the contents, Nathan said, "Anyone care to guess how many cartridges strong, brave Private Raglan Lloyd has here? 40! Not one missing. Not a one. How many you got in your pockets, Raglan? 10? 15? More?"

The point was clear. Lloyd had barely fired a shot. He sat, glaring at Nathan with a mixture of fear and rage.

"That's what I thought." Nathan contemptuously tossed the box back at Lloyd and then stomped back to his place.

10:00 p.m.
Headquarters, Army of the Tennessee, USA
Western outskirts of Rutherford County

As Sherman and McPherson approached the little headquarters cabin together, they could hear Hooker arguing heatedly with A.J. Smith from within.

McPherson groaned, "Bill, you've known Hooker. Does that man ever know when to shut up?"

Sherman shook his head, grumbling, "No, he never quiets himself, not even when he can get his hands onto the girdle laces of some trollop. Just keeps on yammering. That man has more gas in his bag than a newspaper has bile in its press."

When they entered, Hooker stopped in mid-sentence. Flushed and hot, he turned on McPherson and demanded, "General McPherson, why did we not press the attack? And why did we give back the ground we won today?"

Sherman walked behind where Logan sat, exchanging nods, and resumed his former place in the corner. There he took his chair, crossed his legs, and began tapping his foot against the floor.

McPherson mustered up his patience, and said calmly, "General Hooker, first we did not give back all the ground we won, as you know because your flank rests on the mountains you seized earlier this morning. Second, we all have our orders, myself included. Third, I do not owe you any explanations, as well you know."

The implication of McPherson's reply was clear, and Hooker looked at Sherman, who sat in the corner with a flinty look on his face.

"Frankly," Sherman said coldly, "with that storm and with the late hour, I could see but little point to continued hostilities. The boys can't shoot their muskets with the barrels full of water. The day was over, whether I or you or Mac or anyone else damn much liked it or not. The only thing left to do, General Hooker, was to get your flank out of the air for the night. I would have thought you might appreciate that point without being told."

Hooker wore a sour expression, but ultimately said nothing. Good, Sherman thought. All I had to do was give a reminder of what happened last time Joe Hooker left his flank in the air...

McPherson announced, "Now, if you have complaints, I suggest you all confine them strictly to practicalities. You are here to report on the status of your commands, nothing more."

Sherman listened as the corps commanders reported. The figures were only rough estimates at present, but they coincided with his expectations: XV Corps had suffered little; XVI Corps moderately; and XX Corps heavily, especially in the divisions of Butterfield and Geary, whose losses were thought to be 20 to 25 percent. Their reports made, McPherson dismissed them. Hooker stormed out, while Logan and Smith genially bid McPherson and Sherman a goodnight.

McPherson stared at Sherman, who finally asked, "What is it, Mac?"

"I still think Jackson will be there in the morning. Why should he leave?"

Sherman stood up, shaking his head. When he had ordered the withdrawal, Sherman had shared his thinking with McPherson. Convinced that he knew what Jackson was doing in Murfreesboro, he saw no reason to continue pressing an attack that would accomplish nothing beyond lengthening the casualty lists.

He clasped his hands behind his back. "No, no, no. He won't be. This whole blasted thing has just been one big giant raid. We saw most or all of the Army of Tennessee on the field today. Those bastards have already captured Fortress Rosecrans and most likely have stripped it bare by now. I have unconfirmed reports of a large Rebel wagon train moving through south-central Tennessee, in southwesterly direction. My guess is that, come morning, he will have left."

"Well, I hope you're right. And I hope you know what you're doing."

So do I, Sherman thought. He felt that he and McPherson were safe for now, but the blackguard reporters and the charlatan politicians kept grumbling that he had a case of "the slows," and that McPherson should be swapped for the more experienced Hooker. As Sherman's brother kept reminding him from his armchair in the Senate, this was an election year. A defeat or two might change everything politically, leaving them all in the lurch. Worse, if they didn't win victories, Lincoln might lose the election.

"We'll see in the morning. If Jackson has left, I know where he's going, and that gives us an opening. If he is still there, frankly Mac, we are no worse off than we are now and that isn't so bad.

PART III
GET 'ROUND THE LEFT

JUNE TO JULY 1864

CHAPTER 13

June 23, 1864
5:30 a.m.
7ᵗʰ Pennsylvania Cavalry, USA
Smyrna, Tennessee

As the first rays of the sun crept over the horizon, brightening a clear sky, Sergeant Spear quietly led his section of dismounted horse soldiers towards the tree-lined lower end of Stewart's Creek, crawling through tall, wet grass and weeds. Upon reaching the creek's almost vertical banks, he swung his legs around and slid down on the mud and bumpy tree roots. Once he found his footing in the shallow, cool waters, he sprang across to the other side.

Rose, Crowder, and several other men followed. Once they were all gathered behind the shelter of the creek bank, the Pittsburghers slowly climbed back out and crawled into what had been enemy territory the day before. Spear's vanguard edged its way forward, past empty rifle pits and into an area where rows of oversized campfires continued to smolder.

Upon seeing the unattended fires, Spear stood up. "Jim, run back and tell Captain Vale that the Reb cavalry has skeddadled."

After coming up to see for himself, Vale withdrew his probe back across the creek, to where the rest of their regiment was mustered, almost a thousand troopers gathered on the eastern outskirts of Smyrna. There Spear and his squad remounted and joined the waiting.

Spear was sitting astride his horse within earshot of where Colonel Siebert and his staff stood next to their horses when Colonel

Sipes, once their own colonel and now the Saber Brigade's commander, came riding up with General Minty, the brigade's former commander and now at division. Thus, he overheard the top-level conversation.

Sipes relayed his orders. "Jim, the brigade is going in. We'll jump the creek and go straight down the Murfreesboro Pike and the railroad line until we run into something solid. Past the old battlefield and on into town if we can. You've got the center."

Minty, resplendent and buoyant with his plumed hat and rosy cheeks, added, "Klein will jump the creek too, but he is to turn right and move direct south along the other side."

Siebert asked, "And what shall I do if I happen upon something solid?"

Sipes said, "That depends on how determined the opposition is. If it's the whole Confederate army pulled back to a better position, let's say behind Overall Creek, then probe them. If it's a rear guard, pitch in. Don't pull back unless pushed. Make yourself useful."

The Sabers were soon in motion, lines of hundreds of horsemen jumping Stewart's Creek just as soon as those in front of them had cleared and moved on. Spear grinned with the thrill of spurring his horse up to full gallop, and with a cry he jumped his mount over the crevasse, landing on the other side with a jolt.

After reforming, Spear and his men found themselves in the main column, part of a dense parade of mounted blue horseman cantering down the main road between Nashville and Murfreesboro, flags snapping in the early morning breeze. The parade was a short one, however, as just a few miles down the road Spear heard the ragged crackling of scattered musketry, indicating the column's vanguard had run into the enemy. Judging from the sound, Spear surmised the Confederates had picketed Overall Creek. The bugles tooted their orders, and Spear followed as his battalion veered off the road to spread out to the north.

Standing in a reserve line on slightly higher ground, Spear had a passably good location to see what came next. Overall Creek was a more formidable obstacle than Stewart's Creek. Just like at Stewart's, the banks were high and steep, and the enemy's side dominated theirs, but Overall Creek was wider, too wide to jump horses across.

Spear watched as the main line of his regiment dismounted and went forward, firing their Spencers as they went, while the brigade's other regiments, the 4th Michigan and the 4th U.S. Cavalry, rode out to the left and right. Once out on the flanks, they too dismounted and went forward. As soon as the Michiganers and the regulars were across the creek, the butternut skirmishers pulled back out of reach.

A few minutes later, Captain Vale announced, "Alright boys. Those with tools dismount and set to work. We need a ford, so we're making one."

Spear wasn't one of those men who were assigned to carry a shovel, pick, or axe on his saddle, but Crowder was. Smiling Spear told him, "I always knew you were a coffeeboiler at heart, Jim. That's why they gave you that shovel, ain't it?"

With an exaggerated sneer, Crowder said, "With all due respect, Sarge, stick it in your eye."

Crowder then set off to join more than a hundred other men, who were soon busy felling trees and excavating ramps into the banks of Overall Creek, alongside the burnt pilings of the Nashville Turnpike's wagon bridge. With so much experienced labor at hand, the task of building two gently sloping ramps and corduroying them with tree trunks took under twenty minutes. Less than an hour after reaching Overall Creek, the Saber Brigade was moving forward again, through the old Stones River battlefield, but they were soon halted once more by Rebel cavalry, this time on the banks of Stones River itself.

Still watching from the reserve line, Spear heard the hushed grumbles and felt the frustration of the other men in the squadron, amplifying his own irritation at the delays. After a few minutes, Major Jennings, the battalion commander, rode up and summoned his captains, including Captain Vale, and had a brief word with them.

Vale returned and announced, "Boys, Sipes doesn't want to wait on Klein, so we're going in. The regulars and Michigan boys are crossing the river to the north, to sweep those hills north of Murfreesboro. We're going to ride south, cross the Franklin Road, and go over the river there, swinging far around Fortress Rosecrans, coming up on Murfreesboro from the south, and blocking the Rebel line of retreat."

The bugles sounded the call to advance, and they trotted in column south for two miles, before coming upon the Salem Pike and turning east, where they found the wagon bridge over the river intact. Once on the other side, the troopers picked up the pace and rode hard for half a mile, coming upon the crest overlooking the Shelbyville Road. Below them there, about 300 yards away, was a column of grayback troopers, retreating south at the canter.

Major Jennings shouted, "Spencers! Spencers! Fire at will! Shoot 'em down! Shoot 'em down!", orders that were repeated by Captain Vale. As Spear flicked up the sights on his carbine and adjusted the slide for the range, he kept his eye on the Rebels and thought how much the scene reminded him of the patrol around Franklin, just a couple of weeks before. Only now he was with a battalion of a few hundred troopers, not a mere patrol, and there was at least a brigade on the road before them.

He heard the enemy's buglers as they sounded the order for gallop. Spear cocked his hammer and worked his lever. Shouldering the weapon, he didn't bother with proper aiming. He simply drew a bead on the column and squeezed the trigger. Over and over, Spear thumbed back the hammer, worked the lever, and pulled the trigger. In less than a minute, he had fired all seven shots into the fleeing butternuts, prompting him to lower his carbine for reloading.

He gave the small handle on the butt of his Spencer a twist and withdrew the tube. Reaching into his cartridge box, he pulled a handful of bullets and dropped them, one after another, into the hole in the butt of his gun. With seven rounds in, he reinserted the tube, cocked the hammer, worked the lever, brought his carbine up to his shoulder, and resumed firing through the rapidly swelling smoke cloud and into the dregs of the Rebel column.

Spear had worked halfway through his new magazine when Vale started shouting, repeating orders from down the line. The lieutenants joined him, and then Spear himself, struggling to be overheard the cacophony of loud cracks from the repeaters. He lowered his carbine and waved his free hand, yelling, "Cease fire! Cease fire!"

The Pennsylvania troopers rode forward slowly, hesitantly poking through the dense cloud of powder smoke thrown up by firing a few thousand cartridges in less than two minutes. Coming out of the haze, they found the road carpeted with several dozen dead and moaning, wounded men, plus as many screaming, thrashing horses.

Spear stopped before a dying horse. Looking at the corpses or the wounded Rebels, he didn't feel triumphant. He felt nothing for the men in gray, nothing at all. Yet as he looked at this horse, laying there pitifully, its eyes full of terror, he felt a bolt of anguish shoot through him. He drew his revolver, aimed carefully, and shot it between the eye and the ear.

Lieutenant Webster rode up to Spear. "Sergeant, bring the men about. Vale wants our troop to ride down to where the road crosses the Middle Fork, about a mile from here, and picket the crossing."

Spear replied quietly, absently, "Yessir."

10:00 a.m.
Rutherford County Courthouse
Murfreesboro, Tennessee

McPherson and his small band of staff rose up to Murfreesboro's main square, an attractive place of leafy trees and a rich, green lawn, with a fine, three-story brick courthouse topped by a brilliant white, tower-like cupola in the center. McPherson decided it was one of the largest and finest county courthouses he had seen during his time in the South. Just as he arrived in the square, Sherman bounded out the front door.

Well, he looks to be in high feather, McPherson thought as he dismounted.

Sherman grinned broadly, shaking his hand and smacking him on the shoulder. "Mac, Mac, Mac! Lovely morning, is it not? Lovely morning."

"I heard Van Cleve was here, along with most of the garrison, but not General Milroy."

A bitter look replaced Sherman's grin. "Yes, I was just talking to him. Poor fellow. From the sounds of it, Milroy really stuck his foot in it here. However, I doubt those damnable scoundrels in Congress or the double damned news rags will see it that way. They all love Milroy."

"Why did they take Milroy and leave Van Cleve?"

Sherman shrugged. "Milroy has been vigorous in his efforts to root out all forms of disloyalty in his area of responsibility, I'll say that for him. Spies and bandits, secesh agitators and sympathizers, you know the sort. Of course, the Rebels despise him for it. The man has had a price on his head dating from his time in Virginia, and I wouldn't be surprised if someone tells me later his actions in Tennessee have added to the bounty."

"So they intend to put him on trial?"

Sherman tilted his head and grimaced. "Perhaps. Or perhaps to effect some manner of trade. The Rebel government made noise of trying some of our officers for supposed crimes before, but nothing much came of it, and they never tried it with someone so high-ranking. Milroy is a major general of volunteers, ferchrissakes! Anyway, I'm sure poor old Van Cleve will become the scapegoat for what happened here."

"How so? If Milroy was in command and mucked it up…?"

Sherman spoke rapidly. "Because Milroy is a prisoner and Van Cleve isn't. Because Milroy is a fire-eating abolitionist and has powerful friends, and Van Cleve doesn't. God, I loathe politics!" He paused for a breath, then continued. "His health has been poor. I suggested he resign for medical reasons, before the politicians get their carving knives out. Now, what's the word."

"You already know most of it, Bill. We bagged some deserters and stragglers from the old battlefield, and they don't seem to know much. Or if they do, they aren't saying it just yet. The only wounded we've found in the hospitals were those too bad off to move. I'm surprised he left, but Jackson skedaddled pretty darn smoothly."

Sherman grunted. "Good staff work to thank for that. Seems he took his pick of the stores and arsenal here at Fortress Rosecrans too. All the heavy artillery is gone. All of it. Shipped out two days ago."

McPherson winced at that.

Brightening, Sherman declared, "Now! I have some good news." He pulled a folded letter from his pocket and handed it to McPherson. "What do you think of that?"

Sherman lit a cigar while McPherson read the contents. "This is bully news, Bill. The railway from Louisville to Nashville open as of yesterday, and the lead elements of my old corps on the first train!"

Of course, Frank Blair's XVII Corps was smaller now than it was when I had it, McPherson thought. But another two divisions of veteran infantry is always a welcome thing.

Sherman drew a gauntlet and slapped his thigh with it. With his cigar still clenched in his teeth, he exclaimed, "An extra 10,000 of the best fighting men in the world, and under a good man to boot!"

After a big puff, Sherman took the cigar from his mouth. "Now to business. We need to find the enemy. They can't have gone far. Minty I want sent down in the direction of Hoover's Gap and Shelbyville. Grierson will go down by way of Triune and Riggs Crossroads."

The mention of the latter pair of places prompted McPherson to turn his ear. "You don't think Jackson is going west, as close to us as that. That would be a damn risky thing to do."

Sherman said nothing, which raised McPherson's suspicions. "You know something, don't you?"

"I have an idea. For the time being, it's nothing more than that. Issue five days' rations to the men, top up their ammunition. We'll know in what direction Jackson's bastards went this afternoon, and I want to be on the roads and after them before nightfall. Also, draw up a congratulatory order for your army, on their victory at Stewart's Creek yesterday."

"Yesterday was a victory? Just a stalemate if you ask me, moreover because it looks like Jackson accomplished everything he came here to do."

"I'm surprised at you, Mac. Of course it was a victory, insofar as we and the imbecile politicians are concerned. Jackson retreated. We have possession of the field. What more need be said about it?"

McPherson nodded. "Very well."

A voice called out from behind them, "General Sherman! General McPherson!"

Sherman frowned and turned, and he saw a civilian in a cheap brown suit striding up to them, a civilian with a notepad and a pencil. His mood turned from buoyant to sanguinary. McPherson took half a step away from his friend, instinctively moving away from the restrained, spiteful boil he felt there.

"*Chicago Times*, Generals, would you care to comment on the action here at Murfreesboro? Some are already calling it a defeat."

"What is your name? And how did you get here?" Sherman said darkly.

The reporter ignored the question, and asked another of his own. "I have it on good authority that Joe Hooker's corps bore the brunt of yesterday's fighting and gained a good lot of ground that he was ordered to give away. Is that true? General Sherman? General McPherson?"

Sherman took a step forward and thrust his face into that of the reporter, brushing the tip of the reporter's nose with the lit cigar. The reporter yelped and stumbled backwards, barely staying on his feet.

"Oh, my apologies, you sneaking, croaking, venomous harlot! But perhaps you are unaware of my standing orders, a prohibition on all correspondents from traveling with the troops!"

Sherman hollered, "Provost Marshal! Put this louse in irons, and throw him in with the secesh prisoners."

Color drained from the reporter's face, and he half-turned to flee, only to see he was instantly surrounded by blue-clad men. "You can't do that! I have rights!"

"I can and I will. Take him away." The squealing reporter was borne away by provosts. Sherman took the Provost Marshal aside and quietly told him "Jail that parasite until he divulges how he got here. If he refuses, charge him."

2:00 p.m.
Headquarters in the Field, Army of Tennessee, CSA
Eagleville, Tennessee

Jackson stayed out of the summer sun in the shade of a large oak tree, just outside the southern outskirts of the little farming hamlet of Eagleville. Sandie was with him, while Forrest sat under the tree with his hat pulled over his face, having seized the opportunity for an afternoon catnap. In the surrounding pasture were hundreds of escorts, aides, and couriers from Jackson's, Polk's, and Forrest's headquarters, either resting or tending to their business.

Over by the road was Polk with his own people, waving to the passing soldiers of his own corps. His band was there, playing the upbeat, patriotic standard of Bonnie Blue Flag. Those men had been on the road since 10 o'clock the previous night and were consequently trudging more than marching, but even so they waved their hats back and cheered their Old Bishop.

Jackson finished reviewing the congratulatory order that would be distributed and read to the men when they made camp that night. It struck the tone he wanted, sparing floridity for a very plain description of the facts of their victory: the demonstration to the enemy that they were not safe in even the greatest of their fortresses; the deprivation to the enemy of a vast quantity of supplies, either through capture or destruction; the wrecking miles of railroad track and bridges; and the enemy's defeat in battle through the particular efforts of Stewart's Corps and Maney's Division of Polk's Corps.

Handing the paper to Sandie, he said "Good, good. I approve. Use that as the basis for our dispatch to Richmond, and get that to me as soon as you can. Davis and Seddon will want to know of our victory as soon as possible."

"Very good, sir." Tired, but visibly pleased, Sandie took the paper and left.

Jackson turned the word "victory" over in his mind while looking toward Polk, who was still enjoying the pomp of an impromptu review by the roadside. He had no doubts that Providence had graced him with a kind of victory, for he had achieved everything he set out to do. Yet he still felt pettifogged, even more so than after his victory at Lawrenceburg.

Polk's counterattack had not landed as the heavy, concentrated blow Jackson had intended, and he was certain that if it had, Hooker's entire corps would have been swept from the field. Polk had already called on him that morning, protesting Sandie's interference in his command, interference that had sent Maney forward without his sanction.

Technically, Sandie's actions had violated military protocol, but nonetheless he got Maney into battle in time to avert disaster. More important in Jackson's mind, the Bishop had performed poorly, and because of that he now recognized that Polk had performed poorly at Lawrenceburg, too. Yet looking at him, there by the road, Jackson could see that Polk's men adored him.

Of course they do, Jackson thought. We Southrons revere our religious leaders, as any proper, civilized people ought to. Polk is a Godly man, a righteous man, and perhaps that makes him to hesitant to shed blood. Yes, that must be it. He is too cautious. The next time I send him into an attack, I shall stay with him, guide him. It's what Pete has been encouraging me to do all along.

So preoccupied was Jackson that he hadn't noticed the object of his reverie had come from the road and was now standing before him. "The movement has gone splendidly, has it not, General Jackson? The roads are muddy, but not unduly so."

Jackson nodded, but said nothing. The mud was slowing their progress, but it took more rain than what they had seen lately to turn the roads into bottomless channels of mire. As it was, when the enemy cavalry went into Murfreesboro that morning, they had missed what at the time had been the underprotected tail of Polk's Corps marching away on the Salem Pike at a distance of only three or four miles. Once again, he thought, Providence has smiled on this army.

"So, General, now that we have pulled the tail of the Yankee jackal, what is the army's next move?"

Jackson smiled, amused that Polk never gave up trying to pry his plans from him. His expectation was that the enemy would move either to protect Nashville, shadowing them step by step as they did so, or pursue them directly.

Either way, Jackson believed Sherman would be a little rattled now. The man had a reputation as competent, but also excitable to the point of being erratic. He wanted to lure Sherman into battle on ground of his choosing, and he knew of many good places south of Franklin. What was more, that part of Middle Tennessee was not only closer to his base of supply in Tuscumbia, but would also force Sherman to rely upon wagon convoys for his own supply. If Sherman wouldn't attack him, then he would turn Sherman's flank, and cut him off from Nashville.

Jackson knew if he damaged Sherman's Army of the Tennessee badly enough, he could drive it back on Nashville and pen it up inside its works, whereupon George Thomas and his Army of the Cumberland would have no choice but to abandon its drive into

Georgia and come north. And if that didn't work, with some more captures, more preparation, or a mixture of both, he would finally have the wherewithal to sustain a proper late summer or autumn offensive across the Cumberland River.

He shared none of that with Polk, however. "As you know, your corps will camp beyond Riggs Crossroads tonight. Tomorrow, I hope to see you back in your beloved Maury County, General."

As Jackson and Polk talked, a courier arrived and delivered a message to Forrest. Jackson only noticed this when Forrest got to his feet and loped over to them.

Forrest took off his hat, revealing burning red cheeks and clear, sharp eyes. "General Jackson, General Polk, I reckon I need to be leaving you now. Yankee cavalry chased off them pickets I had Red send up to Nolensville. They's up there in force, and got to be met."

Jackson said "You believe Sherman's cavalry means to push through your screen. Where do you intend to stop them?"

Forrest replied firmly. "I know a good patch for a fight, round about Triune. It's a good seven or eight miles from here. That's where I reckon I'll stand in with the bluebellies, if it comes to that."

Jackson eyes lit up. "Very well. General Polk, if he needs it, I want General Forrest to be able to call on infantry from your column for support."

Polk nodded. "Yes, naturally. Of course."

CHAPTER 14

June 23, 1864
3:00 p.m.
Red Jackson's Cavalry, CSA
Hills two miles north of Triune

After riding hard up from Eagleville, Forrest arrived in the crossroads village of Triune. He knew the area well, having once made his headquarters only a few miles away, at Rigg's Crossroads. Triune had once been a prosperous place, with four schools and some fine houses and churches. At least half of those buildings now lay in ruins, burned by one side or another.

Mostly Yankees, Forrest thought to himself as he rode past the ruins of the Methodist Church. We did a little damage ourselves, but it was mostly the Yankees.

Forrest continued north, up the Nolensville Road, and by the time he reached the front, the fighting had subsided to intermittent firing, as dismounted skirmishers traded shots and kept a respectful distance from one another. The clearing showed signs of a fight, a cavalry scrape, with most of the dead and wounded clad in blue. Then Forrest saw Red Jackson waving to him from his horse, with Brigadier General Samuel Ferguson mounted next to him.

After Forrest rode up to him, Red Jackson said happily "Afternoon, sir. A regiment of Yankee cavalry came down from Nolensville, sniffing around. I reeled them in for a proper bushwhack and charged, gave them a good blow in the chops. I reckon they'll be more careful next time."

"Fine news, Red. Afternoon, General Ferguson. I take it it were your boys that gave them Yankees that bloody mouth?"

Ferguson beamed. "Indeed they did, sir."

"Well, that's all fine and dandy, but I reckon we still have a long afternoon before us here. Ain't over yet. Red, have you got men in them hills to the northeast, like I asked?"

"Armstrong's Brigade are holding those gaps like you asked, yessir. I've sent for Ross's Texans to come here. I told Ross to bring everything he could spare from the tail of Polk's Corps here."

Forrest nodded. If the Yankees got through the gaps in those other hills, several miles to the northeast, before nightfall they could swing down like a hammer on the head of Polk's column. Armstrong could fend off a probe, but not a determined assault, so Forrest quickly decided the most important thing was to fix the enemy's attention here, around Triune.

"Red, I want Ferguson here to send some fellows back to Yancey's Knob. That be the big hill on the other side of Triune. Them fellows is to start digging in. Give them all the tools you've got, and take whatever you can find in Triune too. If they got any darkies left in these parts, put them to work, and when Ross comes up, have his boys dismount and join in. When the Yankees come back, you hold them here for as long as you can. Bring up your horse guns, make plenty of noise, and get them good and interested. Fall back on Yancey's Knob when you need to, then dig in your heels."

Red said, "Yessir," while Fergusson nodded and said "I understand, General."

Forrest brought his horse around, barking, "I'll be back shortly. Going to rustle us up some infantry support," before putting his spurs in and galloping away.

He pushed his mount hard all eight miles back to Eagleville, leaving his aides and escorts behind and passing Ross's Brigade trotting north on the way. Reaching the crossroads, Forrest's horse was frothing and spent. Jackson and Polk were gone, but he was gladdened to find long, winding columns of marching infantry still on the road. He went in search of a general and rode straight for the first one he saw, which turned out to be Francis Cockrell.

Cockrell was riding placidly with his staff, alongside his soldiers, when Forrest came thundering up. Energized by Forrest's urgency, he straightened up in the saddle and snapped off a salute. "General Forrest, what are you about, sir?"

Forrest said brusquely, "You're Cockrell, ain't you?"

"That's right, sir."

"I got me a fight brewing right up that road there," Forrest said, pointing back to the north and the Nolensville Road, "and you and your boys are going up that way quick, on General Jackson's orders."

"General Jackson?"

"Yeap. Old Jack gave me permission to call directly on y'all from Polk's Corps for support. Your Missouri boys are in Polk's Corps and you're right here, so I'm calling on you. He said it to me right in front of the Bishop, and he agreed."

Old Jack and the Bishop, Cockrell thought. Good enough for me.

To his aides, Cockrell said, "Sound the bugles to halt the column. Go tell the colonels to step off and clear the road, about face, turn onto the Nolensville Road and head north. Once they are headed north, the boys are to pick up the pace. Force the march."

Forrest nodded. "Now, General Cockrell, I got a favor to ask of you. I need a fresh horse. Can I take one from one of your boys?"

Cockrell agreed. As his Missourians cleared the road and turned around, he started writing a message for his division commander, Samuel French, when French himself came riding up.

French shouted as he rode up, "What in the hell are you doing, General?! Get your boys back on the road and going east at once!"

As French brought his horse to a stop, Cockrell pointed down to Forrest, who was now dismounted. "I have orders to march to the aide of General Forrest's cavalry, sir."

French was indignant. "I've heard of no such thing. Where are these orders?"

Forrest stepped forward, and snapped up the bridle of French's mount. Scowling, Forrest said, "They ain't on paper. I got them spoken like, straight from the commanding general. Polk was there and he confirmed it himself. I can call on any infantry in his corps for support."

"Not in writing?" French sniffed. "Well, I won't have it. Your cavalry's business is your business, General Forrest, but this is something I'll have to confirm with headquarters. I'll allow Cockrell to stay here by the crossroads while we wait."

Forrest radiated blazing anger, prompted French's horse to jerk away. He yanked the frightened animal back with a powerful tug on its bridle, prompting its submission. To its rider, he snapped, "There ain't time for that, and you ain't got no authority to stop me. Cockrell's here and he comes with me, dammit. Now!"

French stared at Forrest and gulped, but he wasn't about to back down to a jumped up, illiterate ex-slave dealer. Forrest glared back at him, injurious intent boiling in his eyes.

Cockrell stammered, "Ahm, General French, sir. This is no oral message delivered by a red-cheeked boy with a single bar on his collar, sir. These are orders from our higher authority, delivered in person by a major general. Now you know this business better than I do, having been to West Point and all, but from my time in this army, I do not believe we can question them. Now General Forrest says there is a fight brewing up that road, and he needs our support at once, so..."

Blinking, French muttered, "Yes, of course. I'm within my rights to seek confirmation, but it was always my intent to cooperate. I did say Cockrell could stay here at first, did I not? If I had known how urgent things were..." Puffing himself up, French continued, "I would always help a brother officer."

Forrest let go of French's horse, said nothing, and stalked away a few steps before jumping up onto a horse borrowed from one of Cockrell's aides. Ignoring French, he said to Cockrell, "March straight for Triune, fast as your feet will carry you." Then Forrest rode off again, his horse's hooves throwing back clods of mud into the attendants who struggled to keep up with him.

The din of a firefight could be heard even before Forrest and his party had reached the eastern courses of the Harpeth River: sharp cracks and rattles from muskets and breechloaders, punctuated by singular muffled cannon shots. Forrest instantly understood from the noise that Red Jackson had withdrawn to Yancey's Knob, just ahead on the other side of the Harpeth Valley, and the Yankees were probing him even now.

"No chance to get the bulge on the blue bastards now," Forrest muttered to himself. "Have to wait, take what they give us, then give it back to them. Give it back to them with a helping of hellfire."

The Nolensville Road ran up and over a low, grassy plateau between two hills of higher elevation. The western hill was the rugged, thickly forested main peak of the knob, while the eastern hill was lower, partly cleared of trees, and crowned by a wide tabletop. Riding up into the gap, Forrest didn't see Red Jackson about, so he got out his binoculars, toured the line, and sized things up for himself.

Reviewing the right and center of Red's line went quickly enough, Forrest riding briskly just behind the rifle pits and low lunettes of the artillery. The horse guns, a mix of six-pounders, twelve-pounder howitzers, and three-inch rifles, were positioned either around the road or up on the tabletop. The Yankees had skirmishers, dismounted troopers, down in the valley, about 200 yards away and behind Nelson's Creek.

Inspecting the forested heights of Yancey's Knob's peak was another business entirely. The track there was too steep and craggy for horses, so Forrest dismounted and went up with just a few aides. Two regiments of Alabamans from Ferguson's Brigade held a 350-yard, fishhook-shaped line that rounded the top of the knob. Here they stood behind trees and rocks, returning fire at bluecoats who in some instances had crept up to as close as 50 yards.

As he walked along behind them, the Alabama troopers hollered, shook their carbines in the air, and waved their hats. Alerted to the presence of a Confederate general, the Union troopers shifted their fire to sniping at him.

Forrest collapsed his body into a crouch, only to have a bullet take off his hat a second later, which in turn prompted him to roll over to alongside the nearest tree trunk.

"God damn!" he shouted to the nearest man, a wiry private. "Damn Yankee almost shot me in the belly!"

The private grinned as he shouldered his carbine. "I saw him. You sit there, sir. I'll get him for you." He waited for the Billy to reappear. When he did so, he fired and missed.

After instructing his aides to hush up the men, so he could move about more safely, Forrest asked, "Trooper, mind telling me your name?"

"Bill Taylor, sir."

"And whereabouts you come from, Private Taylor?"

Busy pouring powder down his carbine barrel, he replied without looking up. "Montgomery, sir."

"Well Private Bill Taylor from Montgomery, may I suggest you squeeze that trigger instead of yanking it like that? I promise you, your shooting will get a mite better for it."

Forrest stayed where he was for a time, wishing he had brought more than just a revolver with him. When his aides returned, he told one of them, "Give my compliments to Old Red. Tell him his dispositions are sound, and he is to hold his ground. Be stubborn. Infantry support will be up in an hour or so."

"Sorry I never got that bluebelly for you, General!"

Forrest grinned. "Never you mind, Taylor. I reckon you'll have more chances, by and by. You take care now, all you fellows, and make sure you hold this ground. Them Yankees come up any closer, you give them six shots with the revolver, then club whoever's left on the head. Understand?"

Taylor and a dozen dirty, grinning faces looked back at him, with some saluting and others saying "Will do, General." Forrest then crept away with his aides, and once out of sight of the firing line, stood up and made his way back down the hill to rejoin the rest of his staff and escorts. That done, he returned to the Harpeth's bridge, dismounted, and sat down on the railing of the wagon bridge. There he waited, whittling away at a stick with a pocket knife.

He only had to wait 20 minutes, by which time he had unconsciously carved his stick into a wicked-looking stake, when Cockrell and his followers came hurtling down the road. Forrest sat calmly as the Missourians came to a thunderous halt, hooves clapping loudly against the planks of the bridge deck.

Forrest raised his voice over the noise. "General Cockrell, you made good time. Good for web feet."

Cockrell cocked his head back and laughed. "Haven't you heard, General Forrest? We're all in the foot cavalry now. Where do you want us?"

Forrest looked over his shoulder. "Lieutenant Coy, take General Cockrell here over to that cemetery, the one we found behind the tabletop. Take that track we used to get back here, and not the main road. It's quicker."

Cockrell detailed part of his staff to point the way and collect stragglers and rode off to the staging area. Forrest waited until the head of Cockrell's jogging column of men appeared down the road before mounting up and joining the Missouri general. Forrest found him standing by a six-foot high monument in the little country cemetery.

"General Forrest, did you see this?" Forrest shook his head, so Cockrell continued. "This here is the grave of Newton Cannon!"

Forrest's face lit up with recognition. "Yep, I remember him. He was the governor hereabouts, when I was a boy. Bitter enemy of Old Hickory, if I recollect. Now, see that notch over yonder?"

"Yes, sir."

"Form your brigade facing thataway. When I send you word, advance through that notch and attack the enemy, wherever and however you find him. Hit him hard, and keep hitting until you chase the bastards back over Nelson's Creek."

"Yessir!"

Forrest rode up to the north side of the tabletop hill, where he found Red Jackson and Ross together, a few dozen yards behind some horse guns, which were trading shots with the blue artillery roughly a thousand yards away. One of the four guns on the tabletop had already been smashed by Northern counter-battery fire. Just as the three generals had exchanged salutes, the volume of fire suddenly surged, and a thick belt of dismounted, blue-coated troopers started forward from Nelson's Creek.

They advanced as a cloud of skirmishers, drawn up three deep, and came on Indian-rush style. The men in the first line found cover and returned fire with their quick-shooting breechloaders, while the second line sprinted past them to new positions. The third line brought up the rear, always close by, standing fresh and ready with full cartridge boxes. Looking down the line, Forrest could see the cloud was much thicker on his left, storm clouds of blue making for the top of Yancey's Knob.

Looking through his binoculars, Forrest declared, "I think that's Grierson down there. Looks like his whole division, or most of it."

"You're sure?" asked Red.

Forrest said lazily, "Yeap. I recognize some of them regimental banners down there from Ringgold Mill. And it looks like General Grierson is making a grab for the top."

Ross said "I didn't think they would try it. Yes, it's the covered approach, what with those woods and all, but it is surely some steep going. Earle and Boyles don't need firearms to hold that place. Rolling boulders downhill will suffice them plenty."

Still watching the blue mass entering the woods for the climb to the top of the knob, Forrest said, "That man ain't no dummy, and he's got bull's balls. Fighting ground is often easier than fighting men, and he knows if he can get up top there, he can stampede us right out of here and into the Harpeth."

Red stiffened, touched with alarm. The Harpeth wasn't deep here, but it was very wide, and there was just that one little bridge. "I have no reserves, General. Shall I try to draw some back?"

Forrest spoke slowly, without concern. "No, see off these fellows here first. Then we worry about Grierson's stab at our left."

The Tennessee cavalryman checked his watch, confirming that it was a little past 6:30, and then dispatched an aide to send Cockrell in. As the aide galloped off, the trio of remaining horse guns depressed their muzzles and disgorged a massed volley of double canister onto the slope before them, chopping down dozens of blue troopers and sending the rest tumbling back down to Nelson's Creek. The advance in the middle was also pushed back by a flood of canister balls and musketry. But then the second line of loosely packed Billies moved through the reeling first, snapping off shots as they went. The third line followed right behind them. The gunners got one more salvo of canister out of their cannon before bullets were dancing among their pieces, felling one crewman after another.

Then Cockrell's Brigade entered the fray, emerging from the notch in a double line of battle, like a roundhouse right bearing down on the corner of the Union flank. Focused on the enemy to their front, for a minute Grierson's troopers were unaware of the presence of the Missourians, and then for another minute only a handful of them were able to bring Cockrell's onrushing force under fire.

The Missouri graybacks swiftly closed up to 150 yards, and there they stopped. Not bothering with dressing their ranks, they dropped to the ground or kneeled and blasted the opposing skirmishers with massed, rapid fire from their Henry Rifles.

Forrest could see Cockrell now, on foot and directing his second line out and farther to the right, to envelope the Yankee flank. Cockrell's efforts were halted when he was counter-attacked by troops from the third line of blue cavalry. For a time, the Northern troopers stood firm in the face of a crossfire of cannons and muskets from the heights above them and quick-firing repeaters from their flank, shooting back briskly with their breech-loading carbines. After a few minutes, however, the leakage to the rear began, and after several minutes the belt of blue skirmishers slowly, grudgingly fell back behind Nelson's Creek.

Turning his attention to the top of Yancey's Knob, Forrest could see nothing, but could hear how hot the fighting must be from the uproar. The clash going on at the peak was loud enough that Forrest could hear it even above the boom of the cannon firing just yards away.

"Captain!" Forrest roared above the din. "Dismount the escort and bring all arms. Red! I need your escort too, so send them up quick as you can."

Forrest then swung off his saddle, snatched up his musketoon, and sprinted for the track leading up to the top of Yancey's Knob. Instead of the easy climb of before, Forrest took long strides, ignoring the burning of his legs and lungs just as he paid no mind to how far behind his escort might be. Minutes of hard, up-hill running brought him almost headlong into a mob of Billies, into a place where the gray line had been broken.

Throwing himself against a tree, Forrest brought his musketoon to his hip, pointed at the nearest clump of bluecoats, and fired a load of buck and ball. He then dropped the stubby musket, drew his revolver, and started firing. Pulling back the hammer with his thumb, he unloaded one shot. At two shots, a bullet struck his tree. Three shots drew more fire toward him. Four shots, and he could see blue troopers moving around on him.

Pulling back the hammer a fifth time, Forrest heard the clapping of pistol and carbine shots from behind him, punctuated by the thump of a shotgun blast. His escort had arrived. Sagging against the tree and struggling for breath, Forrest waved his personal bodyguard on by as they charged into the mass of Yankees and sent them reeling back down the hill. When Red Jackson's own personal escort arrived, Forrest sent them on up to the top of the hill. After several minutes, the attack was repelled, and Forrest sent for the regimental commanders.

Forrest greeted the pair of Alabama colonels with a bear-trap handshake and then jabbed his recovered musketoon down the slope of the knob. "Colonel Earle, Colonel Boyle, get your men ready to charge. We're not letting those bastards get themselves reorganized. Wait for my call, then we all go down the hill together, hollering like demons. Knock them off their heels, get them scared, and drive them across that there creek at the bottom, you understand me?"

Infected with the General's aggression, the colonels yelled back, "Yessir!", snapped off salutes, and went back to their regiments. Forrest counted down the minutes, then looked to his bugler and mouthed the word "Go." The bugler tooted the call to charge, up went a peal of shrieking from several hundred voices, and the butternuts surged forward.

Forrest's hilltop counterattack went forward only about 50 yards before it collided with a hail of bullets, stopping it instantly. Grierson's troopers had pulled back just out of sight, and with plenty of fight left in them, they rammed home a ragged, but still devastating volley of carbine fire at their enemies. The Alabamans and escort troopers slowly worked their way back up the hill to safety, helping those wounded who could be easily moved along with them.

Scowling, Forrest kicked a rock downhill. He wanted a complete victory, and that meant chasing the Yankees off like whipped dogs, tales tucked in between their legs and mewling all the way back to the Nashville works. But he wasn't going to get it, he knew it, and he didn't like it.

Looking up, he could see the hue of the evening sun and knew the sun was setting. Soon it would be dark. He also realized if most or all of Grierson's Division was here, it meant that Grierson hadn't gotten through those hills to the east, and that was their only way of getting in front of or in the middle of Polk's column tomorrow.

So, Forrest thought, I have kept the army safe and I have given Grierson a kick or two, but I ain't licked him. And he needs a licking. That Minty fellow too, lest them two get airs about themselves. But not tonight, no, not tonight.

10:30 p.m.
Rutherford County Courthouse
Headquarters in the Field, Military Division of the Mississippi, USA
Murfreesboro, Tennessee

Sherman paced on the lawn outside the courthouse, hands clasped behind his back and energetically puffing down the cigar clamped between his teeth, as was his habit. He knew that Grierson had been in a fight today near Triune and was lustily anticipating his report, so much so that he couldn't bring himself to focus on anything else.

He looked up at the sound of approaching horses, half-expecting to be disappointed again. "Finally!" he said loudly, relaxing ever so slightly at the sight of McPherson and Grierson riding out of the dark towards him.

Sherman bellowed, "Good evening Mac, Ben. Have you eaten yet?"

Dismounting, the two men came forward. McPherson nodded that he had, while Grierson said "No, Bill, I have not yet had the chance."

While shaking Grierson's hand, Sherman called out to an aide, "Rustle up a meal for General Grierson here."

He regarded the man for a moment, who looked tired and soiled from many road miles in the saddle. Ben Grierson, Illinois music teacher and band leader turned hard-riding horse soldier. Sherman grinned widely at the pluck of it.

"Well, come on in, and tell me about running into that devil today."

The trio retired into the courthouse and into a chamber that Sherman was using for his office tonight. Closing the door behind them, McPherson said, "Bill, I'm surprised you didn't move into Fortress Rosecrans. It would be more secure."

Sherman stubbed out his cigar butt in a half-filled marble ashtray. "You're right about that, but it's too busy. Van Cleve is getting that place back in order. My couriers and business would get tangled up in all that. Now, Ben, what do you have to tell us?"

"My prisoners say I met with W.H. Jackson's whole division today. We got ambushed south of Nolensville, chased that pack of Rebels down to and out of Triune. Since I wanted to get by them for a look around farther south, I attacked them in a position south of that place. We didn't get by them, but I can tell you that Polk's Corps must have been about Eagleville and Riggs Crossroads this afternoon. They brought up infantry support, and I guarantee you Cockrell's Brigade was a part of it. We know from Stewart's Creek that Cockrell's Missouri secessh are armed with captured Henrys, and that's what counter-attacked us at Triune. A thousand screaming sons of bitches armed with Henrys."

Grierson shook his head before concluding. "My estimate is I was fighting five brigades, three of cavalry and two of infantry. We ended the day with a stalemate, which seeing as how my boys were low on ammunition, was the best I could hope for."

Pointing to the map that was pinned up on the wall, McPherson said, "So, if Polk's Corps is here, then it's a good guess the rest is bypassing Shelbyville, since Minty didn't report anything in that direction. That would put them around ... Unionville, Gideonville."

Grierson murmured, "Are they crossing the Duck River, do you think?"

Sherman shook his head. "My guess is they are making for around Columbia, either above or below the Duck. Not that it matters to me! I've got him! Yes, I've got him! I am out of that corral, in open country, and now I've got Stonewall Jackson, dead and buried!" He slapped his hand down on the desk for emphasis, striking so hard he toppled an ink well.

With a quizzical eyebrow raised, McPherson said, "I'm afraid I don't follow you, Bill."

"Look here. When we were in Nashville, we didn't have any room to maneuver. We also had to advance with only an insufficient wagon train to supply us. Insufficient and vulnerable."

McPherson replied slowly. "Yes. I know all that."

"Now we're astride the Nashville and Chattanooga. And as we move west, we hop over to the Nashville and Decatur. By moving west and south from here, our supply line is more secure, and we can sustain an advance. I want you to swing around to the south, get around Jackson's flank, drive deep into his rear, and cut him off from his base down in Alabama."

"But what about Nashville?" asked Grierson.

"What about it? On top of the old city garrison, there are the two infantry brigades Sturgis brought with him, the colored regiments, the 180-day regiments, and throngs of clerks, teamsters, cooks, mechanics, pioneers, and other support troops. Rousseau has a full army corps to man the greatest fortress west of the Appalachians. That place doesn't need this army to protect it, and I'm certain Tom Jackson hasn't realized it yet. We'll steal a march on him before he realizes we're not concerned about Nashville."

Invigorated, McPherson asked, "Alright, Bill, what do you want me to do?"

Sherman jabbed his index finger at points on the wall map. "Ben, you stay about Triune and Nolensville for now, and lend a brigade to Hooker, who is to march down the Salem Pike and pursue the Rebels directly. That ought to keep up appearances, and not show our hand."

Grierson said, "Right. I'll keep probing south and west, and put the bulk of my boys between the butternuts and Nashville."

Sherman went on. "Smith's XVI Corps will move down to Unionville, with the bulk of Minty's cavalry at his front. He is to act like he is in direct pursuit, but his real job is to stand by as a reserve for the two main wings of the army, Hooker and Logan. If Smith's column makes solid contact, he is to break off. Understood?"

McPherson nodded, so Sherman continued. "XV Corps is our whiplash. Logan will march on Shelbyville, with Minty's remaining cavalry. There he will cross the Duck, and seize this road junction at Lewisburg."

It's a good plan, McPherson thought. The three columns would move forward on a 20-mile front, so the entire army could concentrate on any one point inside of a day.

"I have only one question," said McPherson. "When do you want to get started?"

"The men have been issued fresh ammunition and rations?"

"That's right."

Sherman rammed his palms together, making a loud clap. "Before sun-up. Now, Ben, I think you've got a late supper, and Mac, you have marching orders to get out. As for myself, I have some correspondence with Washington to finish."

After his generals left, Sherman sat down at a table, and pulled the glass and bronze oil lamp sitting there closer before putting pen to paper:

*Headquarters in the Field, Military Division of the Mississippi
Rutherford County Courthouse, Murfreesboro, Tennessee
June 24, 1864.*

Lieutenant General U.S. Grant, Commander in Chief.

GENERAL: *I received your letter of June 10, but found myself preoccupied with Jackson's movements in Tennessee. Beyond the hasty scrawls to apprise you of developments in the campaign, I have not been able to respond to your larger suggestions, but they have never been far from my thoughts.*

I know General Thomas is slow of mind and action, but he is judicious and brave, and his Cumberland troops feel great confidence in him. Moreover, his task is to out-maneuver and destroy Bill Hardee, not Jackson or Lee. I think our first plan is still good, amended like so: you go for Lee, I go for Jackson, Thomas goes for Hardee. I'll be with General McPherson as you are with General Meade.

I have ordered a movement to Lewisburg, TN for tomorrow, and expect to be there in two days. McPherson's army is now in open country and on the railroads, and we will continue to move south and around Jackson's right until we either get into his rear or are on the Tennessee. By hard marching and hard fighting, this excellent army will either whip Jackson or force him back to AL, and once I have him there I will endeavor to prevent him from rejoining Hardee.

I agree that a campaign against Mobile, AL should be the chief priority for General Canby. I have directed that once Chalmers and his marauders have been chased out of West Tennessee, Generals Washburn and Slocum are to prepare for raids of their own, targeting eastern Mississippi. As Jackson confronts me out in front of his house, Washburn and Slocum will be at his side door, and Canby at his backdoor. In this way, we can guarantee no troops leave Mississippi or Alabama for other parts of the Confederacy, and I think when Jackson turns around he will find his house burned down behind him.

What is needed out west is a good cavalry hand, especially since I brought Grierson to Middle Tennessee. The only brigade leader in my entire department with the pluck for the job is Colonel Long, and with Colonel Wilder ailing, I hesitate to remove him from Thomas. Can you spare me a fighting horse officer for service in Mississippi?

I am, with respect and your obedient servant,

W.T. Sherman, Major General, U.S. Army

Folding his missive up, Sherman thought about his plans to preoccupy Jackson with concerns for his railroad supply line and his rear, and how they might need a taskmaster to see them along. That sounded like the perfect task for his Inspector General and chief bottlewasher.

So, when the clerk came to collect his letter to Grant, Sherman also told him, "After sending this on its way, wire General Corse in Nashville to pack his things and go to Memphis. His orders will be waiting for him there."

CHAPTER 15

June 25, 1864
4 a.m.
Headquarters, Army of Tennessee, CSA
Bethesda, Tennessee

Sandie raised his hand to cover his yawn as he emerged from his tent. The casualty reports had begun arriving on his desk almost as soon as army headquarters pitched camp yesterday evening, and Jackson had commanded him to deliver a summary on that and various other pieces of business before reveille.

He went over to the mess and asked one of the darkie cooks for a cup of coffee. Freshly made coffee. Even in Virginia, he had never had such a steady supply of formerly Yankee coffee. The very idea of it cleared the sleep from him, even before he took his first sip.

As he took that first marvelous taste from the tin cup, Sandie mused on how it seemed everyone in the army had gotten a half-decent rest yesterday except for himself, the doctors tending the wounded, and those poor souls who drew sentry duty for the night. The day before the army had marched a more reasonable 15 miles on drier, easier roads. That came after fighting a battle and a long march through a night and a day.

Even General Jackson turned in around midnight, Sandie thought. I was up until almost three with this wretched paperwork. One hour of sleep after all that. One miserable hour...

Sandie felt a spasm of grief shoot through him, his thoughts having stumbled over how much of a help James Power Smith had been with his staff burdens. His eyes watered, prompting him to turn away from the darkies and blink down the tears.

Jimmy Smith, Sandie thought, inhaling through his nose and looking up. Good thing it's so dark. No one saw that. Good thing. It wouldn't do.

His feelings under control, Sandie sipped on his coffee and dwelt on Smith for a time. Smith was a late addition to Jackson's military family, having come to them during the Maryland Campaign. All the others, like Sandie himself, dated to the Valley Campaign, if not before. They had become close friends, Sandie and Smith, both being of similar ages and coming from clerical families. And now he was gone.

After draining and returning his cup of coffee, Sandie approached Jackson's tent, and quietly said, "General, sir? Are you up?"

"Enter."

He raised the flap and ducked inside. Jackson was standing and awkwardly buttoning up his coat. Sandie knew better than to offer to help with such matters. Old Jack was very insistent that he get on with most things as if he hadn't lost his left hand.

Sandie retrieved a sheaf of papers from his leather satchel and placed them on Jackson's camp desk. "The casualty figures are all there, sir. I'd call your attention to the figures for Maney's Division and Clayton's Division, both of which were considerably damaged at Third Murfreesboro. The worst is Baker's Brigade from Clayton's."

Jackson spoke in a monotone. "I thought as much. How bad?"

"A third dead and wounded. Another third missing, including General Baker himself. That brigade is all fought-out, sir."

"There are some new Alabama regiments training up. They were intended for Mobile and other such places, but I can assign one of them to the brigade. New regiments have five or six hundred men, so that will fill out their ranks some."

"The most depleted regiments will still need to be consolidated, sir." Sandie hesitated, but then said, "We also need to find a replacement for Baker. The ranking officer in the brigade is now a major, so we can't choose someone from within. May I suggest you ask the War Department for a suitable brigadier in your next communication?"

"Alright, see to it. What about supplies? And the reports from overnight?"

"Counting what the men have in the haversacks, Hawks believes we have food and fodder for 15 days. Allan says our ammunition is sufficient for a major, all-out battle and then some. Our supply situation is excellent. As for field reports, Grierson is between us and Nashville, and Minty is shadowing us from due west. General Forrest describes the Federal pursuit as sluggish since that fight at Triune, with only light skirmishing. They have made no effort to penetrate our cavalry screen."

Perhaps that repulse at Triune quelled their appetites for combat, Jackson thought to himself, saying nothing.

"One last thing. A civilian came into our camp last night. From Shelbyville, sir, with intelligence on the enemy's movements."

Jackson asked skeptically, "A civilian, you say?"

"Yessir, a dry goods merchant from the town. But his son is in the 26th Tennessee. In Brown's Brigade. He is very eager to go visit his son, once we are finished with him. He claims that the entire Federal XV Corps arrived at Shelbyville just before dark and bivouacked north of town. As soon as the sun set, he got on his horse and rode west until he came right onto Buford's pickets. Buford sent him to Cleburne, and Cleburne sent him to me. I only interviewed him myself about three hours ago."

Jackson's eyes began to spark. The man might be wrong about the enemy strength, for what did a civilian really know about that? And Sandie was ambivalent about it. But he the man took great risks riding here at night. Nevermind Buford's pickets, the country was infested with bandits, and he must know that. But most important, there was that lack of energy in the Federal pursuit...

"Does this man, what is his name?"

"Earle E. Wilkinson."

Jackson changed his mind. Why ask Sandie when he could ask Wilkinson himself? "Bring Mr. Wilkinson here. I have questions."

After Sandie left to fetch Wilkinson, Jackson sat down on his cot and wondered about Sherman, and about McPherson. While he felt they might not be particularly aggressive, he had seen nothing to indicate either man was timid or inept. They weren't pursuing him very forcefully, nor were they marching hard to concentrate in front of Nashville. He expected some firm action of some manner from them, either one or the other.

Several minutes later, Sandie returned with Wilkinson. Jackson stood up and offered his hand. "Mr. Wilkinson? I want to thank you for coming to us as you have. You are a civilian, and while you are a good patriot, sir, undertaking such an arduous journey was not your duty."

Wilkinson was a pallid, middle-aged fellow, but his flesh turned bright red above his generous muttonchops. Doffing his hat, and bowing slightly, he revealed a neat bald spot on the top of his head. "You're… you're welcome, General. I had to come, you see. We have still had a Northern garrison in Shelbyville, even after you came to Tennessee. But when all them Yankees came down on the Murfreesboro Road, there was so much confusion… it permitted me to slip out unnoticed."

Jackson said, "I understand. What makes you think all those Yankees you saw were the entire XV Corps?"

Wilkinson spoke hesitantly. "Well, General, it weren't me who said that. It's what they said when I told my story to General Cleburne's people. What I told them was I knew about how the Yankees have those flags, the one that say a division is there."

Jackson said, "A guidon?"

"I reckon so. Well, I know how they have a symbol, and how the flag's field and symbol change colors for each division. I saw those flags down in town, four of them, and each one bearing a diamond with an emblem in the middle that said '40 rounds.' General Cleburne's people said that it meant the whole XV Corps was in Shelbyville. Now I didn't know a thing about any corps. I just knew there were four of those division, er, guidons you called them."

Sandie felt Jackson's body tense up. "Thank you, Mr. Wilkinson. Sandie, summon an orderly to see Mr. Wilkinson here gets a good breakfast, and that he is taken care of until we can send him to see his son. Then come straight back."

When Sandie returned, Jackson was looking down at his map table. Looking up, he said firmly, "Sandie, send orders to Cleburne at once. He is to send whatever part of Buford's cavalry he has on hands to Lewisburg, and to march on Lewisburg immediately."

"That would be Bell's Brigade. Those are Tennesseeans, but my recollection is that they aren't from around these parts."

The one-armed general's face soured, as if he were clearing a bitter taste from his mouth. "Cleburne is to take whatever route is most convenient to him. That is left to his discretion."

Jackson disliked saying that, but he overrode his instinct to dictate Cleburne's route and schedule. He overrode himself because he couldn't know exactly where Cleburne's column might be when the orders reached him, and a couple of hours one way or the other might make all the difference in keeping Marshall County's crossroads and county seat, and with it some leverage on how the next battle might unfold.

I must trust to Providence, he thought to himself, that Cleburne will see the proper path and follow it.

The glow in Jackson's eyes brightened. "That done, Sandie, get back here quick as you can, so we can draw up the marching orders for Stewart, Polk, and Forrest. I want the entire army concentrated around Lewisburg by nightfall."

7:30 a.m.
Headquarters in the Field, Cleburne's Corps, CSA
Farmington, Tennessee

After receiving his new orders from Jackson, Cleburne divided his column into three, their route determined by where they were at time. His wagons and the bulk of his artillery were at the head, and these were instructed to turn south on the best road available to him, the Franklin Turnpike. In the middle, Lucius Polk's Division set off on an old dirt road to Lewisburg, obscure enough that it bore no name on Cleburne's map. Finally, he rode back to the tail of his corps to turn the Tennesseans of Brigadier General Tyree Bell's cavalry and Cheatham's infantry around personally, sending them on a forced march down the Nashville Road to Farmington, a village half a dozen miles northeast of Lewisburg.

Cleburne arrived in Farmington about half an hour after Tyree Bell's troopers, already in a bad mood. The idea of fighting somewhere west of Lewisburg troubled him, since he knew the area was just a grassy plain nestled between the Duck River and the hilly country to the south. It was the sort of land favored by horse breeders, and in Cleburne's mind that made the ground far too open for a proper defense by its very definition. Aggravating him further was his inability to keep up with the cavalry. His bulky old mare just wasn't capable of matching the pace set by the hard-riding butternut horsemen, and even if she had been, his horsemanship was not up to the task either.

Finding Tyree Bell at the village crossroads, Cleburne clambered down off his horse and went over to the beefy, full-bearded horse brigadier, who was talking to some locals.

Saluting, Tyree Bell said, "General Cleburne! I was just inquiring about the lay of the land, hereabouts. May I introduce Mr. Russell, Farmington's blacksmith, Mr. Wyatt, who keeps the local store, and Dr. Locke."

Cleburne shook hands with the Farmington men, all too old for army service, one after the other. He felt his displeasure bubble as he did so. He was impatient with all the interminable pleasantries, but felt constrained by his sense of propriety from cutting them off, so he politely waited.

After what seemed like far too long a time to Cleburne, he was finally free to ask gruffly, "General Bell, your report?"

"Yessir. I have thrown out a screen about a mile and half east of here, on a slight rise in the ground and anchored on the right to East Rock Creek. But when I say that rise is 'slight,' I mean slight. Dammit if this country isn't almost flat. I've sent a patrol down the Shelbyville Road to make contact with the Yankees."

"I want to know as soon as you have word from that patrol. Cheatham's Division is one hour up the road. I'll be studying the ground."

Dismissing Tyree Bell with a nod, the Irishman turned around sharply, got back on his horse, and rode out to examine Farmington's surroundings. He dismissed advancing eastward, since there was nothing there but flat fields full of grass and weeds, bordered by fences and tree fringe. The only ground that offered him any advantage was west of Farmington, where a low ridge ran between Big Rock Creek and East Rock Creek. It wasn't much, but it was something, and as it happened Lucius Polk's Division would arrive on the road that ran right behind Big Rock Creek. He decided that was where Cheatham would dig in.

8:30 a.m.
41ˢᵗ Tennessee Infantry, CSA
Shelbyville Road
6 ½ miles northeast of Lewisburg

Nathan felt grateful as the brigade column turned off the Shelbyville Road and onto a shady country lane, as the turn meant both getting out of the already hot morning sun and that their forced march would soon be at an end. Sweat had soaked through his shirt and shell jacket, leaving dark splotches on his chest, in his arm pits, and down his back. Even his hat band felt sodden. Worse, after ten miles of marching at such a fast clip, he could feel the blisters that had formed on his toes, despite his thick calluses.

Looking over to Halpern, he decided it could be worse. At least he didn't have to corral stragglers, and a forced march produced plenty of those. Unsurprisingly, Lloyd had proved especially prone to breaking ranks and falling behind, prompting the First Sergeant to prod him along at the point of a bayonet.

Over the next twenty minutes, they kept going, passing one regiment after another of Walker's Brigade, until the 41ˢᵗ Tennessee found themselves on the left end of the line. The bugles sounded the order to halt in front of a little white clapboard Presbyterian Church called Bethbirei.

Nathan looked past Willie to Pete, who looked very worn and was already fidgeting with his blanket roll. Willie said over his shoulder, "Pete, don't get comfortable. We ain't been told to fall out yet."

A few minutes later the regiment was advanced a few hundred yards past Bethbirei Church, up and over the gentle ridge to a place overlooking a thousand yards of broad fields, fields that ended only at the winding course of East Rock Creek. There the regiment deployed into a line, and Captain Bell appeared before his company.

"Men! We have been assigned the honor, along with another company of the regiment, of advancing as skirmishers. We shall be the first to meet the filthy invaders, here in Marshall County, where I know some of you men are from. We shall be first, and we shall stop them dead!"

Nathan had to stop himself from spitting on the ground in front of him at Bell's puffed-up little speech, but was relieved all the same that a more senior captain would be in charge. He stepped out to join Willie and Pete, and the three of them went forward as a knot in a loosely ordered skirmish line.

"At least the rich boy knows that some of us ain't from here," muttered Nathan to himself, as an afterthought.

Most of the company's veterans were from Marshall County, but he, Willie, and a few of the others were from Lincoln County. The thought prompted Nathan to recall that Captain Fletcher was from somewhere in the county, and since he had gone home missing half a leg, must be around somewhere.

The Tennesseans advanced about 500 yards before coming to country road with a stone wall on the other side. There they were told to stop. Not even bothering to doff his blanket roll, Nathan dropped to the ground under some shade, and put his back against the wall for a much-desired rest. And there he sat, taking small sips from his canteen and waiting. Down the line, he heard a nervous Raglan Lloyd try to start up some conversation, only to be testily hushed by Halpern.

For almost an hour, all was quiet along the little stone wall. While Willie kept watch and Pete doodled in a patch of dirt with a stick, Nathan grew drowsy in the sultry air and struggled to stay awake. Then the bucolic interlude was broken when Willie whispered sharply "Billies coming."

Nathan crept up to peek over the wall. East Rock Creek was another 500 yards distant, a quarter-mile from them and half a mile from the main line. On the other side of the creek was a throng of Yankee cavalry. At such a distance, the enemy was just a swarm of blue dots, and most of that swarm that was coming across the creek. Other blue dots stayed behind with the horses.

The field was wide open, the only cover coming from tall grass and weeds. As the blue dots grew larger, sprouting arms and legs as they did so, Nathan adjusted his sights. He pushed the bar up to 400 yards at first, and when the enemy came closer with no word to fire, he slid it down to 300 yards and started counting.

About 60 of us behind this wall, he thought, chuckling. And there's maybe only four dozen of them.

Willie picked up the word that came down the line, hissing, "Ready and aim!"

Nathan leveled his musket and lined up a blue trooper. He guessed the range at 250 yards, so he aimed for the groin. His choice wasn't spite, but merely to compensate for the difference between the range and the rifle's sights. He never heard Willie pass on the order to fire, but pulled the trigger as soon as he heard the first musket crack.

Not bothering to see if he hit his target or not, Nathan ducked behind the wall and started reloading. Almost all the Tennesseans did so, and were soon rewarded for their caution when the field before them erupted in flame and smoke. He didn't know which was louder: the sharp reports of the repeater fire or the thwacks from scores of bullets striking the stone wall.

"Sweet Jesus," cried Nathan. "God damned them Yankee repeaters!"

Willie didn't even look up from tamping down his next musket ball. "Blasphemy, Private Grimes. No blasphemy in Old Jack's army."

Nathan pushed the bar on his sights down to 200 yards, shouting back, "Let Old Jack come down here and tell me hisself!"

Looking over the ragged crenellations of the dry stone wall, Nathan saw that the skirmishers had predictably dropped into the grass and weeds. You could guess where exactly they were from the depressions caused by their bodies, but that was still only a good guess. Worse, he understood that because they had repeaters, they didn't need to get up or roll over onto their bellies and fumble to reload. They could lay down, sweet and pretty, and shoot back all the live long day.

He brought his musket up, aimed it at a divot in the grass, and fired. That one shot brought a hail of bullets down around his part of the wall or whizzing overhead, forcing Nathan's head down. It was the start of the pattern that stuck, hard and fast. The bluecoat troopers sought their safety in lying prone and heaping fire on the graybacks, while the graybacks sheltered behind their wall and shot back only as rapidly as safety would allow them.

Twenty minutes into the firefight, Nathan caught sight of another mass of blue dots, mounted blue dots. He shouted, "Willie! Yankee cavalry riding out beyond our left!"

"I see them! I see them! Pete, run down and tell Captain Bell."

Willie hunched down and skirted past Nathan, patting him on the shoulder as he did so, moving to a place where he could keep a wary eye on the advancing cavalry. Nathan kept his attention focused on returning fire on their front, snapping off another shot before dropping down to reload again. He was capping his musket when he heard the bugles sound, and looked out to see their own cavalry charging down on the blue riders.

Still under fire, Nathan, Willie, and the others kept down and cheered as they watched the two masses of horsemen collide, not at a mad gallop like in the storybooks, but at a mild trot. The two fights went on separately for a time, before the Pennsylvanian sabers started pushing back the Tennessee horsemen and cutting into their ranks. Finally, the mounted Johnnies turned tail and galloped off, leaving a good many of their fellows and mounts behind.

The bulk of the Union horse tore off in pursuit, but one company peeled off to behind near a fieldstone house and barn about 200 yards down the dirt track and the stone wall. These troopers dismounted and took up positions in and around the barn and the house.

After sliding off his horse, Spear bent down and sprinted forward, calling out, "To the fence! To the fence!" Upon reaching the fence separating the house and garden from the barnyard, he knelt and pointed his carbine to bear down the length of the stone wall.

As his troopers fell into place on either side of him, Spear pulled back the hammer on his Spencer and shouted, "Fish in a barrel, boys!" and pulled the trigger.

Willie saw what was coming and screamed, "Get down! Get down!" as he threw himself down into the dirt. Spear's bullet zipped into the empty space where he had been kneeling, smacking into the stone before Nathan's face and blinding him with crushed specks and dust.

"Aigh!" shrieked Nathan, falling over backwards. "Sonuffabitch!"

A split second later, repeater fire from the farmhouse and barn tore down along the stone wall, enfilading the butternut skirmishers. Any man who hadn't already gone to ground voluntarily was bloodily knocked down by a bullet. Nathan cleared his eyes and looked up to see Sergeant Marks, his face contorted into a painful grimace, clutching a bloody splotch on his trousers. He had been shot through the lower leg.

Some 50 yards away, Bell crawled forward and grasped his commander, Captain Fonville, by the arm. Bell gulped down his terror, and thinking of his experience from the day before, he shouted, "Captain, are we not intended to withdraw?"

Fonville pulled Bell closer, and whispered hoarsely, "We cannot withdraw in this crossfire. If we get up and leave the wall, it will tear us to pieces."

Despite himself, Bell yelped, "You mean we're trapped!"

"Quiet!" hissed Fonville. "You musn't panic the men! Tillman or Walker will come to our aid."

Bell nodded numbly, but his head was clouded with thoughts of capture and Yankee imprisonment. Nathan was thinking much the same only a short distance away, only he had the memory of his capture at Fort Donelson to ground his bleak imaginings with reality. What was more, Nathan knew it was only a matter of minutes before the Yankees in front of them came over the wall and that would be a vicious business indeed. He looked over to Willie, grasped the revolver tucked in his belt, and braced himself for what he knew would be the short, fatal task of killing anyone who went near his brother.

Then the thunder came, the deep boom of artillery. In rapid succession, four solids ripped through the barnyard and the wooden walls of the barn. Spear jerked his head right and saw the battery of Napoleons, newly placed on the left of the Confederate main line. The polished brass of their heavy tubes gleamed through the haze of smoked belched out by their salvo.

Atop the low ridge, General Cheatham dismounted and strode over to the battery commander. "Captain, aim for the roof of that barn! If you put your cannonballs through the sides, the blasted things go through one side and out the other without hurting even a damned horsefly. Hit the roof, smash the rafters, and the whole barn goes over."

The battery leader shouted, "You heard the General! Elevate the guns for the new target and fire when ready!"

The first gun bellowed, then another, and then the last two at almost the same moment. Three balls crashed through the upper structure of the barn, and with the third one the roof collapsed, prompting a scramble to pull men out from beneath the wreckage.

Grinning, Cheatham smacked the gunner on the shoulder. "Outstanding, Captain, outstanding! Now put some guns on the barnyard and some guns on that house. Drive those fellows out of that farm."

Gritting his teeth, Spear worked his lever, cocked his hammer, and fired the last shot in his magazine. As he stopped to reload, he looked around and observed that not only were they under artillery fire in the barnyard, but the Rebel cavalry had come back.

Spear knew what was coming. He had just fed the last round down the butt of his Spencer when the bugle sounded "To Horse." It was time to go.

"Dammit, dammit, God dammit!" cursed Spear, as he turned and sprinted back to where the horses were being kept. We should have at least captured some prisoners, he thought angrily. Halfway to the horses, he paused and waved his troopers to pass him by, spared a glance to make certain the rest of the troop was doing the same, and then went for his mount.

With the enfilading fire slackening, Nathan sprang to his feet, leveled his musket and fired over the wall at the oncoming bluecoats. He then drew his revolver and shot at the crowd of skirmishers as he stepped up to the wall. Fonville jumped up and yelled, "To the wall! Boys, to the wall!" Bell got to his feet and repeated the order, waving his sword. In an instant, both companies were back on the wall, and with even the officers adding their pistols to the fire, they halted the advance of the Yankee skirmishers.

Thereupon the withdrawal began. The blue cavalry, mounted and dismounted, retreated, going slowly for safety and skirmishing all the way back to East Rock Creek.

Bell called out to Halpern. "First Sergeant! Did we lose anyone?"

Halpern suppressed a groan, wishing Bell had been more discrete. He jogged a few steps over, drew himself up for a salute, and said, "Sergeant Marks took one in the leg, Captain. Looks like just a flesh wound, though. No bones broken. Other than that, we were very lucky. Only a few scrapes and gashes. Very lucky. But I'm afraid someone will have to help Sergeant Marks to the rear, sir."

Bell cast a quick look around, and settled on Lloyd, who in his estimation was a worthless blight on the company. "Fine. Send Private Lloyd back with him, and Fonville's wounded soldiers, too. Maybe he can bring back some ammunition."

Watching Lloyd help Marks hobble back up to the main line, Nathan shouted, "You take care now, Ed, you hear!" He was pleased, not just because Marks wouldn't lose his leg, but also because he hoped that once Raglan Lloyd was on his own and out of sight, the bastard would desert and go back to under whatever rock he had been hiding under these last few years.

Up on the grassy ridge, Cheatham took out his flask and passed it to the artillery captain. "Fine work, captain, absolutely bully! Care for a snort?"

"Yes, sir, thank you very much." After a swig, the captain said, "General, I've had little but pop skull pass my lips since, oh, that Christmas before Stones River. So this fine stuff is much appreciated."

Thumbing down tobacco into his pipe bowl, Cheatham drawled, "Well then, Captain, borrow the flask and enjoy."

"No, sir, I couldn't."

"Captain, I have most of a demi-john of that there whiskey left, so I can spare you a few ounces. Go on, but bring me that flask back. It's a memento."

The captain agreed and left, and the burly Tennessean struck a match and drew air through his pipe. His thoughts turned to the enemy cavalry that rode wide around his left flank during that fight, and were now somewhere in his rear. He wanted to send Tyree Bell's cavalry in pursuit, but if he did that he'd strip his flanks, already in the air and vulnerable, of what little protection they had. No, he could not do that.

Cheatham felt uneasy. It wasn't numbers that bothered him, at least not directly. Most of the army's new recruits had been Tennesseans, and many of them went to him, turning his division into the army's largest. Even without Strahl's Brigade, he had 6,000 men with him. But he had only the single battery of four cannons, the rest being with the corps wagon train, and both his flanks were open.

If Blackjack Logan gets here with just three men to my two, Cheatham thought, that son of a bitch will flank me, easy as pie.

CHAPTER 16

10:30 a.m.
Lucius Polk's Division
Old Dirt Road (Big Rock Creek Road)
Eight miles north of Lewisburg

Coming down the rough, rutted dirt road, Jackson found himself grateful that the ground was still a little soft from the recent rains. It made the ride softer, as well as less dusty.

The tail of Lucius Polk's Division was plainly visible down the road, silver moon banners rustling in the slight breeze, and as Jackson grew closer he spied a group of dozens of men, mounted and on foot, under Cleburne's banner, waving gently in a pleasant breeze. He spurred his horse from a trot up to a canter, as fast as he could handle on a road such as this one.

Jackson slowed down several yards before reaching what he now saw were Cleburne, Lucius Polk, and their people. Adding his own people to the mix brought the total of staffers and escorts to well over one hundred men and a matching number of horses, filling the center of the roadside field.

As Govan's Arkansans continued their march, waving their hats but otherwise remaining silent as they went, Cleburne called out to Jackson from where he was standing. "General Cheatham just repulsed a probe by Federal cavalry, sir! I've given orders for General Polk to deploy on his right, lengthening his line."

Jackson eyes glowed, and he almost barked out the words "Good! Good!" Knowing where Cheatham was, blocking the enemy's path, gave him a vision of the coming battle, and he saw

Providence in it. Earlier that morning, he had directed Stewart to march to Lewisburg by way of the Nashville Road, and that route would bring him down onto the enemy flank. Cleburne, supported by Bishop Polk, would hold the enemy front, while Stewart crossed the Duck River to come down hard on their left.

He was about to say more when musketry began to clatter to the east, beyond the tree-fringed banks of Big Rock Creek. As all eyes turned that way, some of the staff officers became visibly anxious, and the members of the different escort companies for the three generals began sidling over to place themselves between their charges and the creek.

Lucius Polk muttered, "Something is happening with Govan's flankers." Then he barked "Lieutenant, see if General Govan isn't doing something about that. If he isn't, tell him to send more troops."

A minute later, a solid wall of blue-clad cavalry clambered down into the creek and up over the low, sloping banks to emerge on the side, less than 100 yards from the road. Musketry continued to clatter and smack, as the escorts began firing at the Union horsemen, and those horsemen returned fire as they paused to form up.

Cleburne reacted instantly, dashing out into the space between the escorts and the enemy cavalry, jabbing at the Northerners with a map case. "Charge those devils! Charge, charge, charge at once!"

Called out of their surprise and amazement, the escorts awoke to the realization that the army's commander and two of its senior generals were seconds away from capture. Almost as one entity, they spurred their horses forward and plunged headlong at a mass of Northerners who outnumbered them more than five to one, shrieking like demons as they went.

Cleburne then turned on his heels and shouted at Jackson. "Run, sir, run! You and any who are mounted! Run!"

Caught reaching for his pistol, Jackson stopped and said, "I will remain here and..."

Cleburne stepped forward and smacked the flank of Jackson's horse, putting his whole shoulder behind the blow. The animal bolted, taking Jackson along with it, protesting and angrily struggling to assert control as he went.

Jackson yelled, "Stop! Stop!" in bursts as he hurtled across the field, faster than he had dared to go on any horse sense losing Little Sorrel at Chancellorsville more than a year before. Steady pressure on the reins finally cause the animal to slow, but before she stopped she tumbled into a muddy depression in the field.

Becoming stuck, the mare reacted violently. Alarmed, Jackson forcefully jerked back on the reins, only adding to his mount's panic. She bucked and threw him, and with his hand outstretched to instinctively break his fall, he landed badly.

Jackson tried to push himself up and instantly winced as pain shot through his wrist. Instead, he rolled over and sat up, awkwardly using his elbow to help himself up off the ground. Over on the road, the rearmost regiment of Govan's column had turned around and was advancing on the marauding enemy cavalry as a phalanx, bayonets leveled. He also saw that his own horse had freed herself from the muddy quagmire and was standing nearby, shaking terribly.

"That's alright, girl," he said soothingly. "It is not your fault, and it's alright."

No sooner had he said that than Sandie rode up, rolling off his saddle and rushing upon Jackson. "Dear Lord, are you injured sir!?"

Jackson shook his head. "No, no. Well, yes. But not badly. I am afraid, Colonel Pendleon, I have broken my wrist. Can you help me to my feet?"

As he pulled Jackson to his feet, Sandie shouted to Quintard, who had ridden along right behind him, "Captain, help me get the General away from here! We must..."

The rest of what Sandie said was buried by the crash of a massed rifle volley.

Feeble, Jackson leaned on his chief of staff. "No, Sandie. Look there. The enemy leaves."

Stopped by the fierce attack by the escorts and thrown into confusion by the musket salvo, the Federal horse was already withdrawing back across Big Rock Creek. Jackson soon found himself mobbed by not only Sandie, but also Cleburne, Polk, Govan, and many others besides, all inquiring about his injuries and demanding he leave the area.

Still feeling shaken, Jackson forced himself to stiffen up. "No, no. Gentlemen, I appreciate your concern, but you will desist. That is an order. I am not going to be pushed up on a horse and led away at a tether. I will wait on this spot until an ambulance arrives."

Sandie was distracted by a courier, who thrust a message at him. "Message from General Stewart, sir."

Jackson nodded inquiringly, but said nothing and let Sandie read the message. Sandie's eyes widened, and he said, "General Stewart reports that the wagon train of Polk's Corps took a wrong turn and crossed his line of march, clogging up the junction until Stewart rode back and set things right in person."

Jackson's outrage swept away his frailty. He wanted to snatch the scrap of paper away and read it for himself, only he couldn't because of his injury, which only stoked his anger further.

"Who is that man?" growled Jackson.

Sandie blinked. "Polk's quartermaster is Major Thomas Peters, sir."

"Order his arrest. Immediately!"

"Yes. Sir," stammered Sandie. His preference was to wait until the facts were better known before ordering an arrest, but he was not about to argue the matter.

Cleburne came up just then, having jogging across the field. "General Jackson, are you hurt, sir!"

"I fear my wrist is broken."

"No! If only I had realized, I would never have driven your horse so!" cried Cleburne, clearly distraught. "Please, accept my most sincere apologies, I beg you!"

Jackson shook his head. "Apologies are unnecessary. My own inferior horsemanship did me in. And were it not for your prompt response to the crisis, I might have suffered worse, as might we all have. Providence put you where you were to do what you did, and that was good, so let us say no more of it."

10:45 a.m.
Headquarters, Minty's Division, USA
Shelbyville Road
One mile east of Farmington

Minty was giving instructions on where to park his modest wagon train when he saw riders galloping down the road and swiftly recognized the man in their center. Powerfully built and wearing long hair and a broad, handlebar mustache that gave him the air of a Sardinian outlaw chieftain, John Logan cut the kind of style one neither overlooked nor forgot.

He stepped out onto the road, and Logan pulled his horse to a halt in front of him. Coming around, Logan leaned over his mount's neck and thrust forward his hand. Minty took it, and got an iron grip handshake.

Logan liked Minty, although he had only made his acquaintance the month before, just before Lawrenceburg. He thought the Irishman, with his full beard, red cheeks, cocked and plumed hat, and brilliantly polished scabbard and saber, was the closest thing he had seen yet in this war to resemble the flair of the Napoleonic picture books on either side. Yet even with all the showy panache, Minty was no dandy popinjay. The man was a real soldier.

Logan asked, "General Minty, what happens here?"

Minty replied with a grin, "I gave Cheatham a poke for starters. He's due west of here, about two and a half miles, on a low, open rise on the other side of East Rock Creek. He is dug in now, but both his flanks are in the air. Anchored on nothing but a little cavalry on either side. I have put the Sabers and Smith on his front and sent Klein around north on a foray to Berlin, on the Franklin Turnpike, see what's what back there."

"Did you now?! Well done, well done." Logan felt pleased by Minty's enterprise, reminding him as it did of the pluck of the march to Vicksburg.

"What are your orders, sir?" asked Minty.

"John Smith's Division is just a few miles back down the road. They will take your place on the line. That done, I want you to send a full brigade straight up the Nashville Road and occupy Fishing Ford. Let's not forget that the rest of Stonewall's army is north and northwest of here, and I don't want a whole corps crossing the Duck and coming down on my flank."

"I'll send the Sabers."

"Bully choice." Logan swung down off his saddle and looked to his chief of staff. "Major Hotaling, find us a suitable place to set up the corps headquarters." Looking back to Minty, he said "May I have the use of a tent and desk for a time?"

"Yes, of course. Use mine," said Minty, gesturing towards a nearby wall tent.

Logan settled in and composed a dispatch to McPherson:

To A of T HDQRS:

Maj. Gen. James B. McPherson,

XV Army Corps has arrived before Lewisburg as directed, but has encountered Cheatham's Division west of Farmington. My intentions:

1. Cavalry under Brig. Gen. Robert H.G. Minty to screen flanks, secure Fishing Ford, and vigorously reconnoiter for approach of enemy reinforcements.
2. XV Army Corps to extend its line to the south, until friendly line reaches beyond Confederate right flank.
3. Attack Confederate right flank if practicable, drive the enemy back to the north, and secure Lewisburg crossroads.

Confirmation requested.

Your obedient servant,
Maj. Gen. John A. Logan
U.S. Volunteers

Logan handed the paper over to an aide. "Lieutenant, send that message to General McPherson at once."

2:45 p.m.
7th Pennsylvania Cavalry, USA
Nashville Road
Chapel Hill, Tennessee
1 ½ miles north of the Duck River

Spear sat on his horse along with the bulk of his company, inside a woodlot and enjoying the comfortable shade. It's a damn sight better way to wait here for Johnny Reb, he thought, than down there with the others on the road, out in the full heat of the day.

After stopping by the wagons and topping up their ammunition, Spear and his comrades rode to Fishing Ford, half a dozen miles north. The ford was located in a bend in the river, with a shoulder of land on the south bank jutting north. The bulk of the brigade dismounted and started to dig in on some high ground a third of a mile from the ford, neatly sealing up the shoulder, while Jennings's battalion went across the river.

Two of the battalion's three companies were dismounted in a skirmish line half a mile back down the road, alongside a sharp bend in Spring Creek, which flowed south into the Duck. Spear's company had continued beyond that skirmish line for another mile and set up an ambush. Lieutenant Brandt led the troop blocking the road, while the rest of the company waited in the woods a couple hundred yards to the west.

Looking to his men, Spear noticed Crowder gnawing at a cracker and shook his head. He was too anxious for hunger and had never understood how nothing stopped Crowder's appetite in the first place. To chew on some bland old hard bread now, Spear wondered, now of all times. How does he do it?

Spear felt a current of tension shoot through the company and looked to the road to see several dozen butternut troopers cantering down the road from the village of Chapel Hill in a loose mass, an advance guard bearing carbines, musketoons, and shotguns. Brandt's men opened fire from horseback at about 200 yards, prompting the butternuts to dash forward, hollering and firing wildly as they went. Brandt and his troop tucked tail and ran, as intended, and when the Rebels galloped across the front of the woodlot, Captain Vale shouted for his men to charge.

Spear walked his horse out of the trees, drawing his saber and applying the spurs only after he was on open ground. Roaring, he plunged forward with Vale, Crowder, Rose, and the others in the first wave of men in the charge. A few shots cracked out from the Johnnies as they turned about, returned by the blue riders who chose pistols over sabers. Then the charge struck the Rebel horsemen, landing squarely on their face.

Slowing down his horse, Spear passed into the gray ranks before coming to grips with a Rebel horseman. He caught the Rebel in the midst of twisting around in the saddle to shoot him with a revolver. Spear swung his saber, slicing through his enemy's chest and bicep. Passing the wounded rider, he looked over his shoulder and swung again as he went, striking the man in the back and knocking him to the ground.

Not immediately under threat, Spear sheathed his saber, drew his revolver, and cast about looking for another victim. All he saw was that the Rebel cavalry was already in flight. Brandt had turned about and hit them on the side, and with their backs to Spring Creek, the Johnnies broke on the spot and ran. He fired a few shots at the fleeing Rebels, knowing Webster wouldn't order a pursuit, because having bushwhacked the advanced guards, they were supposed to fall back on the skirmish line. Pursuit wasn't any part of it.

As the First Sergeant bellowed "Rally! Rally on the Captain! Rally," Captain Vale shouted "Sergeant Spear! There is one of ours back on that field. See if you can't get him up on his horse."

Spear took note of the bloodletting as he brought his horse around. The clash had left four Rebel dead and wounded on the field, including the man he had cut up, who was now moaning and clutching his wounded arm from the ground. There were others, no doubt, but they had ridden away.

Riding back towards the woodlot, Spear saw it was Dodson, one of the volunteers from '62. A friend, but not a close one. He saw Dodson with his hand over a wet, red spot on his chest, heard his wheezing, and gulped. Dodson was shot through the lung.

Raising his head, Dodson coughed blood. He tried to speak, but the effort only brought on more wet, bloody coughing. Spear grimaced. Lung-shot was a dreadful way to die. At the thought he should put Dodson out of his misery, he clenched his teeth. He knew he couldn't do that, he just couldn't, but neither could he force himself down off his horse, to comfort the dying man.

"It's alright, John. I know. I'll stay with you as long as I can. I'll write your folks, and I'll call on them after it's all over. I promise." Spear didn't get down off his horse, and said nothing more. As the rest of the company rode away, he stayed there for a few minutes more, waiting until Dodson was dead. Only then did he turn and gallop away.

3:15 p.m.
41ˢᵗ Tennessee Infantry, CSA
The Stone Wall
1/3 of a mile east of Bethbirei Church

"On your guard!" Halpern cried. "On your guard!"

Nathan knew an attack was coming, a big one, long before Halpern shouted his warning. The signs of a massing of infantry on the other side of East Rock Creek, just barely within sight, were unmistakable to his seasoned eye. With his sights already raised to 400 yards, Nathan stayed crouched behind the wall and waited for the inevitable swarm of Yankee skirmishers to cross the creek, followed by the ordered host of their main line.

Farther down the wall, Captain Fonville spoke quietly to Bell. "Now Captain, if you will look behind you, you will see not so much as a shrub between this here wall and the main position. The artillery is up now, so when we leave, they will give us some protection. Still, we must leave quickly. When I give the signal, both companies fall back 250 yards. Then we turn and see if we can't discourage them Northrons from following us. You understand me?"

Bell bristled, seeing in Fonville's choice of words a rebuke for his handling of the pickets at Stewart's Creek. But he nodded, saying, "Yes, of course, Captain. It's your command."

The wait went on for several more minutes. Nathan muttered, "Them Yankees sure is taking they's own sweet time," as the first loose row of bluecoats climbed over the creek bank and emerged onto the plain.

It was a minute more when the wall crackled with musketry. Nathan set about loading and firing his musket with practiced briskness and was rummaging his right pocket for the last cartridge kept there when the word came to fall back. He plucked up his ramrod, and without bothering to return it to holder, sprinted off with both, trotting along behind Willie and Pete.

Cannon fire reverberated across the weedy fields, sending shells screaming down onto the abandoned wall. Halfway up across the plain, Fonville called a halt. Nathan turned, knelt, and snapped off a shot.

His pockets emptied of ammunition, Nathan drew a round from his cartridge box and went through the several motions of loading his musket as the stone wall began to crackle with return fire. He shouldered his gun and fired another shot before the crackle surged into the tearing racket of massed, sustained musket fire, sending a clutch of bullets whizzing over or past him with every second.

Fonville ordered a retreat, which Bell repeated to his own company. "Fall back, fall back!" he cried, shrieking the last word as a ball tore through the empty top of his kepi. He stumbled over, and getting back to his feet, Bell restrained his instinct to run for safety. The Yankees might shoot him, but he wouldn't shame himself before the regiment.

They fell back onto the regiment, who were lying in wait just before the top of the low ridge, snug behind the earthworks they had spent the morning and early afternoon digging with tools collected from local farms, tin cups and plates, and their bare hands.

3:45 p.m.
Headquarters in the Field, XV Corps, USA
3/4s of a mile south of the Shelbyville Road

When he launched his attack on Cleburne's Corps half an hour before, John Logan had every expectation of success. His plan was for John Smith's, Osterhaus's, and Morgan Smith's Divisions to demonstrate forcefully against Cleburne's 1 ½-mile long line, while Harrow's Division moved beyond Cleburne's right. Just before the attack began, his own chief topographer had returned from a personal reconnaissance of the Confederate right, reporting nothing but cavalry there.

Harrow's 4,500 men should have pushed straight through that Rebel cavalry to attack Cleburne on the flank. Instead, Logan could hear the terrible din of a pitched battle down where Harrow was, louder than anything his other three divisions were doing.

Logan yelled, "Dammit! Harrow should be rolling the secesh up like an oriental carpet. What in blazes is going on over there?"

Without a word to his staff, he spurred his horse to a gallop and tore off, leaving his officers to scramble after him. A short, hard ride later, he found Harrow studying the enemy with binoculars alongside an Iowa battery of 10-pounder Parrotts, the guns busily and noisily bellowing at what was clearly a battle line of Southern infantry up on the low ridge.

Shouting to be heard as one gun boomed after another, Logan said, "General Harrow, seems like you've come into trouble."

Aware of Logan's presence for the first time, Harrow let his binoculars hang from the lanyard and snapped off a salute. He was a handsome man with intelligent eyes and a fine Roman nose, framed by neatly trimmed hair and beard. Clashing with his appearance was what Logan thought was the whiff of whiskey about him.

Harrow said, "I've come into resistance, sir, that is correct. I had only just started forward when the first of those butternut bastards appeared, but I surmised they would dig in if I didn't pitch in with them, so I attacked. More reinforcements came up, though, so I got pushed back."

Logan regarded Harrow briefly. He had never really liked Harrow, not caring for having cast-off Eastern officers imposed upon him. Worse, Harrow had proven to be the sort of disciplinarian who was cruel rather than strict, and he liked his drink. Yet Logan tolerated him politely, as Harrow was an Indiana crony of President Lincoln. As a politician himself, Logan knew better than to make enemies with anything other than the greatest of care.

But in this instance, Logan could find no complaints with Harrow's conduct. "You acted rightly there, General. I reckon a whole new division has arrived, from the looks of it."

Harrow's eyes shifted nervously. "Yessir. If you look down thataway, you'll see the butternuts extending southward. Now they are out past my flank! So, I've pulled back and started digging in myself."

Logan brightened, thinking of how the first division of the XVI Corps was now in Farmington, standing in reserve, with the other two not far behind. "Well, we've got reinforcements of our own. Yes, we do! I'll be right back, Harrow, and I'll bring Mower's Division with me. But I want you to pay close attention to your left flank, you understand me? You have naught but Smith's troopers and open fields down there. Refuse that flank, entrench it, and anchor it with some guns."

"Yessir," Harrow said, thinking to himself as Logan rode away that he would do no such thing. Oh, of course I will refuse and entrench, of course, but send guns down there? Poppycock. I placed that artillery myself, and see how beautifully the guns pound those Rebel vermin! Lovely. No, Jack Logan can go to hell for all I care. I shall not slacken my fire just to shore up a flank that will have Mower coming alongside it soon enough.

Returning to Farmington by way of the Belfast Road, Logan was confused and angered to see Mower's Division marching north on the Nashville Road. He drove his horse hard and fast into the village, cursing all the way. Even upon finding McPherson and Smith mounted in the crossroads, he was unable to restrain himself.

"Mac! A.J.!" howled Logan. "What in Lucifer's blighted name is going on here!? A.J.'s boys are supposed to be supporting my attack on the Rebel right, so where in hell are they going?!"

Unperturbed, McPherson said, "Good afternoon to you too, Jack. Minty says Confederate infantry is pressing on the Duck River crossings beyond our right flank. We don't know where two of Jackson's corps are, and that ford is six miles away, so if I'm going to do something about it, I've got to do it now. Mower is going to hold those fords."

"Sweeny is not even an hour from here," said Smith, "with Kilby Smith right behind him. You'll get your support soon enough."

Calming himself, Logan said, "It won't wait an hour. More Johnnies have arrived, and they are extending out beyond my flank. If we don't move right now, we'll lose our chance to get 'round their flank and smash them before they all get here. It might damn well be our only chance. Hell, I might be attacked myself in an hour!"

McPherson said, "More?"

"Yes, dammit, more of them. At least a whole division." Logan raised his voice again, pointing south for emphasis. "One of those two corps you spoke of is down on our left, and not across the river on our right."

McPherson paused, struck with a moment's indecision. Logan might be right, but if even one Confederate division got across the Duck to attack his right... he decided that was the more serious threat.

"I'm sorry, Jack, but that is how it is going to be. When the rest of Smith's boys get here, they'll come in alongside your left, and we'll all go down there and see about renewing the attack."

Logan scowled, and muttered, "Yessir." McPherson was being cautious, too cautious, worrying about what harm the enemy might do to him instead of what harm he might do to the enemy. Logan looked away, down the road to Shelbyville, and found himself wishing Sherman was there.

4:00 p.m.
Headquarters, Army of Tennessee, CSA
Farm and Mercantile Bank
Lewisburg, Tennessee

His wrist freshly set in wooden splints, Jackson stepped down from the ambulance and examined the building chosen by Sandie to serve as his headquarters. Located just off the courthouse square, no courier could possibly miss it. Although the white paint on the bank's window frames and its false columns was peeling, the brick construction was solid enough, and the cornerstone read "1838." Nodding his approval, Jackson strode in through the doors.

Sandie was there waiting for him. "Sir, I have an urgent message from General Forrest." The chief of staff then ushered his commander to a clerk's desk by an airy window and made to help him sit down.

"Sandie!" Jackson snarled. "Enough!"

Blushing, Sandie replied quietly, "Yessir. My apologies." He then set the message flat on the desk before Jackson, where it could be easily read.

"Good, good. Now fetch Cleburne, Polk, and their division commanders." Then Jackson looked down to read the message:

2 o'clock, June 25
Headquarters in the Field
In Company with W.H. Jackson's Division, CSA
Versailles, Tennessee

General T.J. Jackson,

While providing security for A.P. Stewart's Corps, troopers of W.H. Jackson's Division discovered Hooker's Corps on the Old Stage Road, well north of the Duck River marching south in the direction of Shelbyville. With your permission, I should want to operate against and harass Hooker's column, while continuing to screen General Stewart's attack on Fishing Ford. I have W.H. Jackson's brigades, in addition to a brigade from Buford's Division, which I believe sufficient to accomplish the two missions.

I have informed General Stewart of Hooker's location, and he concurs with my intentions.

Your obedient servant,
N.B. Forrest
Major General, CSA

Jackson felt flushed. If XX Corps was where Forrest said it was, the largest of the enemy's three segments could only participate in the battle if it turned and attacked Stewart. XVI Corps was likely *en route*, but for the time being that left XV Corps all alone. Whether Stewart came over the river or not, Cleburne and Polk could beat this isolated portion of the Union army, but with Stewart, he could cut it off and destroy it. It would be a Second Kettle Run, only larger.

"Providence," he murmured. "Can this be anything other than Providence?"

First to arrive were Cleburne, Cheatham, and Lucius Polk. After reporting in, Old Pat and Old Frank went to stand outside the door, biding their time with their pipes and amiable chat, while Lucius remained in the bank and called for a cup of coffee. Then Bishop Polk arrived, sweeping into the room followed by an entourage of Maney, French, and a bevy of aides in gold braid.

"General Jackson!" cried Polk. "I was mortified to learn of your injury. Mortified, and the country cannot afford it, I say! Praise be to God you were not captured or wounded in that unfortunate incident."

Jackson got to his feet, slightly embarrassed. "Praise be indeed, but I am not so badly injured. Now, gentlemen, gather around. We attack. We must strike the enemy, strike him while the iron is hot. General Polk, where exactly is your command?"

Polk said, "Maney's gallant boys are up and in line on my nephew's right." Then he looked to French, prompting him to speak.

"Ahm, yes." French cleared his throat. "My division is moving into Lewisburg even as we speak, preparatory to moving onto Maney's right."

Jackson's eyes brightened as he listened and burned like torches when he spoke. "Good. Good. To make the most of the time, we attack *en echelon*. Immediately. General Cleburne!"

Cleburne, already standing ramrod straight, stiffened further. "Yes, General?"

"I want Cheatham to begin this attack. He will advance onto the stone wall and seize it."

Noting Cleburne's expression, which transformed from its customary severity to animation, Jackson nodded for him to speak. "Sir, I already have the bulk of my corps artillery massed behind Cheatham's line, out of sight on the reverse slope and ready to push forward. If you will permit it, I would like to break up that stone wall with a preparatory bombardment of solid shot."

Trained as a gunner, Jackson instantly understood what Cleburne was after. That stone wall was only 500 yards from Cheatham's line, beyond the range of aimed muskets, but an easy, short-range target for artillery firing downhill.

"You wish to blast that wall into pieces, do you? Capital thinking, General Cleburne."

Cleburne smiled modestly. "The idea was that of my chief of artillery, Lieutenant Colonel Beckham."

"Beckham? Robert Beckham? A capable man. I commended him after Chancellorsville."

Standing behind Jackson, Sandie smiled. Beckham had transferred in at Hood's request back in February. He was a Virginia man, and one of the very few gunners Jackson had ever seen fit to praise specifically and by name.

"Very well, I give you 20 minutes for a preparatory bombardment. Then send Cheatham in, then Polk, then Maney. General French, I want your troops in position to the right and rear of Maney's Division, kept out of sight. When Maney starts forward, so do you, advancing onto the enemy left and rear. Do you all understand?"

Cleburne asked, "What of General Stewart?"

Jackson replied flatly "Stewart's Corps is my concern. Is there anything else? No? Then return to your troops. General Cleburne, I expect to hear your cannon directly."

4:20 p.m.
Headquarters in the Field, XV Corps, USA
3/4s of a mile south of the Shelbyville Road

Sherman galloped down the Shelbyville Road in a state of high feather. After putting everything in order from Nashville through Murfreesboro and down to Shelbyville to support the Army of the Tennessee, he was finally free to join that army on its fighting front. Moreover, McPherson's execution of his plan had been a good one, and he felt confident the entire army would be concentrated around Farmington by nightfall.

He arrived at a small cluster of wagons in a field just off the road, a cluster under the banner of the XV Corps. Sherman grinned widely. The XV used to be his corps, and although they didn't have the banner then, he liked its design all the same: a cartridge box emblazoned with the words "40 Rounds." Slowing his horse, he came into the wagon park of a headquarters at a walk and dismounted smartly before McPherson.

Returning salutes, he said, "Jack. Mac. Good to see you both. The last message I got back in Shelbyville is a couple of hours old, so what is the news?"

McPherson motioned Sherman to follow him to a table of improvised from empty ammunition crates, atop which was a map freshly prepared by his topographers. He succinctly explained where Logan's divisions were, that the cavalry were screening his flanks and covering Fishing Ford, and that he had dispatched Mower's Division to shore up Fishing Ford against a strong Confederate force on the north bank of the Duck.

As he listened, Sherman pulled his hat off and ran his fingers through his sweaty red hair, a sense of disappointment bubbling in his gut. His orders had been for Mower and the rest of XVI Corps to support Logan's attack, and while McPherson had the discretion to override those orders as the commander on the spot, Sherman deeply regretted that he had done so. Logan's line was at hand, right here in Farmington, while Fishing Ford was six miles away.

Better to strip the flanks of cavalry and let Minty handle the river crossings, Sherman thought to himself, than to have postponed the attack. He felt in his bones that the delay meant the attack wouldn't happen at all.

Just as McPherson finished his briefing, a courier appeared. "Message from General Hooker, sir!"

McPherson took the note and read it. As he did so, Sherman said to Logan with a suggestive nod, "You had best go see to your lines, Jack."

Handing the message over, McPherson clucked his tongue. "I almost can't believe it. Hooker says two Confederate corps are massed to strike him on the flank. He wants to deploy to the west and stand his ground."

Sherman shook his head. "Cleburne and the Bishop are known to be right here, more Rebel infantry is pressing the Duck crossings off to the north, and Hooker thinks two-thirds of the Rebel army is bearing down on him. Where does he think those troops have come from? General Lee? Tell Fighting Joe to keep moving and get his histrionic ass to Farmington. Send him precise orders to that effect, and I'll countersign it."

Chuckling, McPherson went to find a clerk to draw up those orders. When he returned, Sherman said, "Look here, Mac, you have missed a good opportunity. Perhaps even a great opportunity. You should have supported Logan."

McPherson pursed his lips, but before he could respond, the half-muffled thunder of distant, massed artillery rose from the west. Looking beyond Farmington, Sherman said, "Mac, get on your horse, find A.J. Smith, and get his boys down here as fast as their feet will carry them."

CHAPTER 17

4:15 p.m.
7ᵗʰ Pennsylvania Cavalry, USA
South bank of the Duck River
1 ½ miles west of Fishing Ford

After the ambush, Spear's company fell back on its battalion and dismounted to fight a delaying action north of Fishing Ford, an action fierce enough to force the Confederates to deploy their infantry. Having bought that much time, the Keystoners got back onto their saddles to retire behind the Duck and the entrenchments thrown up by their fellow Sabers. Thereupon, they replenished their cartridge boxes and pockets and were dispatched downriver.

Spear knew where they were going. The oldest hands of the 7ᵗʰ Pennsylvania liked to joke that they had foraged every henhouse and shat in every outhouse in Tennessee, and the boast was almost true, as the regiment had patrolled far and wide in 1862. Just down from Fishing Ford was a summertime livestock crossing, a place where the water was placid and about waist deep, the bottom firm and flat. It wasn't quite a ford, but infantry could cross it easily.

The river bank was lined with trees, and Spear breathed easier when his company wasn't among one of the two that marched out to secure the crossing. Instead, they dismounted behind a large, rectangular wood lot set about a hundred yards back from the river and took up reserve positions there. Rose put his back up against a tree and pulled his hat over his eyes for a nap, while Crowder took his turn as the fourth man who kept the horses.

After studying the ground, Spear went over to Lieutenant Webster. "Sir, I can't say I like this place much. Don't care for it at all, in fact. Look over there. The north bank dominates the south, and behind that are knolls to the right and left. If the Rebels come here..."

Webster finished the sentence. "... if the Rebels come here in any force, they'll shoot down on us like hail. Yes, I know. So does Captain Vale. But you know what they'll say higher up. If the place is an onion, we chew on it all the same."

Having said his peace, Spear settled in to wait and see what came. Men gathered deadwood, built fires in the horse bivvy behind the woods, and brewed up coffee for everyone. The combination of rest and barefoot coffee dispelled some of Spear's weariness, and his thoughts turned to poor, dead Dodson.

Why didn't I get down and comfort the man, Spear thought with some anguish. He couldn't quite rationalize that it was because he might have had to flee from Rebel outriders at a moment's notice, although that was completely true.

Instead, it was the air of death. Not his own death, which he knew with the certainty of repeated proof that he feared only as much as any man did, and perhaps even less so than most. No, what gave him the worst apprehension was seeing the Reaper come for someone familiar, someone he knew. The physical presence of death made intimate. It turned every fiber of his being to unease, so he shrank from it, wouldn't go near it. Just staying with Dodson had required all his courage and control, and even then he felt he only managed because the mercy of God passed through him.

Then the first sounds of a new squabble began: calls of warning interspersed with scattered musketry, the latter growing in frequency as the former died out. Spear could see the sparks and puffs of smoke from the higher, north-side bluffs of the river, and that the Rebel skirmish line there was thickening.

4:20 p.m.
41ˢᵗ Tennessee Infantry, CSA
Near Bethbirei Church

Nathan nestled the side of his head more firmly into his slouch hat and the loose dirt of the earthwork as he pushed harder down on his ear. It was no use though. He had already muffled the roar of the cannon as much as was humanly possible, and it pummeled the insides of his head despite his efforts.

Looking through a misty powder smoke to the busy gunners behind and above them, Nathan admired how smartly it had all been done. With some help from the infantry, the guns had been smoothly pushed forward by hand over carefully chosen routes rather than hauled by horses every which way, unlimbered, and brought around, shaving minutes off getting them into action.

Old Pat and Old Frank were there with some staffers, sitting atop their horses behind the battery posted behind the center of the brigade. Nathan thought the two generals looked as calm as could be, heedless of the occasional bursting shell as they studied the bombardment through their field glasses.

Cheatham smiled and nodded, pleased and relieved with the way things were going. He had been dubious about the prospect of attacking that stone wall, and was just as dubious that the artillery could do what Beckham had promised, but it was working. Most of the shot were striking their targets, and either gouging sizable divots out of the front of the wall or tearing straight through it, spraying the blue infantry with chips of stone shrapnel.

He leaned over to Beckham and shouted to be heard. "Well done, Colonel, well done indeed! You handled those guns as deftly as a steamboat gambler with his derringer!" Cheatham then gave the artilleryman a firm pat on the shoulder for emphasis.

Beckham grinned and tipped his hat back to the Tennessean, but didn't try to make himself heard over the roar of his cannon.

Cleburne had harbored doubts about Beckham's scheme too, but the arguments of the artillery chief he had inherited from his deceased predecessor, John Bell Hood, had been persuasive. Beckham insisted that the short range, gentle elevation, and having the sun at his back would all give him crucial advantages. The gunner also explained that as a dry stone wall was held together only by its weight and friction, cannonballs fired from close range would smash it to rubble. What was more, Beckham had planned the successful artillery charge at Lawrenceburg, and Cleburne found all the reason and method in Beckham's plan that he liked to see in an operation. So, he told Beckham to ready his guns just in case Jackson ordered an assault.

Cleburne withdrew his pocket watch, checked the time, and returned it to its place. Shouting at the top of his lungs, he ordered, "Colonel Beckham! Cease fire! Frank! Prepare your advance!"

Cheatham saluted and nudged his horse around before dispatching aides to his brigade leaders: Walker, Vaughn, and Wright. The battle plan was a simple one. His division would advance down the low open slope, picking the pace up to the double quick once they came under fire. Upon reaching 50 yards distance, each brigade would stop, put a massed volley into the wall's defenders, and charge. On their right, Polk's Division would engage the entrenched Federals to their front, coming on only after Cheatham had taken the remnants of the wall.

The guns quieted, the bugles sounded, and Nathan, Captain Bell, and First Sergeant Halpern all jumped up at the same time, followed by the rest of the company. They formed up swiftly, with Bell and Halpern inspecting the company line as Tillman and the Sergeant Major inspected the line of the entire regiment. Just out in front of them all stood Brigadier General Francis Walker, sword on his shoulder and closely observing his brigade.

"Hurry up! Straighten up!" Walker pointed a finger at the 50th Tennessee, forming up next to the 41st. Half a minute later, he hollered, "Fix bayonets!"

Nathan smirked as he slid his bayonet socket over the muzzle of his rifle. Walker was a good man, as good as Maney had been, and they were lucky to have him.

The smile fell from Nathan's lips as he heard the bugle call to advance, replaced by a tight frown. He had expected a brief speech from Old Frank before they set out. Instead, Walker called out, "For our sweet home, Mother Earth! Forward! March!" and they all stepped off together.

The brigade shouted back as they trod forward in a neat formation, muskets at the shoulder. Nathan picked up the battle cry a quarter beat behind. "Mother Earth! Mother Earth! Mother Earth!"

A shell burst harmlessly, far overhead, fired by guns from the higher ground across the creek, so far away they couldn't be seen except for the puffs of smoke. That shell was followed by another landing behind. Less than a half-minute later, a third bomb exploded in right over and behind another company, felling a pair of men with splinters. Then they were safe from the Northern artillery, down on the plain and out of sight. That was when the bluecoats stood up from behind their ruined wall, leveled their muskets, and fashioned a new wall with the hammers of their musket locks, one made of flame, acrid smoke, and bits of lead.

Standing to Nathan's right was Jim Marsh, one of the fellows Nathan had lost his pay to a few weeks before. Marsh jerked violently and toppled over, his back torn to ribbons by exit wounds. On his left, he felt that Willie and Pete were still there, knew it without looking. He heard Tillman yell, "Double quick! Double quick!" Nathan picked up his pace to a jog and went on.

Through the smoke, Nathan could see the broken wall and the battered ranks of Yankees across the way, and the sight evened his keel, balancing his restrained sense of dread against a new sense of delight. The Yankess have suffered over there, he thought. Oh yes, I can see it. They'uns have suffered.

He could also see them busily reloading. The blue line brought up its arms and fired a second volley. Now Nathan felt the tremor on both sides. At least one man had been shot on his right, but also someone on his left. He saw Willie still standing, still jogging forward, and knew it was greenhorn Pete.

Willie yelped, "Pete got it in the leg!"

A few more fast strides, and the word came to halt, to ready, and to aim. Drawing a bead square in the body of an anonymous, blue-clad figures reloading muskets just on the other side of the cloud of acrid smoke, lazily dissipating in the hot, humid air, Nathan waited. The tick of a clock crawled painfully by, and the first free shots of the fastest loading Billies cracked, and only then did Nathan hear the first half of the next order. Only then did he hear "Fi-!" and squeezed the trigger. The musket butt bit into his shoulder, and the world stopped oozing by. Things very suddenly began to move very quickly.

Mechanically, Nathan lowered his rifle in the first motion of reloading it only to hear the bugle call "Charge!" Without sparing a thought for what to do next, he pushed his bayonet forward, gave a yell that was somewhere between growl and howl, and sprang forward.

Sprinting through the smoke, Nathan reached the rubble of the wall, events rushing by in a frenzy. He jabbed the point of his bayonet past the rock pile, and leapt past to the other side. Then the blurry rush came to a jarring halt, and Nathan realized he was on the other side of the ruined wall alone, encircled by murderously hostile men.

By instinct, Nathan stabbed at where he felt the most menace, slicing through the jacket and fleshy side of his target, who jinked back wildly. He also felt that the man on his hard left was about to club him, and in the corner of his eye, he saw him scream, speared in the back. Willie was there, stabbing from the other side of the wall.

Nathan dropped his musket and stumbled half a step back, reaching for Captain Fletcher's service revolver as he did so. He then lunged forward upon the man whom he perceived as the only one carrying a loaded rifle and elbowed him in the face as he drew the pistol.

But there were still four of them. Too many, far too many. His nerves burned and his gut felt sick, and he knew he was about to be clubbed or stabbed or shot. Then came the dull crack of a pistol shot, then another, and Captain Bell was over the rubble and standing beside him.

Bell came forward wild-eyed, gunning down the Billy that was on the verge of piercing Nathan's back. The Northron dropped to the ground, and Bell shot him a third time, screaming "Die you bastard! Die!"

His pistol free now, Nathan pulled the hammer back and fired at an enemy, not three feet away. He swung his arm around and fired again. Then a third time, and then a fourth, but now at the backs of fleeing bluebellies.

Nathan bent forward, panting with his hands on his knees. He felt dizzy, and noticed for the first time that he had wet himself. God dammit, he thought. How in the blue blazes of Hell did that happen?! Shee-it!

Willie said hesitantly, "Nathan, are you alright?"

Yep," replied Nathan, wheezing. "Yep, I am."

"First Sergeant, rally these men!" bellowed Bell. "Behind the wall, and wait for orders!"

4:45 p.m.
South bank of the Duck River
1 ½ miles west of Fishing Ford

While Cleburne's artillery was still cannonading the stone wall, the musketry along the Duck River crossing became too hot for the forward blue pickets, who were driven back onto the woods. At the same time, the Confederates brought artillery up onto the knolls flanking the crossing and began shelling the woods.

Across the river, A.P. Stewart walked up to the top of an open knoll and into the midst of a very preoccupied gray battery of 12-pounders, busy pelting the front of the woodlot with rangy canister fire. His horse and staff he left behind the knoll, keeping them out of sight so as to not attract Yankee sharpshooters. A thousand yards downriver, a second battery enfiladed the woods, creating a deadly crossfire.

Watching the carnage through his binoculars, Stewart grinned wolfishly. Half of Stevenson's Division was fixing the attention of the force covering Fishing Ford, but the other half was here. Caught in that crossfire, all he needed to do was get some troops over the river chase the Federals off. Do that, and he would flank Fishing Ford. Do that, and he would have Stevenson marching down the Nashville Road in less than an hour.

A captain, the battery commander, waved exultantly. "Old Straight, sir!" he shouted. "Are we keeping it hot enough for you, General?"

"Perfectly hot, Captain!" Stewart then went back down the knoll and sent Reynold's Brigade in.

Brigadier General Alexander Reynolds's mixed outfit of Virginians and North Carolinians was drawn up on a dirt track in a compact column, six men wide. Reynolds, "Old Gauley" to his men, led them tromping down to the Duck River in person, and contrary to the normal practice of sinking back once the advance was well under way, at the fore Reynolds stayed.

Holding their muskets over their heads, the assault column plowed into the cool, meandering waters and over to the other side. Across the river, Reynolds led them storming up the river bank, out of the trees and into the open, where they were instantly halted by a tempest of repeater fire. The head of the column was cut down, and the survivors behind tumbled back to seek shelter behind the river banks. Reynolds himself fell wounded through the forearm and had to crawl back to safety.

Having emptied his entire magazine into the graybacks, Spear put his back to a tree to reload. Not that the tree was especially safe, what with shot and shell ripping through the trees by the left. He knew the Major had sent for reinforcements, and he knew that until those reinforcements came they had to hang on, but he also knew they were in a desperate place.

Thumbing the last cartridge into the butt of his Spencer, Spear cast a quick glance at the men around him, then rolled over and around to fire. A hundred yards away, he could see the Johnnies spreading out along the river bank. He set about aiming and firing on the moving shapes behind the trees, counting down each pull of the lever.

Spear had reached four when the world went bright, dark, bright again, and then came the sensation that his ears were ringing. He was suddenly aware that his face was in the dirt. Spitting bits of leaf and grit from his mouth, he looked up, shook his head, and saw Rose lying with a red stain spreading across his back. A black chunk the size of shot glass was stuck in the middle of his back, and his fingers were twitching.

As he belly-crawled over to Rose, the stench of feces reached Spear. He involuntarily paused and felt his insides churn and quiver. Blood and shit, that awful slaughterhouse smell. Spear took a hard swallow, and inched across the last couple of feet, gritting his teeth.

Rose's eyes were alert, and he mumbled "I can't feel them. My legs." The black thing was a piece of shell iron, and it was stuck in Rose's spine. He might live, but as a cripple if he did.

Steeling himself, Spear clasped Rose's hand. His instinct was to jerk that hand away, but he didn't. Instead, his eyes became wet, and he yelled, "Stretcher bearers! Stretchers!"

He held Rose's hands, repeating, "You'll live, you'll live" over and over until the stretcher bearers came for Rose minutes later. Spear then picked up his Spencer, unscathed from the shell burst, and numbly resumed firing by rote. So numbly, in fact, he missed the call to retreat, and Captain Vale had to come over and shake him on the shoulder.

Getting back on his horse and galloping away restored Spear most of the way to his senses. Arriving on the Nashville Road, he saw thick files of blue-clad foot soldiers marching off the road and towards the river crossing they had just abandoned.

A tall, fit man with a star on his shoulder rode over to Major Jennings, and had a hurried conversation with him. He wore a fierce expression, and with his thick mane and bristly beard, he gave the impression of an angered timber wolf. After talking to the Major, he spoke to the battalion with a booming voice.

"Boys, my name is Joe Mower. The Major here tells me you've got a rough business of it down by the river, but we need to drive those fellows back! And you still have ammunition, do you not!? You can see my infantry right here, and I'm going to send them straight in. Will you ride around their flank, and stick the bastards in the liver while my boys stick them in the chest!? Will you do that for me?!"

Spear felt himself carried along by the revived spirit of his comrades. They yelled together, "Huzzah! Huzzah! Huzzah!" The battalion turned about, riding beyond the flank of Mower's "gorilla guerillas," as men of the XVI Corps styled themselves.

The bluecoats advanced, put the opposing skirmishers to flight, and caught the advancing main line of Rebels in the midst of traversing the deep gully of a 200-yard wide, C-shaped bend in Rich's Creek, a small tributary of the Duck. Threatened with being trapped in the gully for slaughter by the bluecoats, the graybacks withdrew into the field where Crowder and others had previously stood as fourth men, holding horses and brewing coffee behind the woodlot.

Kneeling behind a hedge on the edge of the field, Spear put a Rebel officer in his sights, a man busy putting his troops in line as his regiment readied itself to renew the contest with Northern infantry. Seeing bars on his collar, Spear judged him a captain or lieutenant, but he was too far away to make out if it was two or three bars.

Definitely not just one bar, Spear thought. Sitting behind his woody bramble, he waited for orders to fire. They weren't long in coming.

Spear squeezed the trigger. The officer fell, riddled by more than just Spear's shot. Over 250 troopers were shooting from along that hedge. Spear fired as fast as he could work the lever and hammer of his Spencer, emptying his seven shots in seconds. Hunkering down into his kneeling position, he thumbed cartridges into the butt of his weapon.

When Spear came back up, the blue infantry had arrived to tear at the North Carolinians and Virginians on the front, while the troopers savaged them from flank and rear. The Johnnies on the flank were melting away under the repeater fire, and when Federal buglers sounded that charge, the whole mass of butternuts turned and ran as one.

The butternuts fled back across the river crossing, unmolested for the most part, as Mower's "gorillas" were wary of placing themselves between to the pair of Confederate batteries across the river. They waited for their own artillery to come up before advancing any further.

Exhausted, Spear tumbled around and down. Only after he spent a couple of minutes collecting himself did he look to either side, check to see if any of the boys were wounded. None were.

Suddenly, Spear became aware of the taste of bile in his mouth. His hands trembled. He took his canteen with both hands and took a sip. The water was warm, and upon touching his tongue it made the awful flavor in his mouth much worse, so he spat it back out. After a few moments, the nauseating taste faded, and he sucked down the rest of water greedily.

5:20 p.m.
Headquarters in the Field, Polk's Corps, CSA
The Confederate Right
1 miles east of Lewisburg

Sitting atop his horse, Polk looked on as Jackson stepped down from his ambulance. He smiled genially and offered up his salute, but inwardly resented Jackson's presence.

Finally I have a chance to shine, Polk thought. We have the Federals outnumbered, not by much perhaps, but outnumbered. With our superb Southern manhood, all we must do to drive him from this field on this glorious day is go out and smite him, and God has given me this chance to do the smiting. I do not need Stonewall or anyone else holding me by the hand as I do it!

Despite his brooding, Polk still appeared happy as Jackson reached him. "General Jackson, sir, we are very pleased to have you with us. I trust the ride was not uncomfortable?"

Jackson's face twitched, an obvious sign of irritation. He hated riding in that contraption and was already finding his injured wrist a drain on his patience.

After a moment to restrain his temper, Jackson said, "No, no. Not terrible. General Polk, I want you to supervise General French very closely. It is imperative that he march deep into the Federal rear and seize the Shelbyville Road to the east of Farmington. After he strikes the Federal left and starts them running, get French moving on. Leave pursuing the enemy to Maney and the rest of the army. Do you understand me?"

Of course I understand, Polk thought, growing more annoyed. But his mask of serenity never even so much as twitched.

"Yes, sir. I shall stay close and see to it, rest assured."

"Good, good," replied Jackson, who then turned his attention to directing his staff as to where to set up his tripod and telescope. As he did so, Polk rode forward to where French had massed his division, just behind a dense forest of hollys and beeches. Having just received word that Maney was attacking to his left, French was in the midst of sending forward three of his four brigades: Ector's, Sears's, and Cantey's, this last now under Colonel O'Neal.

Polk stopped himself and his staff long before reaching French, coming close enough to observe his advance, but staying far enough away to avoid direct communication. With a petulant and spiteful sense of glee, he had decided he would avoid interfering in either Maney or French's commands unless absolutely necessary. In a matter of minutes, French's advancing infantry were out of sight, disappeared into the dense forest.

On the other side of the field, General Harrow hadn't strayed far from his Parrott guns since Logan had left him more than an hour and a half before. Pacing back and forth, he watched the Confederate advance upon his line nervously, even though his men were well-entrenched and he had twelve guns in support.

Taking a swig of whiskey from his flask, Harrow observed that his line overlapped the advancing Confederates by a couple hundred yards. "Lieutenant!" he barked. "Go tell Walcutt to not neglect that opportunity. Tell him to blaze away at that open flank. Blaze away, I say! Rake them!"

The message proved unnecessary. As soon as the advancing Confederates came down to within 250 yards, Harrow's entire line erupted with flame and smoke, unleashing a sharp, sudden flood of canister and musket balls. With hundreds of extra rifles aimed at it, the Johnnies standing in Maney's right flank first shuddered and then recoiled, all over the protests and pleading of their leader, Brigadier General William Quarles. The remainder of Maney's Division was soon forced to follow them back to their starting line.

Hampered by the forest, the first brigade of French's Division, Ector's Tar Heels and Texans, came out only after Maney's soldiers were already backing away. Their bearing had them advancing straight onto the corner of Harrow's refused line, but they advanced upon it alone and were easily driven back onto the protection of the woods. Next, Sears's Mississippians came out of the forest, advancing on the leg of the refused Federal line. They too came on alone, and they too were sharply repulsed.

Absorbed with the repulse of his disjointed attack, Polk didn't notice Jackson's ambulance clatter up until Jackson was out of it and almost standing next to him. He only noticed then because one of his aides announced Jackson's arrival.

"General Jackson," Polk said with aplomb, "I..." Seeing Jackson's eyes, Polk was startled into silence. Those eyes, Polk thought in awe, they burn! They positively blaze!

"I have word, General Polk, that Cheatham has taken the stone wall. General Cleburne's other troops still face some stubborn resistance, but they are driving the enemy back on East Rock Creek. You must coordinate your men, drive our enemies from their works, and send General French into their rear, and you must do it now. Now, before he can consolidate a new line behind that creek. Now I say, now!"

Polk felt both cowed and swept away. Suddenly unable to think of anything but obedience, Polk stammered "Yessir!" After sending a courier to Maney with orders to regroup and go forward as soon as possible, Polk spurred his horse into the woods to personally order Ector and Sears to start forward as soon as they saw Maney go in. Only then did he find General French, who was busy bringing Cantey's Brigade into position on the edge of the forest.

French saluted Polk. "Sir, Cantey's boys were marching off in the wrong direction. I'm afraid their new commander mishandled them, and I had to fetch them and bring them back."

Patiently, Polk replied, "That is good, but in the meantime your boys have been going against the Northron's breastworks piecemeal, General. They shall never take those works going in like that, not ever. You have the God-given chance to strike the blow that shall win us this battle, General French."

Polk gestured towards Harrow's entrenchments. "Now look there. The enemy has shifted a whole battery of cannon to the end of their line."

French protested. "I can't go forward against that as I am now, General Polk! I'd be sending Cantey's boys into the teeth of those Federal guns!"

Calmly, Polk said, "You can and you shall. I will go and bring up Cockrell's boys myself, but you will stay here and attack in conjunction with Maney."

Sullenly, French said, "Yes. Sir."

The second attacks began before Polk could return with Cockrell's Brigade. Now better coordinated, the bulk of Polk's Corps pushed up to within 70 yards of the Federal breastworks, where they stubbornly fought it out for almost 15 minutes. Yet

Harrow's troops stood firm behind the protection of their thick dirt embankment, and so it was the Johnnies who wilted and fell back.

Polk waited with French while his troops fell back. To an aide, he said, "Tell General Maney he has fought gallantly, but I require one more effort from him. Tell him Cockrell is on the far right now, and this time we'll get in those works. Be ready to charge."

On the other side of the line, Harrow was celebrating the repulse of the second Confederate attack by taking another pull from his flask. To his artillery chief, he said, "Did you see that, Griffiths! Did you see that?! Your guns did magnificently. If those bastards have the cheek to come at us again, we'll see them off in the same brilliant style. Brilliant! Brilliant!"

"Sir, it's General Logan!" cried Griffiths.

Harrow hid his flask under his coat and turned to face Blackjack as he came thundering up on his great, dark horse. "General Logan, sir! I'm glad to see you. I've just seen off two attacks by an entire corps of Confederate infantry, and I can assure you, sir, that I do not exaggerate. I could use some reinforcements. Can you spare me another battery or brigade, to shore up my left? You were very concerned about my left before, sir."

Logan noted with some dismay that Harrow's face was pink, a sure sign he had been at his bottle. Shaking his head, Logan said, "I have nothing for you, General, except orders. Osterhaus is holding the Rebels up, but we're pulling back our left to East Rock Creek. Now, you know how that creek bends back like a hook, about a mile behind you, yes? Now that you have a lull here, begin falling back on that position at once. Sherman is bringing up Sweeny and Kilby Smith there."

After turning his horse around, Logan spurred his horse and galloped away. Harrow withdrew his flask from its hiding place and took another drink. He was about to issue orders calling for the main body to fall back, leaving triple-strength detachment skirmishers in the trenches, when Maney's Division again started forward from their position on the low ridge, attacking for the third time.

Harrow reacted with a mix of nerves and excitement. "Well, I don't see how seeing off the Johnnies one more time can hurt my reputation! Let them come!" He then drained the remainder of his flask.

Maney's tattered, bloodied butternuts came on, their flags stained and torn and their ranks thinned by their second major clash in four days. Yet they came on all the same, marching steadily forward, despite instantly coming under fire from bursting shells and case shot. Within minutes of Maney starting his advance, French's brigades stepped out of the holly forest.

For this third assault, Cockrell's graybacks extended out beyond the end of Harrow's refused line. On his own initiative, the Missourian led his men out and away from the Federal lines, so as to avoid some fire while coming forward, before turning sharply to bring his men into range for their Henry Rifles. Having maneuvered onto an oblique angle from the big smoothbore cannons anchoring the Yankee line, Cockrell halted his men and opened fire, sending a swarm of .44 caliber bullets ripping in amongst the blue gunners.

In a matter of minutes, canister fire from those guns began to slacken. French rode up to Colonel O'Neal, and told him, "Fix bayonets, Colonel, and charge your brigade. Charge, for God's sake, charge!"

Cantey's Brigade rushed forward, howling and shrieking as they went. A third of the brigade stumbled to a halt when they caught a close-range blast of canister, but the rest rushed in among the glistening Napoleon field guns to chase away the Billy crewmen. Any who stood by their guns were clubbed or speared to death in the frenzy.

French galloped in behind the charge, exultant over what he thought surely must be the highpoint of his wartime career. "Turn the cannons on them! Turn their own cannons on them!" French dismounted and started sponging out the muzzle of a cannon with his own two hands, and soon his staff followers were helping man the captured Yankee guns.

First one and then another blast of canister from the captured field pieces flashed down the leg of the Union line, raking the defenders and smashing them into bloody confusion. When the fire slackened, Sears's Mississippians came roaring forward.

Within a matter of minutes, Polk's entire corps was rushing upon the opposing breastworks. Harrow's men, who had never had much love for the harsh, unfair, and sometimes drunken rule of their division commander, turned and ran.

Polk set out to join his troops, delighted with his triumph. Surely it is my triumph, he thought, as much as it is anyone's. Yes, it is. I'm sure it is.

As he rode forward, he came upon a stretcher party bearing a grisly, soaked and red cargo. "Who is this poor, brave fellow?" Polk asked.

The corporal leading the party of four said, "Colonel O'Neal, sir. God damned canister chopped him into sausage, it did."

In hushed tones, Polk said, "Son, pray for your Colonel, but don't take the Lord's name in vein. Especially not while his spirit finds its way to Heaven!"

Embarrassed, the corporal tipped the brim of his hat. "I shall try, sir."

Upon reaching the breastworks, Polk found French, Maney, and their brigadiers already busy trying to get their men reorganized for the press forward. But they soon discovered their men were exhausted from a full day's marching and fighting, none more so than Maney's, who had only so recently fought so hard at Hell's Hillock. Many were out of ammunition.

Polk sent back to Jackson for permission to wait for the ammunition wagons to come up and resupply his troops. The response was a simple one-line message, delivered verbally by courier "No. Press on for the Shelbyville Road."

6:30 p.m.
Headquarters in the Field, Military Division of the Mississippi, USA
Bills Cemetery
1 ¼ miles south of Farmington

Sherman came upon Harrow in a small family cemetery not 600 yards from where A.J. Smith was putting two divisions in line along the bend of East Rock Creek. Quelling his disgust at finding Harrow without his troops, he rode in among the headstones.

"General Harrow, your report?"

"My report?" Harrow slurred. "My report is these yellow bastards up and ran. No discipline! These western troops, I tell you, they have no discipline! But I'll show them, oh yes, that I promise you. I'll get to the bottom of this, root out the malcontents, and then...!"

"By God, General, are you drunk?!?" snapped Sherman.

Flustered, Harrow shot back, "Why... no! Of course not. Never!"

As Harrow sputtered his excuses, Sherman reached for and lit a cigar, so as to calm his anger. He had never wanted Harrow, much less in command of one of his precious XV Corps divisions, but the War Department sent him with President Lincoln's blessings. The one thing he could not afford right now was a political brouhaha over this drunken hack, and especially not to alienate Lincoln himself.

"Well then, General Harrow, I suggest that instead of planning your inquiry, you see about rallying your men. Kilby Smith and Sweeny are shaking out a line only a third of a mile behind us, but we need to buy some time for them. See to it."

Harrow stared at Sherman for a few seconds, not sure whether he had been rebuked or not. Unable to make up his mind, he saluted and rode away.

As Harrow left, Sherman recalled Lincoln from when they had met in the spring of 1861, before Fort Sumter. Lincoln had asked him about the rebellion in Louisiana, and when Sherman told him the Louisianans were preparing for war, Lincoln had replied, "I guess we'll manage to keep house."

"I guess we'll manage to keep house," snorted Sherman. He had been so appalled by Lincoln's apparent nonchalance that he had washed his hands of the whole business, at least until Sumter had persuaded him to change his mind. He didn't know what quite to make of Lincoln now, who was clearly no political lightweight, but just as clearly still a pure politician.

"Pardon me, sir?" asked Audenried.

Through puffs on his cigar, Sherman said, "Nothing. Come on. Harrow's men loathe him, so if they are going to rally, it won't be because he asked them to do it."

Sherman rode out to the first cluster of troops he could see and was relieved to see they did not seem nearly as downtrodden up close as they looked from a distance. More angry than anything, he thought to himself.

Their colonel, who was busy pulling them together as they fell back, shouted, "Look there! Uncle Billy!"

Sherman tipped his hat to the colonel and noted from the flags that this was the 46th Ohio. "You boys are from Franklin County, are you not? I'm from down in Lancaster, you know?"

Raising his voice, Sherman said, "I know you! We were together at Shiloh! And you were at Vicksburg, and at Chattanooga. You are good boys. Today was hard on you, but I must ask something more. Will you rally and do this for me?"

A dirty-faced captain asked, "What do you need from us, General?"

"Reinforcements are forming a new line behind the creek, but I need more time. You remember Kilby Smith of the 54th Ohio? He's back there now, and you know he is a good man, but I need that time. Daniel Morgan asked the militia for two volleys before they fell back. Will you give me three?"

The Ohioans started chanting, "Four! Four! Four or more!"

Sherman repeated this performance a dozen times, so that by the time Polk's Corps came up, Harrow's Division was reformed, along with its surviving battery of Iowa-crewed rifled cannons. The massed, rolling volleys that met the gray skirmish line was enough to stall the entire advance, forcing the marching columns of tired, thirsty Johnnies to trudge out into line of battle again. When Maney and French's Divisions were ready to attack, Sherman personally led Harrow's division neatly back and across East Rock Creek, behind Sweeny's and Kilby Smith's soldiers to rest and replenish their cartridge boxes.

Stonewall Jackson knew that Stewart would not be able to cross the Duck River at Fishing Ford by that time, and now he also knew at least six Union divisions were dug in or digging in behind East Rock Creek. With only an hour of daylight left, he ordered his troops to leave behind advanced pickets and retire to their starting entrenchments for the night.

CHAPTER 18

June 26, 1864
6:00 a.m.
41ˢᵗ Tennessee Infantry, CSA
Bethbirei Church

Nathan watched as the Sergeant Major collected the roll call reports from each of the regiment's first sergeants, or those that were in camp anyway. Two companies were up in the main entrenchments, a quarter-mile away, and a third was picketing what had been the stone wall, now a dirt and stone embankment fronting a shallow trench.

He had urgent business with Captain Bell and hadn't gotten to him before the assembly. But he waited patiently, biding his time with the agreeable knowledge that Raglan Lloyd had not come back. Most likely, Lloyd had gotten Sergeant Marks to an ambulance, and then promptly deserted.

As soon as the Sergeant Major shouted "Dismissed!", Nathan quickly stepped out and got in front of Captain Bell before he could walk off to the officer's mess.

"Captain, may I have a word, sir?"

Bell blinked groggily and looked Nathan over. "Um, yes, Private. Private Grimes, yes? Yes. Yes, of course. I was meaning to have a word with you anyway. Come with me."

Nathan followed him to the officers' mess, where Bell offered him a cup of coffee before leading him across the dirt road. They moved away from the churchyard, where the regiment had pitched its tents and shelters, and over to the shady quiet of the church cemetery.

"Now Grimes, what is it?" asked Bell.

"I'd like permission to go to the field hospital and check on Sergeant Marks and the other fellows. I can also lay some traps, get us some fresh meat for the cook pot tomorrow. Scrounge around a bit too. Colonel Tillman will send someone soon, you can bet on that, so if you go see him now and suggest me, I reckon he'll send me."

Bell swallowed some coffee, and then said, "Of course, Private, that is a capital idea. I'm sure we can count on you to rush back here in the event of renewed battle today. But, I wish to ask a favor of you. In return for recommending the Colonel give you a full day pass to attend to these errands."

Nathan's eyes became suspicious. "A favor, sir?"

"Yes, just this. If anyone should ask you, you tell them we jumped over that wall together. We were both the first men in the entire division to get over that wall."

Nathan didn't see any real harm in that, as he cared little for bragging rights, although the demand lowered his opinion of Bell by one more notch. "That ain't no thing," he drawled. "Alright, Captain."

"Outstanding!" Bell grinned and slapped Nathan on the shoulder. "Now let me get off to Tillman before someone else does."

Bell walked away very pleased. Nathan was thought to have been first over the wall, not just in Walker's Brigade, but in Cheatham's entire division. That Bell might have been second didn't matter, because being first was what people told stories about, what got written up in newspapers and mentioned in dispatches. With Nathan backing him up, saying that they were both first, the little lie would stick from the first, easily becoming the truth. Bell understood full well that the reputations of great men were built on a foundation of such little lies, half-true stories that became Gospel in their repetition.

Nathan soon had his pass, and after wolfing down his breakfast and retrieving a spool of wire from the quartermaster, he was off. Most of their wounded from yesterday had been carried to the farmhouse and barns of the Whitsell Farm, across Big Rock Creek and about a mile from Bethbirei. Strangely, Sergeant Marks wasn't there, but the company's other wounded were, including Pete, whom he found lying under a canvas shelter between the house and barn.

Nathan was actually glad to see him, especially as the boy still had his leg. "Good morning, Pete. What do the sawbones say?"

Pete propped himself up. "Morning to you, Mr. Grimes. I reckon I'll be alright, and keep my leg, not like them other poor fellows. Doc said the bullet went through the fleshy side of my thigh, didn't hit no bleeders or nothing. He cleaned the hole right up, but I'm here to tell you, that was plenty painful, what with them tools he's got. Said to me that if it don't get infected, he reckons I'll be fine."

Nathan liked the sound of that, since it meant Pete might return to the ranks in late summer. "Pete, may I ask you a personal question?"

"Uh huh."

"What is your last name?"

"Fielding. I'm Peter Washington Fielding."

Smiling, Nathan said, "Now I know, Private Peter W. Fielding. You take care now, hear?"

Nathan left the hospital and headed north, not east back to camp, striking out along the dirt road alongside Big Rock Creek. After a four-mile hike, he turned off onto a country lane, thinking that if this wasn't the right place, he would at least find out where the right place was. But that didn't prove necessary, as the fine, fieldstone farmhouse he had been expecting to see was at the end of the lane.

As he approached, he saw a girl sweeping off the covered porch. Nathan had the sudden and jarring recollection that he hadn't seen a girl even halfway toward pretty since Old Jack had run all the whores out of camp a month ago, and he hadn't the wherewithal to afford their hotly demanded services during that brief opportunity, having lost all of his pitiful back pay at dice. This girl, in her late teens and with her long, shiny brown locks, was a good deal better than half-pretty.

Blushing despite himself, Nathan approached the porch. The girl hadn't noticed him until he spoke. "Pardon me, miss, but is this the Fletcher place?"

With a start, the girl looked up. Nathan could see her tighten her grip on her broomstick as she said, "Army commissary officers came through here the day before yesterday, then again yesterday afternoon. We have no more to give, so you'd best go trouble someone else."

Nathan declared plaintively, "You ain't got a thing to worry about, miss. I ain't commissary, I ain't a bummer, and I sure as hell ain't a deserter. I got a pass, all proper, if you want to see it. No, miss, I'm here to see Captain Fletcher, if that be alright. I reckon you be his kin."

She still looked wary, but relaxed her grip on the broomstick. "We're the Fletchers, that's right. And you are?"

"Private Nathan Grimes, Jr., 41st Tennessee Infantry. The Captain was my commanding officer these past three years, Miss Fletcher, and I knew he lived hereabouts. What with the army in Lewisburg, I thought I'd come and see him."

"Well, you wait here."

When the girl returned, she came back with a matron, an older lady of about 40, and a white and whispy-haired, pot-bellied man past 60. Hobbling up behind them on crutches was Robert Littleberry Fletcher. Nathan hadn't seen Fletcher since Lawrenceburg, and the man had lost weight and looked paler, but that wasn't surprising for one not two months past losing half a leg.

Fletcher beamed, "Nathan! I should have known if anyone was going to find his way up from the army to see me, it would be you. This is my father, my oldest sister Sarah, and my younger sister Elizabeth. Pa, Sarah, Lizzy, this is Nathan Grimes, the best fighting man in the regiment."

The old man extended his hand, giving Nathan a firm shake. "That is praise indeed. I'm pleased to make your acquaintance, sir."

"Thank you kindly, Mr. Fletcher, but no 'sir.' I'm just a common soldier."

Fletcher said, "Sarah, Lizzy, bring out those biscuits from breakfast, and some of that ham we kept back from the commissaries. Nathan here must be hungry." Once the women were indoors, he added "And if I know Private Grimes, I'm sure he has something for us."

Nathan shook his head. "I'm mighty sorry, Captain, but I ain't been scrounging yet. If I was going to come here, I had to come after seeing to things at the hospital, and take care of the rest on the way back to camp. You know how it is."

"I do. How was it? I heard the racket. I know the elephant came for a visit."

Nathan recited the butcher's bill from yesterday's battle and explained where Walker's Brigade had been posted, and the ebb and flow of the fight for the stone wall beyond Bethbirei Church.

Sarah stepped out just as Nathan finished. "Would you care to come in, Mr. Grimes?"

Nathan went inside and was ushered to a seat at the dining table, a simple but heavy and well-finished affair. Looking to the matching hutch and its crockery, he recognized the appointments of a well-off family farm. The Fletchers weren't big plantation owners, but they weren't poor, small-holding dirt farmers or tenants like his father had been either.

"How are things with the company?" asked Fletcher.

Nathan took a bite of a biscuit, wanting to think about how to answer that question before saying anything. The ham was good, aged and salty, and the biscuit had a coat of butter in the middle. It was scrumptious, and after savoring and swallowing the treat, Nathan decided to go with the unvarnished truth.

"Well, they sent us a boy from Bishop Polk's staff, Captain. Bell is his name. He came in with a fancy uniform and a darkie, all set on glory and making a name for himself. Still is. I ain't seen his like since before Donelson. Bell is the son of some big landowner in West Tennessee. I hear old Isham Harris himself lobbied to get him a promotion and a company. He's got guts, but he's stupid. A real rich boy hothead."

The elder Fletcher spat. "Harris."

Fletcher smiled, patting his father's arm. "Now, now. Let's not get into politics." His father was an old guard Whig, and even though the Whig Party was as dead as Julius Caesar, he still had no patience for fire-eating Democrats. But one had to be careful, because expressing such opinions could get a man hanged by Home Guard bandits as a Unionist.

"Well, Nathan, I'm sorry to hear that. And that Ed Marks got hit, although I was glad to hear he made sergeant. The promotion was well overdue. I'm surprised you didn't make corporal, and that they gave it to your brother."

"I don't want no stripes, sir." Wanting to change the subject, Nathan asked, "What are you planning on doing hereabouts, Captain?"

Fletcher leaned back in his chair. "Well, my father here has done an admirable job with the farm, what considering that the two armies long since took all our livestock and our few darkies ran away. We still had one good mule, you know, until the commissary agents from our own Army of Tennessee turned up here yesterday and found him out working with it. I told them the law, protested I was a maimed veteran, cried that there were hungry mouths to feed, and all to no avail. Our own army took our last mule!"

"But I've been thinking that whatever comes, the county is going to be a God-awful mess when it's all over. Back taxes, mortgages unpaid, lost property, and the like. So, I've started preparing cases. No one has any money, so it's all on commission. I am a lawyer, after all."

Nathan nodded knowingly as Fletcher chuckled. What he expected after the war was the rich to use the chaos and poverty to snatch up more land. Whether it was the big Tennessee landowners or the fat Yankee bankers made not so much difference to him, but he thought it suited Fletcher to be in court, helping the folks in the middle keep what they had and make some money off it while he was at it.

Nathan chewed and swallowed the last bite of his dinner. "Much as I'd like to sit a spell longer, Captain, I must go. Traps to lay, bartering to do."

Fletcher got up and steadied himself against the table. "I understand. I appreciate you coming to see me, Nathan, and if you should need anything, anything at all, you only need to ask. Send my regards to your brother, and congratulate him for me on his corporalcy."

Fletcher extended his hand. Nathan hadn't been expecting that, but reached across the table and shook it gladly. He then strapped on his gear and went outside, Fletcher and his family following along after him. A short way down the path, still within sight of the Fletcher house, Nathan turned, fixed his bayonet, and presented arms.

Watery-eyed, Fletcher firmed up his crutches, and saluted. Nathan spun around on his heel and marched down the path as if on parade.

Nathan spent the rest of the morning visiting three separate farms lying between the Fletcher place and the Franklin Pike. Matronly farmwives were running those farms, what with their menfolk either dead, in the army, or on the run from conscription agents, and they didn't have much. Yet Nathan had Yankee greenbacks and other valuables tucked away in his knapsack, all of it looted from dead bluecoats, and was able to barter or buy a jar of moonshine, two big bottles of strong apple cider, a hefty bundle of kale, and several pounds each of ripe cherries and onions.

These he carried with him back to Big Rock Creek, where he spent the early part of the afternoon laying traps along the creek and on the adjoining fields. He was stopped briefly by a patrolling provost, a "turkey driver," but Nathan presented his pass, explained what he was doing, and was left alone.

With his snares laid, Nathan began the return hike up the dirt road alongside Big Rock Creek, the one leading into Lewisburg. Along the way he spied a horse shed in a nearby field, and thinking he might find something worthwhile in it, went over to investigate.

Coming into the open gateway of the shed, Nathan saw a butternut-clad body lying still on the gray, old straw that was thinly scattered on the ground. A bayonet stuck out of his back, surrounded by a dark, old blood stain. Knowing it most unlikely that this Johnnie was killed by the Yankees, given where the body was, he moved closer to investigate. He saw part of the face and recognized the dead man as Sergeant Ed Marks.

The sight shocked Nathan, and he felt a current of grief shoot through him, but it was soon swamped with anger, a cold, dark, and hateful anger. He knew what had happened. Rather than take Marks to an ambulance or the field hospital, Raglan Lloyd had led him away so as to further his escape. He then murdered Marks rather than leave him as a witness and ran off.

Nathan brimmed with rage, so much so it numbed his senses. He left Marks where he found him, and walked back to camp.

He wanted to kill Lloyd, but he also nursed rancor against the army. He decided that Colonel Tillman should have hung Lloyd for the attempted bushwhack on Willie, and that Tillman surely would have, had the need for more men to fight the war not been so great. So now a good man, one of the best men, was dead, and a worthless man was spared to commit murder and go free.

I'll kill Raglan Lloyd, alright, thought Nathan. And I'll do it before the army has a chance to foul it all up again. I'll hunt him down after the war, if that's what it takes.

Nathan arrived in camp, and the hullabaloo going on there pulled him away from his animosity. Several hundred men were milling about the camp, a heavy guard was posted outside Bethbirei Church, and under the Colonel's canvas shelter was not just Colonel Tillman, but also Old Frank, General Walker, and a few other gold braids he didn't recognize.

Willie intercepted Nathan as he entered camp. Seeing his expression, he said "What..?"

Nathan said coldly, "Ed is dead. Stabbed in the back. I found him in a shed just a couple miles from here."

Wille gasped, "Lloyd?"

"Yeap."

Struggling to contain himself, Willie wiped away a tear. "Ed. God rest his soul."

Nathan took a step forward, and Willie snatched him up by the arm. "Nathan, where are you going?"

"Where do you think!?" Nathan barked back. "To report it to headquarters. Fat lot of fucking good it will do. That yellow rat bastard is long gone, you can count on that."

Willie pulled him in close. "Hush! Don't you see what's going on here?"

Nathan muttered angrily, "What do you mean? And get off me!"

"Old Jack is here, you fool! He came in with Old Straight for a service in Bethbirei, that there Presbyterian Church." Seeing no understanding on Nathan's face, he whispered harshly, "Do you think Colonel Tillman will thank you if you storm right in there and tell him Lloyd deserted and murdered a sergeant for good measure? Right in front of Cheatham, Walker, and all that army brass sitting there to hear it?"

Deflated, Nathan said sullenly, "No. You're right. No, he won't."

"I swear, it's a good thing you didn't take these here stripes, Nathan. I reckon your bull-headedness would have lost them right quick. Now, take them vittles you brought in to the commissary, and then let's go find Sergeant Major, and you tell him about poor Ed."

As Willie led Nathan off to find the regiment's commissary sergeant, the church doors opened and local parishioners began emerging. These filed down the church steps to congregate just beyond the line of armed soldiers standing guard. Among the last to come out was Jackson, in company with the minister and A.P. Stewart, and the trio were immediately greeted with applause and cheers from civilian and soldier alike.

Jackson waved with his splinted wrist, smiling awkwardly. He leaned over to say quietly to Stewart, "Pete, I believe you could have wakened me with less savagery during the service."

Stewart smirked. If there was one thing he didn't like at all about his friend and commander, it was the way Jackson would doze off in the midst of divine service, so he took great delight in giving him a sharp elbow or stepping firmly on his foot so as to prevent it.

"If you do not wish the reminder, Tom, then do not require it of me."

"I could order you."

"That you could. And then I'd be guilty of insubordination to the army, but still obedient to the needs of our liturgy."

Jackson laughed out loud at this, breaking into gleeful cackling that took all present by surprise. Quickly recovering some of his composure, he thanked everyone, said his goodbyes, and then went down the church steps and over to where Cheatham and the others were. Stewart followed, and Sandie emerged from the crowd to step in behind him.

Jackson made a half-bow. "General Cheatham. General Walker. Generals Wright and Vaughn. You will understand if I do not salute."

Cheatham smiled pleasantly. "Completely, sir. May I introduce Colonel Tillman? His regiment is camped here."

"Colonel. Your camp is neat and orderly, and your men did their duty yesterday in taking the stone wall. I understand the first man over that wall was from your regiment?"

Tillman beamed. "That is correct sir, although there is some confusion if it was one of our soldiers, or our Captain Samson Bell."

"Well, when you know that, please send it up through channels."

"Yessir, I will do so."

"General Jackson," Cheatham said. "Although I'm sure the men appreciate the day off, I would feel more secure if I could shore up the division's earthworks. Church services in the army must be finished, or nearly so. May I send the boys to work?"

"No," Jackson said firmly. "Providence graced us with a victory yesterday. The Lord must be thanked and praised. This is his day for rest, and the men surely need that rest after their recent exertions. You may begin improving your works in the morning, as ordered."

Having made his case personally, Cheatham let it alone. "Yes, General."

Jackson looked west, towards the crest of the ridgeline. Stewart's Corps had marched through the night from Fishing Ford, arriving just before first light to extend his line southward. The ground here wasn't much to speak of, and he half-hoped that if he did nothing to improve his position, the enemy might be lured into attacking him again. Yet now it was mid-afternoon, and there was little hope of that. Having given the troops most of the Sabbath, he was determined to let them have the rest of it.

7 a.m.
Headquarters, Military Division of Mississippi, USA
Shelbyville Road
Two miles east of Farmington, Tennessee

While Nathan Grimes was hiking out to the field hospital, Sherman was smoking and walking circles around his little headquarters, trying to work the stiffness from his joints. Farmington was too close to the front for setting up his headquarters, and preferring to live simply while in the field anyway, he had bivouacked in the open field the night before. His headquarters reflected this, as the horses present outnumbered the tents. The most settled part was the large telegraph tent, connected by wire to the different corps headquarters along the front and Shelbyville in the rear.

He looked over to his officers, enjoying their breakfasts. The air was thick with the scents of fragrant coffee and savory bacon, but they gave him no appetite. Unlike other men, his vigor never waned for lack of sleep or food. Quite the contrary, the only thing he ever felt he truly needed with any regularity was tobacco, and that was to steady his energetic nature.

McPherson rode up just as Sherman was coming back around to the road. He stopped as he saw McPherson dismount and walk over to him.

"Good morning, Mac. I got your word last night that Hooker is in place on the right. The whole army is up and in line. That's good."

"Morning to you to, Bill. Reports say that Stewart's Corps is over there now. The Rebels army now occupies a five-mile line, east and northeast of Lewisburg. Except that they are entrenched, the position is not especially strong, but it is fairly secure, what with Forrest's cavalry thrown out on the flanks. Those screens extend out to the Duck River on the north, and down to the hills to the south."

"Yes, much the same as with the Army of the Tennessee."

Nodding, McPherson said, "That's right. Bill, there is something I'd like to say before we tour the lines this morning."

Sherman nodded, so McPherson continued. "I thought about what you said yesterday, and I want you to know my concern was only to stop Jackson from bringing another Chancellorsville down on us, and that it was better to contain Stewart's Corps before it got across the Duck. My orders gave me the discretion to do that. But, I can see now that I had other means available to achieve that end, that I didn't need to divert Mower's Division to Fishing Ford, and I should have attacked. If I had done so..."

Motioning for McPherson to stop, Sherman said "War is full of ifs. What attacking with Logan and Mower might have achieved is neither here nor there, and a business best left to armchair generals. We real generals have a job to do."

Putting his hand down on McPherson's shoulder, he continued. "You're the best man in this army. Hell, you saved this army at Lawrenceburg. Yes, yesterday was a defeat and there is no painting it any other way, but we're still here and the Rebels are still over there, and today we get on with the business of whipping them. That is all there is to it. Now, let's mount up and attend to the morning's affairs."

McPherson walked his horse into the little camp, Sherman following behind, finishing his thoughts. He wanted to see the lay of things with his own eyes, of course, but he had already made up his mind as to the army's course as soon as he saw Hooker's XX Corps march down the Shelbyville Road the night before.

The damage done to the railroad around Murfreesboro was due to be repaired the next day, and the 10,000 men of the newly arrived XVII Corps could be concentrated in Shelbyville the day after that. With the reinforcements they would punch through the cavalry screen, and seize the hills around Belfast, a few miles south of the Rebel army. If that didn't work, he would make another wide turning movement farther south and try again to get into the Rebel rear. The one thing he would not do is throw everything into a general assault on Jackson's front.

11 a.m.
Bivouac of the 7th Pennsylvania Cavalry, USA
One mile south of Fishing Ford

After being replaced around Fishing Ford by Mower's Division, the Saber Brigade withdrew and encamped in the open fields. Minty gave them the minor task of patrolling the south bank of the Duck River, but mostly the brigade was spending their Sunday resting.

Spear was cleaning his carbine when an orderly told him that the Major wanted to see him back at battalion. After reassembling his Spencer and stowing it with his saddle and tack, Spear cleaned up his uniform with a horse brush, and then set out for Major Jennings' tent at a brisk walk, about a half-mile across the field, through rather than around the staked and tethered horses of his company.

He stooped to snatch up a thick handful of grass as he went, and paused before his own horse. He let the gelding nibble up the grass, patting forehead and scratching between his ears. "That's good, isn't it Ellis. Yes, that's right. Good boy."

Leaving his horse, he went on to battalion headquarters, which consisted of just two canvas tents, one a pup tent serving as Major Jennings' quarters, and the other set up as an open-sided shelter that was the HQ proper. Such was Uncle Billy's thriftiness that not even majors, colonels, or staffs had proper Sibley tents to call home, and they were only slightly better off than the rankers.

Seeing Jennings behind a desk under the shelter, Spear presented himself. "Sergeant George Spear, reporting as ordered, sir."

Jennings signed the document before him, and set down his pen. "Ah, Spear. Do you know why I sent for you?"

Spear eyed Jennings impassively. He scarcely knew the man. Before making major, Jennings had been the captain of A Company, drawn from Juniata County, out between Lewistown and Harrisburg. "No, major, I suppose I have no idea."

"Well, your company first sergeant, Rothenberger, was killed in that hellish artillery barrage we were trapped in yesterday. You are not just the senior sergeant in your company, but the senior sergeant of this battalion. Furthermore, Captain Vale is very satisfied with you, and I have no reason to overrule him. So, we put you in with the Colonel, who approved. You are now First Sergeant Spear."

The major pulled a pair of folded up chevrons from his pocket, and pushed them across the table. "Go see Captain Vale, and discuss your new duties with him. Then get those sewn on. Congratulations, First Sergeant."

Taking the chevrons, Spear said, "Thank you, sir."

Jennings took up his pen and looked back to his paperwork. "Dismissed."

Spear turned smartly on his heels and strode out, stopping only once he was standing amid the horses again. Only then did he unfold his chevrons. First Sergeant, he thought. It was much more work and only three dollars a month more, but it was something.

With a smile on his face, he started for his company's camp, but then felt some wet pinpricks on his face. Looking up, he saw the rain building up strength.

"Damn," muttered Spear, as he picked up his pace, hoping to reach his pup tent before the rain got worse.

CHAPTER 19

June 27, 1864
7:00 a.m.
Headquarters, Army of Tennessee, CSA
Farm and Mercantile Bank
Lewisburg, Tennessee

Stalking into the bank, Jackson barked at an orderly, "Take that chair, and set it down alongside Sandie's desk. No, not there! On the left side!"

Sandie looked up and pursed his lips ever so slightly. Jackson had been irritable since his wrist was injured. McGuire had since changed his diagnosis from a minor fracture to a bad sprain, but this had not improved the commanding general's mood. Instead, it had grown more short-tempered since the rain began.

This was the second day of near-constant rain, paralyzing both armies with the threat of wet gunpowder and roads turned into bottomless canals of thick slurry. Sandie knew inactivity never suited his chief, so he was more snappish than ever.

Jackson sat down, placing his hand on the desk so the thumb was elevated. Sandie laid the first summary paper before him. "This came to me last night, after you went to bed, sir. It is the Assistant Inspector General's investigation into the charges against Major Peters, Polk's Quartermaster, sir?"

Jackson grimaced with distaste at the mention of Peters. "And what did my IG say?"

"Regrettably, Major Peters was not at fault. The investigation shows that Major Peters became lost because General Polk's chief of artillery, Lieutenant Colonel Samuel Williams, neglected to leave guides after passing through the area, as per standing orders. As for becoming a blockage on the road, he was attempting to move his wagon train off the road, but several of his mule teams were frightened by screaming infantry officers and refused to move."

Jackson grunted. "I believe Peters still should have found his way, guides or no. But fine. Fine. Release Major Peters with the apologies of this headquarters. Place Colonel Williams under arrest in his stead."

Sandie felt his stomach turn cold at the thought of how the Bishop would respond to having first his chief quartermaster, and then his chief artillerist placed under arrest. But he knew better than to suggest perhaps Williams should be let go with a reprimand. "Very well, General."

Setting another paper down before Jackson, Sandie continued. "These are the casualty reports. From Third Murfreesboro, Triune, and Lewisburg, we have suffered roughly 9,000 dead, wounded, and missing."

Jackson looked the figures over. Unsurprisingly, Stewart and Polk accounted for slightly more than two-thirds of that total, their two Corps having borne the brunt of the fighting. The four days had cost him roughly one-quarter of his army. He felt certain the enemy had suffered worse, but also that they had a much larger army.

Have I worn Sherman down enough to make a difference, wondered Jackson. Probably not, what with two fresh divisions waiting in Nashville to reinforce him. If the reports from the Nashville spies and Coleman Scouts are correct about that. Still, Providence will see us through.

Sandie threaded his fingers together, and placed his hands down on the desk. "Have you thought about what to do with Hardee?"

Jackson nodded. Accompanying his report of the debacle at Resaca, General Hardee had attached a formal request that he be relieved of command of the Army of Georgia. In keeping with Hardee's accustomed pedantry, the report lectured at length on his difficulties in facing a larger army, and obliquely tried to shift blame away from himself and onto Jackson.

The Army of Georgia had been bogged down by rainy weather and bad roads for days, much as his own army was mired now. The decision on what to do had been an easy one, as Jackson had never cared much for Hardee and his thinly veiled condescension in the first place.

"I shall endorse it," said Jackson. "Have the letter brought to me, and I shall endorse it at once."

"That raises the question of who to put in Hardee's place. I believe you should discuss who you want to command on the Georgia front, in your subordinate department, if only to help steer the War Department's choice. They should be left on no uncertain terms as to who we do not want, but we will need to make that known through back channels. We should write to General Lee as well, as Davis is certain to seek his advice on the matter."

Jackson half-wished to send A.P. Stewart to relieve Hardee. He had complete confidence in Stewart, and Old Straight could be there in just a few days, despite the weather. The business would be over and done with. But he knew he needed his best lieutenant here, with the Army of Tennessee. Cleburne was proving competent, but Jackson did not yet trust him with independent operations, and the Bishop demanded direct supervision.

So, Jackson thought about Lee's army, which had been defending the gates of Richmond for more than a week now. The first name he came to was Jeb Stuart, and instantly Stuart's handsome, cheery face flashed before him. The plumed hat and cavalier finery. Stuart, who had been killed at Yellow Tavern.

Oh, if only it had been God's design, Jackson thought, that dear old Stuart could have lived and come here.

Jackson realized he was brooding when his thoughts dwelled not just on Stuart, but also Boswell and Smith, and put a stop to it. He turned instead to sifting through the names of several of Lee's general officers, discarding the names of those deemed unfit, and then before casting his mental net into remoter parts of the Confederacy.

"They made Jubal Early a Lieutenant General a few weeks ago, and I'd have him, if Lee will consent to part with him. Richard Taylor in Trans-Mississippi has sufficient rank, and I'd welcome him too. Failing that, my only remaining preference is to promote Robert Rodes into the job."

Sandie murmured, "Lee will never give us Early or Rodes. That leaves Taylor, unless Richmond foists on us someone that we do not want."

"Yes, yes. Someone we do not want. Tell the War Department I want Stephen Lee left where he is, tending to my strategic flank in Mississippi. And I don't want D.H. Hill. He is a good fighter, but too contentious."

D.H. Hill was the brother of Jackson's first wife, now long since deceased, and Sandie recalled how Jackson stood aside when Lee banished the argumentative Hill to North Carolina. He added "I believe we should point out that John Pemberton remains bitterly unpopular with the troops, lest President Davis saddle us with him."

Jackson nodded his head jerkily and said emphatically, "Yes. Yes. No Pemberton."

"Now, Sandie, I have orders for Forrest. I want him to dispatch a patrol to monitor that enemy garrison in Pulaski and reconnoiter the area. A regiment will do. I also wish him to plan to take that fort as soon as the roads dry sufficiently to allow for a fast strike."

Situated 25 miles southwest of Lewisburg, Pulaski had returned to Jackson's thoughts the night before. The fort's rail connection to Nashville had been cut since the Battle of Lawrenceburg, and the garrison was strategically hemmed in by both his army and his installations at Lawrenceburg and Florence. Yet that little thorn of a fort was still there. He wished he had sent a detachment to destroy the fort sometime in May, except he was certain the garrison would have merely fallen back on the much stronger fort in Decatur if he had done so. To have kept Pulaski would have meant garrisoning it, and he lacked the troops for that.

"Yes, sir. I'll write it up, sir."

Jackson stood up. "Good. Good. Now I must get into that … ambulance." He said the last word with heavy vexation. "For my inspection."

Sandie stood up and saluted. "Yes sir. Enjoy the tour." He then motioned to Captain Quintard, who was standing by with a rain poncho and followed Jackson out the door.

June 28, 1864
7:30 a.m.
Headquarters in the Field, Military Division of the Mississippi, USA
Haskins Chapel
Four and a half miles east of Farmington

Once the weather set in, Sherman moved his headquarters to a little church, which he used to house the telegraph exchange, while he moved into a pup tent. Most of the Army of the Tennessee was busy with the tasks of felling timber for strengthening their earthworks and constructing abatis, as well as digging drainage sumps and ditches to keep those earthworks from turning into a network of canals and cisterns. Those not so engaged were assigned to a pioneering detail and were busy felling still more timber to corduroy 15 miles of the Shelbyville Road.

When McPherson stepped into the plain, clapboard chapel, Sherman looked up from the stacks of paper on his desk. "Ah, Mac! Good. Now that you're here, I'm off. It's your army, and I'm sure you will take good care of it while I'm in Nashville."

McPherson put his hands on his hips and smiled. "I was thinking of ordering some several hundred head of cattle slaughtered, enough to put fresh beef on the table for the whole army for supper tonight. It will buck up spirits, what with the rotten weather."

Sherman nodded slowly. "Yes. Indeed it will. Sound thinking, that." Beyond the morale value, Sherman's mind tallied the logistical value of reducing the herd of beeves they drove along behind the army. Fewer cattle meant more grass for the horses and mules, which meant hauling less fodder from the railhead at Shelbyville. The value of grass and fodder rose whenever an army became stationary for more than a day or two.

Pulling on his raincoat and slouch hat, Sherman went outside and jumped up onto his horse. "Look after things here, Mac. I'll be back in two or three days."

Some of the Shelbyville Road had yet to be corduroyed, but that part was the last few miles near Farmington. Sherman and his party of aides and escorts enjoyed a roadbed firmed up by a layer of solid tree trunks all the way to Shelbyville, so the ride took only two hours. Once there, he waited for the train and bided his time by inspecting the new supply depot there. Sherman reached his permanent office, where the staff that oversaw every military department from the Mississippi River to the Appalachian Mountains worked, by 1 o'clock.

There he found Frank Blair waiting for him in the foyer, sipping on a cup of coffee. Blair was unmistakable, what with his fiery red hair and beard. Upon seeing Sherman, he jumped up, stuck out his hand, and exclaimed, "Bill!" Six feet tall, Blair towered over Sherman's five feet, nine inches.

Sherman shook hands. "Good to see you, Frank. Damn good to see you. Are you glad to be away from Washington?"

Blair chuckled. He was a scion of one of the most powerful political families in the country and had spent the winter and spring months serving as a Missouri Congressman, shoring up the conservative wing of the Republican Party while his troops were on furlough.

"That is something I've never quite sorted out about you, Bill. You come from the Ewing household. Ferchrissakes, your own brother is a Senator! And yet you have the worst opinion of politicians."

"Not politicians, Frank. At least not all politicians. Politics. There is a difference. Anyhow, let's go out on the veranda for a smoke."

After both men had lit their cigars and had a few puffs, Sherman said, "Frank, I have a special assignment for the XVII Corps."

"When you told me to wait here in Nashville, rather than to come on down to Shelbyville, that gave me a hint that you might have a trick card in your hat."

"What I want is for you to go to Decherd, not Shelbyville. Once there, you are to march to Pulaski, join Starkweather's men already there, and dig in. Get your men a five-day issue of rations, so you can start immediately and won't be impeded by supply wagons on the march. The roads will be horrible, I know, so form pioneer detachments, put them in the first train you send down there, and corduroy the roads in advance of your main columns. I expect you to manage at least ten miles a day. Ten miles a day, sixty miles, six days total. You can resupply at Pulaski, and your wagons can come up behind you."

Sherman went on, cigar clenched in his fingers, and gesticulating with both hands. "This is a secret expedition, Frank. As of this moment, the only people who know about it are you and me. We will put one of your aides in each locomotive with special orders to send that train onto Decherd. We tell them, give them the written orders, and put them straight on the departing train so word does not get out. No loose lips gabbing our plans out to every Rebel spy in every whorehouse and to every God-damned reporter in Nashville, understood?"

Blair's expression was serious, but inwardly he was very excited. An independent exploit like this could lead to high office after the war, perhaps even the White House itself. "Understood. I won't tell a soul. Until we get to Decherd, insofar as anyone in my corps knows, we're going to Shelbyville."

"Good. You see, Frank, when the rain stops and the roads dry, I'll try to get around Jackson's right flank again. This time, he won't beat me to the next road junction, because you will already be there. With your two divisions plus Starkweather, you will have almost 12,000 men dug in around Pulaski. Jackson would need his entire army to dislodge you, and if he tries, I'll fall on his rear and break him into pieces. He will have no choice but to fall back on Lawrenceburg, or perhaps even to Florence."

Blair said, "And with that, you'll have maneuvered Stonewall Jackson out of Tennessee, or almost so, without having fired another shot."

Sherman smacked his right fist into his left palm. "That's right. That is absolutely right."

July 5, 1864
11 p.m.
Headquarters, Army of Tennessee, CSA
Farm and Mercantile Bank
Lewisburg, Tennessee

Sandie looked across the lamp-lit room at Jackson, who sat at a table awkwardly turning the page of a newspaper, and smiled. His wrist was doing much better, and he had some use of his right hand now. Also, the rain had stopped and the sun had come out that afternoon. Although the air had grown oppressively hot and humid with the break in the weather, the promise was there that in a day or two the roads would dry sufficiently to give the army back its mobility.

Returning to his paperwork, Sandie thought to himself that anything was better than the rain. Not every day had brought a thunderstorm and downpour. Sometimes it misted, sometimes it drizzled, but even though the rain slackened at times, it never stopped. The constant drenching had flooded the creeks and overwhelmed the efforts of the troops to drain the water from their trenches, filling them calf-deep with muddy water.

Sandie's pen stopped as he suddenly wondered about Kate and what the weather might be like in Richmond. His wife's family, the Corbins, had abandoned their estate of Moss Neck and moved to Richmond during the prolonged Battle of the Wilderness, a wise precaution since Moss Neck was in Caroline County, and now well behind enemy lines. In his last letter, Sandie had advised her to urge her family to move again. A city under siege was no place for them.

The thought of his wife filled him with a warm glow. Her hair, her skin, her smile. The glow made him earnestly wish the war was over, but how could it be? Peace with Union was surrender and degradation. Peace without it could only be won now by outlasting the North, and that meant months more of toil, months more of blood.

Suddenly Nathan Bedford Forrest burst into the bank, throwing the heavy double doors open wide. Sandie started in his chair, but Jackson merely looked up and over at the front doors. The only sign he might be disturbed was the iron in his gaze.

Forrest saluted and said loudly, "General Jackson, I came myself. A host of Yankee troops arrived in Pulaski this afternoon. My boys counted them at more than 5,000 before they were driven from their observation posts, and the Yankee banners had the arrow emblem of the XVII Corps."

Jackson got to his feet. "Sandie, summon Colonel Harman and start planning a withdrawal to Lawrenceburg. With Pulaski occupied as it is, we must fall back on Columbia and Mt. Pleasant before turning south. Order General Strahl to bring his men up from Florence to Lawrenceburg, and General Forrest, I require you to dispatch a brigade to reinforce Strahl's Brigade at once. This army moves as soon as the roads have dried out."

Forrest cried, "General, I can't believe you are thinking of retreating! Give me one division of infantry and all my cavalry, and I'll run down there and lick them Yankees before anyone knows I'm gone. This is our chance, to do that thing, you say... you called it... defeat them in detail!"

Unmoved, Jackson said, "With the roads in the state they are in, marching the 25 miles to Pulaski will require a minimum of two whole days. Or we must wait at least two whole days for the roads to dry sufficiently to quicken the march. It is true that with the roads churned up by us, the march will take Sherman even longer. But by the time we reach Pulaski, the XVII Corps will have had those two whole days to entrench."

Forrest's pugnacity began to deflate, as he felt out the truth of the situation. "And this ain't Rosecrans, with a fort built up for a whole army defended by just a few thousand." Sighing, he concluded, "Them 12,000 to 15,000 bluebellies will dig in on a line they can hold against all comers. And then... then Sherman will come up on our rear."

There was a long silence, broken when Forrest brought his first down on Jackson's desk, "God dammit! God damn it all!"

Jackson said softly, "Please, General Forrest. Blasphemy."

"I'm sorry sir, but... it be briarsome to swallow."

Jackson nodded. He understood Forrest's instinctive aggression, and knew how tantalizing the idea of striking at an isolated enemy detachment could be. But it was all a chimera. Dozens of miles and a major river had kept Sherman away from him for his slash at Murfreesboro. Pulaski was just too close.

He admitted to himself that Sherman had managed to very skillfully and quietly reinforce Pulaski. He knew the XVII Corps had left Nashville a week ago, but could only assume they had gone to and remained in Shelbyville. The roads being what they were, no civilians came forward with news of enemy movements from deep behind the lines. It was admirable work, all told.

The room became quiet again, until Sandie said, "I'll send for Colonel Harman, and begin work on routes for your approval, sir."

Jackson replied flatly, "Good. Good."

EPILOGUE

July 6, 1864
9 a.m.
The Executive Mansion
Richmond, Virginia

Davis said, "Please, enter" in response to the knock on his office door.

Burton Harrison stuck his head in. "Sir, Secretary Seddon and General Bragg have both arrived, and are waiting in the dining room. They've already had breakfast, but Seddon asked after some tea, so I had a pot sent in. Also, Secretary Benjamin and Attorney General Davis have both confirmed that they will call on you at 11 o'clock."

Davis got to his feet, buttoning his vest as he did so. "Thank you, Burt. You get some of that tea for yourself, if you want. I'll see myself down to the dining room."

"Yes, Mr. President."

After buttoning up his vest and coat, Davis went down to join his two top war officials, the Secretary of War and his chief military adviser. Entering the dining room, Davis accepted their proper salutations and then bid them to sit down.

"Gentlemen, I'm sure you both know of the news that came in over the wire last night, and I wanted to discuss those events with you first thing. To start with, General Jackson sent us word of his intention to withdraw the Army of Tennessee to Lawrenceburg sometime in the next few days. Second, General Hardee reported that the Federal army under that turncoat, George Thomas, was across the Etowah, and that he is already retreating to Allatoona Pass."

Bragg grimaced. "Frankly, Mr. President, I think the way Thomas has maneuvered Hardee out of those ridges around Dalton and now off the Etwoah River, both perfectly defensible positions, is disgraceful. That man has barely fired a shot in defense of northern Georgia, and given that he clearly wants out of his current post, I doubt that he will. And this over his native state! I urge you to give him what he wants and reassign him."

Davis looked to Seddon, prompting the Secretary of War to say, "I fear General Bragg is correct. Whatever his real difficulties, we cannot expect Hardee to do well at a task he expresses so little confidence in, or enthusiasm for. He must go."

Pursing his lips, Davis found himself wishing he could have it some other way. He had known and respected Bill Hardee for years. As Franklin Pierce's Secretary of War, he had made Hardee a major in the much esteemed U.S. 2nd Cavalry and had asked the Georgian to write his famous infantry tactics book. Davis had spent the last week corresponding with Hardee over the wire, almost pleading with the man to stay at his post and to fight harder. Each message was met with Hardee's polite apologies and a restatement of his wish to be relieved.

"Very well then, gentlemen, very well. Barring giving Beauregard or Johnston the post, there is only one suitable choice, that being Lieutenant General Richard Taylor. As it happens, Taylor and his superior, General Smith, have fallen out as well. It seems to me the thing to do is swap Taylor and Hardee. Based on past experience, I think Jackson ought to get along with Taylor, and Smith ought to get along with Hardee. Perhaps this business will show itself as serendipitous. Do you agree?"

Seddon said, "I completely agree. Taylor is practically Stonewall Jackson's protégé, and Hardee should have just the right temperament for working with Kirby Smith."

"It's an elegant solution, Mr. President," said Bragg.

The three men paused for a moment as the tea service was brought in by a negro servant. After every man was poured a cup, the servant quietly withdrew, and the trio returned to matters of state.

Davis spoke, becoming more animated as he did so. "Now, gentlemen, I do not see these setbacks in Virginia, Georgia, or Tennessee as changing what is otherwise a situation very positive for our country. True, General Lee has been forced back to defend the gates of this very city, but he is holding Grant firmly at bay. Nay, not just holding him at bay, but has given the Union army several sharp reverses in so doing. Stonewall Jackson is no longer on the outskirts of Nashville, true, but he has won two victories, severely damaged the railroads, captured immense supplies and equipments, and is still on Tennessee soil. And with new leadership in Georgia, surely we can hold the Union army there back."

Seddon said, "If Lee can hold the line in Richmond, and I have no doubt he can, and Taylor can hold the line in Georgia, and Jackson stays in Tennessee, surely the Northern people will give up their imperial ambitions and finally let us go our own way. But it will not be easy, the balance of forces being what they are."

Bragg murmured, "The North is war weary. They have always been a soft and irresolute people. We can outlast them. I believe we could even afford to lose Tennessee or Atlanta, but not both. We must keep one or the other if we are to strangle the North's will to continue the war."

Davis drained his teacup. "I'm glad we are in agreement on our first policy, gentlemen."

Seddon asked, "Mr. President, may I inquire... after the events of yesterday afternoon, what do you intend to do about General Milroy?"

Davis said nothing, but instead nodded in a slow, grave manner. Milroy had arrived in Richmond the day before, and his transfer from the train station to Libby Prison had brought out the largest mob the city had seen since the bread riots the year before. Reportedly, many in that would-be lynch mob were refugees from the Shenandoah, where Milroy had enjoyed his reign of terror the year before. The only reason the Northern vandal had escaped hanging then and there was because of his armed escort, originally assigned to guard against his escape.

Judah Benjamin had come the night before, in his role as Secretary of State, to express his concern that prosecuting a Union major general would poison relations with the North, just as the aborted policy to prosecute white officers leading darkie soldiers for inciting servile insurrection had threatened to. He urged that Milroy's trial be indefinitely postponed, and he otherwise be treated as an ordinary prisoner of war.

"What would you have me do, Secretary Seddon?"

"Nothing. Let him rot in Libby Prison, but we do not want to get into the business of judicial reprisals with the United States. A feud of reciprocal trials."

"And what of the $100,000 bounty placed on Milroy's head? Or the bounty leveled by your own state of Virginia? The call for his arrest is a matter of law and cannot merely be set aside."

"No, but it can be delayed. Conduct an investigation, collect evidence. Delay matters. When we have peace, suspend proceedings as part of the peace negotiations. But do not indict Milroy, do no put him on trial, and for God's sake, do not convict him."

Bragg spoke up. "With all due respect, Mr. Secretary, but if this is what we were always going to do when we caught an abolitionist miscreant like this Milroy, a man who gleefully despoils our country in open violation of the standards of civilized warfare, then why did we put a price on his head in the first place? I say prosecute the man! Let it serve as a warning to others like him, like David Hunter or that scoundrel, 'Spoons' Butler."

Davis's eyes came up at the mention of Butler. If it was Butler they had in Libby Prison, Davis knew the man would be sent to the gallows in short order. The only reason to spare him would be to extract a major concession from the North, such as the resumption of prisoner exchanges. So if he would do that for Butler, than why not for Milroy? The one was as villainous as the other, surely.

Davis said very deliberately, "This must necessarily be a military trial, so Mr. Secretary, I desire you to consult with your Judge Advocate General about making the necessary arrangements. Investigate the charges and collect evidence. I want our case to stand up to the closest external scrutiny. But I also want this matter dealt with expeditiously, so I shall place the Attorney General and his people at your disposal as well. I want to see General Milroy in the dock before the end of summer."

AUTHOR'S NOTE

In my last author's note, I briefly examined the style and method that went into plotting *Stonewall Goes West* and layering it with historical detail, and by now readers ought to be familiar with my approach. Even so, some special points deserve some extra comment.

I invested substantial time and energy into getting the geography of my story right, which I consider well spent because it adds so much to the story's color and realism. Most of the details like creeks, hills, and buildings are genuine. Whenever I don't use an authentic, period place name, I use the modern name instead. Some farms I refer to are documented, while others are extrapolations of family cemeteries that I visited and know must have been present in 1864. I know the animal crossing of the Duck downriver from Fishing Ford is there because I talked to the owners of a horse campground in the area about it.

One problem I encountered in this book is that in some instances, I had plenty of evidence that was partly contradictory. The several period maps of Middle Tennessee I consulted were not in complete agreement about the exact location of roads and landmarks, for example. Since this time I venture into the vicinity of the famous Battle of Stones River, I'm sure some will disagree with my interpretations of exactly where this and that might have been. All I can say to that is the sources I consulted don't agree either.

For those wondering how authentic the details surrounding my "boots" characters, Nathan Grimes and George Spear, are, the answer is that their immediate comrades are fictitious. In the case of the 41st Tennessee Infantry, Grimes's entire company is fictional, although the larger regiment is historical. Spear's immediate friends are likewise fictitious, although his company officers and on up were very real.

One of the historical details that might strike some readers as strange or controversial is my mention of the black soldiers who were part of Nathan Bedford Forrest's personal escort, but the existence of these few individuals is well-documented. Similarly, my characterization of Forrest's views on arming slaves is an extrapolation of what is known of the man's actions, sentiments, and character. If Forrest had been present at Cleburne's January 1864 proposal to free and arm slaves to fight for the Confederacy, I imagine he would have supported it wholeheartedly. Like most truly self-made men, Forrest was a hardened pragmatist, and I can easily see him compromising on slavery if doing so allowed for continued dominance over the former slaves.

Another point some might disagree with is the success of Confederate recruiting efforts as described in the story. By the start of active campaigning in 1864, the Confederacy was certainly scraping the bottom of its manpower barrel, and that situation was not helped by sagging national morale. To cite just one example, in most estimations roughly half the troops in Pemberton's Vicksburg army simply went home and never came back.

Yet against this backdrop of defeatism, one must not dismiss the magnetism of a heroic personality or the electrifying effect of a major victory. As late as summer 1864, Joe Shelby recruited at least a couple thousand men in Arkansas and Missouri, and in autumn 1863 Forrest was able to raise two divisions of cavalry in West Tennessee, due largely to their own personal energy and reputations.

So I don't think I overstate the effects on Southern recruiting of having arguably the Confederacy's greatest military hero, Stonewall Jackson, come west, win a major victory, and grab back some territory. In the final analysis, it merely represents scraping the bottom of the barrel with somewhat more success.

Lastly, a brief word on what was oddly the most misunderstood aspect of *Stonewall Goes West*: its length. The average novel is often quoted as 90,000 words long. Against this, the first book was 83,000 words, and this book is just shy of 98,000 words.

www.ingramcontent.com/pod-product-compliance
Lightning Source LLC
Chambersburg PA
CBHW070840250626
47159CB00003B/859